"But what I regret most is that we weren't able to walk away as friends."

He placed a hand to his chest. "I know that's my fault. But things have been really good between us these past few weeks. I was hoping we could build on that this weekend."

Dakota nibbled on her lower lip, unsure of how to respond.

Spending time with Dex again these past few weeks made it evident that she missed the friendship that had been the foundation of their relationship. But for her, being friends again would never be enough. The love and the friendship they'd shared had blossomed together and were inseparable.

I've had enough rejection for one day, thank you very much.

"We can't go back, Dex," she said softly. "But maybe we could forge a new friendship."

"I'd like that." His mouth curved in a tentative smile as he shifted the truck out of park and they started on their way to her father's house.

Dakota turned to look out the window as they traveled through town. Maybe they'd find a way to build some sort of friendship again, but there would be nothing more between them. And in a few months, she'd be gone. Just the way it should be.

So why couldn't she stop thinking of their kiss and wishing it had led to more?

Second Chance
on
Cypress Lane

Reese Ryan

FOREVER

New York Boston

Copyright © 2020 by Roxanne Ravenel
Kiss Me at Sweetwater Springs copyright © 2019 by Annie Rains

Cover design and illustration by Daniela Medina
Cover photographs © Shutterstock
Cover copyright © 2020 by Hachette Book Group, Inc.

Forever
Hachette Book Group
1290 Avenue of the Americas, New York, NY 10104
read-forever.com
twitter.com/readforeverpub

First Edition: December 2020

Forever is an imprint of Grand Central Publishing. The Forever name and logo are trademarks of Hachette Book Group, Inc.

The publisher is not responsible for websites (or their content) that are not owned by the publisher.

The Hachette Speakers Bureau provides a wide range of authors for speaking events. To find out more, go to www.hachettespeakersbureau.com or call (866) 376-6591.

ISBNs: 978-1-5387-3445-2 (mass market); 978-1-5387-3443-8 (ebook)

Printed in the United States of America

OPM

10 9 8 7 6 5 4 3 2 1

For Dimples and Bam Bam: Nonni loves you to pieces.

For my patient husband and family: Thank you for being so supportive and understanding through all of my deadlines and all-nighters. Love and adore you all. XOXO

Acknowledgments

Thank you to my wise, responsive, and incredibly proactive agent, Pamela Harty of the Knight Agency. Working with you is a pleasure. Thank you for your guidance and advice, and for always being there.

Thank you to my editor, Madeleine Colavita, for seeing the vision of Holly Grove Island and for being so invested in making the series and characters come alive.

To the Grand Central Forever team, thank you for all of your support and effort to get the Holly Grove Island series out into the world, onto bookshelves, into libraries, and into the hands of readers.

Second Chance

on

Cypress Lane

Chapter One

• • •

Dakota Jones had learned three things in the past three months, during which she'd landed on the pages of Italian tabloids and *Page Six*, been labeled a homewrecker, and lost her job days before her promotion to weekend anchor was to be announced.

Lesson one: Run a background check on any guy who so much as says hello, let alone one who has a killer smile and a thick Italian accent that turns your knees to Jell-O.

Lesson two: Learn the native tongue of the man you're dating. That way you'll know whether he's conversing with the wife you didn't know he had.

Lesson three: Don't blow all of your disposable income on things that are so...well, disposable.

Because now, instead of settling into her new job or making plans with friends for the long Fourth of July weekend in New York, she was crammed into a crowded, rickety old bus taking her far away from the city she'd called home for the past sixteen years.

Dakota had fallen in love with New York City when her mother had taken her to "the most amazing place in the world" for a shopping trip at the age of nine. "Couldn't you just imagine living here one day?" her mother had mused as they stood in Times Square among the soaring buildings, bustling crowds, and glamorous people.

Mesmerized by her surroundings, Dakota *could* imagine it. And right there on that hot sidewalk, she'd declared that someday she would.

She'd built her entire career on the goal of becoming a lead news anchor in New York, so losing the weekend anchor gig that had brought her one step closer to that dream was devastating. Being left with no choice but to return to Holly Grove Island—the little town in the Outer Banks where she'd grown up and which she had been actively avoiding since the death of her mother five years ago—rubbed salt in the open wound that was once her career.

After eight hours and two bus changes, Dakota was finally deposited with a few of her fellow travelers at the gas station doubling as a bus stop in Elizabeth City, North Carolina, an hour away from Holly Grove Island.

Dakota rummaged in her overpriced designer crossbody bag for a tip for the driver. The bag was a gift from her now ex-boyfriend, Marcello Giovannetti. A token of his affection. She'd been thrilled when he'd given her the thoughtful but expensive gift. But now it was a bitter reminder of how gullible she'd been.

She was an investigative reporter who'd neglected to investigate the man who'd swept her off her feet. But everything about the night they'd met seemed so damn perfect. Like a fairy tale. And for once, it had been nice that there was some mystery to the relationship. That she didn't know every detail about a man before they'd gone out.

And how'd that work out for you, genius?

Disastrously. But she'd gotten herself into this awful mess, so she would get herself out of it.

By running home to Daddy?

Dakota was really starting to hate the little voice in the back of her head. Her father had always predicted that her big-city adventure would go *kaboom.*

The city is a dangerous, cruel place, Kota. It'll chew you up and spit you out.

Returning home with her tail between her legs would only prove her father right. He'd never say "I told you so," but the words would always be hanging in the air between them.

Maybe there was a way she could go home *and* keep her dignity.

On the the long, grueling bus ride, during which her left butt cheek had fallen asleep more than once, she had devised a plan. She'd tell her father she lost her job at the news station because of cutbacks. He could relate to that. The same thing had happened to him ages ago when he worked at a factory. Before he'd gone into law enforcement and eventually become the chief of police on Holly Grove Island, a job he'd retired from a few years ago. This way, maybe her father would never have to know how royally she'd screwed up.

Then there was her other concern. In a town of fewer than a thousand year-round residents, running into Dexter Roberts—her high school sweetheart—was inevitable. Dakota had fallen hard for him. She'd been so sure they were meant to be together she was blindsided when he dumped her after his first semester of college.

After all this time, it still stung.

Marcello had been the first man she'd actually envisioned a future with since Dexter.

She could hear her late mother's voice in that sweet, Eastern North Carolina drawl that Dakota had worked so hard to rid herself of.

You sure know how to pick 'em, sweetie.

Dakota collected her luggage, then moved to the little patio outside the convenience store to wait for her ride. She'd opted for the longer bus trip to give herself more time to prepare for the return home. And for the questions she'd inevitably be asked.

Yet as she stood on the platform awaiting her ride, she felt no more prepared than she'd been when she'd stepped onto the bus early that morning.

"Dakota Jones!"

"Sinclair Buchanan." An involuntary smile eased the tension in Dakota's shoulders as she turned in the direction of that unmistakable twang. After the hell she'd been through the past few months, a genuine smile and a full heart felt...foreign. She dragged her oversize luggage behind her as she made her way toward her friend. "God, how long has it been?"

Sinclair was as beautiful as ever. Her tawny brown skin was flawless, and her natural, rich brown curls had been straightened and hung just past her shoulders, accented by honey-blond ombre waves. Her large hazel eyes practically glowed from within.

Sinclair embraced her so tightly she could barely breathe. "Too long, since your uppity behind decided you weren't coming home anymore." Sinclair finally released Dakota and met her gaze. "If I weren't so happy to see you right now, Dakota Jones, I'd be tellin' you about yourself."

"Missed you, too, Sin." Dakota grinned. "Thanks for picking me up. I know it was last minute and I had no right to ask."

"You know I'd never pass up the chance to usher you back into town. And just in time for the big Fourth of July Festival. Always was your favorite event of the year."

Sinclair threaded her arm through Dakota's. "C'mon. Let's get you home. You must be exhausted."

"And starving."

"Got you covered on that." Sinclair clicked her alarm, and a shiny black Lexus SUV beeped in response. "I packed a little care package for you and your dad."

Dakota turned toward the luxury SUV and cocked her head. "Is that you?"

"Business has been good." Sinclair grinned proudly. "Things are a lot different on the island since you were last here, Dakota. I think you're gonna like being back home."

"I'm not staying, Sin." It wasn't what her friend wanted to hear, but Dakota wouldn't give Sin false expectations. "This is a pit stop while I contemplate my next move."

"You sure, hon?" Sinclair struggled to lift Dakota's bag. "'Cause I swear you got everything you own in this bag, *including* the kitchen sink."

"Sorry. Let me get that. I was dazed by your flashy new ride." Dakota helped her friend lift the bag into the back of her truck. Sin slammed the rear hatch, and they climbed inside.

"Beats the hell out of that rusted-out Gremlin I drove when we were in high school." Sin giggled. "It's a wonder we survived that thing. Remember that board my daddy glued down to the floor? It was the only thing keeping our feet from touching the ground."

"It was a chariot as far as I was concerned." Dakota clicked her seat belt. "At least you had a car."

Sin pulled out of the parking lot and headed toward the highway that would take them to Holly Grove Island. She chatted happily, catching Dakota up on the health of her family, her accidental path into real estate, and some of the changes to the island in the past five years.

They'd once been best friends—practically inseparable until Dakota had gone off to New York to follow her dreams. Within a few years, they'd fallen out of touch. Dakota had been afraid things would feel awkward between her and Sin after so many years apart. Instead, she found comfort in the familiar twang, the incessant chatter, and the irreverent humor of the woman whom she once felt she could tell anything. Even if she wasn't ready to tell Sin *everything* right now.

"So, you wanna tell me why you didn't want your father to know you were comin'?" Sin asked once they'd crossed over Fox Haven Sound and arrived on Main Street.

The question landed in her lap like a ticking time bomb. It was the reason Dakota had been tense, her belly in a knot, the entire bus ride. She didn't like lying to her friends and family, but the truth was unbearably humiliating.

"I wanted to surprise him, that's all." Dakota turned away, focusing on the shops on Main Street as they flew by.

Most of the shops themselves were the same as the last time she'd been home: the bakery, the pharmacy, Myrna's Salon, and Knitty Gritty—the local fiber shop. A used book store in the spot that was once the island's video store. But everything looked brighter and fresher. The buildings were painted in complementary pastel colors and trimmed in crisp white. The windows sparkled, and each building was adorned with newer signs and awnings that amplified the picture-perfect small-town charm.

She could swear she'd stepped into one of her favorite Hallmark movies.

"I know we haven't seen each other much since high school, but we've been best friends since we were in diapers. I know you, Dakota. So I know when something's wrong," Sin said after a brief silence. Dakota opened her mouth to object, but Sin waved a hand and continued. "You're obviously not ready to share whatever it is that's weighing on your chest like a ton of boulders. That's fine. I get it. But if you ever do need someone to talk to, I'm here for you, Dakota. Like I've always been."

Sin's lips curved in a barely-there smile, but the light in her eyes dimmed. The sadness in her friend's voice tightened something in Dakota's chest. There it was—the elephant in the SUV that neither of them had wanted to address. Sin was hurt that Dakota had gone to New York and never returned. That she'd allowed their friendship to wither and die like an untended garden.

"I've been a terrible friend, Sinclair. And I'm sorry." Guilt burned a hole in Dakota's gut over Sin's emails and text messages that had gone unanswered. Set aside to be dealt with later, only later never quite materialized. And eventually, Sin stopped sending them. "I never intended to shut you out. I just got so caught up in school and my career and—"

"And neither me nor this Podunk little town fit into your glamorous new life." Sin grimaced, waving a hand before Dakota could launch into an explanation. "Honestly? If I'd had the opportunity, I probably would've left, too."

"No, you wouldn't have," Dakota said warmly. "You love this place far too much to leave it. You always have and you always will."

A genuine smile spread across Sin's face. "Okay, so maybe you do still know me a little. I do love this place, and I'm gonna do everything in my power to help you realize how much you love it, too." Sin glanced over at Dakota, before returning her gaze to the road. "And as far as I'm concerned, nothing's changed between us. You Joneses are a proud, stubborn bunch, so I thought I'd get that out there, right off."

Dakota's heart squeezed. She was grateful for Sinclair's undying friendship—loyalty she didn't deserve. Sin was right; Dakota had chosen life in the glittering city over her best friend—a choice that had gnawed at her since her last trip home. "When I'm ready to talk, I promise to call you, Sin."

"That's good enough for me." Sin beamed.

Dakota looked into the back seat. "Oh my God, what's in that picnic basket? It smells incredible."

Sin's laugh made it clear that Dakota's attempt to change the subject wasn't lost on her. "A good old-fashioned Southern feast. Fried pork chops, fried okra, fried corn, macaroni and cheese, cornbread, and blackberry cobbler."

"Even the aroma is decadent. I can feel my thighs expanding." Dakota considered swiping a piece of cornbread from the wicker basket, but when she glanced up, Sin had turned onto Passionflower Avenue, then onto Cypress Lane, and there it was.

Home.

The sprawling, pale-pink, four-bedroom Victorian with white trim was way too big for her father. But Oliver Jones wouldn't hear of selling the place. It was where he'd raised his family, and the place held too many memories.

Those memories, many of them painful, were the reason he needed to let the house go. Her father had always taken so much pride in caring for their home. But now the clapboard was overdue for a good paint job, the lawn looked neglected, and the flower bed was overgrown with weeds. The only thing that was exactly as it should be was her mother's prized rosebush.

Dakota's heart beat harder and faster, the sound of it

filling her ears. Why was she so nervous? She was going to spend time with her father, whom she adored.

Sin pulled into the driveway and honked the horn twice. They both giggled, the way they had when they were schoolgirls. Her father had always hated it when her friends blew the horn rather than coming to the front door.

"You ready for this?" Sin turned off the engine and squeezed Dakota's hand.

Dakota ignored the swirling butterflies in her belly. "I'm ready."

They climbed out and unloaded Dakota's luggage. Suddenly, the old wooden screen door slammed.

"Land sakes, Sinclair, what on earth is all this noise about?"

Dakota stepped out from behind Sin's truck. "Hey, Dad."

She searched his face, older and more tired than she remembered it. He'd always been her big, strong father. North of six feet tall, with broad shoulders and a strong jaw. Built like a Mack truck. But today he looked a few inches shorter and frail. Like he needed a good meal.

"Dakota?" His hands trembled as he inched toward the edge of the porch. As if he didn't trust his vision.

"Yes, sir." She stepped closer, barely able to see through the tears that had formed the instant she'd seen him. He was much slimmer than he'd been when he'd come to New York to spend Christmas with her six months ago. "It's me."

"It's so good to see you, baby girl!" He stepped down from the porch carefully, limping a little and holding on to the railing. He opened his arms wide.

Dakota rushed into her father's arms, her tears wetting his shirt. He smelled of Irish Spring soap and Old Spice aftershave.

At least that hasn't changed.

"Why are you limping, Dad?" Dakota asked. "Is everything all right?"

"My right knee has been a little gimpy. Just part of old age. Nothing to worry about." Her father held her at arm's length, his eyes glistening. "Why didn't you tell me you were coming? I would've fixed us some dinner and spruced up the place."

"I wanted to surprise you." She sniffled. "I hope that's okay."

"Of course it is!" He hugged her to him again. "I hope you plan on staying more than a day or two this time."

"Actually, I thought I might stay for a few weeks." She tucked her hair behind her ear. "The station made some cutbacks, and I lost my job. If it's okay with you, I'd like to hang out here until I figure things out."

"These big companies are cutting their workforces everywhere you look," he grumbled, his wiry salt-and-pepper eyebrows gathering. His devastating layoff was still a sore subject for her father. "I'm sorry, Dakota. I know how much you loved that job."

"Thanks, Dad."

It was a gracious thing for her father to say since he'd never wanted her to move so far away or to go into television. He'd spent the majority of his life in their small town. His distrust of big cities had been solidified by his older sister's death at the hands of a mugger a few years after she'd moved to Detroit. And he'd been worried about Dakota going into a male-dominated industry that relied so heavily upon one's looks.

"Doesn't matter what brought you here, Dakota. I'm just glad you're home."

"Ahem." Sin cleared her throat as she lugged the large

suitcase behind her with one arm and toted the heavy picnic basket with the other.

"Sorry, Sin." Dakota grabbed the picnic basket, while her father grabbed her luggage.

He chuckled when he discovered how heavy it was. "Guess you weren't joshing about staying for a while." He turned to Sin and wrapped one arm around her shoulder. "Thank you for bringing my girl home. Best surprise I've had in a mighty long time."

"I told you we'd get her back here eventually," Sinclair whispered loudly.

"I can hear you two. You know that, right?" Dakota called over her shoulder as she climbed the porch stairs.

"Umm-hmm. And we don't even care," Sin taunted.

"Are those your famous fried pork chops and prize-winning blackberry cobbler I smell?" Oliver nodded toward the basket.

"The very same, sir," Sin said proudly. "And I made Dakota's favorite, too. Lemon meringue pie."

"Then I hope you plan on staying to help us eat it."

Dakota's cheeks tightened in a big, genuine smile that she could feel all the way down to her toes. She exhaled, drinking in the sense of comfort that settled over her and eased the tension in her shoulders for the first time since her world had imploded three months earlier.

Her heart wasn't racing and her teeth weren't clenched. She felt centered and calm as she stood on the wraparound porch of the home where she'd grown up, despite the gentle teasing of her father and her childhood best friend.

She couldn't hide out here forever, and she had no intention of giving up her dream of being the lead news anchor in a major market. But maybe spending a few weeks back on Holly Grove Island wouldn't be so terrible after all.

Chapter Two

———•—•—•———

Dakota's eyes fluttered open as the sun warmed her face. Sunlight filtered through the curtains and danced around the room. She surveyed the space for a moment before it registered that she was back home in her old bedroom.

It was a separate suite on the third floor of the large Victorian home. Larger than her cozy little prewar apartment with original floors in the East Village that she'd been forced to sublet. The apartment had barely been as big as a postcard. But it had been all hers, and she'd adored it. Letting go of the place had broken Dakota's heart.

An additional insult to the growing list of injuries.

She stretched and kicked one foot out from beneath the covers. At thirty-four she was living back home with her father, her career in shambles and her love life a complete disaster.

Terrific. She was really going places. Dakota sifted through her luggage, grabbed her toiletries and some fresh clothes, then headed for the bathroom.

After her shower, she took a half hour to check her LinkedIn profile and review the job alerts she'd set up on various career boards. Something she'd done nearly every morning since losing her job three months ago. A task that took much longer given the turtle speed of her father's internet service. Then she made her way downstairs in a T-shirt, a pair of old shorts, and her bare feet. The smell of coffee, blueberry pancakes, and bacon wafted throughout the house. She smiled as she crossed the kitchen and kissed her father on the cheek.

"Everything looks good. Smells good, too. Since when do you cook?" The words struck her as soon as they'd left her mouth, and a pained look crinkled her father's eyes. Her mother had done all of the cooking. What choice did her father have but to learn to cook for himself now that she was gone? "Dad, I'm sorry. I didn't…I mean, I shouldn't have—"

"It's okay, baby girl." Oliver smiled at her warmly. "I know what you meant. Go on and have a seat. I'll fix you a plate."

Dakota slid onto the kitchen chair, her cheeks stinging with heat as an uncomfortable silence settled around them.

Her father set her plate on the table and handed her a fork and knife. After he'd set down his own plate and silverware, he placed the blueberry maple syrup in front of her and a bottle of sugar-free syrup near his plate.

He sat down and nodded toward her still untouched food. "What, you don't trust your old man's culinary abilities?"

"Of course I do." Dakota snickered, picking up her fork. She cut into the light, fluffy pancakes, and took a bite. The pancakes melted in her mouth, and a hint of lemon melded with the fresh blueberries. "Dad, this is really good. Like…"

"Mom's?" Her father chuckled. "Well, that's certainly

the highest compliment I could hope for. Especially since your mom spent the months immediately following her diagnosis teaching me to cook. She insisted that a man living alone needed to be able to cook for himself. I think she was afraid I'd marry the first woman who showed up on my steps with a hot meal if I couldn't."

"Sounds like Mom. Determined to control things, even from the great beyond."

Oliver laughed. "Your mother was a very organized and determined woman. That's for sure. It's one of the things I loved most about her. It's one of the things I love most about you, too." He winked at her.

"I thought my stubbornness drove you crazy." Dakota recalled their last big argument.

He'd rented a U-Haul to collect her things from her college dorm and drive her home after her graduation ceremony. That was when she told him she'd landed a paid internship at a television station in New York, so she wouldn't be returning home. She was moving into a tiny apartment with four roommates—two of whom were male. It was the angriest she'd ever seen her father. Still, she'd stuck to her resolve.

"Sometimes," he acknowledged. "But even then I admired the trait. I was proud of you for making your own decisions. For your conviction and tenacity. I still am."

Dakota bit her lip and her belly burned. If her father only knew what a mess she'd made of her life and career, it'd break his heart. She would have to tell him eventually, but it didn't need to be today. She watched, one brow raised, as he poured the syrup on his pancakes. "Sugar free? That's not like you."

"Watching my figure." He patted his belly, now practically gone, and chuckled. There was something concerning behind the smile, and his laughter felt forced. Besides, her father had always despised diet and sugar-free *anything*.

She was all for her father living a healthier lifestyle, but why the sudden change?

"You're sure everything is okay?" she asked, unconvinced.

"Peachy." He set the bottle down and sliced into his pancakes.

Dakota poured more blueberry syrup on her plate. Something was definitely going on with her father. And she would make it her business to find out what it was.

"Looking forward to the Fourth of July Festival?" He seemed eager to change the subject.

Dakota shrugged, her muscles tense. "I don't know if I'm ready to be paraded around town. I thought I'd hang out here. Decompress. Do some job hunting."

"But you've always loved the Fourth of July Festival. And it isn't small-potatoes stuff anymore. The town goes all out. You should see it."

Dakota could remember everything about the last Fourth of July Festival she'd attended on Holly Grove Island. The heat had been unbearable, and it was sticky and humid. But none of that had mattered to her because she and Dexter had been together. And she'd been head over heels in love with him.

In her head, she'd already mapped out their future together. They'd both go to Texas A&M and get married after she graduated. But they'd hold off on having children until they were both established in their careers. Him as a pro football player and her as a nightly news anchor.

Back then everything had seemed simple. She'd been so sure of what lay ahead for them. But here she was, seventeen years later, decidedly single and with no clue what her future held in store.

"I don't know, Dad."

"Look at it this way," he said. "The festival will give you a chance to get all of those awkward hellos out of the way in a single day. If you don't, you know what'll happen."

She did. If she didn't make an appearance, everyone in town would eventually stop by. One by one.

"You're right. I should get it over with." She shoveled more pancakes into her mouth. They really were delicious. Her mother would be proud.

"That's my girl." Her father settled his big brown eyes on hers and grinned. "Now that you're going to the festival...Lila Gayle has a favor to ask of you."

"How'd Ms. Lila know I was..." Dakota shook her head and laughed. "Never mind. For a moment I forgot where I was." Word of mouth traveled faster here than the high-speed internet she was already beginning to miss. "What's the favor?"

"She was asked to sponsor and judge an event at the festival. But she needs someone to help cover the café booth during the event. She'll have a cook there," he added quickly, likely in response to the look of alarm on her face. "But she's short waitstaff. She just needs you to take the orders, pour coffee. Stuff like that. Should be a walk in the park since you've worked the festival booth for her before."

Dakota had been a server at Lila's Café on weekends and during summers while in high school. So she'd also worked the booth during the Fourth of July Festival.

"She'd pay you, of course."

Dakota waved off that bit of information. "I'm happy to help Ms. Lila out, Dad."

"I'll let her know." Her father munched on a crispy piece of bacon triumphantly.

She had always liked Ms. Lila. It would be good to see her again. Besides, working the booth would ensure that any prying conversations remained short and sweet.

Still, the thought of seeing everyone in town made her a little queasy. In the months before she'd left for NYU to pursue a degree in journalism, her mother had cornered anyone who would listen and compared Dakota to icons like Ida B. Wells and Gwen Ifill, proclaiming that her baby girl was headed off into the world to "make a name for herself." The scandal with Marcello had certainly accomplished that. Just not in the way her mother had hoped. If just one person discovered the truth, the entire town would know within hours what a failure she was, making her humiliation complete.

Her father's place felt safe and comfortable. Outside these doors she'd be a nervous wreck, waiting for the other shoe to drop.

Chapter Three

• — • — •

Dexter Roberts had attended the annual Fourth of July picnic at Holly Grove Island Park nearly every year of his life, except the summers he'd worked during college. Yet he was more nervous than he'd been while awaiting the results of the surgery to repair the devastating knee injury that ended his football career.

A salty morning breeze blew off the Atlantic Ocean, rustling the canvas tents in the Food Alley section of the festival. Dexter hovered between the booths where Ms. Lupita was already preparing all manner of mouthwatering Mexican dishes and Ms. Louise and her daughters were setting out their delectable, handmade fudge and taffy. He tugged down his baseball cap and tried to be inconspicuous as he scanned the early crowd through his dark shades.

"You look as nervous as a long-tailed cat in a room full of rocking chairs, Dexter Roberts." His mother jabbed his side, surprising him. "Skulking around here looking for—"

"I'm not skulking, Mama. And I'm not...*exactly*...looking for anyone. I'm just—"

"Dakota Jones! How wonderful to see you, love." Lila

Gayle Eriksson, owner of Lila's Café, had as thick a British accent now as she'd had the day she'd arrived in town nearly thirty years ago. "I can't thank you enough for popping 'round to help me out."

His attention snapped to the two women the moment he heard Dakota's name. It'd been a long time since he'd seen her. Longer still since they'd spoken.

She wore a simple sleeveless denim shift that hinted at the curvy frame hidden beneath. The midthigh length of the dress revealed miles of smooth mahogany brown skin and toned thighs and calves.

A curtain of glossy, tousled chestnut-brown waves shielded her face from view. But then she tucked her hair behind her ear, making half of her face visible.

She was even more stunning than he remembered.

"You wanna tell me again how you're *not* looking for anyone in particular." His mother stood with her arms folded and one brow hiked. "Nearly got whiplash turning to see Dakota the moment Lila Gayle called her name."

Dexter rubbed his neck, turning his attention to his mother. There was no fooling Marilyn Roberts. It was foolish of him to try. But that hadn't ever stopped him and his younger brothers from trying to pull one over on her, just the same.

"So I wanted to see Dakota. It's no big deal." He shrugged. "We were friends. There's nothing unusual about that."

His mother's expression softened. She rubbed his arm. "I think it's safe to say you two were more than just friends, honey. And no, there's nothing unusual about you being nervous to see her again."

"I didn't say I was nervous," he interjected.

"No, you didn't." She grabbed his hand. "But those sweaty palms, your rapid breathing, and the way you keep rubbing the back of your neck are telling the story loud and clear."

"It's ninety-two degrees out here. Everyone has sweaty palms." Dexter pulled his hand from hers, wiping them both on his board shorts. He swallowed hard, ignoring the rapid beat of his heart, his dry mouth, and the quivering in his gut.

"You should've taken my advice and gone over to Oliver's to see her. Gotten all of the awkwardness of that first meeting out of the way—without the entire town's prying eyes." She glanced around before returning her attention to him. "In a town the size of a postage stamp, you two were bound to run into each other eventually."

Dexter sighed, not acknowledging his mother's I-told-you-so. But she was absolutely right. According to the town gossip chain, Dakota had been back nearly a week. Plenty of time for him to stop by and say hello. But he hadn't. And so here he was, preparing himself for public castigation by the woman who'd once meant *everything* to him.

"Dex, honey, don't let this opportunity to reconnect with Dakota pass you by. She means too much to you."

"That was a long time ago." Dexter frowned. "We're different people now."

"Yet your feelings for her don't seem to have changed." His mother offered an encouraging smile. "Perhaps she feels the same. Only one way to find out."

He glanced at the spot where the two women had stood. They were gone.

Another missed opportunity.

"They stepped inside Lila Gayle's booth," his mother offered, as if she'd read his thoughts. "I believe Dakota is helping her out, like old times." She grinned. "Haven't eaten breakfast yet, have you?"

"No, ma'am." Dexter shook his head.

"Now seems like as good a time as any." His mother winked, then checked her watch. "I'm headed over to the first aid tent to start my shift." She called over her shoulder, "Give Dakota my regards."

Dexter took a deep breath, readjusted the brim of his baseball hat, and leaned against the light pole a stone's throw away from the Lila's Café booth. His heart thudded in his chest and his pulse raced at the thought of reconnecting with Dakota. He'd blown it with her. He couldn't change that. But that hadn't stopped him from wishing he could go back in time and handle things between them differently. Or from wanting her in his life again. If not as lovers, then at least as friends.

There was a solid chance Dakota wouldn't be interested in either. But now that they were both back in their small community, he didn't want things to be awkward.

He'd give it a few minutes. Then he'd head over and order breakfast from the woman who still sent his heart into overdrive without even trying.

———

Dakota was surprised by how easily she fell back into the role of server at Lila's Café, a job she'd held during her sophomore through senior years of high school. There was something comforting about meeting people here, with a wooden countertop between them. Where they couldn't pull her aside and ply her with questions.

The breakfast crowd had slowed down a bit by the time she'd taken over to give Lila Gayle a break. Which made Lila's booth a good place to hide for the rest of the morning.

"Dakota, would you be a dear and get me a refill of coffee?" Mrs. Anderson asked after they'd had all of the expected conversation.

Great to see you.

You're looking a bit thin.

Sorry about your mother.

Her mother had been gone five years. Still, that last bit hit her hard, no matter how many times people had expressed their condolences over the loss of her mother.

"Right away, Mrs. Anderson." Dakota refilled the woman's mug, then turned to replace the carafe.

"I'd love a cup before you put that away."

The familiar voice made her pulse race. Still, when she turned around, seeing him felt surreal. She inhaled deeply and clenched the hand at her side as she bit back the resentment rising in her chest.

"Hello, Dakota." His mouth curved in a soft smile, while his dark sunglasses shielded his eyes. "It's good to see you."

"Dexter." She forced the name caught in her throat past her lips. Grabbing a sleeved paper cup, she filled it with coffee. "What can I get for you today?"

"What's good?" he asked in the same low, sexy growl that once had the power to turn her inside out.

Not today, Satan. Not today.

"Today's special is French toast." She pulled a pad and pencil from the pocket of her apron with all of the indifference she could muster.

"Not what I asked." He didn't touch the laminated menu in front of him. Instead, he slid off his shades and set them on the counter. His gaze was like hot lasers melting her very core. "I'd like to know what *you* think is good."

Not running into the jerk who dumped me while I'm wearing a grease-stained apron. That would be good.

She scribbled quickly on her notepad, then met his gaze. "Waffles, sausage patties, an extra side of bacon, and hash browns. Coming right up."

His eyes widened with surprise and then he chuckled. A broad grin spread across his annoyingly handsome face.

Why couldn't he be balding, sporting a spare tire, and missing a few teeth?

Dakota ripped the ticket off the pad and clipped it to the stainless-steel order wheel. She spun it toward Leo, who was manning the grill, then turned back to Dex.

God, he's handsome.

More than she remembered. But then, he'd been nineteen when she saw him last. But now...She drew in a shaky breath. Her knees wavered and a warmth, which she preferred not to acknowledge, traveled the length of her spine.

Dexter's dark-brown skin looked smooth and warm. His dark eyes glinted with amusement. His sensual lips, framed by a well-trimmed mustache and a neat beard, quirked in a half smile. And he smelled divine, like citrus and sandalwood.

If it weren't for the small matter of hating Dexter Roberts's guts, she'd be inclined to put him on a plate, sop him up with a warm biscuit, then wash him down with an ice-cold glass of sweet tea.

Dakota shuddered inwardly. The quiet, confident, magnetic appeal Dexter had possessed in high school—what Sin had dubbed "the Dex Factor"—was clearly still intact. He'd only been there five whole minutes and he was already driving her insane. But she was older now. Wiser. And in case she'd forgotten the dire consequences of trusting a handsome man with a disarming smile, Marcello had certainly reminded her.

"Your order will be up shortly. More coffee?"

"More coffee would be great." He slid the cup toward her. "But what I'd really like is a chance to talk."

Dexter had never been big on talking. He was the strong and silent type who listened and observed a lot more often than he spoke. Especially around people he didn't know. When he finally opened up to her she was delighted that she'd broken through the wall with which he seemed to surround himself. It had been a coup back then. But she wasn't interested in whatever it was that Dexter Roberts had to say now.

"I'm kind of busy." Dakota lifted one shoulder in a mock apology as she refilled his cup. She replaced the carafe on its warmer.

He surveyed the empty counter and dragged a hand across his forehead. "You're not going to make this easy on me, are you?"

"Like you made things easy for me when you dumped me?" Her voice wavered and her cheeks stung.

So much for my fantasy of playing it cool, if we ever crossed paths again.

"Dakota, I...I'm sorry that I—"

"Forget it, Dex. We don't need to talk about it. *Ever*." Dakota moved to the other end of the counter, thankful that a customer had approached.

She'd made the mistake of revealing that she was still hurt by his rejection. But she wouldn't give Dexter the satisfaction of knowing how shaken she was by seeing him.

Now, if only she could convince her hands and knees to stop wavering.

Chapter Four

— · — · —

$\mathbf{D}$ex peered over his cup at Dakota as he sipped his coffee. His heart slammed against his chest at the sight of the woman who'd taken a huge chunk of his heart with her when she left Holly Grove Island for good.

He aimed to get it back. One way or another.

Dakota cast a nervous glance in his direction as she took another customer's order. He lowered his cup and smiled. She returned her attention to the other customer and tucked a stray curl behind her ear.

He set his cup down, hope slowly flooding his chest.

A few minutes later, Dakota set his food in front of him. "Here you are. Waffles, sausage, bacon, and hash browns. The Dexter Roberts Special." Her tone was matter-of-fact.

"You remembered." He smiled. "I'm flattered."

"Don't be," she replied. "I also remember exactly what Old Man Riley ordered every morning." She folded her arms, her expression hardened.

Dexter's eyes were trained on her mouth. He'd always loved those lips. They'd been soft and warm and always tasted of cherry cola or bubble gum.

He still vividly recalled the taste of her lips and the

feel of her incredibly soft skin on that warm summer night. His pulse elevated at the memory of tugging her lower lip gently between his as he'd kissed her. He cleared his throat. "Old Man Riley died, you know. Couple years back."

"I—I hadn't heard," she stammered, her defensive posture easing as she dropped her arms to her sides. "I'm surprised my dad didn't mention it."

"Oliver hasn't been the same since he lost your mother." Dex raised his eyes to hers, his heart breaking for her. She winced at the mention of her mother. The two of them had been close. "I'm sorry about your mom, Dakota. Ms. Madeline was a remarkable woman. She had such a beautiful, giving spirit. We all miss her like crazy."

"Thanks." She fiddled with the strings of her apron to fill the awkward silence between them. When she settled her gaze on his again, her eyes were shiny with unshed tears. "Let me know if you need anything else."

"I heard you're only here for a few weeks," Dexter called to her retreating back. He'd hoped Dakota would hear him out, allow him to apologize. He'd half expected that she wouldn't, and he'd respect that. But this was something she needed to hear. "Oliver needs you, Dakota."

She turned back to him. "What do you mean?"

"I mean he's lonely, and he hasn't taken losing your mother very well. He misses your mom, but he also really misses you and Shayna," he said, referring to her older sister.

She shifted her eyes to a woman who sat at the other end of the counter, sipping her coffee and awaiting her breakfast order. The woman, who Dex didn't recognize, watched them as if they were a soap opera.

Dakota returned her gaze to him and leaned in, her voice hushed. "I don't want to talk about this here. I'm off duty in a couple of hours. We can talk then. Somewhere discreet. I don't want the whole town thinking…" She let her words trail off, then sighed.

"How about that park bench at the other end of the beach? The one where I…" He cringed when she narrowed her eyes at him and folded her arms.

Asking Dakota to meet him at the spot where he'd asked her to be his girlfriend was a truly stupid idea. But it'd been the first place that had come to mind. It was an easy walk from the booth, would have very little traffic since most of the folks on the island were at the Fourth of July festivities, and was a spot that was familiar to both of them.

Still, suggesting it as a meeting spot was a complete blunder.

Way to go, Dex. Way to go.

A little more than two hours later, Dexter watched Dakota stalk toward the bench where he sat. A trail of smoke practically billowed from her ears.

She was pissed. At him.

Why would he expect anything else after the way he'd ended things between them? It pained him even now to remember the hurt look on her face. He'd broken limbs and torn his ACL playing college football. Nothing had ever hurt him more than what he'd done to her that day. He'd broken her heart. But he'd done it for both of their sakes.

Dex doubted Dakota would see things that way, so it was a topic better left for another day. Right now he'd focus on the issue at hand: Oliver.

But focusing on anything other than how enticing Dakota looked on this hot summer day required a Herculean effort. Her warm brown skin glowed with a light sheen of perspiration. The neckline of her slim denim dress hugged her full breasts and revealed a hint of cleavage. Strappy, black platform sandals highlighted the length of her incredibly sexy legs. A black bandanna held back the beach waves that bounced behind her.

Dex swallowed hard as Dakota got closer. He needed to take it down a notch and play this cool. Starting with shutting his gaping mouth.

———

Dakota's skin felt as if it were on fire beneath Dexter's intense gaze.

Only Dex would have the nerve to ask her to meet him *here*. The very place where their relationship shifted from being friends to something more. If he hadn't been such a jerk to her at the end, she might've considered it sweet that Dex remembered the significance of their spot at the far end of Holly Grove Island Park.

She plopped down on the bench, leaving as much physical space as possible between them. Had this bench always been this small? Maybe it only appeared so because Dexter was taller now and his shoulders were broader. Or maybe it was because her hips weren't as narrow as they'd been the last time he'd placed his large hands on them and pulled her closer.

Dakota squeezed her eyes shut and huffed.

Why did I agree to meet with him?

She rubbed at the goose bumps popping up on her arms, partly because a cool breeze chose that moment to blow off the Atlantic Ocean. Partly because a chill ran through her when his eyes met hers. But this wasn't about her and Dexter.

"You said my dad *needs* me. What did you mean?"

This wasn't a social call. The only reason she'd been

compelled to meet Dexter Roberts here, of all places, was because of her father.

"I'm worried about Oliver," Dexter said. "He hasn't been himself since he lost your mom, and now there's the decline in his health."

Dakota swallowed hard, a knot tightening in her gut. She wanted to tell Dexter to mind his own business because her dad was fine, but the truth was she was worried about him, too.

"A decline in his health?" She echoed Dexter's ominous words. Her mouth suddenly felt dry and the knot in her stomach cinched tighter. "I mean, I know he's lost a lot of weight in the last six months, but he said that he wants to be healthier, so he can live long enough for me to give him some grandkids since Shayna hasn't."

"Sounds like your dad." Dexter chuckled. "So how are Shayna and..."

"Howard," she supplied. "They're both doing fine." *According to Shay.*

But when they spoke by phone, once or twice a month, her sister seemed unhappy, despite insisting everything was fine. Dakota had wanted to fly to California to see for herself, but Shay was always too busy. Not that any of that was Dexter's business.

"Are you saying my dad is sick?" Just saying the words caused a flutter of panic in her chest, but her heart rate doubled when Dexter shifted his gaze from hers rather than answering. "Oh my God, my dad isn't...*dying*, is he?" She whispered the offending word, hating to even put something so awful out into the universe.

Dexter covered her hand with his much larger one. "No, sweet—" He swallowed the word. "No, but Oliver is diabetic. Did he tell you that?"

She shook her head, her eyes burning with tears. "How do you know that when he hasn't told me or Shay?"

"He didn't tell me. I saw him buying diabetic supplies at the pharmacy."

"Why would he keep something so important from us?" she whispered the words aloud to herself, but Dexter responded anyway.

"He probably didn't want to worry you." Dex's reassuring tone drew her attention to his warm smile. "Lila Gayle's been fussin' over him, much as Oliver will allow. Seems to have worked. He's lost a lot of weight, which is great for his condition. But that limp of his has gotten a lot worse. We're all worried about him, but you know your dad."

Dakota's heart ached. She couldn't bear the thought of losing her father, too. Not when the loss of her mother still felt so fresh. She glanced down at the hand Dexter was still holding. Dakota allowed herself the momentary indulgence of reveling in the familiar warmth and comfort of his touch. It had always felt so reassuring when Dexter held her hand in his. Like she was safe. Protected. Loved.

A teenage fantasy back then. A mere illusion now. One she wouldn't fall for again.

She slipped her hand from beneath his.

"I know Holly Grove Island is just a pit stop to whatever you plan to do next. But Oliver needs you right now, Dakota."

"Why are you telling me this?"

He winced, as if he was disappointed that she needed to ask. "I care about Oliver...and about you. I never stopped caring about you, Dakota."

His words felt heavy. Like a living, breathing thing that had taken up residence in the space between them. Her face and neck suddenly felt hot.

How dare he fix his mouth to say something like that? To pretend that he still cared. It was Dex who had broken up with her during Christmas break his first year at Texas A&M.

She'd planned to follow him there, though it meant giving up her dream of going to NYU's journalism school. Because she couldn't bear the thought of spending four long years apart, she'd been willing to defer that dream. Perhaps go to grad school at NYU instead. Or move to New York once his pro football career had ended. She'd been prepared to make that sacrifice because she loved him. But then he'd broken her heart.

Dakota still remembered everything about that night nearly two decades ago. White Christmases were a rarity in the Outer Banks. But that night had started off perfect. The air was cold and crisp. Fluffy white snowflakes fell to the ground but melted on contact. She remembered the green sweater Dex had been wearing and the red peacoat she'd worn with the red, white, and pink scarf Dex's mother had crocheted for her the year before.

They'd been in the middle of exchanging gifts when he'd suddenly blurted out that they were both too young to be tied down. He wanted the freedom to see other people.

She'd been devastated. Thinking of that cold night a lifetime ago still made her heart feel as if it would explode. Dakota bit the inside of her cheek and steeled her spine, sitting taller. She'd been so sure she was past all of this, but suddenly the wound Dexter had inflicted that night felt as raw as ever. She wouldn't give him the satisfaction of knowing how deeply he'd hurt her.

"I appreciate you telling me." It pained her to feel even slightly indebted to Dexter Roberts, but she was grateful he'd informed her about her father's health issues.

She couldn't help feeling guilty about staying away so long, leaving her father to grieve her mother on his own because she couldn't handle the painful memories lurking around every corner: In every single room of their house. At the town gazebo where her mother had sung Christmas carols with the church choir. On the beach where she and her mom would lie in the sun and trade gossip like old girlfriends. At the ice cream shop where her mother would occasionally indulge herself by having two scoops of mint chocolate chip ice cream piled high with whipped cream.

If she needed to extend her stay on Holly Grove Island to see after her father, she could certainly spare a few months. Besides, lying low a bit longer would put more distance between her and the scandal that had tanked her career.

"If it was my mom, I'd want to know." He shrugged.

"Well, thank you, just the same." She stood, turning to leave.

"One more thing, Dakota," he called out, stopping her in her tracks. "I don't know what your eventual plans are, but if you decide to stay on Holly Grove Island for a while, a mutual friend could use your help."

Dakota narrowed her eyes at him. "Who's the mutual friend?"

"Nick Washington. He's now the director of sales and marketing at the new hotel on the island. He's never taken on a job this big before. You know Nick—he's smart and capable, but also a bit cocky. I think he's starting to feel like he's in over his head, but he's too proud to admit it. He needs confident, experienced people on his team. So far the pool has been kind of shallow. And the pay is awfully good."

Dakota wanted to tell Dexter Roberts where he could shove his little job-assistance program. But the truth was, she needed to be here, seeing about her father for at least the next few months. Just until she knew he was on solid footing. And as for Nick's available job... well, she could definitely use the money.

"I'm not staying permanently. But if Nick would consider a temporary arrangement, maybe I can help. But right now my only concern is my father."

"Of course." Dex extended Nick's business card. "In case you need it."

She reached for the card, but Dex flipped it over, revealing a number jotted on the back.

"That's my number. In case you ever want to talk."

Dakota slipped the card into her pocket without looking at it or acknowledging his offer. "I'd better get back before my dad starts to worry." She hiked a thumb over her shoulder toward the sounds of a band warming up at the festival. "Goodbye, Dex."

She hurried back to the event, hoping it was the last she'd see of Dexter Roberts.

Chapter Five

It'd been two days since the Fourth of July Festival, and Dakota had asked her father five different times in five different ways if everything was all right. He'd grunted that everything was fine and changed the subject each time. She could've asked him directly, but then he would've wanted to know who'd told her. And she wouldn't throw Dexter under the bus.

She appreciated him telling her about her dad, even if she hated that he'd been the one to do it. Every time she thought of sitting on that bench a few inches from him, heat filled her chest, her tummy fluttered, and her face heated.

Dakota sighed and fanned herself with an open hand as she glanced at her father's closed bedroom door. Maybe she'd failed miserably where Marcello was concerned, but she'd spent the past six years of her career as an investigative reporter. A damn good one. She'd busted dirty politicians, shady contractors, tricky grifters, and thieving corporations. Surely she could find some evidence to corroborate Dexter's concerns so she could confront her father without pointing the finger at her ex.

Her father had gone fishing early that morning with a

few of his fellow retiree buddies. They'd been gone a few hours already, so he could return any minute. It was now or never.

Dakota sucked in a deep breath, turned the doorknob, and stepped inside her parents' bedroom. She hadn't been in this room in more than five years. Since her mother lay in bed ill, her body slowly being ravaged by cancer.

Her father hadn't changed a thing.

Her mother's makeup and perfume bottles were still lined up against the mirror of the vanity near the far window. The bedding and curtains were the same, and everything was arranged exactly as it had been when her mother was alive.

Dakota didn't dare touch the partially open closet door. She already knew that it would be overflowing with all of her mother's dresses and shoes. Many of which she'd never worn.

Tightness gripped Dakota's chest, and her throat felt dry. She bit her lower lip and fought back the tears that stung her eyes.

How could her father sleep in the room that felt so much like her mother every single night for five years? She hadn't been in the room five minutes and she was on the brink of tears.

Don't be sad, baby. Think of all the great moments we've had together. I couldn't be more proud of you, sweetheart.

Dakota sniffled and wiped angrily at the warm tears that had spilled down her face.

Why did everything have to be so damn complicated? Even a sweet and touching moment at the end of her mother's life detonated a minefield of conflicting emotions.

She was glad to finally hear her mother say she was proud of her, full stop. Rather than pointing out to her where she could be better.

Sit up straight, honey. No man wants to marry the Hunchback of Notre Dame.

Straighten your hair, honey. No studio wants an anchor with a head full of kinky curls.

If they passed you over for that promotion, you obviously didn't want it badly enough. You've got to work harder.

Dakota wrapped her arms around her middle and released a heavy sigh. *Work harder.* Those words were lodged in her brain. They'd been her unofficial motto since she'd entered her first beauty pageant, at her mother's behest, at age five.

No matter how far she'd gone in her career or what she'd achieved, her mother's response had always been *That's great, honey, but…*

But…but…but.

She'd barely had a moment to celebrate the win before her mother would launch into a plan of attack for next time.

Always be the best. Anything else is varying degrees of losing.

Dakota raked her hand through her messy hair and turned her attention toward her parents' bathroom. She crept inside the room, which seemed relatively free of memories. It was sparse. Nothing on the counter but a ceramic container that held her father's razor and toothbrush, the soap dish, and a tube of toothpaste.

She opened the linen closet and eyed the space, feeling guilty about touching anything unnecessarily. There was a collection of meds. She took a quick snapshot of her father's medicines, so she could look them up later. Then a little black pouch caught her eye.

Dakota picked it up and unzipped it. The pouch held a glucose meter, a lance, lancets, and a bottle of test strips.

Dex was right. Her father was diabetic.

What else isn't he telling me?

She grabbed the pouch and crept out of her parents' room. When her father returned, they were going to have a talk.

Dexter's cell rang minutes after he'd ended his last conference call of the day. After a three-hour meeting, he relished the idea of silence. But he was glad to see his cousin Garrett's name and photo pop up on the screen.

"Rett, it's been a while." Dexter put the phone on speaker and continued typing notes from the meeting into a follow-up email for his assistant. "How are you?"

"Things are great," Garrett said. "But the real question is, how are *you*?"

"Fine." Dexter stopped typing and turned to look at the phone. "Why wouldn't I be?"

"Word on the street is your old flame is back in town."

"How'd you...Never mind." Dex dragged a hand across his forehead. His mother undoubtedly had talked to Aunt Ellen, who'd told Garrett. "Yes, Dakota is back in town, *temporarily*. And no, it's no big deal."

"See how defensive you sounded right there?" Dex could practically see his cousin wagging one of his Arsenio Hall–length digits. "If it really wasn't a big deal, you wouldn't feel the need to convince me that it wasn't."

"I'm not."

"You used your Uncle James voice," Garrett said.

Dexter couldn't help chuckling.

His father, James Roberts, was a good man. A solid family provider and the kind of person who would give a neighbor in need the shirt off his back. But the man had a far more difficult time sharing himself with the people who loved him.

As a kid, one of Dexter's favorite sounds in the world had been his father's deep belly laugh. Dex treasured the contagious sound because he'd heard it so rarely. James Roberts was always so serious, with a sober expression and stern tone.

Only two things seemed to truly make James Roberts happy: football and jazz. His father had played the saxophone in a band with a few of his buddies. So Dexter had taken up the sax, too, as a way to get closer to the enigmatic man. And he'd played football, even though he preferred baseball.

He'd had an aptitude for both the saxophone and football, which pleased his father and made him genuinely proud of him. The man had been heartbroken when Dexter's injury ended his college football career and extinguished any hopes of a professional one. And yet all Dexter had felt when he'd finally learned his fate was a deep sense of relief.

"I wasn't using my Uncle James voice," Dexter said. Because in their family, that was definitely a thing. "Just being clear."

"I don't know," Rett said. "Sounds like my boy needs me. Say the word and I'm there. I know how hard the breakup was on you. It couldn't have been easy seeing her again."

"It was fine, and I'm fine."

"But is she still *fine*?" There was playfulness in his cousin's tone.

"She's beyond fine. She's gorgeous. Seeing her again after all this time . . . It knocked me on my ass for a minute, if I'm being honest," Dexter admitted with a sigh. "But what's crazy is that she looks so much like her mother now. I swear, she could be her twin."

"If you ask me, Dakota's mama thought they were twins. I've heard of parents wanting to live vicariously through their children, but the woman took it a bit far," Rett said, then added, "God rest her soul."

"You know that doesn't give you a pass for speaking ill of the dead, right?" Dexter pointed out.

"Wasn't speaking ill of her, bruh. Just stating facts. Let the chips fall where they may," Rett said matter-of-factly. Neither of them spoke for a minute. Then his cousin broke the silence. "You sure you're good?"

"Positive. We've already gotten through that first awkward meeting. We even spoke privately." Dex clenched his fist, remembering how good it had felt to hold Dakota's hand again.

"Her idea or yours?" Rett's interest was obviously piqued.

"Mine. I wanted to talk to her about an issue with her father." Dexter cleared his throat, then added, "Told her she should hang around town for a while. For Oliver's sake."

"Wait, you snitched on her dad, then guilted her into sticking around longer?" Rett whistled. "That's grimy."

"It's not like I did it for me." His cheeks heated and his pulse quickened, even as he denied his cousin's claim. "I was looking out for her dad. Besides, she has the right to know."

"Speaking of Dakota's right to know..." Rett quickly transitioned to the topic they both knew he didn't want to discuss. "Don't you think Dakota has the right to know what *really* happened between you two back then?"

Dexter heaved a sigh and tapped his thumb against the blotter on his desk. The pain in Dakota's eyes and the tears that streaked her cheeks, red from the frigid weather, were as vivid in his mind as they'd been that day seventeen years ago.

"She knows what happened. I broke up with her. It was my decision, no one else's. It was the best thing for the both of us." Dex gritted the words out.

"Say it a few more times and maybe you'll start believing it." Rett's words were firm but empathetic. "But the truth is that we both know you regret how you handled the situation."

That much is true.

They both knew it, so there was no need to confirm it.

"You missed a great Fourth of July Festival," Dexter said instead. "The new committee has outdone itself. I can't wait to see what they'll do for Founders Day." Dexter lightly rapped his finger on the desk. "You should come home for it. Aunt Ellen would be thrilled."

"We'll see. I don't know if I'm up to being grilled about my love life and hounded about producing grandchildren for my mother," Rett said.

"You don't have a love life, so it'll be a short conversation. But if she asks about your sex life... well, that would be a conversation and a half."

"Or maybe you don't know me as well as you think you do. Maybe I'm ready for something more," Rett countered.

There was a beat of silence; then they both broke into laughter.

"I could barely say that with a straight face," Rett said. "You know I'm all about that bachelor life."

"I do. Which is why I don't understand why you're pressing me about Dakota. Seems like it goes against your bachelor code."

"Being a quintessential bachelor is the right move for *me*. For a marshmallow-soft dude like you...not so much." Rett laughed.

"You didn't even like Dakota when I was dating her," Dex reminded his cousin.

"I didn't dislike her *personally*. I was selfish, and I didn't appreciate sharing my best friend and wingman." There was regret in Rett's voice, but he quickly recovered. "Besides, after that chick you were going to marry, I'd much prefer that you get back with Dakota."

"Evelyn wasn't that bad." Dexter felt the need to defend her. His ex was high maintenance, but she wasn't a bad person. And it was him who evidently hadn't been ready to commit to her. Because they weren't the right fit.

"She who shall not be named or she who was a piece of work will do just fine," Rett responded quickly, then sighed. "Seriously, you and Dakota were good together. I didn't recognize it then, but I do now. And if there is any chance that the two of you are still right for each other...well, seems like it'd be worth investigating."

"We were kids then. We didn't have a clue about love."

"Maybe," Rett conceded. "But you made each other happy. And from what I hear, you could both use a little of that in your lives right now."

"Could you please tell me where my real cousin is and put him back on the phone?" Dexter teased. "The sentimental sap on the line right now is giving me the blues."

From the moment he learned that she'd returned to town, he'd been in his head and in his feelings about how badly he'd screwed up with Dakota. The last thing he needed was for Mr. Quintessential Bachelor, of all people, to point out the very thing that was constantly on his brain. His desire for a second chance with her.

"It was a momentary lapse. I promise to be the same annoying prick you know and love the next time we talk. Deal?"

"Deal."

"So..." Rett dragged out the single syllable. "If Dakota is back, she's probably hanging out with her girl Sin again."

"From what I hear," Dexter said. "Why? You still sweet on Sin?"

"I was never *sweet* on Sinclair Buchanan." Rett put a little bass in his voice. "She was a pain in my ass that I was forced to spend time with while you and Dakota were together."

"Oh, so we're gonna pretend that all that bickering you and Sin did back then wasn't one big game of juvenile flirtation?" Dexter laughed when his cousin stammered in response. "That's what I thought." Dexter glanced up at his assistant, who'd knocked on his open door. "Gotta go. But you should come home. In the meantime, I'll tell Sinclair you said hello."

"Don't you dare—"

Dexter ended the call, still chuckling at how flustered Rett had been around the topic of Sinclair Buchanan. He answered his assistant's questions about the recent conference call, then got back to work. But his cousin's words kept cycling through his brain.

Don't you think Dakota has the right to know what really *happened between you two back then?*

Maybe she did, and maybe it would absolve him of some of the guilt he felt. But it would be devastating if she learned the truth. And he wouldn't hurt her again.

Chapter Six

* * *

It'd been a long time since Dakota had eaten fried catfish. Or fried anything. The additional pounds didn't translate well on camera. But she was unemployed, feeling sorry for herself, and she deserved a bit of down-home goodness.

Her father had returned with the fish he'd caught that morning already cleaned and filleted, for which she was grateful. She didn't mind eating fish or meat. She just didn't like the idea of meeting her meat while it still had eyes and a mouth. She wouldn't have minded cooking her father's catch, either. But he'd insisted on cooking it himself.

"The meal was delicious." Dakota took the final bite of catfish. "But I'm beginning to think that you secretly doubt my cooking abilities." Dakota poured herself a glass of sweet tea—something else she hadn't allowed herself to enjoy since her last trip home. She'd probably drank five gallons of the stuff the week she came home for her mother's funeral.

"It's no secret." Her father chuckled. "You have many talents, Kota. God knows cooking has never been one of them."

"Dad!" Dakota balled up her napkin and tossed it across the table at her father.

He caught it, both of them laughing.

"Speaking of secrets..." Dakota put down her fork and produced the pouch she'd hidden on the seat beside her. She shoved it across the table. "Can we talk about this?"

"You went through my things?" Her father frowned, furrowing his white and gray brows.

"I was looking for the heating pad. I think I might've tweaked my back rearranging the furniture in my room."

Mostly true.

"All right, Dakota." Her father sighed, obviously doubtful of her story. He shrugged. "So I'm diabetic. Shouldn't be a shock. My father was and my brother, Phil, is."

A twinge tugged at her gut. Her grandfather had suffered multiple amputations before his death twenty years ago. And her uncle Phil was a noncompliant diabetic who suffered with debilitating nerve pain. Neither would happen to her father as long as she could help it.

"Then why didn't you tell me? Even before I came home, we talked several times a week. You never once thought you should mention this to me?"

"You were busy, living your life in the big city." His eyes didn't meet hers. "I didn't want to be a burden or to make you feel you needed to come home to see about me. I have everything under control."

"Well, I'm certainly not busy now, and I'm right here." She reached across the table and squeezed her father's hand, forcing him to drag his gaze to hers. "If it's completely under control, why hide it from me?"

"I wasn't hiding anything." He pulled back his hand. "Some things are just private."

Dakota groaned quietly. "How long have you known?"

"About six months, and I'm doing well." He patted his belly. "Down thirty pounds."

"That's great. Still, you should've told me. What if something had happened to you?"

Her father's expression shifted to one of recognition. "This isn't like what happened to your mother, sweetheart." He placed his hand over hers.

Dakota's heart thudded in her chest and tears burned her eyes. Her mother had concealed her illness from Dakota and her sister until her father insisted on telling them. By then she'd had only a few months left. But her mother hadn't told them that, either.

"I'm fine. I promise. Well, except for—"

"What else is there?" Dakota tried to keep her voice measured, despite her growing panic.

"I've been putting off knee-replacement surgery."

"Why?"

"I have the rental properties to look after. Besides, it's not the kind of thing you want to go through alone," he admitted with a shrug.

He'd had the other knee replaced ten years ago. When he'd still had her mother.

Her father was a proud, independent man. His body seemed to vibrate with the discomfort of revealing his vulnerabilities to her.

"You're not alone, Dad." Dakota squeezed his hand. It broke her heart that she needed to say that. Didn't he know she would've dropped everything and come home had she known he needed her?

"You shouldn't be hobbling around in pain when there's a simple fix. Call your doctor today. Ask for the soonest date you can get on the schedule. I can help out with managing the rental properties, and I won't leave until after you've had your surgery and you can get around on your own again."

"You don't need to do that, Dakota. I can manage." He tried to tug his hand away, but she wouldn't let him.

"If it were me who needed you, wouldn't you have come to New York to take care of me, despite how much you hate the city?"

"Of course. I'm your father. It will always be my job to make sure you're all right."

"Well, we're family. And it's my job to look after you, too. Shay has Howard. We only have each other. So will you please stop being so difficult and let me do this for you?"

He gave her a grateful, if reluctant, smile. "All right, baby girl. I'll call the doctor's office and see how soon they can get me in." He pulled his hand back and grabbed another piece of fish from the plate. "But if you get another job offer, don't think twice about accepting it. I know how things go in television. If you sit on the sidelines too long, it's easy to be forgotten."

He wasn't wrong about that. Only, that was exactly what she needed. Enough time and distance for the scandal to blow over and be forgotten. But if she was going to move back to New York or a large market on the West Coast, she needed to find a way to earn money while she stayed here on Holly Grove Island.

She was a Class A screwup, but she wouldn't become a financial burden to her father.

"I'm not leaving here as long as you need me," she said firmly. "End of discussion."

"I appreciate that, Dakota." A small smile lifted the edges of his mouth and his eyes glistened. "But that won't stop me from taking you out in a game of cornhole. That is, if you think you're still up to it. I imagine it's been a long time since you tossed a bag."

"Oh, you're talking smack, huh?" Dakota stood, gathering their plates. "Well, I'd be happy to wipe that smug smile off your face, *Old Man*. Best three out of five?"

Her dad chuckled. "You're on."

Yes, she was stuck in Tiny Town, USA, for the next few months. But on the upside, she enjoyed spending time with her father and hanging out with Sin a couple of nights a week. As long as she kept busy and avoided Dexter Roberts and the town's gossiping hens, she'd be fine.

Chapter Seven

Sweat trickled down Dakota's face and neck as she ran along the coastline. It had been more than five years since she'd gone for a run on this beach, but the familiar taste of the warm, salty air filled her mouth. Strands of hair that had escaped her messy ponytail stuck to her face. Her thighs burned and her feet ached, but she was determined to make it to the end of the beach.

It'd been two weeks since Dakota had returned to the island. Yet despite the fresh air and idyllic setting, she was anxious and restless. Worried about the uncertainty of her future. Unable to shake the pain of her past. Her mother's death. The breakup with Dexter. Here on the island, all of it felt far too immediate. No longer distant hurts she could easily shake off.

Focus on the endgame.

Dakota repeated her mother's admonition in her head. The goal was to become a lead evening news anchor in one of the major markets. Preferably one that would put her in a position to get noticed by one of the national news networks.

She'd been ready to take the next step in her career.

She'd stumbled and fallen from grace instead. But she hadn't lost sight of her dream. The one that she and her parents had worked hard and sacrificed for.

When Dakota was ten years old, she'd declared that she wanted to be a "news lady." Her older sister had scoffed. Her father had smiled, patted her head, and said, "You can do anything you put your mind to, baby girl." Her mother had made it her life's mission.

Madeline Jones had died before Dakota could achieve that goal. But the determination to reward her mother's belief in her had driven Dakota whenever she'd encountered a bumpy road along the way. She'd battled sexism, racism, and nepotism. But the past few months had been the bumpiest yet. And the wound she'd sustained had been completely self-inflicted, leaving her no choice but to return to the island.

There was something surprisingly comforting about being back at home. Still, a twinge of guilt burned in her stomach whenever the topic of her old job came up. She couldn't bring herself to tell Sin or her dad the truth. But not telling them made her feel like the kind of awful, scheming person the Italian tabloids made her out to be.

Dakota stopped, her chest heaving and her lungs burning. Sweat trickled into her eyes, blurring her vision. She wiped her face with the back of her arm and blinked, her eyes stinging.

"I wondered when you'd start running again."

She jumped at the voice behind her, but she had no doubt as to whom it belonged.

Dexter seemed to have a knack for catching her at moments when she looked her very worst. She wished the ground would open up and swallow her whole.

Slowly, she turned around and raised her gaze to his as she

shielded her eyes from the sun. He was running...shirtless. His skin was slick with sweat, yet he still managed to look good enough to adorn the cover of a men's health magazine. And those biceps and pecs. The boy she'd known and loved hadn't been packing this muscled bod. One thing was for sure, the man was no stranger to the gym.

"Been stalking the beach looking for me?" she asked.

A wide grin parted his handsome face, his eyes shielded by mirrored sunglasses. "Stalk the daughter of the town's former police chief? That'd be an ill-advised move."

Dakota propped her fists on her hips as she stared at her reflection in his lenses. She looked even worse than she'd imagined. She brushed loose strands of hair from her face. "Then what brings you here?"

"A lot of things have changed since you've been gone, Dakota, but this is still a public beach." His smirk made her want to either kiss him or smack him. She wasn't sure which.

"Still a smart-ass, I see." She folded her arms, narrowing her eyes at him.

He removed his sunglasses and tucked the arm inside the waistband of his shorts. Good Lord! Was he trying to make her stare at him...*there*? "Guess there's something about you that still manages to rile me up."

Now, there's something I'd like to rile up.

She raised her eyes to meet his. The flare of his nostrils, his heated gaze, and his lopsided smirk indicated that he'd seen her checking out his...package. A blaze of heat crept up her neck and bloomed across her cheeks. She needed to get away from Dexter before she embarrassed herself any further.

"I should go."

"Dakota, wait." Dexter stepped closer, his expression

shifting from amusement to deep concern. He glanced around, as if to ensure that no one would overhear him. "How'd everything work out with your father?"

"Oh. Good, thanks." A tiny part of her was disappointed by the question. The way he'd stepped in closer, she expected his question to be about them. "We had an honest conversation about his health and a few other things. So thank you again for that."

"I'm glad." Dexter cleared his throat after an awkward beat of silence between them. "Look, we're running in the same direction. Why don't we run together?"

Because I'd rather walk barefoot on hot coals.

Running together was how they'd first gotten to know each other. He was trying to increase his footspeed for football. She'd run track and wanted to shave some time off her mile. Sinclair had suggested they run together. Mostly so Dakota would stop asking Sin to run at what her friend considered an ungodly hour.

Dexter had been quiet and closed off in the beginning. They'd done a lot of running but very little talking. But Dakota had worn him down with her chatter and myriad questions over the weeks they'd run together. Ever curious, she'd considered it her personal challenge to get Dex to share at least one thing with her each time they'd run together.

Little by little, he had. And she'd fallen for Dexter Roberts right here on this beach. She had no intention of doing it again.

"It's been a long time since I've run. I'd only hold you back." She released her hair from the messy ponytail, shook her head, then secured her hair in a topknot.

Maybe that would stay put.

"I don't mind the slower pace. In fact, I could use the

break. Besides, my mother is making breakfast this morning and my sister is coming over, too. They'd both love to see you."

Dakota stood there for what felt like an eternity. The little voice in her head and a little voice emanating from...somewhere decidedly lower...debated. Their relationship was ancient history. She should be over him. But the hurt she felt over their breakup still ached deep. And the overwhelming desire she had for him teemed beneath her flesh, making its way down her spine and fluttering low in her belly.

After all this time, there was still something about his deep voice and reassuring smile that drew her in. But the warm, nostalgic feeling was like the lure on the end of a fishing line. It only appeared real. In the end, it was dangerous.

"Thank you for the offer, but I'd better get back. My dad's expecting me at home for breakfast. Please tell Em and Ms. Marilyn I said hello. I'm sure I'll catch up with them at some point while I'm here. Enjoy the rest of your run."

Dakota turned and ran back up the beach toward her father's house, as fast as her legs could carry her.

———

Dex pulled his shades out of his waistband and put them back on as he watched Dakota running up the beach away from him.

Couldn't resist being a smart-ass, could you?

He sighed and resumed his jog back to his mother's house. Okay, so maybe he'd lied about not stalking the beach looking for her. The beach near his condo wasn't as long or as level as the beach here, but he'd always been content to run there. Yet since Dakota had returned to the island, he'd been running on this beach each weekend morning, hoping to run into her.

Dexter was still drawn to her, and he wanted to repair the damage he'd done. Knowing she was there on the island, hating his guts, tore him up inside.

Only he'd finally run into her, and he couldn't resist shooting off his stupid mouth and scaring her off. Even after he'd razzed her, she'd nearly agreed to go back to his mother's house. He was sure of it.

He picked up the pace and tried not to think of how beautiful Dakota looked. Her skin glistened with sweat. Her body was toned yet curvy in all the right places. And when she'd let down her natural mahogany curls and shook them, he'd practically had to rely on Jedi mind tricks to keep his body from reacting in his flimsy shorts.

Did she have any idea how such a small gesture still affected him? Maybe she did and it was her way of torturing him. If so, it was working.

Now he needed to get back to his place and take a cold shower.

Chapter Eight

— • • • —

Dakota and her father usually ate breakfast together at home. But this morning they would be doing a cleanout of one of his rental properties there on the island. So her father suggested that they forgo cooking in the sweltering kitchen and grab breakfast over at Lila's Café before they got to work.

Dakota couldn't help noticing that her father's smile widened and his eyes shimmered as Lila Gayle approached their table at her little café on Main Street.

"Good morning, Oliver." Lila's eyes seemed lit from within.

"Lila." He nodded, not taking his eyes off her.

Lila Gayle turned to Dakota, still beaming but her tone decidedly less flirtatious. "Dakota, I can't thank you enough for helping me at the festival. It's so good to have you back home." She filled Dakota's coffee cup. "I haven't seen your father this happy in years."

Dakota studied her father's face. Ms. Lila was definitely flirting with her dad. Something she often did playfully with the customers. But from the look on her father's face and the tone of his voice, it was more than just teasing to him.

Did her father have a thing for Ms. Lila?

When his eyes met Dakota's again, he cleared his throat, shifting uncomfortably under her scrutiny. He buried his face in his menu.

"Thanks, Ms. Lila," Dakota said. "I'll only be here a few months, but it feels good to be home. I didn't realize how much I missed the beach. And the people," she added quickly.

"Well, however long you're here, I know Oliver is thrilled to have some company while he's rattling around that big old house. Still, I'm sorry about what happened with your job."

A loud clang echoed through the small café when Dakota dropped her fork and it crashed against her coffee mug. Her cheeks stung and her heart beat double time. "Sorry?"

"I hope you don't mind that your dad told us about you getting laid off. I was terribly sorry to hear it. I know how much you loved your work."

The front door opened suddenly. A tourist couple and their two small children entered. Lila welcomed the couple before excusing herself and rushing over to seat them.

It took a full two minutes for Dakota's heart rate to level off again.

"Everything okay?" Her father stared across the table, his expression laced with concern.

"Yes." Dakota gripped her coffee mug with both hands, as if it were an emotional shield, but she didn't drink from it. "Why?"

"You seem upset. Are you angry that I told Lila Gayle about you losing your job?"

"No, of course not." She sipped some of the steaming hot coffee. "My career has always been a huge part of who I am. Now here I am, thirty-four years old, no job prospects, living back at home with my dad. Let's just say that none of this was on my bingo card for how my life would turn out." Dakota put the coffee cup down, her gaze not meeting her father's. "Can you imagine what Mom would have said?"

"Work harder," they echoed simultaneously.

Her father sighed and sipped more of his coffee. "I loved your mother, sweetheart. She was a wonderful woman, but she wasn't always right. So stop talking as if you're a failure."

"Aren't I?" Dakota frowned.

"No, you are not." Her father's tone was adamant. "And I don't want you thinking that. Your mother and I were so proud of you. I *am* proud of you." Her father's voice wavered. "Losing your job because of corporate reorganization doesn't change that. In fact, *nothing* could change how proud I am of you, Dakota. Don't ever forget that." He squeezed her hand.

Dakota bit her lower lip and nodded. Her father was a blur through the tears filling her eyes. If only he knew how badly she'd screwed up her life and her career. "Thanks, Dad. That means a lot."

"Morning, Ms. Lila."

Dakota's gaze snapped toward the familiar voice.

Dex.

"Hey there, sugarplum!" Lila hugged both Dexter and the man accompanying him.

"Is that Nick Washington?" Dakota asked incredulously.

Her father turned around in his booth and looked over his shoulder. "That's him. The boy is tall as a tree and as mischievous as ever." He chuckled. "Not much has changed."

"Well, I haven't seen him in eight or nine years, Dad. So

a lot has changed since then. Before he was this awkward, gangly kid. Now he looks like a freaking model. He's not the little Nicky I used to babysit anymore."

"Guess not," her father said. "He moved back a few years ago."

"Is he still best friends with—"

"Dexter's little sister, Emerie? Yep. The two of 'em are thick as thieves."

"Is Em still a tomboy?"

Oliver laughed. "Yes, but she's also grown into a lovely young lady. Not that our boy Nick seems to notice."

"Chief Jones, Dakota. How are you?" Dex stood over them in a navy-blue suit that hung so well on his athletic frame, it had to have been tailored just for him.

"Doing well, Dex," her father said. "And you?"

"Great. Nick and I stopped in for a quick bite to eat before we hit the road."

"Why don't the two of you join us?" Her father slid over in the booth. "We were just about to order."

Dakota considered kicking her father's shin beneath the table. But nothing in the world would make him recant his offer once extended. She narrowed her eyes at him to let him know she didn't appreciate his spontaneous invitation to Dexter.

Her father had the unmitigated gall to grin. They would have a long talk about this once they were alone.

"Sure, if we're not imposing." Dex's eyes seemed to plead with hers.

"Not at all." She shrugged, then added, "It'd be good to see Nick again."

Dex waved Nick over, and Dakota quickly stood, blocking Dex's entrance to her side of the booth as she raised her arms to Nick.

"Nicholas Washington, I can't believe that's you." Dakota hugged him. "Gosh, look at you. All grown up now."

"If you ask my dad, that's still debatable." Nick laughed, the dimples in his cheeks more pronounced with his wide grin.

"Nick's being modest," Dex said. "He was recently named director of sales and marketing for the new Holly Grove Island Resort, opening soon."

"Congrats, Nick. You have to sit down and tell me all about it." She pulled him into her side of the booth. A move that wasn't lost on Dexter, based on the amused look he gave her.

"Guess I'm over here with you, Chief Jones," he said.

"Sure thing, son." Oliver stood. "But I need to ask Lila Gayle something." He stepped out into the aisle and gestured for Dex to slide into the booth. "Go ahead and take the seat by the window. Too much sun for me, anyway." He winked at Dexter and walked away.

Great.

Now she was seated directly across from Dex. That was even worse than sitting next to him. Dakota turned to Nick and forced a smile.

"So, Nick. How'd you get into marketing?" Dakota squirmed beneath Dex's heated stare.

"That was my major in college. I interned with a Hollywood studio two of my four years at SoCal. After graduation I worked for a smaller indie film studio for a few years before Em finally talked me into moving back. Said she was sick of flying out to LA."

"It's great that you two remained best friends all these years. How is Em anyway?"

"Fantastic. She's an unbelievable graphic artist. I'd love to hire her, but she's a freelancer and she loves it. Besides, she says she's not cut out for working for *the man*. Especially this one." He poked a thumb to his chest. "She doesn't think our friendship could survive it."

Dakota grinned. "Em's probably right about that."

Oliver returned to the table, and Lila Gayle took their orders, then went to the kitchen.

"Speaking of working with friends...Have you given more thought to working for me?" Nick asked.

Dakota looked over at Dex, who was smiling, then back at Nick. "So you and Em can't work together, but we can?"

"Hey, I can handle it, if you can deal with the guy you babysat being your boss." Nick smirked.

"Is that a challenge?"

"It's a genuine offer." Nick's expression turned serious. "We're opening soon and I could use someone who's done PR and knows the island and the people here. You'd be doing me a favor."

"I was an investigative reporter, Nick," she said.

"You were a TV personality, you minored in public relations, and I'd imagine you have press connections," Nick said without missing a beat.

Nick was good. And honestly, she'd interned in the station's sales and public relations departments before she'd been offered a job behind the scenes in the newsroom. She had no doubts about her qualifications for the job, but did she really want to work for a friend?

"I don't know, Nick. I'm not moving to the island for good. I'm only here while I figure out my next move. If an opportunity comes along, I'd have to leave you high and dry."

"We often use contract employees at our Myrtle Beach location, where Dex is assistant operations manager." He nodded toward Dexter. "So if you're interested, I can make it work."

"Sounds intriguing," she admitted, "but I'm already helping my dad out with his rental properties while I'm here. In fact, we're doing a cleanout after breakfast."

"I appreciate your help, Dakota," her father interrupted. "But I've decided to hire a management company to deal with the day-to-day stuff. Besides, you've been antsy all week. You've already rearranged the furniture, organized the pantry, and cleaned out the linen closets. You need something to do, and you know it."

"Dex and I will be in Myrtle Beach the next couple of days, but I'll be back by the end of the week. Take the next few days to think about it," Nick said. "Then swing by my office Friday afternoon at one. I'll treat you to a late lunch and give you a tour of the place. We'll see where things go from there. What do you say?"

Nick was as persuasive now as when he'd talked her into letting him stay up past his bedtime when he was six.

"You had me at lunch," she said. "It's a date, but I can't commit to taking the job."

"Fair enough." Nick flashed his million-watt grin.

The food arrived and they settled into a comfortable rhythm, eating and talking. Dakota avoided conversing with Dexter, directing most of her comments to her father or Nick. But Dexter wouldn't give up.

"Dakota, when was the last time you got down to Myrtle Beach?"

"Probably thirteen years. Right, Dad?" Dakota looked up from her meal and shrugged. "Isn't that when we took that family trip there the summer after Shayna graduated from USC?"

"Sounds about right. Wasn't much inclined to go back

after I spent the entire week beating off half-clad men with a stick," Oliver grumbled.

"I'll bet you and Shay were up to all kinds of mischief." Nick laughed.

Like her father, Dexter was not amused by the story. His brows furrowed and a small frown marred his handsome face.

Dakota found *that* amusing.

"We were young and single. It was the first summer it was legal for me to drink, and my sister was about to move to California for work. So, yeah, we might've been up to a little mischief." Dakota smiled sweetly at her dad, who was frowning. She held up her index finger and thumb about an inch apart and peeked through them. "Just a little, Dad. Nothing serious."

Oliver mumbled something under his breath, and Dakota and Nick snickered.

"A lot has changed since then. You should come down one weekend," Dex said, then cleared his throat when she glared at him and her father raised one furry brow. "I meant you and Sin should come down. It'd be fun."

"You work in Myrtle Beach, three hours away, but you still live on Holly Grove Island?"

"I have a place in Myrtle Beach, too. But I'm here most weekends. What can I say?" Dex shrugged in response to her incredulous stare. "I lived away from the island for seven or eight years. I spent most of that time homesick. I missed our little town and the beaches here. I missed the people of Holly Grove Island. And I missed"—he raised his eyes to hers—"everyone. Here is where I want to be."

Dakota's heart thumped in her chest and her mouth went dry. Something in his penetrating gaze warmed her chest and made her tummy flutter. Her hand drifted to a burning cheek. Dex hadn't said that he'd missed her. She hadn't even been living on the island until a couple of weeks ago. So why had his words felt so personal?

Dakota poked at her eggs. "Oh."

"Heard you bought yourself a fancy new car, Nick," Oliver said quickly.

Dakota could have kissed her father for the much-needed reprieve. He gave her a quick smile before returning his attention to Nick.

"I did." Nick beamed. "It's outside. You should come out and see it."

"No time like the present." Her father grinned.

Nick hopped up from the table, and he and her father headed for the door as Nick excitedly rattled off the features of his new muscle car.

Dakota picked at her Belgian waffles, though she was already full. Anything to avoid talking to the man who still had the ability to send her pulse racing with a simple stare.

"So you're just going to ignore my invitation?" Dexter leaned back against the booth.

"Your invitation to Myrtle Beach?" Butterflies fluttered in her belly. She hated that Dexter's sultry voice and heated gaze still affected her. "I assumed you were just being polite."

"No. I'd really like it if you…two…came down one weekend."

"Thanks, but I'm not sure how long I'll be here."

"Well, it's a sincere and open invitation, should you change your mind. If not, maybe we'll cross paths on the beach again."

"It was good seeing your mom again at the festival." It seemed best to change the subject. "She looks amazing."

"I think she shed fifty pounds and ten years after the divorce." He gave her a pained smile. "By the way, she says if you don't stop by for a visit, she's going to hunt you down."

Dakota laughed. She'd hugged the woman and chatted with her briefly at the Fourth of July celebration. But Ms. Marilyn had made her promise to drop by for a proper visit. "Tell your mom I promise to stop by soon."

"She'll like that." Dex finished the last of his breakfast sandwich. "You know, I just saw your partner in crime this morning."

"Sin? Where?"

"At the gym. I'm surprised she hasn't dragged you there. She's practically a gym rat."

"Yeah, she can't stop talking about the handsome men at her gym." Dakota pretended to ignore the narrowing of Dex's eyes and the tightening of his jaw. "I'm not looking. And as you already know, I'm not crazy about other people seeing me sweaty and panting."

"Believe me, even then you're still gorgeous." His eyes twinkled. "On second thought, maybe it's best you stay away from the gym. Otherwise your dad might be forced to pull out that stick again to beat the morning meatheads away."

She stared at him, blinking. Goddammit, she'd come to town with a plan where Dexter Roberts was concerned. She'd be polite but aloof. Show him that she didn't care enough to still be angry about their past. Not give him the satisfaction of knowing that he'd left an indelible mark on her heart. She was failing miserably.

Nick and her dad returned before she could ask Dex why he was going out of his way to be so nice to her. Dakota was thankful for the interruption. Because it didn't matter why. She and Dexter weren't lovers *or* friends. They were just two people from the same little town who would occasionally cross paths.

"We'd better head out, Dad." Dakota stood. "It was great seeing you, Nick. I promise to think about your offer. I'll see you for lunch on Friday either way." She hugged him.

"Great. See you then." Nick turned to Dex. "We'd better hit the road, too."

Nick and her dad headed toward the door and Dakota followed.

"Dakota." Dex's voice was low enough that her father and Nick didn't seem to hear him.

She turned around. "Yes?"

"I just wanted to say that I'm glad you're home. For your dad, I mean." Dexter ran a hand over his closely cropped hair. "He looks good, happy, since you came to town."

As much as she still resented Dexter, her heart sank a little when he made it clear he was glad she'd returned for her father's sake, not because he'd missed her. It was vain and immature, but she wanted him to want her.

What power did her rejection have otherwise?

"Lila Gayle said the same earlier. Thanks again for telling me about my dad." She turned to walk away, but he caught her wrist.

Dakota's skin prickled with heat beneath his touch as she met his gaze.

Dex had something to say, but he seemed unsure of how to say it. Not atypical.

He hadn't been gregarious and outgoing in high school. But he was warm and friendly. Good-natured, thoughtful, and observant. It shouldn't surprise her that Dex wanted to return to the island full-time. He'd always been reserved around people he didn't know well. Around those he did, he was animated and at ease.

They'd once known each other well in every way imaginable. Had been able to talk to each other about almost anything.

Dakota had been thrilled when she'd first gotten Dex to open up to her. He was mindful and mature, well served by his observant nature. And despite his calm approach to life, he seemed to feel more deeply than most. So when he'd declared that he loved her, she'd believed him. But that had all been so long ago. They were mere strangers now, despite their unbearably painful past.

"I'm sorry about what happened between us, Dakota," he finally managed. "I never wanted to hurt you. You have to believe that."

"Do I?" She tugged her arm from his grip. "It doesn't matter, anyway. Like you said, it was a long time ago."

"It matters to me." He stepped closer. His expression was pained as his dark eyes searched hers. "So I need you to know that I am genuinely sorry for hurting you."

Dakota frowned. Why did her feelings matter so much to him now? They obviously hadn't mattered to him then.

"You coming, Dakota?" Her father poked his head inside the café, his gaze shifting from Dakota to Dex, then back again.

"Yes, sir." Dakota cast one last glance at Dex before hurrying out of the restaurant.

Nothing either of them could say would change the past. And that was where any lingering feelings she had for Dexter Roberts needed to stay.

Chapter Nine

- • • • -

Dex sat across his desk from his boss, Mike Warren, who'd requested to meet with him before the office opened on a Friday morning. As the assistant director of operations at the Myrtle Beach Resort, he did most of the hands-on work. He'd even taken on an increased amount of Mike's duties as the director of operations. Dexter ran a tight ship, and everything was going well at the resort. So what had prompted the need for what sounded like a serious meeting?

Mike folded one leg over the other, as if he had nothing but time. Still, Dexter wouldn't cave and ask why Mike had wanted to sit down with him.

Don't blink first.

"You're not going to ask what this is about, are you?" Mike sounded slightly impressed.

"I figured it was like salary negotiations." Dexter shrugged. "The person who initiates the topic loses."

A reluctant grin spread across Mike's face. "I'm here to offer you a new position."

"What's the position?" Dex leaned back in his chair and rubbed his whiskered chin.

"Director of operations at the Holly Grove Island Resort," Mike said in a tone reminiscent of a game show host declaring that a contestant had won a new car.

"I thought Jacobsen was offered the job." Dexter kept his tone and facial expression neutral, leaving the other man confounded.

Dexter had applied for the job—equivalent to Mike's position in Myrtle Beach. But despite his qualifications and track record with the organization, the company had opted to go with a well-known exec who planned to defect from one of its competitors. When the man's daughter became ill, he opted to keep his family in Chicago, close to the girl's doctors. So the resort went with plan B, another strong outside candidate who worked for a popular hotel chain.

"He was, but his current company offered him a new position with a salary and benefits package he couldn't refuse." Mike straightened his tie, slipping easily from game show host back into his usual business-only tone. "Corporate called to tell me a couple of days ago."

"Hmm…" Dex steepled his fingers, not wanting to seem overly eager. Yes, he *really* wanted the position. But he also wanted to ensure that he'd be fairly compensated for it. "And now you've decided to hire someone internally?"

"Not someone, Dex. *You*." The man pointed at him. "For the record, you always had my vote. The damn higher-ups thought it would be better to go with a big-name candidate with more experience. I've seen how you run things here. You're approachable, and the staff loves you, but they know you won't take any bullshit. You're conscientious, yet ambitious. Plus, you're a native of the island. You're the perfect fit."

"Thank you for your confidence," Dex said warily. Mike was a generally decent guy, but if he was such a perfect fit for the job, why had it taken them two failed hires to give him a shot? And why hadn't Mike gone to bat for him from the beginning? There was definitely more to the offer than Mike was saying. "But why do I feel like there's another shoe about to drop?"

"And you're incredibly perceptive. Did I mention that?" Mike chuckled, leaning forward. "You would be the *acting* director of operations over at the HGI Resort." Mike waved a hand. "Think of it as a trial period. You just do what you do here, and the powers that be will be as convinced as I am that we couldn't possibly find a better person for the job."

He didn't like that he wasn't being offered the position permanently. But he *was* the best man for the job, and he was prepared to prove it.

"Okay. Let's say I'm on board with the plan. When would I start at Holly Grove Island?"

"We need you at the HGI Resort right away. We're behind the eight ball already with this musical chairs routine. In fact, if it weren't for your help, the HGI Resort wouldn't be as far along as it is now."

"Who would take my place here?" It made Dex uncomfortable to suddenly abandon ship. True, Mike was the one in charge, and he'd still be here. But in reality, Dexter managed the day-to-day operations of the resort while Mike spent much of his time on the road.

"Marla Rose." The man practically mumbled the name.

Mike's niece. *Of course.* The man had slowly been giving her jobs with increasing responsibility over the past five or six years. She was currently managing the accounting department.

Dexter held back the remarks churning inside. What would be the point? Marla Rose couldn't run a newspaper stand, let alone an operation of this size. And they both knew it. But apparently familial ties were more important than job qualifications.

Their small group of resorts was still owned by an ultra-wealthy family, and many of its members worked for the organization. So rules prohibiting one from hiring or managing blood relatives were notably absent from the company policies.

"Of course, she will need extensive training, but she catches on quickly," Mike added, clearing his throat when Dexter raised an eyebrow in response.

"You want me to do this job *and* run the new resort." It wasn't a question.

"Just until Marla is comfortable in her new role." The man shifted in his seat, like he couldn't get comfortable. "I'm sure you wouldn't have to pull double duty for long."

"And what if, in the end, the higher-ups decide to go with another outside candidate for the position at the HGI Resort?"

Mike's cheeks flushed, and he glanced down at his hands for a moment before returning his attention to Dex.

"It wouldn't be fair to displace Marla from the position," he managed to say with a straight face. "So your current position would no longer be available. But we'd find you a spot comparable to your current one at one of our five resorts. Florida maybe."

A knot tightened in Dexter's gut. He was trying to get closer to home, not move farther away. Despite what his mother and sister might think, they needed him. And he cherished his role as Uncle Dex, so he liked living an easy distance from his brother Steven and his family in Wilmington and his brother Ellis and his family who made their home in Carolina Beach.

Dexter wanted the position. He'd worked his way up through the company with this very opportunity in mind. And he was anxious to move back to the island full-time. But there were two issues that gave him pause. One: He'd be taking a big risk if they decided to go with someone else. Then he'd end up with a lesser position or he'd have to relocate. Either situation would be a devastating setback. Two: As the director of operations at the Holly Grove Island Resort, he would be prohibited from dating an employee. Despite how Dakota had left things between them at the diner, he was holding onto the hope that she would stay on Holly Grove Island and that she'd eventually give him another chance. But if she accepted Nick's job offer, Dakota would be strictly off-limits.

He sighed. Since Dakota clearly wanted nothing to do with him, a second chance with her was more of a delusion than a probability. Was he really going to pass up an opportunity like this for a relationship that had little chance of ever becoming a reality?

"I'd essentially be running both locations. That's a lot to ask of one person," Dexter said.

"For which the company is prepared to compensate you handsomely." The man had the decency not to object to the fact that Dexter effectively ran the Myrtle Beach Resort. "But there's something else you should know."

Dexter leaned forward, hands folded on the desk. Mike had already dropped the other shoe, so would this new bit of information qualify as an ax?

"There's another reason I was able to convince the board to give you a shot." Mike's lip curled and he wrinkled his nose, as if he suddenly had a bad taste in his mouth. "Some of the locals are up in arms because they'll have to share the beach and endure more traffic. They're afraid that the resort is going to mean the end of their *precious* way of life."

The muscles in Dexter's neck tensed. Did Mike realize that he sounded like an ass and that his resentment of the locals was obvious? He doubted it. But now wasn't the time to point it out. He'd put that in his back pocket for another day. A day on which they weren't discussing his future with the company.

"We've had pushback from some of the diehards on the island since before we broke ground." Dex shrugged. "We're two weeks to open now. So why the concern?"

"There was a brawl at one of the events over at the Pleasure Cove Resort. It's fired up resistance to the Holly Grove Island Resort. We figured—"

"That bringing in a local boy who knows the island and the people will help squash any opposition."

"You know how this game goes, Dex," Mike admitted begrudgingly. "But this provides you with the perfect leverage to show them what you've got."

And double—maybe even triple—my workload.

"Opening a new resort is quite an undertaking," Dexter reminded the man.

"It is. And I can think of no one better prepared to handle it. I'll be honest, Dex. We desperately need your help. You've got us over a barrel."

He'd have to endure even more commuting between the properties for now. But if he was named the permanent HGI director of operations, he'd eventually be able to settle in back on the island full-time.

He'd be closer to his family. And to Dakota. At least for as long as she decided to stay on Holly Grove Island. She hadn't seemed inclined to take Nick up on his job offer, but even if she did, maybe they could still forge a friendship. He'd rather have her back in his life as a friend than not at all.

"So...what do you say?" Mike asked.

Dexter rubbed his chin and studied the man silently as Mike shifted in his seat again.

Mike chuckled and straightened his tie again. "Maybe we should talk about the compensation package first."

Now the man had Dexter's full attention.

———

Dakota followed Nick back into his office following a delicious lunch at the resort's four-star restaurant and an impressive tour of the new Holly Grove Island Resort on Friday afternoon. He'd shown her the resort's rooms and palatial suites, two swimming pools, a state-of-the-art fitness facility, the luxury spa, and two on-site restaurants. The resort's decor featured a muted, beach-inspired color scheme, accented by vibrant seascape murals, teak tables, and lighting and decorative accents that incorporated sea glass or pieces of coral. It was a lovely place to work, and everyone on Nick's team seemed genuinely excited to be a part of the new resort.

Dakota checked her watch as she returned to the comfy leather chair in front of Nick's desk, where their meeting had begun nearly two hours earlier. She'd been so enamored with the resort that time had gotten away from her. Sin had badgered her into getting dressed up and going for a girls' night out later that evening, and she would need to change.

"So what do you think?" Nick practically beamed, like a man at a poker table who was confident he held the winning hand.

"The resort is stunning, and you seem to have a fantastic team in place."

It was still hard to believe that the boy who'd once been a hell-on-wheels practical joker who would give Dennis the Menace a run for his money had grown into a competent, responsible human being. And possibly her boss. At least temporarily.

"I agree. But I'll admit that after two false starts, I'm a little nervous about who will be chosen as the new director of operations. Hopefully, whoever they select will be a good fit." Nick took his seat behind the desk. "Now, in terms of the corporate and community relations manager position, as we discussed, the job would entail coordinating the hotel's marketing efforts, managing and establishing community and media relations, and developing community and corporate partnerships to maximize the resort's exposure. You've seen our facility. There's nothing like it around here. The place practically sells itself. Our soft opening is in a couple of weeks, but bookings have been steady."

"And you'd really be okay with me taking the position on a temporary, contract basis?" Dakota leaned forward in her chair.

"Obviously, I'd prefer that you take the position permanently. But I need the help now and I'd rather have a competent, experienced professional I trust at this critical stage. From where I'm sitting, that's definitely you." Nick leaned forward, his forearms pressed into the leather blotter on his desk.

"And you're willing to meet my salary requirements?" The job seemed almost too perfect. And whether it was a job or a man, nothing that had seemed too perfect at first blush ever really was. There had to be a catch, and it was better she know now what that was.

"It's a little more than I'd budgeted, but I've got some leeway," Nick said.

"And would I have the flexibility to work from home a few days a week while my dad is recovering from his knee-replacement surgery?"

"Absolutely. I'll want to meet up sometimes, but as long as the work is getting done and everyone is being kept in the loop, I'm fine with it." Nick shrugged.

"Guess I'm all out of excuses," Dakota muttered more to herself than to her friend. She hadn't expected to actually want the job. But more importantly, she *needed* it.

The past few months of unexpected unemployment had seriously diminished her savings. And though she was crashing in her old bedroom, she wouldn't become a financial burden to her father. Yes, he was doing well enough with his beach rental properties. But she was too damn old for handouts from Dad. The job Nick was offering was a godsend, and after seeing the place and meeting the staff, she was excited about the challenge the position presented. But first there was a major issue she needed to address.

Any competent employer would do at least a cursory internet and social media check of a potential employee. If she accepted this offer, Nick learning the truth would be inescapable. What would he think of her?

"I can tell you're intrigued by the job, but you're still hesitant. Why?" Nick broke into her thoughts.

Tell him. Now.

Dakota swallowed past the lump in her throat and walked a few paces away from Nick's desk, wringing her hands. "There's something I need to tell you."

Nick walked around his desk and sat on the front edge. "Okay."

"The real reason I lost my job at the station in New York

is because they felt I'd become a liability after I got caught up in a scandal. I was dating this guy, an Italian movie director." Dakota sat in her chair again, her eyes lowered. "We dated for a few months, but it turned out that he was separated, not divorced, from his wife. Suddenly there were pictures of us together in Italian tabloids and in *Page Six*. His wife started making the rounds on Italian entertainment shows accusing me of trying to break up her marriage."

"You never suspected?" Nick's tone wasn't accusatory, which she appreciated.

Dakota met her friend's gaze. She needed him to know that she was telling the absolute truth. "I would *never* have started seeing him if I'd known he was still attached to someone else."

"And your station didn't take the fact that you were blindsided into account?"

"The station manager felt badly and said he wished there were some other way, but they didn't want the bad publicity." Dakota groaned. "Every other station in town felt the same, except the radio station that wanted me to become a late-night radio personality and use the handle DJ Scandalous."

If it hadn't been such a crushing defeat, she might've actually found that last bit funny.

Dakota's ears were filled with the sound of the blood rushing in her veins as a heavy silence descended over them.

Finally, Nick spoke. "I'm sorry this happened to you, Dakota. But thankfully, their loss is our gain. So if that's the only thing holding you back from accepting my offer, it looks like you really are all out of excuses."

"You'd still hire me?" Dakota's voice broke slightly. "Despite my baggage?"

"You didn't commit a crime, Dakota. And you told me the truth. I know that wasn't easy. I respect your honesty. It confirms what I already know...I want you on my team, for however long you're here. Do we have a deal?"

"Yes." Dakota nodded, relieved. The tension in her chest eased. "Definitely, yes."

"Good." Nick shook her hand. "Let's head over to human resources so they can get you started on your paperwork."

"Yes, of course." She stood, smoothing down the skirt of her sleeveless blue dress. "Thank you, Nick. By the way, no one else on the island knows. Not even my dad or Sin. I'm not ready to talk about it with either of them yet. So if it's possible—"

"This is just between us. You have my word." Nick squeezed her shoulder and gave her a reassuring smile that made her want to hug him and break down in tears. But in a good way. Not like when she'd broken down in tears when he'd filled his mother's bathtub with sand or when he'd disassembled her prized bicycle.

Nick's computer dinged, and he walked over to look at it. A big smile spread across his face, and he laughed. But when he glanced up at her, suddenly he frowned. "Before we go, there's a new development here at the resort that I need to tell you about."

"Since I accepted the offer thirty seconds ago?" She laughed nervously.

"Actually...yes." Nick adjusted his tie, looking uneasy. "There's been a slight change in the chain of command here at the resort."

"Oh?" Something in Nick's eyes told her she wasn't going to like what he had to say.

"Like I said, the two outside candidates chosen to

manage the resort backed out. Moments ago, an announcement went out—"

Nick was disrupted by a knock on the partially open door. "Got a second, Nick?"

Dakota's spine stiffened at the sound of the familiar voice.

Dexter.

He was on the management team at the Myrtle Beach location. *What is he doing here?*

"What's good, boss?" Nick stood and shook Dexter's hand. "Just read the announcement a moment ago. Congrats. I know you've wanted this for a long time."

Nick called Dexter boss. *As in* the-man-he-works-for boss?

Did Nick work directly for Dexter? Neither of them had mentioned that before.

"Thanks, Nick. I didn't realize the email had gone out. I was hoping to tell you myself first." Dexter shifted his attention to her. "Hello, Dakota." He gave her a sheepish smile. "Sorry to interrupt your meeting."

"You're the new director of the resort?" Dakota stammered, pointing at him.

"I am." Dex sounded apologetic. "I've been named the acting director."

"They'll make you the permanent director. It's what they should've done in the first place," Nick said. When his gaze met Dakota's, he straightened his tie. "Speaking of good news, Dakota has agreed to come on board…on a contract basis. I was about to walk her over to HR, but first I wanted to update her on the change in hierarchy."

"I see." Dexter seemed disappointed. An odd reaction, given that he'd been the one to suggest that she take the job.

"Well, that certainly is great news." Dexter's smile was perfunctory and his posture stiff. He turned back to Nick. "I almost forgot, I ran into your assistant as she was leaving for the day. She mentioned that you should be heading out for a dental appointment."

"Crap." Nick checked his watch. "Time got away from me. Dakota, I'll walk you over to HR on my way out."

"Why don't you let me walk Dakota over?" Dexter offered before she could respond. "If you get on Doc Mason's shit list, you'll be forced to go to a dentist off island."

"Right." As the men traded a look, Nick's reluctance was obvious. There was definitely a shift in the dynamics between him and Dexter. Nick turned to her as he slipped on his jacket. "I look forward to working with you, Dakota. I'll be in touch."

Dakota remained seated. Still stunned, she'd barely been able to react quickly enough to thank Nick before he hurried out of the office. Nick and Dexter's conversation had floated past her like remnants of a cloud.

"Seems congratulations is in order." Dexter sat on the edge of Nick's desk. He smoothed down the navy tie he wore with a tailored gray suit.

Why did he have to keep showing up when she least expected it, looking as delicious as the last slice of red velvet cake?

"For both of us, it seems." Dakota folded her arms. "When you told me about this job, you failed to mention that you would be Nick's boss. That I'd essentially be working for you."

"I was offered the position just this morning. It was completely unexpected." He kneaded the back of his neck. "To be honest, it still feels kind of surreal. Besides, you were adamant that you wouldn't take the job," he reminded her.

She had been, and if she'd known Nick was his direct report, she wouldn't have accepted the job. But the reality was that she *needed* this job, and it was something that she actually wanted to do.

Still, this town was barely big enough for both of them. She kept running into Dexter everywhere she went: the Fourth of July Festival, the beach, Lila's Café. Now she was expected to work with him, too? No, to work *for* him. She was trying her best to put their past behind her and move on. How was she supposed to do that when Dexter always seemed to be right there, being helpful and reminding her of what might've been?

"This was a mistake." She stood, turning to leave, but Dexter's voice halted her.

"Dakota, I'm sorry if this complicates things. But I couldn't *not* take the position. It's a big opportunity for me. Don't make your decision based on any lingering animosity you might feel toward me."

Lingering?

Right about now, that animosity had staked a flag in the ground and set up shop.

Keep your head high and never let them see how much they've hurt you.

Her mother had drilled those words into her head when she was on the junior beauty pageant circuit and a clique of mean girls had teased her. She'd run to her mother crying. But Madeline Jones wouldn't abide tears or allow her to feel sorry for herself for one moment.

Dakota steeled her spine and lifted her chin, doing her best to keep her tone and expression neutral. "I expected you to be working in Myrtle Beach, not here."

"I know, but I've been asked to head up operations here for the foreseeable future. Besides, Holly Grove Island is my home. It's where I want to be, so I'm going to do everything in my power to make this move a permanent one."

Dakota stood, frozen, like an insect trapped in amber. The impetus to stay and the compulsion to flee weighed on her equally. In just a few weeks, her view of Dexter had softened considerably. He'd reminded her at every turn of what a good and kind person he'd always been...until he wasn't. Her still-bruised heart urged her to walk away. But her brain and her dwindling bank account reminded her that she *needed* this job.

"This position is ideal for you, Dakota. And Nick really does need your help." Dex took a few steps closer. "You've always been great with people, and you know the folks on the island. You're perfect for this role. Don't walk away from it because of your feelings toward me."

"I don't have feelings for you one way or the other." Dakota clenched her jaw as she forced her gaze to meet his. "You're simply a part of my past. But you're right. It would be silly to let that prevent me from taking this job."

Only the momentary furrowing of his brows indicated that he'd been hurt by her insistence she had no feelings for him.

Maybe it wasn't exactly true—*yet.* But she would follow her mother's advice, as she had that day on the pageant circuit and later in the newsroom.

Fake it till you make it, baby. Eventually it'll become your truth.

"Nick will be pleased, and so am I." Dex gestured toward the door. "I'll walk you over to human resources now."

"Before we go..." She forced herself to meet his gaze. "I need to tell you that I'm grateful you let me know about my dad and about this job. But if you've done all of this because you expect me to feel obligated to you somehow—"

"Dakota, you don't owe me anything." He winced, as if her words had cut into his skin like a jagged blade.

For an instant she regretted saying them. But she needed to make it clear to both of them that there would never be anything between them again. Neither love nor friendship.

"You're helping us out of a bind. So Nick and I are grateful to you."

Dakota nodded and stepped through the door, hoping she wasn't about to make the second-biggest mistake of her life.

Chapter Ten

◆—◆—◆

How'd your meeting with Nick go, honey?" Her father glanced up from where he was slicing oranges in the kitchen.

"The meeting with Nick went well." Dakota forced a smile. She'd taken a moment in the car to gather herself and shake off any outward display of her anxiety about taking the contract job. She washed her hands at the sink, then swiped a slice of the fragrant, juicy orange.

Her father handed her another slice, his brows furrowed with concern. "But?"

"But Dexter showed up. And guess who is the newly appointed director of operations at the Holly Grove Island Resort."

"Good for him." Her father nodded approvingly.

"He's Nick's boss now, which means, indirectly, he's my boss now." Dakota propped a fist on her hip, dismayed that her father didn't seem to grasp the magnitude of the situation.

"You said you're over him, so what does it matter?" The look on her father's face was a mixture of amusement and feigned innocence.

Dakota gave him her sternest look, but her father chuckled. "Would you have considered the opportunity if you'd known?"

"No." She slid into the kitchen chair and fiddled with the place mat. "Still, Dex should've told me *before* I met with Nick."

Oliver sat at the table, too. "So why didn't he?"

"He was just appointed to the position this morning. Also, he didn't want me to pass up on the opportunity because of any animosity I might feel toward him."

What was it with men thinking it was their job to decide what she should and shouldn't be told? Her father, Marcello, and Dex all behaved as if they needed to filter the truth for her.

"Are you still angry with him?" Her father's brows knitted with concern when she didn't answer. He sighed softly. "You know, your mama always said that hate isn't the opposite of love; indifference is. Don't seem like you're feeling too indifferent about Dex."

"If you'd asked me a month ago, I would've sworn I was. But now..." A mixture of emotions swirled in Dakota's chest.

"Seems you've got much deeper feelings for him than you're willing to admit." He held out another slice of orange.

She accepted it gratefully, thankful for the time to quietly reflect on her father's words.

Why couldn't she let go of her hard feelings toward Dexter? She wasn't that brokenhearted teenage girl standing in the snow, unsure of herself, anymore. But maybe she was so angry with him because the humiliation of the scandal and losing her job made her feel like that powerless young girl whose world had been upended all over again.

Her feelings for Dex were as ambiguous as her future in broadcasting. That didn't bode well for either.

"Dexter meant a lot to you, honey. I can only imagine where your head is at right now, being forced to finally confront those emotions after burying them so deep for so long. Seeing you again has probably brought up all kinds of complicated feelings for him, too." He rinsed the cutting board and his hands, then dried both with a towel. "Have you considered telling him how you feel about what happened between you back then? Maybe if you did, you'd both feel better."

Her life was enough of a shitshow already. Sitting down with Dex and hashing out what had happened between them back then felt like more than her fragile ego could take. Her mother had taught her not to reveal her hurt and pain. To stuff it down inside as she focused on achieving the success that would be her ultimate revenge. But decades of trying to be strong, shoving the lid down on her pain, and persevering with a smile were coming back to haunt her. Being forced to finally confront her and Dexter's past felt like enough to make the entire barrel of bitterness and pain explode.

"I don't know, Dad." Dakota tucked her hair behind one ear. "Maybe some things are better left in the past."

Her father frowned, worry creasing his forehead. Still, he seemed to concede for the moment. He squeezed her arm and offered a pained smile. "Sounds like you accepted the job."

"I did. And Dexter and I came to an understanding about it. Still, us working together feels like an awful idea."

"Yet you two seemed to have forged an alliance since you returned to town. He told you about my health situation and Nick's job offer."

Dakota froze, her mouth gaping open. "How'd you know—"

"I saw the boy in town not long after you *discovered* my meds and glucose meter and read me the riot act." Her father chuckled, taking a sip of water. "He told me that he'd run into you at the festival. I asked point-blank if he'd mentioned seeing me buy my glucose meter and some other supplies. Considering that you two hadn't spoken in a good, long time, it never occurred to me that I needed to tell him to keep that information under his hat."

"You do realize that *boy* is a thirty-six-year-old man?" Dakota shook her head as she poured herself a glass of filtered water from the pitcher. "So what did Dex say when you asked?"

"He admitted it without apology." Oliver raked a hand through his thinning hair. "It wasn't his business to tell, but I admire his honesty." He looked at her thoughtfully, his eyes filled with sadness. "I misjudged Dexter back when he was sweet on you. Seems you're making the same mistake now. He's a fine man, Dakota. I could do far worse for a son-in-law."

"Son-in-law?" Dakota nearly choked on her glass of water. "Listen to me carefully, Dad. There is *zero* chance of me and Dexter getting back together. Nothing is going on between us. Nor will there ever be again. That ship has set sail, caught fire in the harbor, and sank like a rock to the bottom of the sea. Are we clear?"

"Whatever you say, darlin'." Oliver chuckled before taking another drink of water. The corners of his mouth lifted in a mischievous smile. "But I can't remember the last time I've seen you this fired up about anything."

That, she couldn't deny.

So it was safer if she kept her distance from Dexter Roberts. Despite the fact that they'd essentially be working together.

Dakota sighed. Suddenly, she could use a night of fun with Sin and a few stiff drinks.

———

It was late afternoon and Dexter was seated at his new desk, going over some of the plans for the resort. He'd had a long day, beginning with his early morning meeting with Mike, continuing with travel between the two properties, and ending with walkthroughs with senior members of the HGI staff. The hotel's soft opening was in two weeks, and a handful of minor renovation projects weren't quite complete. But he was more concerned about his earlier encounter with Dakota.

The stiffness of her shoulders when she recognized his voice and the anger that flared in her eyes, even if it was for only a moment, kept replaying in his head. The memory was filed beside the heartbroken look on her tear-stained face that night he'd ended things between them.

He could still hear her strangled words.

Is there someone else?

His heart ached as he recalled the tears that streamed down her cheeks, her mascara running. He'd had to fight the urge to take her into his arms, smooth back her dark, curly hair, and tell her the truth. He didn't mean a word of what he'd said. The last thing he'd wanted was to watch her walk out of his life. He'd comforted himself all these years by convincing himself it had been the right thing to do. But things no longer seemed so clear.

He was startled by a knock on the frame of his open door.

"Hey, boss. Could we talk for a minute?" Nick sounded apprehensive. *Very unlike him.*

"Sure. Come in."

Nick stepped inside and closed the door behind him. *Not good.*

His friend's shoulders bore the weight of a man gearing up to say something he'd rather not. Dex closed his laptop, settled back in his chair, and gave Nick his complete attention.

Nick slid into the leather chair and sighed. "When you helped me get this job, you made me promise that I wouldn't allow our friendship to prevent me from saying whatever it is I needed to say in my role as sales and marketing director."

Dexter gritted his teeth and released a quiet sigh. "If this is about Dakota—"

"I'm thrilled to work with Dakota. In fact, I'm damn lucky to have her. But are you sure your history won't be a problem?" Nick barreled past Dex's warning look. "Because this feels like a ticking time bomb that's going to blow up and take out innocent bystanders. Like me."

"Relax, Nick. Dakota and I talked." Dex calmly loosened his tie. "We're both sensible adults. We can handle this."

Nick leaned forward in his chair, his clasped hands between his knees. "Are you sure this isn't just about you wanting Dakota back?"

Heat flamed in Dex's face and neck. He tried to strain the irritation he felt from his voice. "I'd like to think you know me better than to think I'd recommend Dakota for this job for selfish reasons. Besides, now that we've both accepted our new, temporary positions, I'm her superior.

Which means Dakota is off limits. So even if I did have any hopes of reconnecting with her…" Dexter sighed gruffly. "It's no longer an option."

"I know the reasonable, logical, professional Dexter Roberts who thinks with the head above his shoulders better than that. The guy who is thinking with his heart and parts I don't even want to think about…That guy I'm not so sure about."

"You're overreacting, Nick."

"I saw the way you looked at her at the diner, the way you looked at her earlier today. You've got it bad for her." It wasn't a question, so he wouldn't insult either of them by denying it. "Love and work don't mix, Dex. A very wise man made that clear to me when he interviewed me for this job."

Dexter groaned quietly. He'd warned Nick that the resort wasn't his personal hunting ground to troll for dates. Now that speech was coming back to bite him in the ass. No, the circumstances weren't exactly the same. He and Dakota had already been involved. Had history. Still, if he made that thin-as-a-razor-blade distinction he'd look like a hypocrite. Not the best way to earn respect from his staff as the acting director who had aspirations of being named the official appointee.

Dex rose from his seat and walked over to the wall of windows. He watched as the waves broke against the shore. "I understand your concern, Nick. And I won't deny that I still have feelings for Dakota." He turned to face his friend. "But I won't allow those feelings to interfere with our work here. I promised Dakota that, and I meant it."

"She knows you're still into her?" Nick quirked an eyebrow.

"She knows I'm fond of her and that I'd like to be friends again," Dex said carefully.

"We both know that's only half the story. What happens when the other half comes knocking?"

Usually, Dexter appreciated Nick's what-if, worst-case scenarios. Right now he wanted the man to stop raining on his parade. He finally felt a bit of hope that perhaps they'd be able to forge a tentative truce. Maybe a casual friendship. Though he'd be lying to himself if he didn't acknowledge the wish for something more.

Nick was determined to ruin that tiny bloom of hope with reality.

"Leave that to me," Dex said.

"I care about Dakota, too, Dex. I don't begrudge you for walking away back then. But I don't want to see her hurt again. She's been through enough."

Nick was pushing the boundaries, but Dex admired his sense of obligation and friendship.

It'd been nearly two decades, and he still couldn't forgive himself for hurting her. He certainly didn't want a replay of the scenario.

"I don't want to see her hurt again, either," he assured his friend. "I accepted this position knowing that meant any play for Dakota was off the table. And I have every intention of sticking to that."

The road to hell is paved with good intentions, son.

Those words, once uttered by Dakota's mother, echoed in his head.

"Fair enough." Nick seemed satisfied. "And for the record, I do hope you and Dakota become friends again."

"Thanks." Dexter forced the vision of Dakota in that sleeveless blue dress that hugged her enticing curves from his brain. "Now, is there anything else?"

"No, sir." Nick took the hint and headed toward the door. He turned back and asked, "Does this mean I can ask out that cute bartender we hired?"

Nick barely escaped the room before the book Dex threw sailed across the space and slammed against the door frame. The sound of his friend's laughter trailed down the hall.

Maybe hiring his friend and his ex *weren't* the best ideas he'd ever had.

Chapter Eleven

───•──•──•───

So you did ditch the sweats and flip-flops." Sinclair laughed as Dakota stepped up into her SUV. "And as much as I enjoy sitting on my couch drinking and watching movies with you, I'm glad you finally agreed to get dressed up and go out."

"Shut up and drive." Dakota strapped on her seat belt. Her friend was wearing a lovely green dress that picked up the flecks of green in her hazel eyes. "Pretty dress."

"It's new. Got myself a little something to celebrate a big sale I made today."

"Congrats, hon. Residential or commercial property?"

"Commercial. Old Man Higgins finally agreed to sell that dilapidated bait shop of his." She made a face as if the aroma of bloodworms and mullet filled the cabin.

Dakota laughed. "That bad, huh?"

"You have no idea. In fact, I tried to get Captain Grumpypants to lower his asking price because the place was in such bad shape and smelled wretched. He wouldn't put a penny into fixing it up. Yet he insisted it was worth his asking price because he had one of the sweetest locations on the sound."

"So you're saying the client knew more than you did?" Dakota smirked.

"One time in seven years. Give me a break, all right?" Sin said. "Worked out pretty well for both of us."

"Who bought the place? Are we finally going to get a national chain in here?"

"On Holly Grove Island? Did you start drinking without me?" Sin scoffed. "You know that the folks in this town would rather shutter the entire place than allow a big box store in here. It's part of what makes us exclusive and able to charge top dollar for crappy old bait shops." She grinned. "Daniel Eriksson bought the place."

"Lila Gayle's son? I thought he moved back to the UK?"

"He did, a little more than five years ago. But he missed home. We started his search for a house and space for his proposed business while he was here last Christmas visiting his mother. Don't tell her, by the way," Sin said. "He wants to surprise her."

"That's sweet. She's going to be really happy to have him back." Dakota couldn't help smiling. "What does he plan to do with the place? Open a new bait shop?"

"He's going to start a water sports shop. You know, rent kayaks and water skis. But he also plans to give lessons. It's a smart move, and his timing is perfect. The resort is going to bring in a lot more visitors."

"Danny always was a clever guy." Dakota smiled. "Is he still using that adorable accent to charm the pants off every girl who comes to town?"

"Didn't hear anything his last couple of visits. Maybe living back in the UK has settled him down a bit. Or maybe he's finally learned to keep it in his pants." Sin Groucho Marxed her sculpted eyebrows, lifting them up and down. "Speaking of Ms. Lila, wasn't that her car in your driveway?"

"They had pot roast at the diner today. She knows how much my dad loves it, so she brought us leftovers." Dakota studied the Cheshire cat grin on her friend's face. "Why?"

"She didn't just drop it off. Seems she stayed for dinner." Sin switched the radio station.

"She's been bringing us dinner a couple times a week since I've been here."

"Particularly on Friday nights—the night you usually hang out with me," Sin pointed out.

"Yeah, I guess." A knot tightened in Dakota's gut. "Why? What's the big deal?"

A mischievous grin lit Sin's face. "She's taken quite an interest in you two, that's all."

"Ms. Lila is thoughtful. Sweet. Giving." Dakota dug in her handbag and opened her compact. "Besides, I think she's a little lonely since both her sons moved off the island."

"She's giving, all right. And a lot less lonely these days." Sin could barely hold back a grin. "They've been spending a lot of time together, even before you came back to town."

"You're saying that Ms. Lila…and my dad…" A boulder settled in the bottom of her stomach. "No?"

Dakota wasn't completely clueless. She'd teased her dad about how enamored he'd seemed with Ms. Lila the day they'd had breakfast with Nick and Dex. But he'd dismissed it and changed the subject. Maybe she'd given him a pass because she wanted it not to be true.

"I think it's cute…your dad and Ms. Lila. They're both really good people who've lost their life partners, and they've been lonely. Don't you think they deserve some happiness?" Sin glanced at her briefly.

"Yes, but..." Dakota sank her teeth into her lower lip and sighed.

She'd enjoyed Ms. Lila's visits. But it was nice spending time with her father. Maybe it made her sound like a spoiled toddler, but Dakota wasn't keen on the idea of someone else riding in and replacing her mother—not even someone she liked as much as Lila Gayle.

"I was in my dad's room the other day. Everything is exactly as my mother left it. He hasn't gotten rid of any of her stuff. That tells me he isn't ready to move on. There's nothing wrong with that."

"No there isn't," Sin said gently, her eyes on the road. "But it has been five years since we lost your mom, Dakota. I don't see anything wrong with him wanting love and companionship, either. Do you?" Sin spared her a quick glance.

Companionship? Sure. *Love?* The thought made her shudder.

She couldn't imagine her father loving anyone other than her mother. Her parents had been married for more than thirty years. Yet they'd still been affectionate toward each other. As kids, she and Shay had been grossed out seeing the two of them kiss and cuddle.

Her parents hadn't just loved each other. They'd been *in love*, right up to her mother's death. It broke her heart to think of her dad with anyone other than her mom.

Dakota studied the waves of the Atlantic Ocean as Sinclair navigated Jessamine Drive, the winding road that made a circuit along the edge of the island. She still hadn't responded.

"Kota, I know you miss your mom. Obviously, your

father does, too. But would you rather he spend the rest of his life alone than with someone as sweet and caring as Ms. Lila?"

"He isn't alone. We have each other," Dakota corrected her friend.

"Until you're back to New York or off to some other faraway city barely able to spare any of us the time of day." Sinclair sucked in a breath and pressed a hand to her chest. "God, I'm sorry, Dakota. I shouldn't have—"

"No, you're right." Sin's words hit Dakota like a sucker punch to the gut. Sinclair was right to be upset. The distance between them all these years had been totally her fault.

She and Sinclair had been best friends most of their lives, but she went off to school in New York while Sin stayed on the island and worked for her father at the hardware store. They'd both tried to stay in touch at first. But the separation, her ambitious course schedule, and the city nightlife had eventually made it difficult for Dakota to keep in contact.

She had honestly intended to call Sinclair, but there was always some obligation or distraction that kept her from picking up the phone. Sin was the one who kept making the effort. But eventually they'd lost touch. Dakota had apologized to Sin the day she'd picked her up from the bus depot, but she was obviously still hurt about it.

"Sin, I really am sorry that I allowed our friendship to lapse while I was away. Yes, I was overwhelmed by my school schedule and life in the city, but that's no excuse. I should've made time for you. Called. Visited. I got so caught up in—"

"Living your best life?" Sin snorted. "Guess that's my fault. I did buy you that book of Oprah's as your going-away present. That's exactly what I wanted for you. I just never imagined that you'd be living your best life without me."

Dakota's chest ached with both shame and regret. As angry as she'd been with Dexter for the sudden breakup, how could she not have realized that she'd essentially broken up with Sin the same way? Or how much pain she'd caused her best friend because of it?

She placed a gentle hand on her friend's shoulder. "Sin, I really am sorry. I promise, no matter where I go or what I do, I will never, ever neglect our friendship again. It means too much to me. *You* mean too much to me. Forgive me?"

"God, I can be so freaking easy sometimes." Sin sniffled and fanned her teary eyes so she wouldn't ruin her makeup. Their laughter broke the tension between them. "Of course I forgive you. But if you ever drop me like that again—"

"I won't. I promise," Dakota said, and she meant it. She'd genuinely missed her bold, funny, thoughtful, and irreverent friend. "Now, will you please tell me where we're going?"

"Such impatience," Sin scolded. "Fine. If you can't wait a few more minutes, I'll tell you. We're going to the Foxhole."

"Seriously?" Dakota folded her arms and stared at her friend. "I got dressed up and put on these shoes"—she pointed at her feet—"just to wade through three inches of peanut shells on the floor and wear a lobster bib?"

"Ye of little faith." Sinclair nodded up ahead as their old hangout came into view.

Dakota's gaze followed Sin's to the end of the road. "That isn't the Foxhole," she said, despite the large sign declaring that it was. "This place is—"

"Gorgeous. I know!" Sinclair pulled into the newly

paved parking lot, which was once all gravel, and parked the truck. "I sold it to Drew and Lydia Halliday three years ago. He still plays pro football out in California, but Lydia's family has been running the restaurant."

"It doesn't even resemble the old place. It's incredible, and it has to be at least twice as big as it was before. And check out all those windows overlooking the water."

"I know. Drew sank a ton of money into the place. There's a gorgeous deck in back, all strung with lights. It's a wonderful space for weddings and special events. They have all kinds of events during the year, and they bring in live musicians on Friday nights."

"Who's playing tonight?" Dakota stepped out of the SUV and straightened her dress.

"Guess we'll have to find out." Sin shrugged, but the mischievous twinkle in her eye left Dakota wondering what other surprises her friend had in store.

Chapter Twelve

• • •

Dexter nearly fell off his barstool when Dakota Jones walked through the door wearing a black-and-white dress with one asymmetrical shoulder strap, which highlighted the shimmering brown skin of her toned shoulders and her long, elegant neck. The body-conscious cut of the dress and the slim belt at her waist played up her ample curves: full, round breasts and generous hips, which swayed as she walked.

His heart raced thinking of those curves and the expanse of her legs, elongated by black and silver high-heeled sandals with straps tied in a black bow above each ankle.

Good God. Was the woman trying to kill him?

He turned back toward the bar and swigged his beer, her image burned into his memory. The visceral sensation of those long legs wrapped around his waist as he'd made love to her shot down his spine, hitting him with the force of a two-ton battering ram. The sensory memory was so vivid, he shuddered. Dex gulped from his bottle of beer to cool down the heat rising in his chest.

Nick, seated on the stool beside him, gave him an odd

look and placed his own beer on the bar. He turned toward the door. "Ahh...I see." He turned back to his friend.

"What?" Dex asked. "This is the hottest event on the island tonight. Lots of people we know will be here. Em's coming tonight, isn't she?"

Nick glanced at his watch. "Yeah, but *I* invited her. I didn't trick her friend into bringing her here. Besides, you know I don't think of your sister that way. We're just friends."

"And I'm the one that's delusional?" Dex muttered the words under his breath.

"Look, whatever, man." Nick waved him off. "And don't think I don't see what you're doing here." He pointed at Dex with his beer. "I'm not *that* easily distracted."

A gorgeous blonde with a skirt that was more like a postage stamp and a prayer strode past them and grinned at Nick. He watched the pronounced sway of the woman's hips as she and a friend walked away.

"You were saying?" Dex raised an eyebrow.

"We'll talk about my issues later." Nick finally dragged his gaze back to Dex. "Right now we're talking about you and Sin scheming like Lucy and Ethel to get you and Dakota back together. Remember, bud, those harebrained schemes always backfired. I get the distinct feeling this one will, too. Besides, didn't we just talk about this a few hours ago?"

"First, I'm not scheming to get Dakota back. *Anymore*," he added in response to his friend's pointed look, which called bullshit on his claim. "Obviously, the situation has changed. I meant what I said earlier about her being off-limits. I do hope that we can at least be friendly again. Especially now that we're all working together. Otherwise, things would be awkward around the office, and none of us wants that. Second, yes, I did suggest that Sin bring Dakota out to the Foxhole tonight. But that was weeks ago, and she never confirmed that they'd be here. With everything that's been going on this week, I'd kind of forgotten about it."

Nick chugged the rest of his beer before setting it down on the bar and indicating to the bartender that he'd like another. "Fine. Keep telling yourself that, *friend*. But don't say I didn't warn you when things go sideways."

"You're making a big deal out of nothing, Nicky." Dex smirked when Nick narrowed his eyes at him for using his childhood nickname.

"You know I hate it when you call me that." Nick pointed at him.

"You don't seem to mind when my sister calls you that," Dex pointed out.

"Em's not a big, hairy dude." Nick smirked.

"Nicky. Dex. Hey!" As Sinclair waved from across the room, Dakota flashed a look of displeasure at her best friend.

Nick gave him an *I told you so* look, then rose to greet them. "Sin, Dakota. What brings you to the Foxhole tonight?"

"When do I ever say no to a fabulous party?" Sin elbowed Nick. "Besides, we're celebrating my girl Dakota's new job and my sale of Higgins's Bait Shop."

"You finally unloaded that rattrap? Well, good for you. This does call for a celebration." Nick wrapped an arm around Sin's shoulder and squeezed. "Looks like it's been a good day for all of us. Tell you what, first round is on me. What are you ladies drinking tonight?"

"Thanks, darlin'." Sin batted her eyes. "I'll have a cosmo. Kota, what're you drinking?"

They all turned to Dakota, who had yet to speak. One

hand gripped the elbow of her other arm, her expression equivalent to that of a rabbit who'd wandered into a foxhole. She cleared her throat and stood a little taller. "A French 75."

Nick and Sin exchanged looks, as if they hadn't heard her right. They both shrugged.

"I'll see if they have it," Nick said.

"I'll come with." Sinclair ran her fingers through her hair. "I've gotta see what's in this fancy drink Dakota ordered."

Nick and Sin left, leaving Dex alone with her. An awkward silence filled with all the words he wanted to say to her settled between them.

I'm sorry.

Forgive me.

Give us another chance. I promise I won't blow it.

But the way she wrapped her arms around herself made it clear that those weren't words Dakota was ready to hear from him.

Nick was right. Now that he was Dakota's boss, what he'd planned for tonight was an incredibly bad idea. But he couldn't regret the fact that she was standing here with him now.

Dex pulled out the barstool Nick had vacated. "Have a seat?"

"Thank you." She put her purse on the bar and slid onto the stool. The hem of her thigh-length dress rose. She tugged at it, drawing his eyes there momentarily. "What brings you and Nick here tonight?"

"I'm usually here when they host the Friday Night Jam Sessions." He sank onto the barstool again, trying to stay relaxed and casual about the fact that she was sitting here beside him. Like two old friends shooting the breeze, as his father liked to say.

"Jam sessions?"

"Informal jazz sets in the tradition of those held in New York during the early forties." It was a topic he could talk about endlessly. "Jazz musicians who were able to secure regular, well-paying gigs at high-class hotels or radio shows often didn't have the freedom to play the music they really wanted to play. And, of course, most of the bands were segregated. At these jam sessions, usually at a club like Minton's Playhouse or Monroe's, musicians of all ethnicities would get together after their shows and play. You never knew who might drop in on any given night. Artists like Dizzy Gillespie, Miles Davis, Benny Goodman, Bill Evans, and Thelonious Monk."

"You seem to know a lot about it." Her voice had a teasing lilt, which he'd missed. It was the most relaxed she'd been in his presence since her return to Holly Grove Island. "When did you become a jazz aficionado?"

"My great-grandparents were well-known jazz musicians. My great-grandmother was a jazz singer and my great-grandfather was the leader of his own band. So I've always had an interest in the subject." He took another swig of his beer. "And my grandfather was a jazz pianist. He played venues all over the world before they settled down and got married. He talked about his glory days all the time."

"I never knew that." Dakota seemed saddened by the realization. "But then, you didn't talk much about your paternal grandparents."

"Didn't know them very well back then," he admitted. "My father and grandfather had a falling-out when my father was young. They didn't speak for years. When we were"—he cleared his throat—"when we knew each other, I'd only met my grandparents a few times. But when I went to college in Texas, they lived a short distance from my dorm. I started visiting them regularly. Had dinner with them nearly every Sunday. Granddad and I would sit on the porch and talk for hours after dinner. I think he was trying to make up for all the years he missed with my dad."

"Must've been a pretty big argument to cause that kind of rift. Did they make up?" Her gaze was warm. Sincere. It reminded him of how comforting her presence had always been.

If he'd had a bad day, he'd known he could talk to Dakota about it. But even if he hadn't wanted to put words to whatever he was dealing with, being with her eased the tension.

He missed that, and he missed her. But she hadn't been the one to walk away. He had. Even though he'd done it for all of the right reasons, he would never stop regretting the decision that brought them here. As two strangers who'd once promised to always love each other.

"They did," he responded finally. "The weekend I graduated from Texas A&M. I didn't give them much choice. I wanted them both there. It forced my father and grandfather to hash things out."

"Here you are. A French 75." Nick approached with Dakota's drink in hand, a lemon rind spiraled around the long stem.

"Thanks, Nick." She accepted the drink. "Here, you can have your seat back."

"Keep it." He held up a hand. "There's someone I need to say hello to."

Nick excused himself and headed to the corner of the room where the blonde and her friend were seated. Nick definitely had a thing for blondes, and brunettes, and redheads.

"I wonder where Sin went." Dakota craned her neck, searching the room. She blew out a breath that sent her side-swept bangs fluttering, then took a sip of her drink. "Not bad."

"When'd you start drinking fancy drinks from old movies?" Dex grinned. "*Casablanca*, right?"

The spark in her widened eyes indicated that she was impressed he'd recognized the connection between the old black-and-white film and the drink she'd ordered.

They'd watched the movie together one summer night under the stars, when it was played on a projector at Holly Grove Island Park. Dex didn't remember a lot about the movie, but he remembered everything about being with Dakota that night. What she wore. Her wild, natural curls pulled into a high ponytail. The root beer lip gloss he'd stolen a taste of when he'd walked her home. And the fact that she'd mused about one day trying all of the drinks ordered in the movie—especially the French 75.

"It's been a long time since we drank together, Dex. You didn't think I was still sneaking wine coolers under the high school bleachers, did you?"

He chuckled. "No, I s'pose not."

"I see your palate hasn't changed much." She indicated his beer bottle.

"There's plenty of night still ahead, woman." He winked at her, then put the bottle to his mouth and downed the rest of the warm liquid. "A man has got to pace himself."

"I suppose." Her dark-brown eyes twinkled as she reined in a mischievous little smirk that made his heart dance. He couldn't help remembering all the times he'd seen that smirk before and the intimacy they'd once shared.

He fought back the desire to lean in and plant a kiss on her full lips, as he had so many times before. Because he was her boss now. And as long as he was, friendship was the extent of their relationship. But at least in this moment, friendship felt like more of a possibility than a far-fetched fantasy.

"Dakota Jones? Is that you? Oh my gosh. Look at this, folks. We've got ourselves a real-life celebrity in the house."

Dakota's shoulders tensed and her nostrils flared as Angela Gilson—the owner of the shrill voice—approached.

The muscles in Dexter's back tensed. He clenched his jaw and gritted his teeth as he clutched the empty beer bottle. Restrained himself from uttering the words he wanted to say.

Go away, Angela. No one has time for your mean-girl, high school bullshit here.

Their mothers had been close friends, but by high school, the relationship between Dakota and Angela had already been a tense one. When Angela had become head cheerleader, she'd seemed to believe that earned her the right to date him—the starting quarterback of the football team. When he and Dakota had started dating, Angela seemed to consider the action as an open declaration of war. She'd been horrible to Dakota every chance she got.

Talk about someone who has trouble letting go of the past.

Dexter opened his mouth to tell Angela to grow up and drop the mean-girl act, but Dakota subtly shook her head. She turned to face her high school nemesis.

"Angela," Dakota said flatly. "I see you're still right here where I left you."

Dakota was prepared for the fight. *Good for her.* Angela was like a shark. The woman could sense fear and she could smell blood in the water at nearly six hundred yards.

"And I see you're right back where you started."

Angela glared at Dakota, her arms folded across her chest. Suddenly she broke out in a loud, hyena-worthy laugh and waved a manicured hand. "I'm just teasing you, girl. Had to get a shot in for old times sake." She gave Dakota a Hollywood air kiss. "Great to see you."

Dakota seemed unsure how to react, but graciously accepted the gesture. Still, her response was measured and the smile she returned was tepid, at best. "You, too, Angela."

Angela grinned. "Well, looka here. Girl, you ain't been back in town but five minutes and you two are right back at it."

Dakota's eyes widened. "No, this is not... *that.* I'm here with Sinclair Buchanan and he was already here with Nick."

"I don't see Sin or Nick." Angela crossed her arms. Her gaze of disbelief shifted between Dakota and Dex.

Dakota looked to him, as if pleading for help.

"It's true, Angela. Sin and Dakota arrived a few minutes ago. I was already here." His eyes met Dakota's, lingering there. "Crossing paths tonight was a pleasant surprise."

Dakota shifted on her stool beneath his gaze, before turning her attention back to Angela. "See?"

"Oh, I see, all right." Angela cocked one hip and frowned. "Dakota happens to show up here on the night when—"

"Angela! Well, land sakes. I ain't seen you in a month of Sundays, girl." Sinclair wrapped an arm around the tiny sprite's shoulder and steered her away from them. "Been meaning to ask if you're finally ready to move out of your mama's house and buy a place of your own. I just put a gorgeous condo on the market that's got your name written all over it." Their conversation faded as they slipped into the crowd.

Dakota was visibly relieved by Angela's departure. She released a breath, turned back to the bar, and took a deep gulp of her drink. "Not much has changed around here," she muttered.

"You're not going to judge the entire town by Angela Gilson, are you?" Dex smiled. "Where's that objective reporter?"

"Guess that isn't fair of me." She met his gaze. "If I'm being honest, things have changed a lot, even since my last visit home when..." Her voice trailed off, and she looked away momentarily. "Take this place, for instance. I can't believe how different it looks now. Sin said Drew and Lydia bought the place."

"They did. Lydia and the kids are here during the off season. Drew prefers Cali. He bought his parents and sister a place out there. Only Lydia's family is still on the island."

She nodded but seemed lost in her own thoughts. He wanted to take her in his arms and comfort her. Tell her again how sorry he was about her mother. That wasn't an option, so he did his best to distract her instead.

"There's been new development all along this road"— he gestured in the general direction of it—"since we started building the resort. Other places, like this one, have changed ownership or been updated. You came back home at an exciting time in the town's history." He mentally chastised himself for sounding like a convention bureau brochure.

Her polite smile betrayed waning interest. She scanned the room. "Have you seen Sin?"

Didn't think it would be easy to win Dakota over, did you?

"She's over there." Dex tipped his chin in the direction of the bandstand, where Sin was talking to a few of the musicians who were setting up. "I'll walk you over."

"Thanks, but that isn't necessary. It was kind of you to keep me company, but your wingman already has you set up with a sure thing." She nodded toward where Nick was flirting with the blonde and her friend.

Was that a hint of jealousy in her voice?

"I'd much rather stay here and talk to you, Dakota. I think you know that."

There was a flash of hurt and perhaps anger in her dark eyes. But why?

He'd admitted that he preferred her company to the woman across the room staring at him like she was dying of thirst and he was the last watering hole for miles.

Dakota's mouth twisted in a controlled scowl, and he could almost see the memory of that day—the day he'd told her they should see other people—scrolling across her face. "Nice of you to choose me this time."

The sarcastic reply was sharp and cut deep, like jagged glass ripping at his skin. Dexter swallowed back an apology. He'd apologized to Dakota more than once. He doubted she wanted to hear another. What she needed was to work out the resentment she felt toward him. If launching a well-placed barb at him would help her get over the anger she still held on to, he'd gladly endure the hit.

"I'd better mingle, or Angela will have everyone convinced I'm being snooty. Besides, best not to fuel the rumors she's sure to start about us." She grabbed her drink and took one last glance at the brunette before turning to him with a half-hearted smile. "Have fun, *boss*."

Dexter groaned quietly as she sashayed away in the fitted dress. Sex was off the table, but he missed Dakota, and he'd rather have her in his life as a friend than not at all.

Chapter Thirteen

Dakota pushed her way through the crowd. Most of what was left of her drink sloshed onto her dress and splattered on her expensive shoes, remnants of her former, glamorous life. She gulped down the remainder and set the empty glass on a nearby tray. Then she headed toward the ladies' room and stood in front of the mirror, sifting her fingers through her hair.

She was going to strangle Sinclair. First she made her get all dressed up and dragged her out on a Friday night when she would rather be on the couch splitting a bag of microwave popcorn and watching home improvement shows. Then she dished her off on Dexter Roberts, of all people, and disappeared.

Maybe it was a mistake to return to the island. Dakota heaved a sigh. *No, coming home was the right thing to do.*

She needed to be here to keep tabs on her father's health. She'd already lost her mother far too soon. Dakota couldn't bear the thought of losing her father, too.

Her relationship with her sister had grown distant since Shay had gotten married. Without her father, she'd be completely alone in the world—a devastating prospect.

A chill ran down her spine and her arms prickled with goose bumps at the thought of something happening to her father.

She would stay long enough to make sure her father's health was on track. But staying on Holly Grove Island a moment longer than she needed to...that would be a mistake.

Honestly, the place might as well be called Dexter Roberts Island, because the man was everywhere she went, looking finer than ever and saying and doing all the right things. Making her want him, when that was the very last thing she should want.

Dakota turned sideways and checked herself out in profile in the black-and-white dress.

If she had to run into Dex twice in one day, she could at least take comfort in the fact that both times she'd looked good. She was glad she'd taken Sin's advice to dress up.

Judging by the way Dexter's eyes drank her in as she approached him at the bar and when he'd seen her at the office earlier that day, he'd certainly liked what he'd seen.

Good.

He'd probably end up going home with the brunette, but maybe she'd at least given him a moment's regret. She didn't care if it made her petty or immature. She wanted Dex to regret the day he'd broken her heart. To wonder if he'd made the right choice.

"There you are." Sinclair entered the restroom. "Everything all right?"

"Now you show up, after you abandoned me with Dexter. Did you know he'd be here?"

"I saved you from Angela, didn't I?" Sin batted her hazel eyes and avoided answering the question. "Besides, it looked like you two were gettin' on fine. What happened?"

"I was being polite, and so was he." It wasn't a lie. She *was* being polite. But for a moment she'd also been reminded of how much she'd once enjoyed Dexter's company. Once she'd gotten him to open up to her, they'd been able to talk about everything from movies and music to sports. Or whatever new topic he was obsessive about at the time. The only subject Dexter hadn't discussed much was his relationship with his father. "In fact, he's probably wrapped around that leggy brunette in the killer red dress by now."

Sin leaned closer and folded her arms. Her eyes danced with amusement. "You aren't jealous, are you, darlin'? Because I distinctly remember you telling me—"

"Oh, shut up." Dakota smacked Sin's arm and sighed. "You don't get to use my words against me. *Ever.* That's best friend rule number five or something."

"Guess I need to dust off the old handbook and refresh my memory." Sin grinned. "Anyway, the show starts soon, and it's always amazing. Trust me, you don't want to miss it. I snagged us a table near the stage, but my friend isn't going to hold it forever. So do whatever you gotta do and let's get back out there."

"Fine." Dakota pouted and stomped off toward a stall.

She'd seen Dex not once but twice today. They'd even managed to have a decent conversation like two perfectly mature adults. She could certainly survive the rest of the night.

They settled at their table near the bandstand and ordered another round of drinks and some appetizers. A woman strode toward the stage in a pair of pin-striped, black dress slacks, a white button-down shirt, and a loose tie.

Dakota peered at the woman for a minute, trying to

place her face. Suddenly, she turned to Sin. "Oh my gosh, is that Dexter's little sister?"

"She ain't so little anymore." Sin grinned.

"My God, she's grown into such a beautiful young woman." Dakota choked up a little. Her eyes stung with emotion. Emerie had always been so sweet. She'd been like a little sister to Dakota. Dex would sometimes let her tag along when they went for ice cream or to the beach.

"She's as much a tomboy now as ever," Sin lamented.

"What does it matter as long as she's happy?" Dakota gave Sin her evil eye. "Besides, I love her look. My dad said she and Nick are still best friends."

Nick and Emerie had met when she and Dexter had taken Em to some kid movie and she'd decided to bring Nick along. The two of them hit it off and they'd been friends ever since.

"I'm just saying, the girl is classically beautiful. Model gorgeous. I would kill to have her cheekbones and that figure," Sin groused.

"And she and Nick are definitely just friends?" Dakota glanced over at him laughing with another group of women. Nick Washington was definitely still a charmer.

"I swear, sometimes I think the two of 'em were dropped on their heads or something. It's obvious there's sexual tension there. She's always touching him. And you should see how he roughhouses with her when we're at the beach. You'd have to be blind not to see what's up with the two of them."

"If it were obvious to Nick and Em, they'd probably have done something about it by now." Dakota ignored her friend's incredulous eye roll and concentrated instead on Em, who was welcoming the crowd and announcing that it was time to start the evening's jam session.

"Of course you'd say that. You can't even see that you're still in love with Dexter," Sin whispered loudly, pinning Dakota with a pointed look that dared her to object.

Better to ignore the dig.

The server arrived, delivering their food and another round of drinks, and Dakota was grateful for the distraction of food. Anything to get Sin off the topic of her and Dexter and her complicated feelings for the man who was now her boss as well as her ex.

Dakota picked up one of the crispy, buttermilk-fried green tomatoes, dipped it in the tangy sauce, and took a bite. Not acknowledging her friend's earlier comment, she returned her attention to the stage, where Em was introducing the musicians.

"Tonight we have a collective of truly amazing local musicians. On the drums, my best friend, the incredible Nicholas Washington. On the piano, the superbly talented Quinton Carson. The intrepid Jay Montgomery on the bass. On tenor saxophone, we have the remarkable Rich Vargas. Then last, but not least, on alto sax, my big brother, the brilliant Dexter Roberts. Fellas, take it away."

Dakota sat there blinking, mouth open, unable to speak. Dexter had stripped off his suit jacket and stood onstage with a black and gold saxophone strapped across his body. One corner of his sensuous mouth curved in a half smile when his dark eyes met hers—widening with surprise. Then he put the mouthpiece to his lips and blew.

The sound Dex elicited from the instrument was soulful and sensual. As unique and expressive as the human voice. Something about the piece they were playing spoke to her.

Dexter's eyes were closed during much of the song. When they weren't, they always managed to meet hers. As if he were somehow speaking directly to her. Finally, she recognized the song they were playing. "Breakin' My Heart (Pretty Brown Eyes)" by Mint Condition. A song he knew to be one of her favorites. The lyrics about a woman who outwardly rejects a man she secretly harbors deep feelings for couldn't be more apropos of their current situation.

When he met her gaze again, she'd never felt more vulnerable. Like Dexter could see inside her head. Like he was privy to all of the conflicting emotions weighing on her chest and making it hard to breathe.

Was he playing the song for her?

Dakota swallowed hard, her pulse thumping. It all felt so surreal. Dexter Roberts was a jazz musician—an incredibly good one. What else didn't she know about him?

Dakota realized Sin was staring at her, amused by her stunned reaction.

"Dexter's not bad, huh?" Sin grinned.

"Not bad? He's *incredible*. They all are," she added quickly, ignoring Sin's smirk.

She'd known that Dexter's father had played the sax and his mother played the piano. Dex had told her that his parents had required him and his younger siblings to take music lessons from their parents as kids. But she'd had no clue that Dexter had this level of talent.

She'd never heard him play an instrument, despite asking him to play for her. He'd always downplayed his abilities and said she wasn't missing anything. Clearly that wasn't true.

"Has he always been this good?" She could barely take her eyes off Dexter. There was something incredibly sexy about the way he handled the instrument and the confidence with which he played.

"Don't know." Sin shrugged. "I first heard him play a

few years ago, when Nick talked Dex and the guys into playing here once a month. I honestly couldn't believe my ears. You know I'm a country music girl all the way. But what that man can do with that instrument is amazing. Look at the thing... It's downright sexy. And so is he." Sin looked around. "Apparently, we aren't the only ones who think so." She nodded toward the blonde Nick had been flirting with and her brunette friend, who only had eyes for Dexter.

Dakota was really starting to hate that woman.

She cursed under her breath, hoping Sin hadn't noticed her giving the woman her death stare. Because she was being absolutely ridiculous.

Why should she care if the woman was interested in Dexter?

Dakota had no claim on Dexter's affections. Nor did she want any. So why was she gritting her teeth and clenching her fists on her lap beneath the table?

Jealousy, plain and simple.

She no longer had any claim to Dexter, but deep down, a part of her hadn't come to terms with that.

Sinclair swiped one of the fried green tomatoes from the plate, her mouth curled in a self-satisfied grin.

"This is why you brought me here, isn't it? Did you think I'd fall into Dexter's arms because the man can play the sax?"

"I brought you here because Friday Night Jam Sessions are *the* premier event on the island. People come from all over the Outer Banks for it. Besides, you've been stressed since you've returned home. I'm not prying," Sin added quickly, in response to Dakota's involuntary frown, which accompanied the quickening of her pulse, her heart beating a mile a minute. "I promised that I wouldn't push you, and

I meant it. We can talk about whatever is bothering you whenever you're ready."

The fight-or-flight response that had kicked in when her friend alluded to the troubles that had brought Dakota back home simmered down. But her heart was still in her throat, and she could barely speak. She nodded her thanks to her friend, bringing her glass to her lips and taking a sip of her second drink of the night.

When she'd first arrived on the island, she'd spent every waking hour stressed, in expectation that someone—everyone—would learn the truth. That she'd been stupidly naive and had come crashing back down to earth from the pedestal her mother had put her on when she'd bragged about her daughter the reporter. But as the weeks elapsed, she'd grown more comfortable. Settled into life on Holly Grove Island. Worried less about the day when she'd eventually have to at least tell her father and Sin the ugly truth.

Earlier that day, she'd been compelled to admit the truth to Nick. And as terrifying as it had been, it had also been the tiniest bit freeing. Nick had been supportive, he hadn't judged her, and he'd promised to keep her secret. Somehow, that had made the burden she'd been carrying feel the slightest bit lighter. But Sin's allusion to it now—even though her friend didn't know exactly what *it* was—had sent her into full panic mode again. If only for a moment.

"I wanted to take my best friend, who I've really missed, out for a fun night on the town." Sin finally nibbled on her fried green tomato. "Don't tell me you're not enjoying it."

Dakota exhaled softly, her attention drifting to Dexter onstage again. "I am. And maybe you're right. Maybe I should get out more often. Now that I'm working at the resort, I don't have much of a choice."

"It's for your own good." Sin squeezed her hand. The candlelight was reflected in her hazel eyes. They both returned their attention to the stage as the song ended and the club filled with thunderous applause.

Dakota couldn't help clapping, too. The band was amazing—especially Nick and Dex. She still couldn't get over the fact that the two of them were such exceptional musicians.

She'd been so busy with her own life and pursuing her own dreams that she'd completely disconnected from this place. From all of the people she'd known here. Good people who'd always cared for her, supported her, believed in her.

Dakota's gaze drifted to her friend, who watched the stage intently. Sin was a ride-or-die kind of friend. The one who offered a shoulder to cry on but was also ready to take off her earrings and heels and brandish a baseball bat if the situation called for it.

Sinclair had welcomed her home and resumed their friendship, despite how hurt she'd been by Dakota pulling away after she'd moved to New York. Her friend had been willing to put aside any resentment because Dakota needed her.

Sin was a better friend than she deserved.

The realization made Dakota's eyes burn with tears. She was glad that she and Sin had talked on the way here. That she'd given her friend the apology she deserved.

Dakota hugged her friend, seated beside her at the table. "Thanks for getting me out of the house tonight, Sin. I needed this."

"I knew you did." Sinclair nodded toward the stage. "Listen to Dex. He ain't just playin' that thing. He's makin' love to it, and just about every other girl here is wishing he'd make love to her like that, too." She shuddered and took a sip of her cosmo. "I wish I had a man who knew how to blow an instrument like that."

"Sin!" Dakota's censure came out louder than she'd intended, but no one seemed to notice. They were all too taken with the band.

Her friend giggled and held up a hand. "Easy, tiger. I'm not talking about your man in particular. I meant in general."

Dakota took a sip of her drink and watched Dexter as he played the instrument, his eyes closed, seemingly lost in the evocative melody.

She was behaving irrationally. Still, she couldn't help feeling a sense of possessiveness over Dexter. It was an odd dance: the push and pull of the past and the present.

For the past seventeen years, Dexter had been firmly lodged in her brain as the villain who'd callously broken her heart. But each encounter she'd had with Dexter since her return to Holly Grove Island had reminded her of all the reasons she'd once adored him.

He'd been the star quarterback of their high school football team. But Dexter hadn't been the stereotypical jock. He was confident without being arrogant. Athletic, but also studious. Dex was the strong, silent type. Pensive and observant. But once he'd gotten to know someone, he would open up to them. He was protective of her and his younger siblings. Loyal to his small group of friends. And he adored his mother.

She honestly couldn't help falling in love with him.

But that was why his abrupt insistence that he no longer wanted to be locked into an exclusive relationship had been so unlike him. It was the opposite of every promise he'd made to her during their two years together.

I will always love you, Dakota. No matter what we do or where our lives take us.

It was a promise they'd made to each other. Yes, they'd been young. Their parents had often warned them that they were too young to know what love really was.

Still, she'd meant every word. Dexter obviously hadn't.

Dakota tore her attention from Dexter and nodded toward Nick. "I remember Nick banging on those drums next door all the time as a kid," Dakota said. "It drove my dad insane. He was thrilled when Nick finally went off to college."

"I remember." Sin laughed. "Apparently it paid off. Nicky played paid gigs as a side hustle while he attended school in Louisiana. Em says he played a little of everything. Jazz, rock, hip-hop. But he fell in love with jazz. Apparently, he was in demand on the local music scene."

"Nick's awfully good. I'm surprised he didn't pursue it," Dakota said, over Nick's drum solo. His hands were a blur, and he played with so much energy.

"He did for a while. In Vegas, LA, and New York. He lived hard and fast for a few years. I think the life was a bit much for him." A sad look crept across Sin's face, but then she forced a smile. "So he came back home. Dex gave him a job at the hotel in Myrtle Beach, and he's worked his way up the ladder."

Dakota wanted to ask what it was that Sin wasn't saying, but the song ended on a crash of Nick's cymbals and the entire crowd erupted in applause. When she looked up at the stage, Dex was staring at her. His sexy, one-sided grin made her heart flutter and evoked happier memories.

There was something hypnotic about that smile. He'd always had a way of making her feel it belonged to her and no one else. And his stare. *Holy hell.* Had someone

suddenly turned on a four-hundred-watt lightbulb? Her
skin was warm, and she could barely breathe.

She turned toward Sin instead. Her friend grinned like
the cat that stole the canary and ate it for lunch with a side
of biscuits and gravy.

"What?" Dakota fiddled with her bracelet, a graduation
gift from her mother.

"Looks like Nicky and Em aren't the only folks around here
in complete denial." Sin hiked a brow, her mouth twisted.

Dakota pointed a finger at her friend to object to her statement, but the bassist played the familiar opening chords of
another of her favorite songs, drawing her attention.

Dexter stepped into the spotlight at the center of the
small stage. Eyes closed, he played the soulful notes she'd
recognize anywhere.

"'Cupid,'" Dakota whispered beneath her breath.

Sinclair listened intently; then a dreamy smile lit her
face. "Yes! You listened to that song so much it drove us
all crazy. He's playing it just for you, Dakota. God, that is
so sweet."

Dakota swallowed hard, trying to dismiss the nostalgic
memories of the summer she'd fallen in love with that song
by the group 112. She'd played it so often that her parents
and Sin hated it and Dexter complained that he heard the
song in his sleep.

She tried to push down the unsettling cocktail of
emotions that bubbled in her chest as Dexter played every
note with so much passion. The song had always reminded
her of how Dexter had first professed his love for her. He'd
been so nervous and unsure, but also incredibly sweet and
sincere. Even now it moved her.

Dakota smiled involuntarily at the memory, but quickly
dismissed it.

"Dex isn't playing the song for me. He's playing it for the audience." Dakota gestured to the people around them. "Because it happens to be a great song."

But when she glanced up and his eyes met hers, she realized that what Sin said was true. He *was* playing the song for her. Speaking to her through the ballad that had always meant so much to her, as he once had.

They were playing an instrumental version of the song, but Dakota remembered the lyrics word-for-word. In the song, the man pleaded with his love interest to believe his genuine declaration of love and trust that if they took that leap of faith, their love would work out.

Dakota's eyes drifted closed, and she could almost feel Dexter's arms around her waist, her cheek pressed to his chest as he sang the words softly in her ear. The love and affection she'd felt for him in that perfect moment came rushing back with the force of a rapidly moving stream.

A knot churned in her belly, and her chest ached at the bittersweet memory.

"Sweetie, are you okay?" Sinclair touched her arm, her voice heavy with concern.

"Yes, of course." Dakota forced a smile. "Why?"

Sinclair trailed two fingers down one side of her face.

Dakota touched her cheek, gasping with surprise when she found it wet with tears. Her face heated with embarrassment. Had she honestly been sitting here crying?

"I'm fine. I just need some fresh air." Dakota forced a smile to reassure her friend. Then she grabbed her purse and excused herself from the table, making her way toward the exit.

She stepped out into the chillier night air. It was a relief against her heated skin; her face and chest burned with intense embarrassment. How could she have let herself get so wrapped up in the past that she'd shed actual tears right there in the club? In front of everyone?

Dakota took a deep breath, inhaling the salty breeze blowing off the Atlantic Ocean. The wind rustled her hair, blowing it across her face.

A sudden hand on her shoulder startled her. She whipped around.

"Sin. God, you scared me." Dakota splayed her fingers against her chest.

"Sorry, sweetie. I didn't mean to startle you, but I needed to make sure you're all right."

"I'm fine. Embarrassed, that's all." Dakota brushed her fingertips over her cheek.

"Don't be. The room is dim. The audience was watching the stage. And Dex and the band are completely absorbed with their performances." Sin ticked each reason off on her fingers. "I doubt anyone else in the room even noticed a few tears."

"Two drinks in, and I'm a mess." Dakota swiped a finger beneath one eye.

She'd been overwrought with emotion and nostalgic about the past. Being at the Foxhole tonight had made her realize how much she'd missed her close friendship with Sin. And that some small part of her still missed Dex. Pining for Dex was foolish. Regardless of his sweet, sentimental display tonight, the truth was, when it counted, Dex had let her down. She'd believed that he loved her. Had been willing to defer her own dreams to be with him as she supported his. But he'd flatly rejected her.

That was all she really needed to remember about Dexter Roberts.

"It must be overwhelming for you to be back here after all this time. You've been through a lot...losing your job,

I mean." Sin lowered her gaze and tucked a few strands of her ombre-blond hair behind her ear. "This is your first time being back home since you lost your mom. It's a lot to deal with. It's only natural that you'd feel some kind of way about everything that's going on. You've held up remarkably well, considering."

Dakota drew in a shaky breath and nodded. She hugged Sin. "You're a better friend than I deserve. Thank you for not giving up on me."

"I can't afford to abandon my best friend. I can be a lot, and not everybody has the constitution to put up with all of this." Sin rubbed Dakota's back. "Why do you think I'm still single?"

Before Dakota could disagree, they were both startled by the door crashing open.

"Dakota, are you all right?" Dexter's chest heaved as if he'd run the entire way.

"Dexter?" Dakota blinked. For a moment she wondered if she was imagining him standing there. But Sinclair looked just as stunned to see him. "What on earth are you doing here? You're supposed to be onstage right now."

"We took a quick, unscheduled break." He waved off her concerns. "I had to make sure you were okay. I thought you'd like hearing our rendition of your favorite songs. I'd never have arranged for us to play them if I thought for a moment that it would upset you."

"So you were expecting me to be here tonight?" Dakota glared in her friend's direction. She'd suspected as much.

"Guess that's my cue to leave." Sin hugged Dakota again, whispering in her ear, "This man is keeping an entire club full of half-drunk folks waiting, because he was worried about you. He obviously still cares an awful lot about you, too."

Sin patted Dexter's arm on her way back inside the club.

Dakota and Dexter stood outside the club's entrance, their eyes meeting in an awkward dance. He shoved his hands in his pockets and moved a few steps closer.

"I'm sorry, Dakota. The last thing I wanted was to upset you. That certainly isn't why I arranged for us to play those songs," he said.

"Why did you play them, Dexter?" It was the question that had been burning in her brain from the moment she realized he was playing "Cupid" for her. "What did you hope it would accomplish?"

He dropped his gaze, sighing heavily before meeting her eyes again. "I won't lie. I'd hoped that…" He frowned deeply, letting the words die on his lips.

He didn't need to finish them. His song choice and performance made it clear that he'd hoped to reignite things between them.

"I updated the set with those songs right after I saw you at the Fourth of July Festival. Before my promotion and before you accepted the job." Dexter ran a hand over his stubbled chin. "Obviously, as of today, the circumstances have changed. I was so preoccupied with everything going on today that I didn't even consider changing the set list."

"Dex, there you are." Nick popped his head outside. "We have to get started up again soon." His tone was urgent, but the look he gave them both was apologetic.

"I'll be right in, Nick. I promise. Give me two minutes." Dexter turned to her once Nick had gone back inside. He hiked a thumb over his shoulder. "I'm sorry, Dakota. I'd love to finish this conversation now, but I really need to—"

"Go. I don't want to be the reason your club full of adoring fans starts to riot," she said, only half-teasing. "You're incredibly good, by the way."

"Thanks." Worry lines were etched into the space between his thick, neat brows—a feature of his face she'd always loved. "And you're sure you're good?"

"I will be." She forced a pained smile. "Thank you for checking on me, and for the songs. It was a sweet gesture. But maybe it's better if we don't revisit the past."

"Maybe you're right." He shrugged, a pained look in his dark eyes. "But I'm still really glad you're here."

Her belly fluttered as she watched him turn and jog back inside. Dakota's head reeled with thoughts she shouldn't be having about her ex, who was now also her boss, once removed.

She appreciated Dexter's concern and the time and effort he'd put into arranging this thoughtful surprise. But any feelings of attraction or affection evoked by nostalgia or a sense of gratitude were best shoved back into the little box from which they came and buried deep.

He was a colleague, a fellow islander, and maybe someday they'd manage to be friends again. But the little voice in her head that wondered, even for a moment, if there was the possibility of them becoming anything more was a recipe for disaster.

She'd come back home to regroup while she took care of her father and strategized her next move. It would be hard enough walking away from Sin and her dad again. Dakota didn't need any more reasons to get attached to life on Holly Grove Island.

She wrapped her arms around herself and waited until the music started again before she made her way back inside.

Chapter Fourteen

* * *

Admittedly, Sin had dragged Dakota to the Foxhole kicking and screaming. But for the first time since she'd returned home, she felt like she'd been able to let loose, shut off her brain, and have some fun.

Of course, the three cocktails she'd had probably had a little to do with it.

Still, the music was phenomenal, and the atmosphere of the revamped space was lively, yet intimate. She hadn't laughed this hard in months. Her legs were tired from dancing. Dakota hadn't intended to get out on the floor, but the older man they'd befriended at the next table had convinced her to join him. She'd relaxed and had a little fun. Ten minutes later, her gorgeous shoes were tucked under the table and she was dancing with someone else. It seemed as if she'd danced with just about every unattached man there, except for the members of the band.

The band took a break, and she was thrilled to finally get off her feet. She collapsed onto the chair next to Sinclair, both of them giggling.

"You must be exhausted," Sin teased. "But you look

happy. In fact, that's the biggest smile I've seen on your face since you've been home."

"I know." Dakota nodded gratefully. "Thank you for tonight. You have no idea how much I needed it."

Sin's expression indicated that there was something she wanted to say, but then she decided against it. "I'm glad I could help you out, Twinkle Toes. And you know I'm always here if you need me. For anything. No matter what it is. Seriously."

"I appreciate that, Sin." Dakota felt like a liar, keeping the truth from Sin and her dad. But she still wasn't ready to talk about what a fool she'd been. She'd sabotaged her entire career over a hot Italian man whose warm brown eyes and thick accent had turned her brain to mush. Dakota reached under the table for her shoes and strapped them on. "I'm going to the powder room."

"Okay," Sin said, in a tone meant to remind her that they'd revisit the subject.

It was an olive branch that Dakota would eventually accept, but not tonight. Tonight she felt amazing, and she wanted to keep floating in this warm, happy bubble.

"Should I order more drinks?" Sin asked gleefully.

"Maybe we should switch to food for a while. Why don't you put in an order of fried calamari? Put it on my bill."

"Tonight is my treat, remember?" Sin's words were slightly slurred.

Looked like they'd be taking a cab home. Two drinks was her limit, and Sin was definitely well over hers—whatever that might be. For a tiny little thing, the girl could drink her weight in alcohol.

"Yes, ma'am." She'd let Sin win this battle. Then maybe her friend would give in easily when she insisted they take a ride share home. "Be back in a sec."

Dakota turned around and collided with a hard wall of muscled man.

She tottered on her heels, but Dex placed his large hands at her waist to steady her. Dakota inhaled the notes of cedar, patchouli, and citrus in his cologne, which she'd caught the faintest whiff of when she'd been seated next to him at the bar. The heat radiating from his tall, muscular body enveloped hers. Dakota's pulse quickened and her skin tingled beneath his touch through the thin fabric of her dress.

"You all right?" Dexter's voice was sexy—low and gruff, the way it had sounded on those late-night telephone conversations where neither of them wanted to be the first to hang up. His voice had done things to her then. And she could feel her body reacting to it and the nearness of him now. "I didn't mean to surprise you like that."

"I'm fine." She took a step back, prompting him to drop his hands from her waist. "You know I've always been kind of a klutz. I should've looked where I was going."

Dex shoved his hands into his pockets and smiled. "The band is on dinner break. If you don't mind, I thought I'd grab a quick bite with you and Sin."

"You're welcome to join us," Sin interjected. "We're about to place an order."

"Thanks, Sin," Dex responded, but his eyes never left hers. He seemed to be seeking her permission.

"Like Sin said, you're welcome to join us. Be right back." Dakota headed to the restroom, hoping Dex hadn't noticed the beading of her nipples through the thin material of her dress.

She made her way to the washroom, trying to calm her breath and reminding herself that Dexter Roberts was her boss and that she absolutely did *not* have feelings for him.

Despite the fact that every part of her body was screaming otherwise.

———

Dex watched as Dakota walked away, her sashay sexier than ever. The string bean he'd dated in high school was gone, replaced by a woman whose body was tight and toned, yet voluptuous and sensual. His fingers curled instinctively beneath the table as he recalled how it felt to grip her waist, even briefly.

His only thought at the time had been to prevent her from falling. Now all he could think about was how it would feel to slide his hands a little lower and cup that—

"Tonight's going well, right?" Sin jogged him from his less-than-pure thoughts.

He cleared his throat and turned his attention to her. "Dakota seems to be enjoying herself. I get the feeling she needed a night like this."

"Me too. I know there's something going on with her, but she won't talk about it."

"Even best friends deserve some privacy, Sin," he said kindly. "Don't take it personally. If something is wrong, I'm sure she'll talk to you when she's ready. In the meantime, just be the friend she needs."

The server suddenly appeared, distracting Sin from further discussion on the topic, and they both placed their orders.

"Look who I found." Dakota finally returned to the table with his little sister, Em, in tow. "She was at the bar all alone, so I invited her to join us."

Dakota was evidently determined not to let Sin leave them alone again. She'd brought reinforcements. *Smart woman.* And with Nick sitting at another table with the blonde and her friend, Em wouldn't be going anywhere anytime soon.

"I see your *friend* is otherwise occupied." Sin nodded toward Nick and the two women.

Em seemed oblivious to Sinclair's undue emphasis on the word *friend.*

"You know Nicky." Em shrugged. "He always goes for the out-of-towners. I'm pretty sure he'd rather cut off his big toe than be involved in an *actual* relationship."

"Every man believes that, honey. Until the right girl comes along and knocks him flat on his ass." Sin slapped the table for emphasis. "He'll be head over heels and he won't even see it coming until he's been toe-tagged and body-bagged."

"Dramatic much, Sin?" Dakota laughed.

Emerie snorted. "I'll have to see it to believe it. But it'd be good for Nick. So I hope he does eventually fall hard for some girl. Anyway, I normally bring my friend Kassie to these things. But tonight she went to a formal dinner off island with her boyfriend's family. Ooh... is that fried calamari?" Em pointed as a server floated past with another table's order. "I want that."

Dex couldn't help laughing. Sinclair was completely outdone by the fact that Em couldn't care less about Nick's love life. She narrowed her eyes and kicked him under the table, which only made him laugh harder.

"What is it?" Em's gaze shifted around the table.

"Nothing. These two are clowning, that's all," Dakota said quickly. "The waitress walked past. You should catch up with her and place your order."

As soon as Em was gone, Dakota gave Sin and Dex the same look his mother had leveled at him and his brothers when they'd gotten fidgety in church as kids. "What's wrong with you two? You're going to give the poor girl a complex."

"Seems like Em is blissfully content with the situation," Sin said. "I hope she feels that way when some woman comes along and puts it on that boy. *Then* she'll sit up and take notice, only it'll be too late."

"Either way, it's none of our business. So lay off the matchmaking, all right?" Dex pressed. "As much as I like and respect Nick as a friend and coworker, I don't know how chill I'd be if he and Em ever became a thing. The guy isn't the settling-down type."

"Fine. I was only trying to help." Sin huffed. "Anyway, I see a man I need to talk to about some commercial space I've had my eye on." She was gone before Dakota could question the wisdom of talking real estate while completely buzzed.

"Looks like it's just us. *Again.*" Dakota glanced around the room as she took a sip of what looked like club soda.

He winced, remembering how they'd once lived for moments like this.

They'd both been busy, overscheduled high school kids. Between school, football practice, family obligations, and their after-school jobs, it'd been tough to make time for each other. Which was why they'd treasured every single moment they'd spent together.

But that was a lifetime ago. Now that their only option was friendship, taking a stroll down that part of memory lane wasn't the wisest move.

The server brought the order of calamari to the table, and Dakota nibbled on a piece.

"So when did you become a concert-worthy saxophone player?" she asked.

"I'm flattered you think so." Dex couldn't help smiling at the compliment.

"You know I started playing when I was about ten because my mother insisted that we all take up an instrument. She played the piano, but that didn't appeal to me, and they wouldn't go for the drums." He chuckled. "My dad was a professional sax player until my mom got pregnant and they settled down to start a family."

He shrugged, as if it were a minor detail to the story. But that decision had been the first domino to fall in a long succession of them.

He was grateful his parents had chosen to have him and to start their family. But his father had spent most of his adult life saddled with regret over a life interrupted. His mother loved each of her children. But she'd endured an unhappy marriage in order to keep their family together. His parents' misery, for the sake of him and his siblings, had always plagued him with guilt. He was the reason that both of them had spent so much of their lives unfulfilled.

Most adult children would be upset about their parents divorcing. But for Dex, the news had actually caused him to breathe a deep sigh of relief.

Better late than never.

His parents seemed happier since they'd filed for divorce immediately after Em had graduated from UNC. In fact, they'd never gotten along better.

"So you picked the sax because it was the instrument your dad played," Dakota prodded.

He hadn't delved deeply into his family dynamics when he and Dakota were together. But she'd known that his father had been a stoic man and that they hadn't been close.

"It was a way for me to hang out with my father while also satisfying my mom's music requirement." Dex thanked the server who'd brought out his meal. "There were two things my dad loved. Pro football and the saxophone." Dex shrugged. "I did my best to excel at both, but I couldn't play quarterback and be in the marching band. I went with football because it gave me the best shot at a college scholarship."

"And the best shot at collecting groupies like Ms. Brunette in the Red Dress over there. She's staring at me like she's considering giving me an appendectomy with a fork."

"Dakota, I'm spending my dinner break here with you because I have zero interest in her." Dexter didn't turn to look at the woman. Despite their current employee-employer status, he had eyes only for Dakota. And it pained him that she failed to see how important she still was to him. "I'm much more concerned about repairing our friendship."

She stared at him, blinking. As if she was unsure whether or not to accept his words at face value. Dakota dropped her gaze and nibbled on more of the calamari.

"I wish you had let me hear you play back when we were…friends. There were a lot of topics you never seemed to want to talk about."

"That's something I regret," he admitted. "But playing the sax and being into jazz weren't the kinds of things the high school football team captain bragged to his buddies or his girl about."

"Not much demand for sax players in high school garage bands, I suppose," she agreed. "Still, it's cool your dad taught you to play the sax. And for the record, if you'd trusted me with that part of your life, I would never have laughed at you about it."

Her warm smile melted his heart.

Tagged and bagged? Yeah, this woman did that to him and more. She had since the first day he'd laid eyes on her. Warmth filled his chest and he fought back the urge to touch her hand.

"Openness and vulnerability...that wasn't something I was accustomed to seeing in my family," he admitted.

His father was closed off with his emotions, except when he was commiserating about the missed opportunities of his past or projecting his own wishes onto his children's futures. Dexter's mother, on the other hand, had always been warm and open. They'd never doubted her love for them. But she walled off her own pain and loneliness.

So it was no surprise that he'd built a stone wall around his own deepest thoughts and feelings, suppressing them and keeping them to himself. But it was as if Dakota had sensed something deeper in him and been drawn to it.

She'd been like an insistent dripping of water with the power to carve a path through those hardened walls over time. He'd liked having someone to share thoughts with that he kept from the rest of the world. Dakota had been his safe space. But more importantly, he'd treasured being hers. That she'd trusted him with her own raw, unfiltered emotions.

"You taught me the beauty of being open and letting people in, Dakota. Still, I wish I'd been even more candid with you. In fact, there are a lot of things I wish I'd done differently."

"Thank you for saying that, Dexter, but like I said earlier, maybe it's best if we focus on the present and keep the past behind us, where it belongs." Dakota sighed softly. She gestured toward an older man beckoning her from the dance floor. "I'd better go. I still need to hit the restroom, and my unofficial dance partner for the night is calling. But it was nice catching up."

"You, too." He forced a smile, his jaw tight and his voice strained by the constriction of his throat. Dex wanted to beg her to stay there with him. To tell her that he'd be content to sit there and reminisce about their past all night. That he wanted her to be part of both his present and his future. But that would only push her away when they were finally making some progress. And it would feed his desire to be more than just friends with Dakota. Something he couldn't afford given the probationary status of his promotion at the Holly Grove Island Resort.

Dexter tried his best to divert his gaze from the smooth brown skin of her thighs, revealed when she crossed her legs to remove one shoe, then the other, before sliding them beneath the table.

"Save a dance for me later?" he asked.

She studied him for a moment, then shrugged. "Sure. You're about the only person in the room I *haven't* danced with tonight. Might as well go home with my punch card full."

It wasn't an enthusiastic acceptance, but beggars couldn't be choosers.

Dex shoved a bite of steak into his mouth and chewed as he watched her dance with someone else, wishing it were him instead.

Chapter Fifteen

• • • •

Dakota thanked Gerald—the older man who'd been her dance partner for most of the evening—then made her way back to the table. She slid into the chair, happy but exhausted, and slipped her shoes back on.

It was well after one in the morning. The crowd had thinned considerably, but there were still plenty of people on the dance floor, hanging out at the bar, and scattered around the tables and the sofas that lined the space. But she didn't see Sinclair anywhere. In fact, she hadn't seen her friend for a half hour or more.

Pulling out her phone, Dakota called Sin. The phone rang until it rolled over to voice mail. She called the number again and got the same. The band had ended their set a little after midnight and a DJ had taken over. With the music blaring, it would be difficult to hear her cell phone ring, even if Sinclair had it with her.

She checked beneath the table and chairs. Her friend's shoes and purse were gone.

"Where are you, Sin?" Dakota's eyes swept the space again. She sighed. She'd have to hunt her friend down the old-fashioned way.

Dakota made her way through the club, checking the dance floor, the other tables, the couches around the perimeter, the bathroom, and the patio. She checked with the bartender, who hadn't seen her friend for a while, either.

There was no sign of Sinclair anywhere, and now she was beginning to worry.

They'd expanded the Foxhole, but still, the space wasn't so big that she shouldn't be able to find Sinclair. What if something had happened to her?

When Dakota and her friends went out in New York, they'd always employed a buddy system. No wandering off alone. Don't accept drinks from strangers unless you watched the bartender make it yourself. No hookups with random dudes who might turn out to be ax murderers. She and Sinclair hadn't established any rules tonight. It was Holly Grove Island.

When her father ran the island's small police force, drunk and disorderly conduct or kids trespassing in an abandoned property were the most dangerous situations they'd encountered. So it hadn't seemed necessary to establish rules of engagement. But now she wished they'd made the rules clear.

Still, Sin was smart and savvy. She wouldn't have left with someone without telling her.

Something is definitely wrong.

Panic gripped Dakota's chest. Suddenly it seemed as if everything was moving faster. The music and the people talking and laughing around her seemed so much louder. Her heart thudded as she glanced around the room.

"Sinclair, where are you?" Dakota whispered the words aloud as she typed them into her phone and sent the text message.

No response.

She glanced toward the door. Maybe Sin had gone out to her SUV for some reason. It was the only place she hadn't checked. Dakota hurried toward the exit, when she heard her name being called. She whirled around.

"Where's the fire?" Dexter teased. "I was hoping to claim that dance you promised me."

"I...I can't. I have to—"

"Dakota, what's wrong?" His teasing expression morphed into one of deep concern.

"I...It's Sin. I was about to call a ride share service to take us home because we've both been drinking, but I...I can't find her anywhere, and I've searched *everywhere*," she stammered, her hands shaking.

"Are you sure you've looked everywhere? The place is a lot bigger than it was when we came here as kids."

"I know," she snapped. "And yes, I've looked *everywhere*. The patio. At the tables. In the sitting area. The restroom. I even asked one of the bartenders if he'd seen her. I'm telling you, Sinclair isn't here."

Dexter placed his large hands on her shoulders, commanding her attention and calming her down a little. "Just take a deep breath. I'm sure Sinclair is fine, but I'm going to help you find her. And then I'll take both of you home myself, all right?"

Dakota bobbed her head, her heart still racing. She'd never been so glad to see Dexter.

"Have you checked outside yet?"

She shook her head. "No, I was headed there next."

"Good. I'll come with you. We'll find her, Dakota." The look in his eyes and the tone of his voice was so confident. "I promise."

She wanted to believe him. To believe that everything would be all right. But the image stuck in her head was a board in her old newsroom with photos of missing women, most of whom had vanished from local nightclubs. It was a story her team had reported on. They'd helped make a break in the case, giving the police crucial evidence in nailing the guy they'd suspected of human trafficking. But not all of the women had been found. And the ones who had been recovered would never be the same.

She'd never forgive herself if she'd allowed the same to happen to her friend right under her nose, while she had fun out on the dance floor.

"Dakota, c'mon." Dex was already headed toward the exit.

She joined him, and they scanned the large front porch. There were a few people milling around, including a couple canoodling on the porch swing. But Sin wasn't among them.

"Where'd you guys park?" Dexter asked, turning toward the lot.

"Over here." Dakota led the way toward Sinclair's luxury SUV.

Her friend wasn't in the front seat. They pressed their faces against the darkened back windows, peering inside the vehicle. There was still no sign of Sinclair.

"She isn't here. She isn't anywhere." Dakota's breathing became shallow, and it was more difficult to draw in air. Her eyes stung with tears. "I need to call my dad right now. He'll know what to do."

"Are you *sure* you've looked everywhere inside the club?"

"Yes, I'm sure."

"Before you wake Chief Jones, why don't we check the place one more time?"

"And what if Sinclair is bound and gagged in the back of some nondescript sedan getting farther and farther away while we waste time rehashing what I've already done?" She propped a fist on her hip.

"If we call the police right now, they're going to suggest that we check the place again. Your father probably would, too. If we look again and we still don't find her, I'll call the station myself. All right?"

"We should get Nick and Em to help us," she said.

"Em went home a little after our set ended. Nick left with his new friends not long afterward. For right now, we are the cavalry. If we split up, we can cover the place more efficiently."

Dakota nodded, and they made a quick plan to divide up the search.

She started with the patio, then checked the sofas in the lounge area before heading for the restroom again. Sinclair was nowhere to be found. Dakota stepped out into the hall, tears staining her cheeks.

How did you feel once you discovered that your friend was missing?

God, she'd asked the loved ones of victims that stupid ass question more times than she could count. She hated asking it, but her producer insisted. The pain they felt was etched in their faces. Their voices trembled with it. It was a completely unnecessary query meant simply to get an emotional rise out of the interview subject. Now, more than ever, she felt like a jerk for all the times she'd asked it.

A door marked EMPLOYEES ONLY opened suddenly. Dexter's wide shoulders backed out of the room. A cascade of brown hair with blond highlights tumbled over one shoulder.

"Sinclair?" Dakota hurried toward the end of the hall and held the door open for Dex, who cradled her friend in his arms. "You found her. Is she okay?"

"Sin's fine. Just knocked out. Guess she partied a little too hard tonight. She complained of a headache about an hour ago, and one of the bartenders gave her permission to take a nap on the sofa in the employee lounge. The conversation happened while the bartender you talked to was on break," Dexter explained.

Tears of relief wet Dakota's face.

"I'm just glad she's okay." Dakota brushed hair from Sin's face as her friend snored quietly. "I need to get her home, and I could use your help. I'm sorry. I'm sure this isn't how you'd planned on ending your night."

"I promised I'd get you two home safely tonight, and that's what I'm going to do," he said. "Here's her purse. The keys to her SUV should be inside."

Dakota rummaged around in Sin's bag for her keys. She held them up. "Got 'em."

They got Sin in the back seat of her truck, still asleep; then Dex opened the passenger door for Dakota before going back to retrieve his sax.

"How will you get back to pick up your truck?" Dakota asked once he'd settled into the driver's seat.

"Nick or Em will bring me back here sometime tomorrow. It's no big deal. People leave their cars here all the time. The Foxhole does a great job of coordinating ride share services during Friday Night Jam Sessions so everyone gets home safely."

They rode in silence for the first several minutes as she watched the ocean on the other side of Jessamine Drive. It was a clear night, and the moon was high and bright in the sky.

Dakota peeked at Sin, who was still fast asleep in the back seat. Mouth open and head tipped back. She considered taking a photo to torture her friend with. It would serve Sin right for scaring her to death like that.

She turned toward the handsome man seated behind the wheel of her friend's SUV. "Thanks, Dexter. If you hadn't come along when you did—"

"Sin would've been fine," he interrupted. "All I did was ask the right person the right question. You would've eventually done the same." His eyes were still on the road.

A typical Dexter Roberts response. He'd always been low-key. In interviews for the school newspaper, he'd never crowed about the amazing numbers he'd put up in a game. Instead, he'd used the opportunity to praise his running backs and receivers. The offensive line for protecting him and giving him enough time. The defense for keeping them in the game when the team was off to a slow start. The coaches for keeping them ready and calling the right plays.

She'd never been sure if he was uncomfortable taking the credit or if he was simply farsighted enough to recognize that sharing the acclaim would endear him to the town, his teammates, and his coaches. That they would all work that much harder for him the following week.

It was one of the traits she'd adored about him. He was confident enough in himself that he hadn't needed to talk shit about the other team or crow about himself in order to be noticed by college scouts.

"Well, thank you anyway. If Sin were conscious right now, she'd thank you, too."

"I knew Sin was probably fine." He shrugged. "I did it for you." He glanced over at her momentarily. A small smile curved one side of his mouth. "I was afraid you were going to blow a gasket back there."

"Accurate." She sighed, looking out the window again. "When you've seen, up close and personal, how awful human beings can be to one another, even to the people they claim to love…" She shook her head trying to erase all of the ugly images that came to her mind. "Well, let's just say I'm not as optimistic as I once was."

He was quiet for a moment. "That's a shame. I always loved that about you. It's one of the greatest things you taught me. To look on the bright side of things and to never give up."

Dakota regarded the man's profile as he stared ahead, focused on the empty road that stretched out in front of them. She wasn't sure how to respond to the compliment. It was the second time tonight he'd claimed that she'd had a lasting, positive impact on his life.

Unsure of what to say, she changed the subject.

"I'm going to spend the night at Sin's place. Once we get her settled in bed, I can bring you back to get your truck. I'll be fine by then."

"Not necessary."

"Well, at least let me take you home," Dakota insisted.

Dexter laughed. "I guess Sin didn't tell you."

"Didn't tell me what?" Dakota's shoulders tensed. She'd had enough surprises tonight.

"Sin and I are neighbors. My condo is on the second floor of her building."

"No, she never mentioned that." Dakota glared at her friend, innocently sleeping in the back seat. "Well, that's good. Still, one of us can take you back to get your truck in the morning. It's the least we can do."

"Knowing you're both okay is all the thanks I need, Dakota." Dexter's voice dipped to a low, sultry tone and his intense gaze met hers as the vehicle idled at a stoplight.

Heat crawled over Dakota's skin and drifted down her spine, settling into the space between her thighs. She felt the sudden need to press her knees together.

Words caught in her throat, her chest rising and falling rapidly. The sound of her pulse reverberated in her ears.

Dakota turned back toward the window, her eyes drifting shut.

Would there ever be a time when she wasn't susceptible to the Dex Factor?

———

Dexter carried a still-sleeping Sinclair into her luxury condo on the top floor of his building. He followed Dakota into the master bedroom.

He'd last seen the place five years ago, when Sinclair had been trying to sell him his condo—a fixer-upper that was a gaudy tribute to the seventies. He'd bought it as an investment property, but a couple of years ago, he'd bought a bigger house as a rental property and made this condo his weekend home.

The girl always had style. And while the place had looked nice when he'd last seen it, she'd taken it to the next level. The decor and finishes were stunning. Like something out of a magazine.

Sinclair barely stirred as he lay her in her bed after Dakota pulled back the duvet.

When Dakota slipped off her friend's shoes, Dexter moved toward the door so Dakota could get Sin out of her club attire.

"Give me a minute to get her into her pajamas." Dakota rummaged through one of the dresser drawers. "And I'll be right out."

It was late, and it had been an incredibly long day, so he'd planned to go back to his place to get some much-needed rest. But unable to pass on spending a few more minutes with Dakota, he returned to the great room and waited instead. The layout of their condos was similar, but the footprint of Sin's place was about five hundred square feet larger than his. Plus, the view from the top floor was incredible.

Dexter slid the patio door open and stepped out onto the balcony. He leaned over the railing and stared down at the empty stretch of beach beneath them. It was beautiful. Peaceful. Calm. A few of the many reasons he loved living here.

His condo on Myrtle Beach was a stone's throw from the coast, too. But the beach there was much busier. The city no longer had the calm vibe they still enjoyed here on the island. He could understand why some of the locals were so passionate about maintaining their quiet, calm way of life. They feared that having the resort here would change Holly Grove Island for the worst. But the world was changing, and the island needed to change with it. He'd do everything in his power to ensure that any growth related to the resort would be good for the island and for the people who called it home year-round.

The patio door slid open, and he turned around. Dakota stepped out onto the balcony in her bare feet. Her eyes widened as she regarded the clear, starry sky and the bright, beautiful moon. "I'd forgotten how lovely the island is at night."

"The New York night skyline is pretty spectacular, too." He didn't know why he'd said it. He wanted Dakota to stay here on the island. Not return to New York.

"It is," she agreed. The wind whipped her hair across her face. She tucked it behind her ear. "They're both beautiful in their own unique ways, I suppose." She turned, studying him for a moment, as if he were a mystery she was trying to decipher.

But not as beautiful as you.

Though, to be honest, anyone could see how beautiful Dakota was on the inside and out. She'd always been compassionate, going out of her way to make kids who didn't quite fit in feel welcome. She'd treated everyone the same. Given everyone the benefit of the doubt. She'd been affectionate toward her friends and family. Toward him.

"So I promised you a dance tonight." Her mouth quirked in a half smile. "And I'm a woman of my word."

Dexter rubbed his jaw. There was nothing he wanted more right now than to hold Dakota in his arms under the stars on this beautiful night. But the fact that they could never be anything more than friends as long as they both worked at the resort pained him.

"I appreciate the offer, but you must be tired."

"I am. But not too tired to honor my word. Besides, it feels like the right way to thank you for what you did tonight."

"A dance beneath the stars with the most beautiful girl in the world." He uttered the sincere words without thought. "I'd be a fool to turn that down."

"You're laying it on a little thick, pal." Dakota flashed an almost shy smile.

"Only calling it like I see it." He stepped forward, snaking an arm around her waist and grasping her hand. Her sweet scent filled his nostrils, and though he maintained plenty of space between their bodies, he could still feel the heat from hers.

Dakota tipped her head back to meet his gaze and placed a hand on his shoulder. "It's too late to play music out here on the balcony. We'll just have to use our imagination."

"Or…" He pulled her closer as he sang the opening lines of Frank Sinatra's "The Way You Look Tonight."

Her back tensed when he first started to sing. But by the second stanza, she'd relaxed in his arms as they moved together beneath the stars.

They'd both fallen in love with the American standard while watching the romantic comedy *My Best Friend's Wedding*. The scene where Dermot Mulroney's character sang the song to Julia Roberts's character as they danced on the ferry had been a favorite of Dakota's. And he hadn't hated it either.

He could still quote the words from the scene they'd watched together so often.

If you love someone, you say it. Right then. Out loud. Otherwise…the moment just passes you by.

Dakota had turned to him one day while they were watching that scene and she'd done just that. She'd told him she loved him, quickly adding that she didn't expect him to say it back.

But he had. Because he did. He just hadn't known how to tell her until that moment. He'd refused to let the moment pass him by.

Even after all of the time they'd spent apart, he still loved her. Maybe not the same way he had then, because they weren't the same people they were then. But he cared deeply for her, and he always would.

When he finished singing, they stopped swaying, and he expected Dakota to retreat. Instead, she tipped her chin, her gaze meeting his expectantly.

Dexter studied the full, lush lips he'd kissed hundreds of times what felt like a lifetime ago. His own lips tingled with the vivid memory of the taste and feel of hers. He wanted to pull her body flush against his as he tasted her mouth again. Satisfy the curiosity that had plagued him since that day at the Fourth of July Festival.

But instead, they stood there frozen until Dakota slipped out of his arms, leaving a noticeable chill as an ocean breeze swept across the balcony, rustling her hair. Dakota rubbed at the goose bumps that had popped up on her flesh.

"The songs the band played at the club tonight," she said finally. "Are they part of your usual set?"

"Most of them. But 'Pretty Brown Eyes' and 'Cupid' were recent additions," he admitted.

"Oh." She gazed out at the sea again, and an awkward silence engulfed them.

There were so many things he'd planned to say to Dakota. So many things he *needed* to tell her. But the unexpected promotion and her acceptance of the contract position had derailed his plans. He was her boss now. Getting involved with Dakota could complicate matters and jeopardize his chances of being named the new director of operations. Something he'd been working toward his entire career.

Even if he was willing to sacrifice the opportunity for the chance to be with Dakota, she had no intention of staying on Holly Grove Island. In a few months, she'd pack her bags and walk away. He honestly didn't know if he could handle losing her again.

"It's late. I should go." Dex slid the patio door open.

"Yes, it is late," she agreed, her voice faint and her eyes filled with disappointment. "And it's been a long night."

He grabbed the sax she'd carried up for him and stepped out into the hall. "Good night, Dakota. Be sure to lock up."

"I will. And, Dex..." She followed him out into the hall and hugged him, her cheek pressed to his chest. "Thank you. I appreciate everything you've done."

He inhaled the sweet, floral scent of her hair, frozen at the unexpected gesture as he savored the sensation of her warm, soft body pressed to his. Dexter draped his free arm around her. "Anything for you, Dakota," he whispered. "All you have to do is ask."

She nodded, neither of them speaking. Finally, she pulled away and ducked back inside Sin's condo, wishing him a good night.

Dexter groaned as he made his way toward the elevator, wishing he hadn't let the moment pass tonight.

Chapter Sixteen

Dakota rushed into the office, her messenger bag and purse both slung across her body as she tried not to spill the coffee she'd picked up for her meeting with Nick.

It was her second official day working for the resort, but with the impending opening, she'd had to hit the ground running. She'd spent the days before she officially started familiarizing herself with every piece of information on the resort. Nick had also given her access to all the stats she needed. The expected occupancy of the hotel, how the increased traffic would impact the island, and most important, the additional revenue that the town and its small business owners could expect.

Now she, Nick, and Dexter were meeting with the mayor, the town historian, and several local business owners who still objected to the opening of the resort. While the mayor had been all for the project in the very beginning, he was much less vocal about that support with the small business owners airing their many gripes about the resort. The complaints of those business owners, plus a few of the diehard locals, had created an unwanted groundswell of discontent, slowly shifting the opinions of the townsfolk.

The beach will be too crowded.
There will be too much traffic.
An influx of strangers might mean an increase in crime.

With the soft opening drawing closer, the ill will of local residents was the last thing the resort needed. The group of discontent townsfolk couldn't stop the opening, but their complaints could create an avalanche of bad press, which would divert from any positive press about the opening of the resort. And the town council could make their lives miserable as they planned various events going forward. They had to get ahead of this before things got any worse.

Dakota had been hearing similar objections for as long as she could remember. It was the reason the town had fought so hard to keep chain stores and big box retailers at bay. They hadn't wanted to sacrifice their way of life. The longer Dakota had been back home, the more she understood why holding on to the quieter, slower pace was so important to them.

Nick and Dexter had laid out most of their formal presentation, but they'd saved the summary for her.

Dakota recapped all of the benefits the resort would bring to the island. But before she could finish, she was interrupted by Cleta Gaines, owner of the town's fabric and fiber shop, Knitty Gritty.

"I'm sorry, Dakota, but how is it we're supposed to believe that the three of you could truly understand what's at stake here? You didn't value the island's way of life. That's why none of you stayed. You especially. You've lived in New York nearly as long as you lived on the island. You couldn't wait to leave this place, and you're only back here now because you lost your job."

Tension rolled off Dexter, who was seated a few feet

from her. Mrs. Gaines's blanket statement about the three of them had barely registered a reaction from him, but when the woman had homed in on her, his jaw tightened and he gripped the armrests.

"Mrs. Gaines, that was completely un—"

Dakota touched Dexter's shoulder, signaling that she could handle Mrs. Gaines herself. She appreciated his protective nature and that he'd been willing to go to bat for her, even though it wouldn't be in the best interest of his relationship with Mrs. Gaines and the others. But she could certainly handle the grumpy older woman.

The woman's accusation smarted. Mostly because it was true. She hadn't valued the slow pace of life in their small town. In fact, a few months ago Dakota probably wouldn't have considered it an insult that Mrs. Gaines regarded her as an outsider. At the time, she'd considered herself the quintessential New Yorker, and she'd been damn proud of it.

But being home for the past several weeks had reminded her exactly what made the island so special. The beautiful green space of Holly Grove Island Park. The quirky little festivals. The familiar shops on Main Street filled with people who'd known Dakota her entire life and genuinely cared about her well-being. The pristine beach with a lovely view of the ocean's rolling waves. The calm of Fox Haven Sound on the other side of the island.

Dakota swallowed back her initial anger and opted for honesty.

"You're right, Mrs. Gaines. I have been an outsider for a very long time. As a teenager, I felt I was missing out on so much because of our slow island lifestyle. And it's true. There was a lot I was missing out on. I love the hustle and bustle of New York City. The culture. The nightlife. But in my work as a reporter, I got a front-row seat to the much uglier side of city living: the stress, the loneliness one often feels despite being surrounded by hordes of people. The traffic, the pollution, and dangers I'd never had to worry about when I lived in the safety of our friendly little town."

Dakota's eyes burned remembering how terrified she'd been when she'd thought something had happened to Sin. She cleared her throat, then continued.

"Being back home for the past several weeks has made me realize that not everything I was missing out on was something I truly wanted. Yes, Dexter, Nicholas, and I spent several years living in big cities across the country, but we never stopped being Holly Grove Islanders. And Nick and Dex have spent the past few years in Myrtle Beach, a stone's throw away, waiting for an opportunity like this that would bring them back home. Close to the people they love and respect. To the beach we all adore. Do you really think any of us would knowingly do anything to hurt Holly Grove Island?"

Mrs. Gaines frowned, subtly shaking her head as she folded her arms and looked out the window to the beach.

Dakota took that as a small victory. Now they needed to convince the other two ringleaders: town historian Leland Gaston, who took his job far too seriously, and Dalton James, owner of several rental homes in town.

"Maybe you wouldn't knowingly do anything to hurt the town." Leland tapped the table with his index finger. "But not living here has skewed your thinking. We don't want the commercialization of this island. We're proud of our history and the island's independence. We don't want the kind of changes we've seen in Myrtle Beach and that they're beginning to see in Pleasure Cove," he said, referring to the state-of-the-art Pleasure Cove Resort, Holly Grove Island Resort's direct competitor.

"I get that, Mr. Gaston." Dakota kept her tone upbeat. Now wasn't the time to point out that the man was overreacting about one little fight at the volleyball tournament hosted by the Pleasure Cove Resort. Or to argue that Pleasure Cove had seen countless benefits from the opening of the resort. "But the world is changing. Whether we like it or not. What we're doing here is making gradual changes that will benefit everyone in the long run. This way we can control the narrative. Preserve the elements that make our little island town so special while ushering in changes that will benefit everyone."

"And just how is it benefiting me?" Mr. Dalton asked. "My bookings are down since the resort started taking reservations."

"Your rates are too high, for one thing," Mrs. Gaines muttered.

The man shot her a look, but a few of the other people in the room nodded in agreement.

"Do any of your children live on the island, Mr. Dalton?" Dex asked. "Or yours, Mr. Gaston?" He walked toward the front of the room, his arms folded. "What about you, Mrs. Gaines?"

He shifted his gaze to each of them in turn.

"You know they don't, Dexter." Mrs. Gaines's response was pained. "There aren't any opportunities in her field for my Ella. Same as Leland's and Dalton's boys."

"Exactly." Dexter sighed. "I would've returned home the minute I graduated had there been an opportunity in my chosen field. And I'm sure it's the same for many of the kids who grow up and leave the island. This resort and the resulting growth of the town will provide viable career opportunities for residents who might leave otherwise."

"And not just the resort itself," Nick jumped in. "There will be opportunities for other businesses here on the island as a result of the additional tourist traffic."

"And as for you, Mr. James," Dakota said. "Maybe you'll have to lower your prices a bit to stay competitive— which I know you can afford to do. But that dip you're experiencing is temporary. I can guarantee you that as the island becomes a more popular destination, you'll make up that traffic, maybe even see it rise. The same thing has happened in Pleasure Cove."

The man grunted, but Dakota could tell he was mulling the information over in his head.

With all of their objections quelled for the moment, they wrapped up the meeting. Mayor Newbury, the last to leave, approached the three of them.

"That went better than expected." The man's voice was low, as if he feared the others might hear him from out in the hall. "You should sponsor the town movie later this month. Bring goodies. Give this same talk. I think you just might win over a few more folks."

"Great idea, Mayor Newbury. We'll be in touch." Dexter shook the man's hand, then turned to the two of them once he was gone. "Good job, you two. And, Dakota, that heart- felt appeal you made was brilliant. It really turned the tide. Lunch is on me."

"That isn't necessary." Dakota gathered her papers and shoved them into her portfolio, trying not to think about how good Dex smelled or how distractingly handsome he looked.

Dex seemed to peer straight through her with those dark,

brooding eyes. "It would be a working lunch to strategize this impromptu meeting with the town."

"Oh." Dakota's cheeks warmed. *It's just business, not a lunch date.* "Then sure."

"I'd love to join you two, but I have a late lunch scheduled with my group sales manager and a few sorority committee members. We're hoping to host their next Founders Day event." Nick zipped his messenger bag. "Dakota, take notes and you can bring me up to speed this afternoon." He turned to Dexter. "We're going to make one hell of an impression on the town at that talk, Dex. Don't worry. We'll make you look good."

Nick was gone before Dakota could blink.

She turned to Dex and forced a smile. "So...lunch."

"Is Lila's Café all right?" He stared at her for a moment, something unreadable in his expression. His eyes didn't travel her body. They never left hers. And yet his stare made her feel naked. Vulnerable.

Since she'd returned to town, Dex had slowly been wearing away at her defenses. Reminding her of what a kind and thoughtful person he'd always been. Sparking fond memories of the companionship they'd once enjoyed. Dexter still exuded the same quiet strength she'd always admired and was fiercely protective of the people he cared about.

Since that night at the Foxhole, she couldn't help thinking of everything that had happened that evening. The songs he'd played that meant so much to her. How he'd dropped everything to help find their friend. Dancing together on Sin's balcony. And she'd found herself reminiscing over sweet moments they'd shared in the past. Memories that had been overwritten by the painful anomaly of the night he'd broken up with her.

Dakota nodded. "Lunch at Lila's Café sounds perfect."

"Great. I have to make a quick call, but I'll meet you in the lobby in thirty minutes."

Dexter pulled out his phone, and his long legs carried him from the room, leaving Dakota to admire the retreat of his broad back and firm bottom.

A shiver ran down her spine and her breath caught as she was suddenly struck by the memory of how enticing his lean, athletic body had looked without clothes.

Not helpful, Dakota. Not helpful at all.

She released a breathy sigh and pressed a hand to her heated forehead.

Her father would have his surgery in a couple of weeks, and she anticipated being on the island for only another few months. Surely she could show some restraint for that long.

But as warmth filled her face and electricity skittered down her spine, causing her to clench her thighs, it was increasingly harder to deny the truth. A part of her had hoped that Dexter would kiss her on that balcony. But despite the thoughtful compliments, the grand gesture of playing those songs for her at the Foxhole, and what seemed like flirtation, Dexter was only interested in repairing their friendship and burying any past hurt feelings.

Fine.

They were both better off that way. He was the resort's director, after all. And she was in town to lick her wounds while she made plans for the rest of her life. The last thing she needed was to get tangled up with Dexter Roberts.

Her involvement with a seemingly sweet man was the very thing that had sabotaged her career. It was the reason she found herself at the bottom of the heap, broken and bleeding. Forced to claw her way back up.

Dakota inhaled a deep breath, shook off her unsettling

attraction to Dexter, and headed toward her desk to wait until it was time to meet with him.

———

Dexter finished the last bite of his crab cake sandwich as Dakota made notes of all the ideas they'd discussed for sponsorship of the town's outdoor film and their brief talk that Friday.

He'd been impressed with how Dakota had handled the meeting with Mayor Newbury and the three ringleaders of the growing resistance to the Holly Grove Island Resort. Dexter was usually pretty even-keeled during moments of high stress, when the tempers of those around him spiked. He could take anything those three hurled at him. But when Mrs. Gaines had gone after Dakota...he'd felt that far more personally than he might've about any accusation launched directly at him.

So...yes. He'd lost his cool momentarily. He'd been blinded by a temporary flash of anger, prepared to tell the older woman—whom he generally admired and respected—that her attack on Dakota was completely uncalled for and she needed to back off.

It wasn't as if he hadn't gone to bat for his employees before. He had on many occasions. He didn't permit employees to be treated harshly by fellow employees or supervisors. Nor would he allow a customer to berate a hotel employee. Even if it meant losing a prestigious event or a wealthy client. But he made the decision logically, with a calm head and heart.

So why had he felt fire building in his chest and his muscles tensing when Cleta Gaines made that dig at Dakota earlier?

Because it was Dakota.

One of the three women in the world he would do just about anything for. His mother and sister being the other two. Even after all this time and distance between them, he still cared for her deeply. Ached for her. Both physically and emotionally. He had lain awake many nights, regretting how he'd handled the situation between them. Wishing he could claim a mulligan so he could go back in time and approach things differently. But the past was the past. Nothing he could say or do would change that.

He draped one arm across the back of the booth as he studied her. Dakota was beautiful in a simple sleeveless, knee-length floral dress that hugged the sweet curves of her hips. The V-neck showed the tiniest hint of cleavage and skimmed over her full breasts.

Dakota dragged her fingers through her shoulder-length hair and flipped it to one side so stray locks wouldn't fall across her eyes as she leaned forward, scribbling on a pad.

"I know we covered a lot of ground, but it seems you're writing a lot more than we discussed." Dexter sipped his sweet tea.

"I'm creating a mind map." She continued scribbling furiously. "The concepts we discussed earlier spurred some additional ideas for events at the resort."

She put her pen down and looked up for a moment before grabbing her fork and diving into her shrimp and grits, which had likely gotten cold.

"Why don't we have that reheated?" He nodded toward her bowl.

"I'd forgotten how good Ms. Lila's shrimp and grits are," she murmured, her eyes drifting shut.

The way her eyes fluttered closed and the sensual sound

she made in appreciation of the meal sent a shudder down his spine. The visceral memory of how she'd done the same while lying beneath him on a smoldering summer night filled his head with the sweetest vision. A vision that had been running in his mind more nights than he cared to admit since their dance on Sin's balcony. For a minute, he seriously thought he might lose it.

He adjusted his position in the booth and tried to think about things he hated. *Cauliflower. Fake bacon. Skinny jeans. Centipedes.* Anything but the gorgeous temptress sitting across the table from him innocently enjoying her meal, oblivious to how turned on he'd been all morning by sitting so close to her that he could smell her sweet perfume.

"Exactly. And a meal like that deserves to be enjoyed hot." Dexter got the attention of the server and kindly asked if she wouldn't mind reheating Dakota's food, then turned back to her.

"You were incredible in that meeting today, Dakota. Not that I'm surprised. I recommended you for the position because I knew you'd be good at it. But you were exceptional—even-tempered, quick on your feet. I think your fresh storytelling perspective is exactly what we need to break through with folks who see the resort as a threat to Holly Grove Island's way of life. You're quite an asset to the team."

"But a temporary one," Dakota reminded him, drinking her tea. "Hopefully, by the time I leave, this won't be an issue anymore."

"Hopefully." He tilted his head as he studied her. "Or maybe you'll change your mind about leaving. After all, you made a pretty compelling case for life here on the island."

"That was for their sakes. Not a declaration that I've suddenly changed my lifelong career aspirations."

"I did," he said. "And I'm much happier because of it. Besides, what you said to them in that meeting…it sounded sincere and deeply personal."

"It was," she admitted, gliding a finger down the condensation on her glass. "But you're not being fair. Your career change wasn't a voluntary one." There was apology in her brown eyes. "I heard about the ACL injury. Sorry things didn't work out as you'd hoped. I know how hard you worked to go pro as a football player."

True. But the most disappointing thing to happen in his life hadn't been the decimation of his pro football aspirations. That distinct honor went to losing her.

"I'll let you in on a little secret." Dexter leaned forward, his voice lowered. "Going pro wasn't my dream. It was my dad's. And other than my propensity for the saxophone, it was the only thing I did that really seemed to impress him."

His father's utter devastation over the premature end of his career flashed through Dexter's brain. "He'd hoped to go pro when he was in college, and my mom wanted to be a doctor. When she got pregnant with me, they both dropped out. Suddenly they had a family, and neither of them ever attained their life dreams."

"I know you don't believe for one minute that your mother regrets having you." She'd lowered her voice, too. Her expression was kind. "Your mother adores you. All of you. You must know that."

"I do, and we're lucky to have been born to such a loving, selfless woman." Dex tapped the table with his thumb. "I just wish she'd been able to achieve what she wanted."

"You feel guilty about your parents, don't you?" Dakota tilted her head, assessing him.

"Doesn't matter." He thanked the server, who'd returned with Dakota's steaming bowl of shrimp and grits.

"It does matter, Dex," she said once the server was gone. "I know Ms. Marilyn wouldn't want you to take on the responsibility for a choice she made—one I'm sure she doesn't regret. Have you ever talked to your mother about how you feel?"

"No, and I don't intend to." Dex frowned. Any guilt he felt was his own issue, and he'd deal with it. He wouldn't burden his mother with his feelings, especially not now that she was finally living her life on her own terms.

"Okay," she conceded softly, sounding as if she regretted bringing it up. She lifted a forkful of the savory mélange to her lips, blowing on it to cool it.

He shut his eyes against the visual. Seriously, he needed to get his mind out of the gutter. But ever since their dance on the balcony beneath the stars as he sang to her and the lingering hug she'd given him, thoughts of Dakota Jones in his arms and in his bed kept filling his head.

"I appreciate what you're trying to do, Dakota. I don't mean to discount your concern in any way. But my family is...my family." He shrugged. "And if there's one thing the Robertses are good at, it's burying our feelings."

"Is that why you never told me that you were playing football for your dad, not because you wanted to?"

"That and I didn't want you to see me as this pathetic dude desperate for his father's approval." Dexter winced, hearing the words out loud. "Enough about me. I'd love to hear some of these grand ideas you've been scribbling for the past half hour." Dexter sipped his coffee, eager to change the subject.

"They're still kind of rough." She ate another forkful.

"I'll keep that in mind." He set his mug on the table and interlocked his fingers.

Dakota released a nervous sigh, then surveyed her notepad. "The two ideas that I feel most strongly about revolve around creating festivals that would draw people here to the island for a long weekend."

"What kind of festivals are we talking? We already have our big Fourth of July Festival and Founders Day," he reminded her.

"Which are a big deal *locally*." She emphasized the last word. "But neither would draw much of a crowd from outside the island community. And that's great. We should have events that are just for us. But I'm thinking of events that would put Holly Grove Island on the map as an annual destination. Festivities that would create a broad enough interest to draw people from across the country. Maybe even entice travelers from abroad."

"I'm all ears." He leaned forward a little more, waiting patiently as she finished the last of her meal and pushed her empty bowl aside.

"The first idea is a jazz festival. I've been studying ones around the country and in the Caribbean. They tend to have huge, loyal followings. That would really be to our advantage and would help us build a strong, steady base of repeat guests," Dakota said.

"A jazz festival." Dexter repeated the words as he rubbed his jaw. "That could work. It'd bring in a stream of guests for the resort and for rental owners. Plus, it'd mean a boost to the island's economy."

"Exactly." Her brown eyes lit up in response to his

enthusiasm. "Lila's Café, the Foxhole, and other local eateries could establish booths. We could also bring in food trucks from Wilmington and a few other nearby locales. And local businesses could set up vendor booths."

"It would be a win for everyone." Dexter shook a finger at her as he reviewed the possibilities in his head. Dakota's suggestion was a stroke of genius. The kind of endeavor that could put the HGI Resort on the map and help solidify his appointment as director. "That idea is an absolute winner. Let's begin putting a formal proposal together right away. I know we can fast-track this idea, and I'd like to be able to announce next year's event within a few weeks."

"Shouldn't we run this by Nick?" she asked. "I mean, I know you're his boss, but..."

"This is a hot idea. I don't want to waste a minute and risk the Pleasure Cove Resort announcing one of their own. So let me worry about Nick." Dexter tapped out a note on his phone to remind himself to talk to his friend. It was a phenomenal idea. He had no doubt that Nick would be on board with it. "Now, tell me about this other idea."

"This one isn't quite as well defined," she said. "But I was thinking that maybe we could do some sort of family-oriented festival. Family Fun Weekend, maybe. Our resort is family-oriented, while Pleasure Cove is designed as more of an adult playground. We should use that difference to our advantage. Create a weekend meant to celebrate families. Maybe have a kid-oriented music festival and lots of sports and games designed for extended families. That way we encourage grandparents to come along too, which has the potential to double our bookings."

Dexter considered her proposal. "I like the idea of

playing off our contrast to Pleasure Cove, rather than trying to compete with them head-on. Let's table that one for now, but we'll definitely circle back to it, because I think that one could be a winner, too."

"Will do." Dakota flipped through her pad for a clean page. "Maybe there's a music festival happening somewhere soon that I could attend to get a better feel for what we want to implement here."

Dexter picked up his phone again and scrolled through it. Finally, he came across the item he'd been looking for. "The Newport Jazz Festival is this coming weekend. If there are any tickets and hotel rooms anywhere, my assistant will find them."

Her eyes widened. "For me and you?"

"Yes. Separate rooms, of course," he added, though that should've gone without saying. "Problem?"

She sank her teeth into her bottom lip and assessed him. "No, but I'm surprised you're ready to move so quickly on this."

"You shouldn't be. This could be huge. You've done great work today, Dakota. So well done." He scrolled through the apps on his phone and opened his calendar. "The Newport festival is on the weekend, of course. Friday through Sunday. I need to know if you're in. If so, I'll have Tiffany begin searching for tickets, flights, and hotel rooms right away."

"I'm in." She sipped her tea and scanned the calendar on her own phone. "My dad's surgery isn't until the following week, so the timing is perfect."

"Great." He kept his voice even, careful not to betray the spark of electricity that ran down his spine at the thought of spending the weekend with Dakota. "Ready to head back?"

Dakota nodded and grabbed her things from the table. But she halted at the sound of a familiar voice.

"Hello, beautiful! How are you today?"

Behind the counter, Lila Gayle blushed, then nodded in the direction of their table.

"Dad?" Dakota made her way toward Oliver. Her head swiveled between her father and Lila Gayle. Both of them wore a guilty expression, like teenagers busted making out under the bleachers.

"Hey, Kota." Oliver laughed nervously, wrapping his daughter in a quick hug. "Dexter." He nodded toward him. "What brings you two here so late in the day?"

"Lunch." Dakota folded her arms and stared at her father. "How about you, Dad?"

"Same." He took a seat at the counter. "Time got away from me. Didn't realize how late it had gotten." He patted his stomach. "You know I shouldn't go too long without eating."

"I made you lunch. Leftovers from dinner, remember?"

"That's right. You did." Oliver took a sip from the glass of water Ms. Lila had set on the counter in front of him. "Guess I forgot. No worries, darlin'. I'll eat it tomorrow. Promise."

"We'd better head back to the office, Dakota. I have a phone call scheduled in less than an hour." Dexter stood beside her. "It was good to see you, Mr. Jones." Dexter shook the man's hand, and Oliver gave him a grateful smile. They exchanged their goodbyes and headed back to Dexter's truck.

Dex and Dakota rode the short distance to the resort, mostly in silence.

"Are you okay, Dakota?" he asked finally, when the resort came into view.

"Of course. Why wouldn't I be?"

"Maybe because you've gone into a shell ever since we saw your father at the diner. More specifically, since you overheard him calling Lila Gayle *beautiful*."

"And why should that bother me?" She turned toward him. "It's true. I'm pretty sure that she and Helen Mirren"—who could practically be the woman's twin—"are aging in reverse." Dakota's tone was bitter. "So why would that possibly bother me?"

Dexter debated whether he should voice what he'd been thinking. He sucked in a deep breath and hoped he wouldn't regret what he was about to say. "Isn't that what your father always called your mother?"

Dakota frowned, her eyes suddenly misty. A twinge of guilt tugged at Dexter's chest. He almost regretted bringing it up.

"I'm fine," she repeated.

Dexter parked the truck, and they both climbed out and entered the building. She turned to him as they approached her department. "Thanks, Dex."

"For lunch?" He straightened his tie. "It's the least I could do after what you did in that meeting today. And your idea for the festival? It's going to be great for the resort and the town."

"For your confidence in me on this project." She tucked her dark-brown hair behind one ear. "After what happened with my job..." She sighed. "Let's just say that I really needed a vote of confidence right now, so I appreciate it."

"It was well placed." Dexter patted her shoulder and smiled. Then he made his way to his office to get his assistant started on hunting down tickets, flights, and hotel rooms for the quickly approaching event.

Planning to spend a long weekend with his ex was either one of the most brilliant or one of the dumbest moves he'd ever made. Right now he wasn't sure which. He only knew that he looked forward to every moment he'd get to spend with Dakota.

Chapter Seventeen

I realize that you two seemed to have called a truce since that night at the club," Sinclair said. "But I had no idea we were at the spend-the-weekend-out-of-town-together stage in the relationship already. You two move pretty quickly." Sin poured more of the frozen strawberry daiquiri from a pitcher, topping off both of their glasses.

"You're supposed to be helping me pick out my wardrobe for the weekend, not practicing for amateur comedy hour." Dakota elbowed her friend in the ribs. "And like I told you before, this isn't a date weekend. It's a business trip."

"Then why aren't you traveling to this thing with Nick? After all, you work directly for him, not Dex, right?" Sinclair laughed when Dakota gave her the evil eye. *"Exactly."*

"Nick happens to be playing a gig in New Orleans this weekend. He's filling in for a drummer friend of his who's getting married," Dakota said.

"Whatever you say." Sinclair sipped her daiquiri. "Those are the pajamas you're taking?"

"Yes. What's wrong with them?" Dakota looked down

at the cartoon-character pants she'd just packed in her overnight bag. "No one but me will see them."

"I wouldn't bet on it." Sinclair rolled her eyes and took another sip of her drink.

It wasn't worth debating, so Dakota ignored the implication of Sin's statement.

"For a job that Nick and Dexter had to beg you to accept, you certainly seem to be enjoying it." Sin sprawled on Dakota's bed beside the overnight bag.

"I am." She couldn't disagree with her friend.

So far, working at the resort had turned out to be a pleasant surprise. She'd expected to miss the hustle and bustle of the newsroom and doing work that was important and meaningful. Yet working with Nick on marketing for the resort and collaborating with him and Dexter on creating plans that would satisfy the local residents was far more interesting and rewarding than she'd anticipated. And quite frankly, it was fascinating to watch Nick put that sweet-talking Southern charm of his to use for something other than getting groupies to take him home at the end of the night.

When she'd taken the job, she'd dreaded the idea of seeing Dexter every day. But that night at the Foxhole had shifted her perspective. Or perhaps it was more accurate to say it brought her perspective of him full circle. Reminded her of how kind, thoughtful, and protective he'd always been. Made her appreciate those things about him again.

And, if she was being honest with herself, maybe a small part of her was excited about spending time with Dexter during this research trip to New England. Not that she would tell Sin that. It would only encourage her.

"This old town ain't so bad after all, huh?" Sinclair chided, leaning back on her elbows.

"Believe me...no one is more surprised than I am by how much I'm enjoying the job so far. But it's early. Next week I'll probably be standing around the water cooler bitching about how much I hate my wet-behind-the-ears boss and his full-of-himself superior." Dakota laughed.

"Maybe," Sin said. "Now, can we talk about the fact that you're going to be spending three whole days with your ex? The man who planned his entire set at the club around songs that mean something to you?"

Dakota gave her friend a pointed look, then returned to her closet. Sinclair didn't need to remind her of that night. Dakota hadn't been able to stop thinking of it. And she often found herself stealing longing glimpses of Dexter ever since. There was a battle raging between her head, her heart, and her body, and her head definitely wasn't winning.

"If spending a long weekend with your ultra-fine, super sweet ex doesn't give you butterflies, you'd better see a doctor, honey. 'Cause I'm pretty sure your heart has turned to stone," Sinclair said.

"Of course I'm a little nervous. Which is ridiculous, right?" Dakota sank onto the mattress beside her friend. She tugged her hair over one shoulder. "This is strictly a business trip. He's obviously not interested in anything more than that, and neither am I. The last thing I need is to get involved with someone else."

"Someone *else*? As in you're already involved with someone?" Sin raised one eyebrow, her eyes widening.

"No, of course not." Dakota's heart thudded in her chest, the perpetual knot in her gut tightened, and her mouth suddenly went dry. "But I don't know where I'll be living three months from now. So starting something here with Dexter—or anyone—what would be the point?"

"I can respect that." Sin sat up beside Dakota, her gaze narrowed. "But that doesn't mean that you aren't attracted to him."

Dakota paced over to the window. What was the point in lying about it? Her friend could read her like a book. "Okay, yeah. I know I shouldn't be, but…yes, I'm attracted to Dex."

"And why shouldn't you be?" Sin challenged.

"Because he's my boss, and because I've seen this movie before. It ends with me crying on my front porch in the middle of winter." Dakota waved a hand. "No thanks. Maya Angelou said 'When someone shows you who they are, believe them the first time.' Dex showed me who he was that day. He isn't someone I can count on in a relationship when things get tough. So getting involved with him again is a mistake I have no intention of making."

Sin frowned. "Maybe you're mistaken about what Dexter's actions revealed that day. Have the two of you ever discussed what happened?"

"He's tried." Dakota shrugged. "But it's not a conversation I want to have."

"Maybe you should give him a chance to explain himself," Sin said.

"Why are you suddenly so invested in me getting with Dex?" Dakota folded her arms. "Back then I had to physically restrain you from going to his house and keying his car."

"I—I know. And I was furious with him for breaking my best friend's heart. But since then I've come to realize that he was young and dumb, like we all were back then. He made a mistake, Dakota. A choice that he's wished he could take back ever since. Besides, everything he's done since you returned to town...isn't it obvious how much he cares about you?"

Dakota didn't respond.

She understood the consequences of bad choices more than most. Only she didn't have the luxury of blaming her youth for her grave mistake.

"Yes, he's been thoughtful and helpful," Dakota agreed. "And was I moved by his performance and him finding your missing-in-action behind at the club that night? Yes. But getting involved with Dexter would be a mistake. My life is already enough of a disaster. I'll pass on the additional drama."

"Okay, so maybe you're not ready for anything serious right now. Dex was engaged about a year and a half ago. Maybe he's not ready for anything serious again yet, either. But that doesn't mean—"

"Dex was engaged?" It was irrational of her to be surprised and, frankly, a little hurt by the news. After all, he'd broken up with her so he could see other people. But she was.

Dakota sank onto the mattress again. "Why didn't they go through with it?"

It was none of her business, but she couldn't resist asking.

"Dexter broke it off with her. His official story is that she's an amazing woman, but they weren't a good fit," Sin said.

"But?" Dakota turned to face her friend and sat cross-legged, the way they'd sat on those little mats when they were in kindergarten together.

"I think the real reason he couldn't go through with marrying her is because she wasn't you. You're the one he really wants. Then, now, *always*."

"Did Dex tell you that?" Dakota frowned. Her cheeks were hot, and her pulse raced.

"He didn't need to." Sin shrugged. "And if I had even the slightest doubt in my mind about it before, everything that happened at the Foxhole that night only confirmed it. I said it before, and I'm saying it again. Dexter Roberts is head over heels in love with you, Dakota. And if you weren't so stubborn, you'd realize that you're still in love with him, too."

Dakota winced, tension spanning her forehead. Her friend seemed determined to torture her with talk of her and Dexter reigniting their past flame. Didn't she see it was something Dakota clearly didn't want to talk about? But making a big deal about it would only prove that she was much more sensitive about the subject than she was willing to admit.

"You've had one too many daiquiris." Dakota trudged back to her closet and grabbed a few more clothing items to stuff into her bag. "Good thing you're spending the night."

"Speaking of which, I'm exhausted. I'm working with residential clients right now who seem determined to see one hundred perfectly good houses before settling on one. I'm meeting them in the morning for round four of our search, so I'd better get some shut-eye or it won't be so easy to maintain this charming personality."

"Go." Dakota laughed. "I don't want to be the reason you end up on the news for assaulting your clients. Besides, my wardrobe is pretty much set. And it's not like this is a date weekend. I just need to look presentable."

"Keep telling yourself that, sweetie." Sinclair refilled her glass, then set the pitcher down again. "And since you're gonna be gone for the weekend, why don't we do movie night at my place on Thursday before you leave?"

"Fine," Dakota agreed, wishing her friend good night as

Sin headed for the spare bedroom in Dakota's third-floor suite, which had been Sin's second home when they were in high school.

Dakota was slightly annoyed with her best friend. Mostly because what Sinclair had said was true. Not about Dexter and her still being in love with each other. That was ridiculous.

But there was lingering attraction and nostalgic memories between them. Nothing as serious as what Sin was intimating, but they'd have to learn to navigate the powerful pull of their shared emotions.

She and Dexter had a good working relationship and a single purpose for this trip. It was strictly business. Nothing more.

Dakota repeated the words in her head. Then she grabbed a couple of pretty nightgowns out of her lingerie drawer and slipped them into her bag. *Just in case.*

Chapter Eighteen

Dexter walked through his condo, reviewing his mental checklist. He double-checked that he'd packed everything necessary for his long weekend in Newport, Rhode Island, with Dakota. Then he ran through a mental checklist of all of the work-related items he needed to handle before they left.

Everything was in order. The slight anxiety he was feeling wasn't because he'd forgotten something. It stemmed from the fact that he'd be spending the next three days with Dakota.

This is a business trip, not a lovers' getaway. Get a hold of yourself, man.

Dexter had been telling himself that for the past three days. But it hadn't stopped the quickening of his pulse whenever he thought about spending three days alone with the woman he adored a little more each day. Not just because she was the first woman he'd ever fallen for or because he'd been her first. It was because Dakota was incredibly smart. Full of fire. And more beautiful than ever. She was good with people because she genuinely cared about them. Which also made her easy to talk to. It was no wonder she'd always had a way of getting him to open up to her more than he did with anyone else.

And God help him, because he still wanted her. More than he'd ever wanted anyone.

He'd been engaged to Evelyn for six months, and they'd dated for more than two years before that. Yet he'd never loved her the way he'd loved Dakota.

Dexter had hoped that Dakota's return to Holly Grove Island would result in one of two things. Either he'd finally realize that his lingering feelings for her were part of a quixotic schoolboy fantasy that he needed to let go of. That he'd put Dakota Jones on an unrealistic pedestal. A part of him hoped that she really had changed, as some of the locals had opined. That she imagined herself too important to make time to return to their little town. A princess attitude would definitely knock the stars out of his eyes.

Or…he would discover he'd been right all along. That Dakota was the one woman he wanted in his life. Then maybe they could reconcile. Perhaps even pick up where they'd left off all those years ago.

It was clear now that he was no less enamored with Dakota. But his unexpected promotion to the DOO of the Holly Grove Island Resort had changed his plans to woo Dakota back. The company's nonfraternization policy was clear. As a member of the resort's senior executive staff, he had no business getting involved with an employee. It was the same advice he'd given Nick.

Dexter cursed under his breath for having suggested that Nick hire Dakota in the first place. Something he'd never have done if he'd known he'd had a shot in hell at the position after being turned down for it twice in the past six months.

He'd been working to get to this level in his field his entire adult life. Was he willing to give that up for a woman who was insistent that she wouldn't be sticking around? Then what would he have? No Dakota and no job. Which would also mean he'd be forced to leave Holly Grove Island.

No, it was too big a risk. Too narrow a chance of a reward.

Stay the course, Dex. Stay the course. Just be grateful she doesn't hate you anymore.

In a few months, Dakota would go on to the next big thing in her life, and he wished her the best. Then his life would return to normal. Maybe he'd even let go of his pipe dreams about them resuming their relationship and he could finally move on.

He was picking her up at her father's house in little more than an hour so that they could drive to the airport together for their midmorning flight. Which gave him just enough time to make himself breakfast and clean up.

Dexter was laying out the eggs, bacon, and cheese on the counter when a sudden knock at his door startled him. The sun had yet to rise.

Who on earth would knock on my door at this hour of the morning?

He peeked through the peephole, surprised by who was standing on the other side. Dexter took a deep breath and opened the door.

"Dakota." He scanned her lovely face. It was before six a.m. Yet this woman managed to look beautiful in a simple T-shirt, a pair of jean shorts, and sandals. Her hair was pulled back in a high, tight ponytail. Dakota smelled like coconut and vanilla, like she was fresh out of the shower. She wore only a hint of pink lip gloss and a dusting of eye shadow. "Did I get our plans mixed up? I thought I was supposed to pick you up at your dad's place in an hour."

"You were, but our movie night went late, and I ended

up staying over at Sin's place. Rather than waking her at this ungodly hour to take me home, it made sense to catch you before you left. We can swing by my dad's place and pick up my bags, then head to the airport. I hope that's okay."

"Of course." He stepped aside and gestured for her to enter his condo. Dex jerked a thumb over his shoulder. "I was about to make myself breakfast. You hungry?"

"Starving." She rubbed her stomach, and his errant eye-balls went straight for the swell of her breasts and the flesh bared by her V-neck T-shirt. "What's on the menu?"

"Bacon, egg, and cheese croissants. Sound good?"

"Sounds amazing." Dakota followed him inside. "How can I help?"

"You're a guest." Dexter returned to the kitchen and washed his hands. "Have a seat. Or look around. But you're not helping me cook. Not on your first—" Dex cleared his throat. Saying that this was her first visit was a bold, presumptuous statement. It implied he expected her to return. Nothing could be further from the truth. In fact, he was still a bit stunned that she was standing in his home. "I'd give you the penny tour, but time being short and all..." He took out a bowl and started to crack the eggs. "Scrambled okay?"

"Perfect." Dakota set her small purse on the counter and walked through the great room, glancing around. "The layout of your place looks a lot like Sin's, but it's—"

"A little smaller," he confirmed. "When I first bought the place, I thought I'd use it strictly as a rental investment. But I bought another rental property and now this is my primary residence. Eventually I'll upgrade and buy either a townhome or a house on the beach when the opportunity arises. But for now it's the perfect—"

"Bachelor pad?" Her pouty, pink lips curved in a half smile, but her expectant expression indicated that she was hoping he'd deny it.

"Nothing as exciting as that," he said truthfully. "But it's a great setup for a person living alone or an active couple without children."

"You don't have a second bedroom in this unit?"

"I do, but it's small. Just big enough for my desk, the built-in bookshelves I built, and a small reading space." He added a splash of milk to the eggs. "I use it as my office."

"You built the bookshelves yourself?" Dakota raised an eyebrow. "I'm impressed."

"Something else I learned from my grandfather while I was in Texas. Don't believe me?" He chuckled in response to her incredulous stare. "You're welcome to take a look for yourself. The office is down that hall. First room on the right."

"Not that I don't believe you," she said, "but I'd love to see them." Dakota wandered down the hall in the direction of his office.

Dex wasn't sure why, but something about having Dakota in his personal space unnerved him. She'd been in his office and in his truck. Each time his heart had beaten a little faster, heat traveling down his spine because of her close proximity. But he hadn't experienced this kind of raw vulnerability then. Maybe it was because his mother had always preached that one's home was an extension of oneself. And it felt like he was baring a little of his soul to her by having her here. Especially by allowing her to venture into his office unaccompanied. The only space more private was his bedroom.

When several minutes had gone by, her silence while she explored the room gnawed at him. It was a small space.

Not much to see. Did she hate the bookshelves or the office itself? Is that why Dakota, who had the gift of gab, was stone silent?

He put the strips of bacon on a baking sheet and into the oven, then washed his hands. When he turned around, Dakota was standing on the other side of the counter looking as if she'd seen a ghost. She clutched something in her arms.

"Dakota, what's wrong?" He walked around the counter, his voice trailing off when he recognized the item she held to her chest.

Dex swallowed, wiping his slightly damp palms down the front of his jeans. He hadn't thought of that album when he'd said it was okay for her to go into his office. And since he kept it high on the top shelf, he certainly hadn't expected her to retrieve it.

"You still have this?" She held up the black leather photo album with a silver frame on the front, which housed a candid photo, taken by Sinclair, of the two of them kissing on the beach at sunset. Dakota had given him the photo album for Christmas *that* day.

The day he'd broken her heart.

"Why would you keep this after all this time?" Her voice was shaky.

"Honestly?" Dex ran a hand over his head, the sound of rushing blood filling his ears. "Not keeping it has never been an option."

"Not even when you were engaged?"

She knew. Not that he'd tried to keep it a secret from her. And he should've expected that Sin would've mentioned it.

"Even then I couldn't bring myself to get rid of it," he confessed, the words heavy on his tongue.

Dakota's eyes widened. As if she was unsure how she should feel about his inability to part with the final memento she'd given him. "That must've gone over well with your fiancée."

Dakota set the photo album on the counter and settled onto a barstool.

He rubbed his jaw, unsure of exactly how honest he should be with her about that. But there were enough secrets between them already. This one wasn't worth keeping.

"It didn't. In fact, that album is kind of the reason I didn't go through with the marriage."

"She was that angry that you'd kept it?" There was hesitation in Dakota's question. Like she both wanted to know and feared the answer.

Dexter returned to the stove and set the timer for the bacon. Then he melted butter in a skillet. He poured the eggs into the heated pan and sprinkled the shredded Italian blend cheese over it, stirring the mixture with a wooden spatula.

Dakota folded her arms on the counter and patiently awaited his response.

"Evelyn wasn't necessarily angry that I'd kept the photo album," he said finally, turning toward her. "But she wanted me to get rid of it, and I just…couldn't."

"You allowed your engagement to end over an old album of photos with your high school girlfriend?" Dakota's tone was a mixture of wonder and incredulity. "Why? There was no connection between us. We hadn't seen or spoken to each other in more than a decade. Why would you let this"—she tapped on the book—"destroy your relationship?"

Dex sucked in a deep breath and met her questioning stare. He'd hoped to skim the surface and give Dakota the basics. But the same inquisitive nature that made her a damned good investigative reporter wouldn't be satisfied with a superficial response.

"The relationship didn't end because I wouldn't get rid of the album. I wouldn't let go of the photo album because my future with Evelyn wasn't as important to me as that book of photos from my past." He shrugged. "It only confirmed some of the nagging doubts I'd had about us."

"Like?" Her warm gaze bored into him, demanding the absolute truth and nothing less.

He wasn't sure either of them could handle the unvarnished truth, but this he could give her.

"I'd started to wonder if Evelyn and I weren't *settling* for each other. We'd dated for a few months during our senior year of college. But then we encountered each other at an alumni event and struck up a relationship again." He turned back to scramble their eggs. "I suspect we were both feeling a little lonely at a time in our lives when our college friends were all settling down and starting families. Then there was the comfort of our familiarity. It was nice reminiscing over the past and tapping into that connection to our younger selves."

Dex turned off the gas and moved the pan to another burner on the stove. He put a top over it to keep the eggs warm until the bacon was done, then turned back to Dakota.

"Neither of which were good reasons for us to commit to a lifetime together. I realized that the engagement was a mistake. We both deserved more. So I ended things and returned the photo album to its designated spot on that shelf. I can't recall the last time I looked through it. I guess I just find solace in knowing that it's there, if ever I do want to look back."

He opened the container of fresh-baked croissants he'd picked up at the Bakery on Main the afternoon before. "Toasted?"

"Please." Her eyes didn't meet his. After a few beats of silence, she said, "So, indirectly, I'm responsible for the dissolution of your engagement?"

"This wasn't about you or your gift, Dakota. It was about me not being ready to move on."

"From us?" She huffed, her brows wrinkled with confusion as she studied his face. "Because of a stupid photo album I gave you on the day you ended our relationship so you could move on with someone else?"

"There wasn't anyone else, Dakota." Dexter stalked around the counter, less than two feet separating them. His eyes searched hers. Dakota's accusation burned deep in his gut. She couldn't be more wrong about there being someone else. He'd loved her and only her. In fact, he'd loved her so damn much he would've done anything to ensure she got the life she deserved. But telling her the truth—all of it—would only cause her more pain.

Dexter fought back the desire to take Dakota into his arms and kiss her until he'd erased any doubts about how much he cared for her then and now.

"You said you wanted to see other people." There was so much pain in her voice. The heartache they'd both suffered that night was obviously as fresh in her mind as it was in his. "*That's* why we broke up."

"But I didn't see anyone else," he assured her. "Not for more than a year."

"No. I don't believe you." Dakota glared at him as she shook her head angrily, her palm flattened against her collarbone. "Why would you say you wanted to see other people if you weren't interested in someone *specific*?"

"Would you have gone along with it if I'd just said we needed to take a step back? That I loved you, but I didn't want you to give up your dream of attending NYU for me?" Dexter surprised himself by uttering the words that had gone unspoken between them for nearly two decades.

He honestly hadn't intended to say them. But now that he had, he was glad she knew the truth. He'd only been trying to protect her. To stop her from making a grave mistake. A sacrifice that would've eventually made her resent her life with him—the way his father did.

"No," Dakota whispered, blinking repeatedly, her eyes watery.

"I couldn't let you give up everything you'd worked so hard for to be with me. You deserve the world, Dakota. Everything you ever dreamed of." He forced a pained smile, one hand reaching out to cradle her soft cheek. "I couldn't be the one to take that away from you."

Still seated on the barstool, Dakota grasped his shirt and tugged him down, their faces inches apart. Her watery gaze met his, and Dex held his breath. He should pull out of her grip. Put some space between them. His head was fully aware of what he *should* do. But when Dakota's eyes drifted closed, and she pressed her mouth to his, all of the things he should do were forgotten in an instant.

Dex closed his eyes as he cradled her face in his hands, losing himself in the comfort and release of *finally* tasting Dakota's soft, full lips again. Of holding her in his arms. Heat filled his chest as he angled her head, greedily taking control of their unexpected kiss.

She parted her lips in response with a soft moan. Dex swallowed the sound, savoring the warmth and the sweet cinnamon taste as his tongue glided against hers. He claimed her mouth in the way he'd imagined from the moment he'd laid eyes on her at the Fourth of July Festival. It was everything he'd hoped it would be and more.

The heat from Dakota's fingertips seared his skin through his thin cotton shirt as she moved her hands to his back. She leaned into him, and an inadvertent sigh escaped his lips. Dakota's thighs bracketed his, and she looped her arms around his waist, bringing their bodies as flush as their positions would allow.

Dexter reveled in the sensation of Dakota's lush curves cradled against the planes of his chest. She sat on the edge of the barstool, the heat between her thighs pressed to his growing length—straining against his zipper and aching to be buried inside her.

He removed the band from her hair and it tumbled down around her shoulders. Dex tangled his fingers in the soft, silky strands he'd been aching to touch as he kissed her.

God, he wanted this woman. More than anything.

Suddenly, the opening chords of Donny Hathaway's "A Song for You" blared, startling both of them. They pulled away from each other, chests heaving, as they turned toward her purse on the counter.

"It's my dad. He's probably wondering why I didn't come home last night, especially since my luggage is sitting by the front door." Dakota whispered the words with a hint of apology. She rummaged inside her small purse for the phone and answered the call as Dex tried his best to slow his breathing, hoping Oliver wouldn't hear him and wonder what the hell was going on.

"Good morning, Dad. How are you?" Dakota raked her fingers through her disheveled hair. The same glossy strands he'd sifted his fingers through moments earlier. "Yes, I'm fine. We fell asleep during the second movie, so I just spent the night at Sin's. I'm having breakfast now.

No, I don't need you to pick me up," she added after a few moments of silence on her side of the conversation. "Dex lives in Sin's building. I'll catch him before he leaves, and we'll swing by to pick up my luggage before we head to the airport." A smile spread across her face. "You know I wouldn't leave without saying goodbye, Dad. See you in a little bit. Thanks for checking on me."

Dakota ended the call and set the phone on the counter. She slipped her arms around Dexter's waist, pulling him forward again. Her eyes gleamed and her sexy little smirk made his heart—and other parts of his anatomy—dance with anticipation. "Sorry about the interruption."

She leaned in again, but before his lips met hers, the oven timer blared angrily. Dexter groaned, forcing a rush of air from his nostrils.

Damn oven timer.

He rushed over to the stove to shut off the noisy reminder before it awakened all of his neighbors. Dexter removed the bacon from the oven and transferred it to a plate covered with paper towels.

Eyes drifting shut, Dexter heaved a sigh, not turning to face her.

He wanted Dakota in the worst way. But this road was fraught with danger—for both of them. He hadn't initiated the kiss, nor had he expected it. But he'd welcomed it. And since he lacked the willpower to say no, the universe had obviously dropped one shoe and then another on his hard head.

First Oliver had called just as their ill-advised kiss had started to escalate. Then the oven timer blared before they could resume their kiss.

It was a sign. Or at the very least, a reminder.

He'd finally told Dakota why he'd really broken things

off between them. But the rest he wasn't prepared to tell her. Not yet.

No matter how badly he wanted Dakota, he realized that they could never have anything real as long as he was keeping the truth from her. Even if he was doing it for her own good. So he was prepared to tell her everything, if it came to that. But she intended to walk away in a few months. And he wouldn't hurt her again for the sake of a temporary fling. So he'd keep his secret, and his hands, to himself.

Dex turned around slowly and shoved his hands into his pockets. He leaned against the counter beside the stove, needing the distance between them.

She opened her mouth, an impish grin on her face. But when her eyes met his, her playful expression crumpled, disappointment sliding into its place. It seemed she already knew what he was going to say, but he needed to say the words anyway. For himself, if not for her.

He dragged a hand across his forehead, the sound of his heartbeat pounding in his ears. "Dakota, I—"

"I shouldn't have come here, and I shouldn't have kissed you." She pressed a hand to her forehead. "I don't know what I was thinking."

"Dakota, please don't take this as a rejection. If it weren't for—"

"I get it. You don't owe me an explanation." She held up a hand. "In fact, I'd really appreciate it if we didn't talk about it again. Like...ever." Dakota raked her fingers through her hair. "I must look a mess. Is it okay if I use your restroom?"

"Of course." Dex gestured toward the hall and gave Dakota instructions on where the guest bathroom was located.

She grabbed her phone, purse, and the elastic band he'd

removed from her hair. Then she hurried down the hall and away from him.

Dexter ran a hand over his head and groaned quietly. He'd done the one thing he'd promised himself he wouldn't: He'd hurt her again.

Dakota had been worried that she looked a mess. But the truth was that she looked absolutely radiant with her glowing cheeks, flushed skin, and kiss-swollen lips. In fact, there were few things in the world that could render her anything less than gorgeous.

He'd wanted to tell her that and so much more. But he bit back the words, knowing they would've only further complicated an already awkward situation. Instead, he stood there, his hands clenched at his sides, wishing the situation were different. Knowing it never would be.

———

Dakota stood in front of the mirror in the small, beautifully decorated guest bathroom in Dexter's condo, her skin hot and her hands shaking. She pressed her palms to the cool countertop on either side of the vessel sink and focused on taking in deep breaths and slowing her racing heart rate.

"You kissed him, you goof." She pointed an accusatory finger at her reflection in the mirror. "What the hell were you thinking? You just made everything ten times worse."

Dakota sighed and pulled out her phone. Her first instinct was to call Sin. But her friend had been sound asleep when she'd left. Besides, she was thirty-four freaking years old. She needed to get her shit together. If she wasn't capable of handling an inadvertent kiss with her ex at this age, would she ever be?

She took a deep, cleansing breath. It was just a stupid

mistake. A reaction to seeing that damn photo album and remembering how much she'd once loved him, coupled with all of the sweet and wonderful things he'd done on her behalf since she'd returned to the island.

And then there was the blow of learning the truth about why he'd broken up with her.

A part of her was angry that Dexter had taken away her choice in the matter. Yet, if she was being honest, nothing he could've said at the time would've deterred her from following him to college in Texas.

She was so in love with Dexter back then. Spending the next four years in a long-distance relationship seemed unbearable. So despite her parents' pleas, she'd been determined to attend the same university as Dexter. Even if she had to attend on a scholarship or work her way through college because her parents refused to support her decision.

Dakota sighed. She'd spent so many years angry with Dexter over the breakup. But he'd done it for her. To ensure she remained on the path she'd chosen for herself.

Maybe he was lying. Maybe he'd just fallen for someone else. But she was inclined to believe what Dexter had said. Because making that kind of sacrifice for someone he loved... *that* was the Dexter Roberts she'd always known. The boy she'd fallen in love with.

No wonder she'd kissed him. She'd simply been responding to the overwhelming swell of emotions that had been building between them.

And so had he.

Dakota pressed her fingertips to her lips—still tingling from their kiss.

God, he's an amazing kisser.

Dexter had always been a good kisser. He'd kissed her like kissing was the endgame, not something he was forced to do if he hoped to get to third base. Still, he'd certainly upped his game in the interim since their last kiss more than a decade and a half ago.

She released a long, slow breath, opening her eyes and trying to force their kiss from her brain, which was playing it over and over on an endless loop, like some internet meme.

Why couldn't he have become a terrible kisser? That would definitely have helped.

Forget about the kiss. It was a one-time deal. Never to be repeated.

She reached for the ponytail holder on the counter, then froze. A shiver rolled down her spine as she recalled how Dex had removed it, gliding his fingers through her hair. How he'd fisted the strands as he'd deepened their kiss. That momentary feeling of possession had made her burn with desire for him. Dakota shuddered with the sensory memory, her eyes squeezing shut.

Dex had always liked her hair down. He'd preferred it when she'd worn it natural. Had loved tangling his fingers in her unruly curls as he'd kissed her.

She'd started straightening her hair once she got into television and was actively pursuing an on-screen reporting gig.

Your natural hair is lovely, dear. But no news exec wants to worry that your hair will draw up like a cotton ball when you're on camera.

Dakota could hear her mother's voice in her head as clearly as the day she'd said it. They'd been standing outside of an expensive salon in Manhattan during one of her mother's visits. She'd "surprised" Dakota with a hair appointment with one of the city's hottest stylists.

It'd been more of an ambush than a genuine surprise,

because Madeline Jones had known that Dakota wouldn't like the idea one bit. They'd discussed it before. Dakota had insisted that she shouldn't have to conform her look to mimic mainstream, European-centered concepts of beauty. Her mother agreed, in theory. But she contended that though it wasn't fair, Dakota's naturally curly hair was the only thing keeping her behind the camera rather than in front of it.

"I know this isn't what you want to hear, sweetie. But if you want the studio execs to take you seriously, you'll have to make sacrifices for now. When you become the face of the station, you can fight the good fight, make demands, and help level the playing field for the little brown and black girls who will one day watch you on television and decide they want to follow your path. But you won't get to do any of that if you allow your hair to be a barrier to achieving your dream." Her mother's eyes pleaded with her as she tugged on Dakota's hair.

What her mother was asking had gone against everything she'd believed. That people should be accepted for who they are. That it was categorically wrong to discriminate against someone because of their race, religion, disability, how their hair grew from their heads, or the hairstyle they chose to wear. But she'd given in that day, walked into that salon, and let the woman straighten her hair—though she'd refused to have it altered chemically.

Sadly, it seemed her mother was right. Within six months of changing her hair, she'd been given her first shot at doing a story on camera.

Dakota raked her fingers through the shiny, flat-ironed strands that fell to her shoulders and tried to create some semblance of order. She decided against pulling her hair back. Not because Dex obviously still preferred it down. Because it was easier.

She finished up in the bathroom, washing her hands and fussing with her hair one last time. Dakota took a deep breath, then exhaled.

You can't hide in here forever. So put on your big-girl panties and get this over with.

Dakota made her way down the hall and returned to her seat at the breakfast bar, where Dexter had her plate waiting.

He stepped out of the kitchen carrying his plate, a sheepish look on his handsome face. "I really am sorry. I shouldn't have—"

"We agreed never to talk about it again, remember?" Dakota tucked her hair behind one ear. "I promise you, we're fine."

"Okay. Well…great." He forced a wooden, lifeless smile that barely stirred the muscles of his face.

Dakota turned her focus to the still-warm bacon, egg, and cheese croissant in front of her. She cut the sandwich in half and took a bite.

"This is so good," she mumbled, covering her mostly full mouth with one hand. The eggs and bacon were cooked to perfection. The croissant was light and flaky. It tasted freshly made.

"Glad you like it. Coffee?"

"Please." Maybe if she'd had her first cup of coffee before she'd arrived on Dexter's doorstep, she wouldn't have made the colossal mistake of kissing him. "Cream, if you have it."

"Of course." His smile seemed a little more genuine now, and his shoulders relaxed. "I only have Italian crème–flavored creamer. I hope that's okay."

"It's my favorite." She tried to ignore the fluttering in her belly when their eyes met.

"As you wish." He winked, pouring a steaming mug of coffee. He set it and the bottle of creamer on the counter in front of her.

Dakota couldn't help giggling in response to his reference to *The Princess Bride*—one of her favorite movies. He'd teasingly called her Princess Buttercup after he'd watched the movie with her for the third or fourth time. Dexter laughed, too.

The familiar teasing between them eased the tension that had settled in the pit of her stomach. It had filled the space around them like insidious black smoke, silently choking them and making it difficult to breathe.

But their laughter seemed to clear the air, replacing the darkness with the light that had once been a hallmark of their relationship.

As they ate their croissants and drank their coffee, Dexter shifted the conversation to something safe: work. He updated her on what he'd learned about the festival they were attending and a few others on the East Coast they'd have to compete with for attendees. After they'd eaten, Dakota helped him clean up the breakfast dishes. He grabbed his carry-on, and they made their way to his truck.

Once his luggage was loaded, he settled into the driver's seat and glanced over at her as she adjusted her seat belt.

"I regret a lot of things about the day our relationship ended, Dakota. But what I regret most is that we weren't able to walk away as friends. I know that's my fault," he added, placing a hand to his chest. "But things have been really good between us these past few weeks. I was hoping we could build on that this weekend."

Dakota nibbled on her lower lip, unsure of how to respond.

Spending time with Dex again these past few weeks

made it evident that she missed the friendship that had been the foundation of their relationship. But for her, being friends again would never be enough. The love and the friendship they'd shared had blossomed together and were inseparable.

I've had enough rejection for one day, thank you very much.

"We can't go back, Dex," she said softly. "But maybe we could forge a new friendship."

"I'd like that." His mouth curved in a tentative smile as he shifted the truck out of park and they started on their way to her father's house.

Dakota turned to look out the window as they traveled through town. Dexter was her boss. Maybe they'd find a way to build some sort of friendship again, but there would be nothing more between them. And in a few months, she'd be gone. Just the way it should be.

So why couldn't she stop thinking of their kiss and wishing it had led to more?

Chapter Nineteen

Dexter turned his truck onto Cypress Lane, the familiar pink-clapboard house coming into view. Just seeing the place again brought back a rush of memories. The first time he'd kissed Dakota was on her front porch after walking her home from a beach party. And the first time they'd made love was upstairs in her bedroom, the weekend her parents had gone to Asheville for her mother's high school reunion.

His heart thudded in his chest with the memory of that warm summer night and the taste of her salty skin as he'd kissed her neck and shoulders. Going all the way had been Dakota's idea, but he could still remember how she'd trembled as they'd undressed in the dark, the moonlight filtering in through the small captain's window in her bedroom. She was beautiful, and she'd given herself to him. It was the most meaningful gift he'd ever received.

He'd fumbled his way through, making love to her awkwardly and impetuously, hoping she didn't realize how nervous he was, too. Everything about that night was permanently etched in his memory. He'd never forget the feeling of being inside of her. How her warm, slick skin had glided against his in the hot room as he called out her name in the throes of utter bliss. Or the way she'd whimpered his.

He'd loved her fiercely and couldn't imagine a future without Dakota in his life. But little more than a year later, everything had gone wrong between them.

It'd been a devastating blow from which it had taken him a long time to recover, if he ever really had.

Dex pulled into the driveway and put the truck in park, staring up at the window to her room. He could tell himself that this trip was only about business, but no matter how many times he repeated the words, it wouldn't make them true.

He loved her still. Nothing would ever change that.

"I'll be fifteen, twenty minutes tops." Dakota opened the truck door and hopped out. "I showered at Sin's place. I just need to do a quick change, put on my makeup, and grab my bags. They're already packed and right by the front door. You're welcome to come in."

Before he could answer, Oliver appeared on the front porch with a steaming mug of coffee in hand.

"I wouldn't have minded picking you up." Her father gave Dex a pointed glare before shifting a look of concern toward his daughter, who seemed amused by his over-protectiveness.

"Relax, Dad. Dex lives in the same building. It made more sense to catch a ride with him and let both you and Sinclair sleep in." Dakota jogged up the steps and kissed her father on the cheek, careful not to jostle his coffee. "I'm gonna change before I go. Keep Dex company for me?" She had hurried inside the house before her father could respond.

Dexter drew in a deep breath and climbed out of the

truck. He made his way toward the porch, where Oliver stood with his coffee cup in hand as he assessed him.

Dexter chuckled inside. Not much had changed. The old dog was still guarding the door.

. To be fair, he could only imagine how this must look to the older man. Him bringing his daughter home while the sun was barely up. Whisking her off for a long weekend.

Of course Oliver wanted to look him in the eye and size him up. Suss out his intentions.

"Good morning, Chief Jones." Dexter shook the older man's hand.

"Morning, Dexter." Oliver sat on the rattan sofa and gestured for him to take a seat in one of the Adirondack chairs across from him.

The man studied him for a moment, his mouth pulled into a tight line. "So you two are off on a business trip, eh?"

"Yes, sir."

Oliver stared at him without speaking. As if he expected Dexter to say something more. When he didn't, Oliver held up his mug. "Coffee?"

"No, sir. Dakota and I already had…" *Shit.* Dexter wished he could take the words back the moment they left his mouth. He cleared his throat. "I was making breakfast when she knocked on my door this morning, after she left Sin's place," Dexter clarified. "So we've both already had coffee and breakfast."

Dex and Dakota were in their midthirties. Well beyond the age where Oliver Jones had any say in whether the two of them were together. Yet sitting here with Oliver a couple of floors below where he'd first made love to the man's daughter struck him with a sudden sense of guilt. Like he was that teenage boy sneaking out of his girlfriend's house all over again.

Did Oliver know what had happened between them back then?

"Dakota has some great ideas about how we can create events that will be beneficial for the resort and for the town," Dexter said. "So when the opportunity arose to see a similar event in action, we didn't want to waste any time."

"Hmm…" Oliver scratched the gray hairs on his chin. "Well, I'm certainly glad Dakota seems to be enjoying the job."

"She's a real asset to our team," Dex assured the man, trying to ignore the bead of sweat trickling down his back beneath Oliver's intense stare. He'd almost forgotten that Dakota had inherited her "death stare" from her father, the town's former chief of police. "So, how is the rental business going, Chief Jones?"

"Got no complaints." Oliver set his mug down on a small, round table beside the sofa. "And unlike Dalton and some of the others, I don't oppose the resort. I'm farsighted enough to see the potential it offers to the island." He looked over his shoulder toward the front door, then leaned forward and lowered his voice. "But before Kota comes down, there's something I'd like to talk to you about."

Dex sat taller in his seat, shoulders tense. "Yes, sir?"

"It's no secret I didn't much like you back when you were dating my daughter. Nothing personal, mind you," he added. "It's hard for a man to watch his daughter go from being daddy's little girl to dating some teenage boy. Especially since we were once teenage boys ourselves." He shrugged. "I don't think there's a boy alive I would've believed worthy of my daughter back then. But that was a long time ago. I've gotten a chance to see the kind of person you've become. How you treat your parents and your siblings. The folks in this town. You're a good man, Dexter. I believe that."

"Thank you, Chief Jones." The unexpected compliment took him by surprise. "That means a lot to me coming from a man I admire as much as you."

Dexter wasn't blowing smoke. He meant every word. He'd always admired Oliver Jones. He was a no-nonsense but fair man. The model of the husband and father Dexter one day aspired to be. Still, Dexter had the sense that this was only the first part of a sandwich. He expected the filling to be a healthy dose of Limburger cheese.

"I don't know what your intentions are with this job or this project you two are working on, but you broke my daughter's heart once. And something tells me that, as strong as she is, she isn't in a place in her life right now where she can afford to take another hit like that."

Dexter had run into Chief Jones countless times in the years since things had ended between him and Dakota. They'd never once talked about his relationship with his daughter. The man's anger and resentment toward him had been obvious in the years immediately following the breakup. Over the years, the boiling-hot rage in the man's eyes had eventually faded to a tepid, lukewarm reception. But then, a few months before his wife died, his attitude toward Dex had gone from *meh* to cordial.

Dexter hadn't understood the reason for the change, but he'd been grateful that they'd been able to move past the man's anger without having the uncomfortable discussion they were having now.

"I understand, sir. Believe me, I do," he offered.

"Do you, Dexter?" the man asked, though the question was clearly rhetorical. "I think I know you well enough to believe you would never intentionally hurt my daughter.

But my Dakota has always had such a big heart, and she wears it on her sleeve. She's in deep before she even realizes that the tide is rising. So whatever this is, son…all I ask is that you be honest with her about it this time."

This time?

Did that mean he knew the truth about why he'd walked away from Dakota?

"Sir, I—"

"I think I might've set a record." Dakota appeared in the screened doorway out of breath. She stepped outside, toting her luggage behind her. The scent of coconut and vanilla wafted off of her, and she'd pulled her hair up into a neat topknot. She wore another sleeveless dress that hugged her curves and skimmed her toned thighs. This one was navy blue. A powder-blue sweater was draped over her arm. "I promised you I wouldn't be long."

"You did." Dexter stood, reaching for her bag, which she gladly surrendered.

"Okay, Dad. I'll see you in a few days. Behave yourself while I'm gone. I'll know if you've raided my snack stash." She gave her father a big hug, then kissed his cheek again.

Oliver peered at him over Dakota's shoulder as he hugged his daughter. A silent *Don't forget what I said.*

He wouldn't. How could he? It was all he'd be thinking during their plane ride.

————

There was definitely something bothering Dexter. They'd had very little conversation since they'd left her house earlier that morning. And once they'd hit cruising altitude an hour ago, Dex had put on his headphones and had been silently reading and replying to email on his laptop.

Not that she couldn't find a way to amuse herself during their flight. But for a man who'd proclaimed that he hoped this trip would mend their friendship, Dex seemed especially withdrawn.

Dakota shook off the thought. This was business travel, not some misguided trip down memory lane.

No good could come from that.

Look what had happened after she'd run across the stupid photo album. It was on such a high shelf that she'd almost missed it. She'd had to climb the rolling ladder to reach the book.

And as she thumbed through the album, every photo had transported her back to the moment in time when it had been taken. To memories she'd buried deep and hadn't contemplated in years. They were so young back then, and so very much in love.

It felt like a lifetime ago. And yet all of those emotions had started brimming to the surface. Compelling her to do something incredibly stupid. She'd kissed him, making an already difficult situation even more awkward.

Without turning her head, Dakota glanced over at Dex. He was still wearing his headset and seemingly oblivious to her thoughts about him.

Dex had made it abundantly clear that he wasn't looking for anything but friendship from her. She'd been the one who'd crossed the line. She should be grateful that Dexter had had the presence of mind to put a halt to it.

What if things had gone much further?

Talk about awkward.

Unable to take the weird silence between them, she'd slipped on her own noise-canceling headset. She was listening to one of the many books on her phone—a steamy romance. She'd only been half listening, thoughts of Dexter and the kiss rolling in her brain. But the couple was suddenly embroiled in a particularly hot love scene that had her complete attention, leaving her hot and bothered.

Her cheeks and forehead warmed, and she was suddenly paranoid that Dexter would overhear the sexy passage. The scene sent flashes of her and Dexter's embrace rushing through her brain. Only in her head, they hadn't stopped at that passionate kiss.

Dakota hit pause and dropped her headset in her lap, as if it had set fire to her ears.

Note to self: Maybe don't listen to an erotic romance while seated next to your hot-as-habaneros ex on a business trip.

"Sorry I haven't been much company." Dexter's voice startled her. He tilted his head and narrowed his gaze at her when she nearly jumped out of her skin. "Got a lot on my mind."

"You must have a lot riding on this project."

"More than you know," he said quietly, turning to look out the window.

He'd never indicated as much, but she could only imagine how big a deal this promotion must be for him. Especially since he'd lost his bid for it twice before.

She didn't doubt that Dex had worked hard for his job, as she had for hers. But the promotion gods giveth and taketh away. She'd learned that lesson the ass-to-the-concrete way. She could guess how much stress Dexter must be feeling to prove he was worthy of the shot he'd been given. Dakota knew from experience that when a person of color was given such an opportunity, they were often also permitted only the thinnest margin of error. Expected to fail so that the higher-ups could pat themselves on the back and offer their "failure" up as proof that they'd *tried* to make their management team more diverse.

We have to do twice as much to get half as far, Dakota. Never, ever forget that.

Words both her mother and father had repeated to her throughout much of her life. She hadn't wanted to believe them, but on more than one occasion, she'd found them to be true.

"Your idea for a music festival could really put our little town on the map. And the resort would be at the center of it all. If we do this right, there's the potential for exponential growth."

"Too bad some of the town council is still so reluctant to expand the public beach and go after a younger crowd."

Dex grunted. "Mayor Newbury sees the potential. But he's scared of his own shadow, afraid to stand up to the folks who are still living the old glory days, determined to keep Holly Grove Island a closed-off community."

"Getting the resort built was quite an accomplishment. And we made headway at the meeting," she reminded him.

"We did. Thanks to you." He nudged her with his elbow and flashed an appreciative smile, flooding her chest with a surge of unexpected warmth. "I realize that the folks who oppose the resort aren't deliberately trying to be a pain in my ass. They love our town, but so do I. I just wish they'd stop living in the past."

"Then we need to show them how good the future can be if they're willing to bend a little," Dakota said.

"That's exactly why I need your help on this, Dakota. Dalton is as pigheaded as a sow. I've lost my temper with him a time or two at town planning meetings."

"He has a way of getting under people's skin." Dakota laughed. "But I'd think a smooth-talking charmer like you would know better than to let him get you riled up."

"Nick's the charmer, not me. I'm more to the point. Maybe a little too direct sometimes."

"But if you want cooperation from Dalton and the others, you're going to have to use more finesse. Maybe Nick would be willing to give you a few pointers. He's the master of schmooze."

"Is that what we're calling bullshitters these days?" Dex chuckled.

Was Dex jealous of Nick?

"I don't think that's quite fair. Yes, Nick could sell ice at a stand in the middle of the frozen tundra. But he would do it without being dishonest. I overheard some of his conversation with those girls at the club last week." Heat filled her cheeks at the memory of some of the direct language she'd heard that night. "He might've turned up the I'm-with-the-band charm, but still...he was pretty straightforward about what he wanted. And so were they."

She fanned her collar, heat rising in her neck.

"I can imagine." He pinned her with his gaze. The smirk he was trying his best to restrain indicated that he had a good idea of how those conversations had gone. "And I didn't mean to imply...I'm not knocking Nick. His way of doing things undeniably works for him. Why do you think I recommended him to head up sales and marketing?"

Good point.

"I'm just saying that I'm not Nick. I don't have his gift of charm."

"True."

"Thanks," he said incredulously, one brow raised.

Dakota laughed. "That wasn't an insult, Dex. I just

meant that you're caring and genuine. People pick up on your sincerity and your concern for others."

"It means a lot to me that you see me that way." His soft gaze was filled with gratitude, and a heavy silence lingered between them before he finally spoke again. "Anyway, I shouldn't have to charm Dalton and the others into accepting something that has the potential to double or even triple the town's revenues."

"Like you said, some of the older islanders don't want to let go of the past. It's one of the reasons I was so eager to get out of town as a teenager," she added. "We need to approach the situation delicately and spell out the benefits clearly. Put together case studies and gather plenty of data."

"I like that idea. If anyone can persuade those stubborn troublemakers, I'm betting it's you." He winked at her before putting his headset back on and tapping away on his laptop.

Dakota put her headset back in place, too. But she couldn't help the smile that started deep in her chest and tightened her cheeks. Nor could she shake the niggling feeling that the joy she now felt stemmed purely from being with Dex.

Chapter Twenty

•—•—●—•—•

After they checked into their hotel and received their room keys, Dexter offered to walk Dakota to her room.

"I lived alone in one of the largest cities in North America." Her eyes glinted with amusement. "I can take care of myself, you know."

"I don't doubt that. But your dad would have my head if anything happened to you." Dexter headed toward the elevator, punching the number for her floor. "So consider it self-preservation."

"Far be it from me to discourage you from being a gentleman," she said with a smirk.

He walked Dakota to her room, checking it to ensure no one else was there. His gaze lingered on the plush king-size bed. The memory of their first time together commandeered his thoughts. He blinked back the memories, sounds, and sensations that had been cycling through his brain since they'd kissed at his place that morning.

But standing a few inches from the bed she'd be sleeping in filled his mind with images of the two of them together. Not sweet memories of the past. A blazing-hot desire for the present: to make Dakota his again and worship every inch of her soft, beautiful, brown skin.

No matter how much he told himself he was content to be friends, the truth—that he ached to be with her—lurked inside his head and gripped his chest.

Don't start what you can't finish, son.

How many times had his father told him that?

He was Dakota's boss, and she was leaving soon anyway.

Neither of them needed more pain or aggravation. And that was all that could possibly come of them taking things beyond that kiss.

"We've got a long night, and I'm exhausted. I'm going to have something delivered to my room and catch a nap before we head out tonight. Order whatever you'd like and charge it to the room." Dexter moved toward the door, where he'd left his own luggage.

"I will, thanks." She leaned against the open door, offering a small smile. There was a hint of disappointment in her voice. "Will we grab dinner together before the festival?"

She was beautiful, and he couldn't possibly say no to those pleading brown eyes.

"Sounds great." He smiled. "Meet you in the lobby at six."

Dex hurried down the hall and stepped into the elevator. Glad to be alone, he pressed his back against the glass wall and released an anxious breath.

He'd escaped Dakota's room as quickly as he could, not trusting himself to do what was in the best interests of both of them. He'd had the presence of mind to put a halt to things between them that morning. He doubted he'd have the strength to pull it off a second time.

The elevator dinged and the doors flew open. A young family entered. He greeted them, answering the myriad questions asked by the older of the two children.

Dexter exited on the next floor and went to his room. He set up his laptop and sat behind the desk to respond to a few more emails before he ordered lunch. But he couldn't dismiss the contented look of that couple as they held hands in the elevator, surrounded by their two small children. Or how beautiful the woman looked with her glowing smile and burgeoning belly. The couple appeared to be in their midthirties, too. Perhaps even younger.

If he and Dakota had stayed together, would that be them now? Three kids in and still very much in love?

Dexter kneaded the tension at the back of his neck and sighed. He'd blown it. No amount of wishing or regret would erase that. And life seldom afforded one do-overs.

What if he told Dakota the whole truth about their breakup? Would she be more likely to give him another shot? Dex groaned, dragging a hand over his head.

Doubtful.

More importantly, telling her would only hurt her. And Dakota didn't deserve that.

When she'd arrived in town, he'd had hopes of a second chance with her. It was still what he wanted. But with his promotion, he now faced an all-or-nothing proposition. Because this time he wouldn't just lose Dakota. He'd lose everything he'd been working toward for the past ten years.

So he would keep his secret. Try to convince her to stay. Then, if she did, he'd take the risk, tell her everything and try his best to win her back.

———

Dakota flopped onto the bed in her hotel room. She was exhausted, but it was a good tired. The kind that came with the feeling of accomplishment. A feeling she'd missed in the interim between leaving her job at the news station and starting her work at the resort.

She'd gotten up early and it was going to be a long and grueling day, since she hadn't gotten much sleep the night before. She and Sin had stayed up late watching movies. She should be taking a nap, but she couldn't. Her entire body buzzed with energy, and her brain wouldn't calm down long enough for her to drift off to sleep.

Did her restlessness stem from her and Dexter's kiss that morning? Or from having spent the entire plane ride with him? Either way, Dexter "Why'd He Have to Look and Smell and Taste So Damn Good?" Roberts was the common denominator.

Since Dakota couldn't rest, she showered and slipped on a tank top and a pair of old shorts. She checked in with her father. Then she spent a few hours outlining ideas for the two festivals she'd proposed, identifying mutually beneficial opportunities for the resort to collaborate with the town.

Dakota couldn't help smiling as she reviewed her list. She felt exhilarated by her work with Dex. Or maybe it was the thrill of working closely with a man for whom she obviously still felt *something*.

She checked her watch. She'd been so preoccupied that she'd forgotten to order something for lunch. And now it was precariously close to time for them to grab dinner.

There was a knock at her door. Dakota grabbed the remote and muted the home improvement show that had been playing quietly on the television in the background as she worked. She approached the door warily and checked the peephole.

Dexter.

He was more than an hour early. She looked a mess in her tattered shorts and faded college tank top. But compared to how she'd looked the day they'd crossed paths while running on the beach, she looked like a movie star.

Dakota opened the door. "Hey."

"Hey." He smiled softly, his hands shoved in his pockets.

"I thought we weren't supposed to meet for another hour."

"We weren't. But I never did get around to grabbing lunch, so I'm starving. I tried to call to see if you'd be open to an earlier dinner, but—"

"My phone is charging by the bed. I guess I didn't hear it vibrating over the sound of the television," she said quickly. "Earlier is fine, but as you can see, I'm not dressed." She indicated her casual attire.

Dexter's gaze glided down her body momentarily before his eyes met hers again. He cleared his throat, his cheeks flushed.

"Or maybe I'm overdressed." He glanced down at his dark-wash jeans and pale-blue T-shirt worn underneath an open, floral-print button-down shirt. One arm of his mirrored sunglasses was tucked inside the breast pocket.

"No." She shook her head. "You look perfect for the occasion." Their eyes met as they stood there for a moment. Butterflies danced in her belly, and neither of them spoke for what felt like minutes.

"Sorry, I should've invited you in," she said finally, opening the door wider and waving him inside. "I already took a shower. Give me maybe a half hour to get ready and do something with my hair." She raked her fingers through her damp curls, which she'd planned to dry and flat iron before meeting Dex in the lobby.

"I didn't mean to throw you off. We could meet downstairs later, as planned," he said.

"It's fine," she insisted. "As long as you don't mind waiting while I get ready."

Dexter stepped inside. He seemed to be working hard to keep his eyes above her neck.

Dakota tried to suppress a self-satisfied grin. Her ego appreciated the boost.

She invited him to have a seat on the upholstered chair in the corner, then retrieved everything she needed. "Did you decide where we're going to eat?"

"We've got a couple of options." He settled onto the chair. "We can either go somewhere really nice, like the seafood restaurant here at the hotel or a nearby steakhouse."

Dakota wasn't feeling especially fancy today. She'd done plenty of that back in New York. It was Friday night, and she would be attending her first music festival in more than a decade, even if it was for work. She would prefer something fun and low-key.

"And the other option?"

He seemed relieved that she was passing on the fancy meal. "We could head over to the festival site early and check out their food truck rodeo."

"Let's do that," Dakota said excitedly. "I'd love to incorporate a food truck rodeo into our event."

He grinned. "That's what I was thinking, too."

"That was easy. Hopefully it'll be as simple to figure out what to do with my hair."

"I like it that way." Dexter indicated her damp, natural curls. "Always have."

She sank her teeth into her lower lip, and without thought, ran her fingers through her damp hair and tucked a few strands behind her ear. "Thanks."

The first time he'd said that to her, he'd sifted his fingers through her hair and pulled her in for a kiss—their first. Heat rolled along her neck and shoulders as the memory of his lips on hers nearly took her breath away.

Without uttering another word, she turned and rushed inside the bathroom, shutting the door behind her. Dakota took slow, deliberate breaths, willing her heartbeat to slow down. She sat on the edge of the tub to gather her thoughts.

It was the second time today she'd found herself hiding in a bathroom after an encounter with Dexter Roberts.

You really need to pull it together.

But the truth was she wanted Dexter. Even though she shouldn't and nothing could possibly come of it, there was still a part of her that wanted to believe it was possible.

Dakota put on a pair of black, dressy, tie-waist shorts and the matching top, meant to give the outfit the look of a single piece. She gathered her dark curls into a low pony-tail and twisted it into a bun. Then she applied her makeup. A simple, fresh-faced summer look. After all, this was a casual business dinner, not a date. No matter how much she might want it to be.

———

The festival grounds were already bustling with people by the time Dex and Dakota arrived. In addition to the food truck rodeo, a variety of food vendors sold everything from crab cakes to Italian sausages and sushi.

Dakota had ordered crab rangoon from one of the food trucks and Dex had gone for lobster ravioli from another. They sat at one of the picnic tables as soon as two festival-goers abandoned their seats.

"This place is packed," Dakota said as she carefully opened her box.

"Our event would be small potatoes compared to this, but that could be good. There are probably a lot of people who'd like to attend a music festival but wouldn't want to negotiate a crowd this size." He leaned toward Dakota, seated beside him, so he wouldn't have to shout over the blaring music that had started up on a nearby stage.

"True." She nodded thoughtfully. "But this festival started off small, too." She shrugged. "Who knows where our event might end up ten or twenty years from now? It would be an amazing legacy to leave the town long after we've both moved on."

"Never considered that. Leaving a legacy, I mean." He stuffed a forkful of the lobster ravioli in his mouth and chewed, savoring the explosion of flavors on his tongue. "I like the idea of leaving our mark on the town that made us."

More importantly, he liked that they'd be leaving their mark on the town *together*. That they would always have that connection. An observation it seemed prudent to keep to himself.

"My God, this crab rangoon is amazing." She picked up one of the crispy fried wontons filled with crab meat and cream cheese, broke it in half, and extended a piece to him. "You *have* to taste one of these."

Dex tilted his head, assessing her for a moment. Dakota had fallen in love with the appetizer when they'd gone to a Thai restaurant off island the summer before he left for college. She obviously still loved them.

His lips quirked in an involuntary smile. Dakota had the same determined expression on her face now that she'd had when she'd insisted he try them that night long ago.

Disagreement was pointless. She was beautiful, as determined as her mother, and as stubborn as Chief Jones. No wonder she made a damn good investigative reporter.

He leaned forward and accepted the morsel she held out, his teeth playfully nicking her fingers.

Her teeth sank into her lower lip as she watched him chew.

"Wow. That is good," he muttered, resisting the urge to lick the savory cream cheese from her thumb. "I'll take that other half."

She blinked, staring at him before picking up the other half of the filled, crispy fried wonton and setting it on the edge of his plate.

He pierced one of the raviolis with his fork and held it up. "Would you like to try some of mine?"

Dakota nodded, leaning in to take a bite. She chewed thoughtfully, her eyes drifting closed momentarily.

His heart raced in response to the sensual scene. He swallowed hard and sucked in a slow, deep breath. "Good?" he asked finally.

"Incredible." She licked the creamy sauce from her lower lips, her eyes lingering on his.

Dexter's gaze slid down to Dakota's mouth again as she chewed, then followed the column of her elegant neck as she swallowed. He shut his eyes against the hint of visible cleavage before opening them to trail down the rest of her body.

We're coworkers and old friends. That's all.

He repeated the words to himself, conveniently leaving out the part about them also being former lovers.

A sudden burst of heat seemed to swirl around them. Dexter tugged on the collar of his T-shirt, in need of a hint of the cool air coming from a nearby fan. He cleared his throat. "Guess we both chose well."

"Would you mind if I had another ravioli?" she asked.

He pushed his food toward her and she speared another piece with her fork.

"Some of my fondest memories are of sharing a meal with you," he said. "And there are so many foods I would never have tried if it hadn't been for you."

A range of emotions passed over her face. A wide-eyed look of surprise; a soft, appreciative smile; then a frown that dimmed the light in her brown eyes.

Dexter immediately regretted revealing that after all this time, his most cherished memories still revolved around Dakota. It made him sound lovelorn and pathetic.

"We'd better hurry if we want to browse the craft vendors section before our show begins," he said, abruptly, before she could respond to his statement.

They finished their food in relative silence before relinquishing their seats. Then they walked toward the row of craft vendors selling handmade jewelry, clothing, art, and more. They visited several of the stalls, examining their wares, an awkward silence hanging between them.

"Did my dad threaten you or something?" She stopped walking suddenly and turned toward him.

"Why would you think that?" Dexter frowned, shoving a hand in his pocket.

"You've been quiet and a little standoffish since we left my dad's this morning. He didn't ask you if I spent the night at your place?"

"No," he offered quickly. "He definitely didn't ask me that, nor did he threaten me. Besides, I'm a little old for the Chief Jones intimidation routine."

"I don't know." Dakota laughed, walking toward another booth. "My dad had you quaking in your boots a few times."

"A: The man wore a gun and was the chief of police."
He held up one finger, then another. "B: Those weren't any
old boots. They were my favorite pair of Timbs."

"How could I possibly forget?" She placed a gentle
hand on his arm above his elbow. Her warmth seeped
through the layers of fabric, and little sparks of electricity
danced along his skin. "You were obsessed with them."
She glanced down at his feet. "I'm surprised you're not
wearing a pair right now."

"Oh, I still love my Timbs." He chuckled. "I considered
bringing them on this trip, but I figured you'd be more
impressed by the Cole Haans."

"The shoes were a good choice." She met his gaze instead of looking down at his feet again. Her lips quirked in
a mischievous smile. "You wore them to impress me?"

Shit.

He needed to put a lid on his mouth to give his
brain a shot at catching up. This was why he preferred to
think more and speak less. But there was something about
Dakota that had always put him at ease and encouraged
him to say whatever was on his mind—without running it
through his usual filter.

Dex turned and walked down the aisle of craft vendors
again. "Are you telling me you didn't select that"—he cleared
his throat—"very *fetching* short set with me in mind?"

"I honestly didn't." She turned away from him, but he
still caught a glimpse of the adorable smirk that curved her
sensual lips. "Sorry to disappoint you."

"Well, you've impressed me nevertheless." He stopped
walking this time, turning to meet her gaze and return her
broad smile. "And you could never, ever disappoint me."

The words, meant to be a compliment, seemed to cause
her distress.

"Thanks," she muttered, her head turned away from him as she surveyed a booth. She turned and continued their trek past the row of vendors selling their wares.

"We have to do a craft vendor area like this. It could really be a boon for some of our local business owners. Other coastal Carolina businesses might be interested in buying booths, too," he noted, wanting to ask her what he'd said wrong but deciding against it.

"Great idea." She tapped notes into an app on her phone. "I like that the food and craft vendors are in separate areas. We should emulate that, too."

"Definitely." He stopped to try on a few hats at one of the vendors. "Didn't think to bring a hat," he said. "How about you?"

She shook her head and continued typing out her notes, completely focused on the task.

They hadn't come out to the festival grounds until late afternoon. But for the next two days, they'd be there much earlier in the day. The sun would be grueling.

He took off the hat he'd tried on and settled it on Dakota's head. He held his hands up, as if framing her for a photo. "There. That one looks much better on you." He winked.

"I'll take your word for it." She went back to typing out notes on her phone.

"Don't." He tugged her by the elbow and nodded toward the mirror situated on the table stacked with hats. "See for yourself."

Dakota turned reluctantly and looked at herself in the mirror as he tried on a different hat. Her mouth curved in a soft smile and she tilted her head, stepping closer to the mirror. She adjusted the lightweight, wide-brim fedora and smiled.

"This hat is really cute," she conceded. "And you're right. It'll be broiling out here for the next two days." She reached inside the purse strapped against her body for her wallet.

"I've got it," Dex insisted to the vendor as he tried on a third hat and studied himself in the mirror over Dakota's head. "And I think I'll take that one." He met her reflection in the mirror. "What do you think?"

"Another good choice." She offered a faint smile and repositioned the hat on her head. "And thank you for the hat. I appreciate it."

"My pleasure," he said, handing the man his credit card.

As they turned and walked away, he resisted the urge to take her hand, as he had so many times before when they'd strolled together at carnivals or amusement parks. When they hit the end of the craft vendor aisle, they turned around and made their way back up the other side.

Dakota tapped out more notes about the best locations for the event and where the craft and food vendors should be set up. He listened carefully and offered feedback when required. But mostly, he found himself completely enamored with Dakota Jones. Not just because she was beautiful and looked good enough to eat in that little outfit that showcased her toned legs and made his temperature skyrocket every time the top rose, offering a peek of her midriff. He was fascinated by the lightning speed at which her brain worked and her curiosity about everything around them. He loved watching her interact with complete strangers, whom she instantly put at ease. She chatted with them as if they were old friends, her interest in them genuine.

Dakota had always had a way of making everything seem so much more intriguing than he'd thought upon first glance. They'd walk past an old building in town or a statue in the park, landmarks he'd seen his entire life and never really thought twice about, and she'd stand there grinning, as if she knew a secret that the rest of the world didn't.

The moment he'd ask what she was smiling about, she'd launch excitedly into some obscure but fascinating piece of history about the place. Stories that made him see a run-down old building or a neglected statue in a whole new light.

"You are a fascinating woman, Dakota Jones," Dex marveled, his mouth stretching in a smile. "You always have been."

"I feel like that's code for *weird*." She giggled. "But thank you, I think." Dakota checked the time on her phone, then slipped it into her pocket. "Our concert starts soon. We should find our seats."

Dex nodded toward one of the bars. "Can I get you anything? I doubt they're serving French 75s here, but maybe a cranberry juice and vodka?" he teased.

"No, thank you. But I will take another sweet tea." She held up her nearly empty cup.

They got in the shortest beverage line and he ordered another sweet tea for her and an overpriced beer for himself.

She sipped her drink as she entered the line to the venue ahead of him. "I've barely been back home a month and I've already gotten addicted to this stuff again. I swear I can feel it going straight to my thighs."

His gaze dropped to her legs. It was difficult enough to ignore the sashaying of her hips and how sexy she looked in those shorts. Now his attention was drawn to the smooth brown skin of her thighs and his heartbeat went into overdrive.

Cauliflower. Fake bacon. Skinny jeans. Centi...

actually...His gaze floated up a few inches, assessing her bottom. *That ass would look spectacular in a pair of skinny jeans.*

Not helpful.

He shook his head, shifting his gaze and his thoughts away from Dakota's body.

"It's one of those things, I guess," he managed finally, rewarding himself with a long swig of his beer. "It reminds you of hot summers as a kid."

"Yeah, I guess so." Dakota suddenly sounded a little sad. "My mom made the best sweet tea. She'd make it with lemon and blueberries, or sometimes blackberries or peaches. Her sweet tea was always this happy surprise. You never knew exactly what she might throw in there, you know?" Her voice broke slightly.

Dex had the sudden urge to wrap his arms around her and tell her everything would be okay. Instead, he put a gentle hand on her shoulder. "It's okay, Dakota, I realize how much you must miss her."

She swiped a finger beneath her eye and sniffled. "Let's talk about something else. Anything. Please."

"Sure. What would you like to talk about?"

"What made you go into the hospitality industry?"

He groaned quietly, his right knee suddenly throbbing. "Got hit by a particularly aggressive cornerback on one of the last plays of the season opener during my senior year. He ended up with a lucrative NFL contract and I got two screws in my right knee. You may have noticed that it makes air travel much more fun."

"I'm sorry, Dex. That must've been tough."

"Thanks, but don't be." He shrugged. "It ended my NFL hopes, but that was never my dream anyway. The injury was tough, and yeah, sometimes it still hurts like hell. But in a way, it freed me. I stopped worrying about what my dad wanted for me. And for the first time, I considered what I wanted for myself."

"And what was it that you wanted?"

You.

He swigged his beer. "I spent my summers during college as a paid intern at a hotel near campus instead of coming home for summer break. I enjoyed the work, and my manager said I was a natural. He encouraged me to pursue it as a career. Said he could easily see me working my way up in the industry. So that's what I did. I got a job at that hotel, first at the front desk, then in group sales, and eventually on the operations team. By that time, I was really beginning to miss home. So when I learned about a small hotel group that had plans to build a luxury resort on the island, I applied to their Myrtle Beach property, so I was closer to the island. Closer to my family. Thought it gave me the best shot at eventually getting a top exec position at the Holly Grove Island Resort."

"Looks like everything is working out for you." She seemed genuinely happy for him.

He couldn't help smiling, thinking of how different this conversation was from the tense one they'd had when he'd encountered her at the Fourth of July Festival.

"I'm glad you found a career you enjoy, that you get to be back home, where you want to be," she said.

"Does being a news reporter make you happy?" he asked after they'd shown their tickets to an usher and followed her directions to find their section.

"I enjoy making a difference in people's lives," she said after a careful pause. "Getting justice for those who've been wronged. But for everyone I've helped, there were plenty I couldn't. It's heartbreaking. I remember every one of them, even now. Years later. I can't say I enjoyed those instances, but telling their stories was important. I'm proud to have done that."

"I'm sorry you lost your job in New York, Dakota. But I'd be lying if I said I wasn't glad that it brought you back home. Even if it's only for a little while."

She gazed up at him from beneath the brim of her hat. "And why is that, Dex?"

Because I want a second chance with you, Dakota.

Dex choked back the words.

"Because you're a vital addition to our team," he said instead. "And because I've been hoping to mend our friendship."

"Oh." The light in her eyes dimmed. She pointed toward the section listed on their tickets. "I think this is us."

They showed their tickets to another usher, who led them to their seats. He sat beside Dakota, wishing he'd been able to tell her the truth. He wanted her in his life again, but he wanted to be much more than friends.

Chapter Twenty-One

$\bullet\!-\!\bullet\!-\!\bullet$

Dakota tossed her purse on the corner of the bed and buried her face in her hands, stifling the urge to scream. The concert had been amazing, and what they'd learned from just the first day of their visit had been invaluable. It was well worth the cost of their trip. And she'd truly enjoyed Dex's company.

So much so that when they returned to the hotel and Dex insisted on walking her up to her room, she'd hoped that he would kiss her good night. Maybe even come inside for a nightcap. But he hadn't. Instead, he'd been a perfect gentleman. He'd ensured that no one was lingering in her room, then said good night and taken his leave. And she couldn't help being a little hurt by it.

What are you thinking, Dakota? You're falling for Dex all over again.

She understood why Dexter had really broken up with her back then, and they'd made amends, but what they'd shared was a lifetime ago. They were different people now. And now, just as then, they were on very different paths in their lives. He wanted to stay on Holly Grove Island. Her aspirations would take her far away from home. There was no way to reconcile those competing goals. And yet, she couldn't help wanting him.

Dakota blew out a frustrated breath as she flopped onto the corner chair. Dexter Roberts was the king of mixed signals. And hell, maybe she was, too.

One minute she was sure he wanted to kiss her. The next he was stressing that he only wanted to be friends. Then, in a momentary lapse in judgment, she'd thrown herself at Dex in his condo that morning, only to have him politely reject her after giving her a kiss that turned her inside out and left her knees weak.

Maybe it was the vulnerability caused by the loss of her job and being shamed publicly. But she felt like the same insecure teenage girl whose heart Dexter had broken. The girl who always wondered if she was good enough, and if she ever would be.

She couldn't allow herself to return to that dark place. Yet she could feel herself descending into that morass of insecurity, and she was weary of keeping the secret of what had really happened in New York. Of constantly wondering when someone in town would find out.

She needed a lifeline.

Dakota picked up her phone, and dialed Sinclair's number.

"Hey, hon." Sin's voice was bright and cheerful. "How are things going at the festival?"

"Better than I could've hoped," she said, though her voice betrayed that she was on the verge of tears.

"You don't sound fine, Kota." Sin's voice was heavy with concern. "What happened?"

"Nothing, and that's the problem." Dakota laughed bitterly as she slid the elastic band from her hair and ran her fingers through it. "But there's something I need to

tell you first. It's about the real reason I came home from
New York."

"Okay, shoot." Sinclair didn't seem surprised that there
was more to the story than Dakota had indicated. "Whatever it is, I'm here for you, hon."

Dakota sucked in a deep breath, her hands trembling
and her eyes welling with tears as she told Sin the
truth: She hadn't been the victim of a random layoff.
She'd sabotaged her own career through carelessness and
naïvete. She told Sin about the handsome Italian director
she'd fallen head over heels for, how she'd lost her job
at the news station, and why she hadn't been able to find
another job in New York.

Her friend listened without interrupting, and Dakota felt
as if a weight had been lifted from her chest.

"I'm sorry I didn't tell you the truth when I first arrived,
Sin. But I was ashamed to tell you what happened, what a
fool I'd been." She sniffled, then blew her nose.

"Dakota, you have nothing to apologize for. You didn't
do anything wrong. I'm sorry that you had to go through
this. I wish I could've been there for you then. I wish I were
there with you right now so I could give you a huge hug
and tell you that everything is going to be okay, because
it will," Sin said. "I can only imagine how devastating it
must feel right now, honey. But like every other scandal,
it'll eventually pass."

"I wish I believed that." Dakota tossed the tissue in a
nearby trash can and then grabbed another, dabbing her
wet cheeks.

"People have short memories. One celebutante will steal
another's man or some athlete or politician will say something incredibly stupid and everyone will forget about this.
I promise you. You just have to be patient and wait it out.

And while you do, I'm glad you decided to come home to the people who care about you," Sin said reassuringly. "Speaking of which…how are things going with you and Dex?"

"Honestly? We had an amazing day together. In fact, things have been really good between us since that night at the club. Maybe too good." Dakota's heart raced at the mere prospect of saying the words aloud to someone else. "Sin, I think I'm falling for Dex again. Which is crazy after all we've been through, right?"

Dakota needed her friend to give her a hard dose of reality, so she could get her mind right and stop mooning over a man who clearly wasn't into her anymore.

"No, honey, it isn't." Sinclair's tone softened. "Dexter is a great guy, Dakota. He's honorable and trustworthy. He cares about the people in his life, especially you."

"I know. He's been so sweet and thoughtful. Going out of his way to see after me and to make sure my dad was okay. And now that we've been spending time together again, it feels like he's that same amazing guy I fell in love with, only better." Dakota twirled a strand of hair around one finger, nervous about how her friend would take what she was about to say. "I can't help wondering if this terrible thing that happened, if maybe there was purpose to it or, at the very least, a silver lining. Like Dex and I were meant to cross paths again at this point in our lives."

"Serendipity," Sin said in a breathless, awestruck voice. "I'm getting goose bumps just thinking about it. And I'm betting that he's falling in love with you again, too."

"That's just it." Dakota sighed. "Dex doesn't feel the same way."

"What makes you say that?" Sin asked in disbelief. "Have you seen the stars in that man's eyes when he looks at you? My God, Dakota, the man arranged an entire show at the Foxhole in honor of your return home."

"I know. I thought the same thing. But then this morning at Dex's condo, I kind of…kissed him." Dakota pulled the phone away from her ear when her friend squealed.

"Then what happened?" Sin could barely contain her excitement.

"He kissed me back and it was…intense and amazing and…" Dakota sighed. "Then it wasn't. He made it clear that he's my boss now and that he just wants to be friends."

"But he didn't say that he didn't have feelings for you, Dakota," Sin pointed out. "What I'm hearing is that he's concerned that if people find out he's dating an employee of the resort, it could jeopardize his career. Especially now that he's got a real shot at becoming the permanent director at the Holly Grove Island Resort."

"I can respect that. I understand how important this job is to him. How hard he's worked for it. Besides, I'm only passing through." A wave of sadness settled over her. "Dex wants to be home and I want to be…" Dakota sank her teeth into her lower lip and sighed. For the first time since she was ten, the answer didn't come readily.

When she'd arrived in town, she had planned to return to New York as soon as possible. Or maybe settle in LA, where her sister, Shay, lived. Or perhaps even Chicago. But since she'd been home, things had slowly been shifting. The thought of leaving her father, Sin, and Dexter hurt. Suddenly the excitement of what she'd be running to no longer outweighed the sadness over the people she'd be leaving behind.

"Maybe Dexter isn't the only one who wants to come home for good," Sin said.

"I've invested so much time and energy into my career. I can't give all that up," Dakota said more to herself than to Sin. "I wish I didn't feel this way. I already know it can't end well, and I can't go through this again with Dex. Not when the first time hurt so much."

"He was your first love, Dakota. That's hard to get over. But ask yourself if you're closing yourself off to the possibility of a future with Dex because it really isn't what you want anymore or because you're afraid."

"After what happened with Dexter the first time and then this disaster with my most recent ex, I have good reason to be gun-shy." Dakota sat on the edge of the chair.

"What happened with Marcello Giovannetti was unfortunate, Dakota, but it wasn't your fault. Don't shut out the possibility of finding something special with Dexter because of what one wavy-haired, one-hit wonder did."

"I know in my head that it isn't my fault. But there's a part of me that doesn't trust myself any—wait...What did you say about Marcello?" Dakota stood suddenly and placed a hand on her hip.

"I said you can't let what he did to you cause you to miss out on a second chance with Dex," Sin said.

"Yes, but I never mentioned his name, Sin," Dakota said.

"You must have." Sin's voice was unusually high pitched.

"I *didn't*," Dakota insisted. "Because I know you, Sin, and I didn't want you mailing fifty pounds of fresh cow manure or something to the guy." She sank onto the chair again, suddenly nauseous. "Tell me the truth, Sinclair Buchanan. How long have you known?"

Sin was silent for a moment; then she heaved a quiet sigh. "After you called me to say you'd be coming home, but before I picked you up at the station."

"Oh my God." Dakota pressed her hand to her mouth.

Her skin was hot, her head was spinning, and it was suddenly harder to breathe. "Sin, why didn't you tell me you knew instead of letting me make a fool of myself?"

"Because you're my best friend, Dakota." There were tears in Sin's voice. "You were obviously already embarrassed. I didn't want to make it worse. And we hadn't seen each other in such a long time. We were feeling each other out. I wasn't sure how you'd react, and I didn't want to scare you off. I figured you'd tell me when you were ready."

"That's why you kept saying you were there whenever I was ready to talk." Dakota rubbed her throbbing temple and sighed. "I should've realized then that you knew."

"Have you told your dad?" Sin asked after a beat of silence between them.

"No." Dakota whispered the word.

"Even on *Gilligan's Island*, they had a transistor radio, Dakota," Sin warned her. "Don't let your father hear about this from someone else. He loves you, and he'll understand. But if he hears it from someone else—"

"He'd be devastated." It broke her heart to think of it.

"What are you going to do about your dad and about Dex?" Sin asked.

"I don't know," Dakota said. "But I'd better figure it out soon."

Chapter Twenty-Two

•—•—•

Dexter returned to his seat with Dakota, their drinks in hand. He should be exhausted. The previous long day had been capped off by a long, sleepless night. He'd tossed and turned, thoughts of Dakota filling his head. By the time he finally dozed off to sleep, the alarm on his phone woke him.

After meeting for breakfast, he and Dakota had headed over to the festival grounds, where they'd been all day. They'd spent time talking to festivalgoers, especially those who attended every year. And they'd chatted with vendors about what made the event one they looked forward to participating in.

Work aside, they'd also managed to have a good time. The festival was a great experience, but there was no mystery to why he'd enjoyed himself so much. He and Dakota had slowly been getting to know each other again since she'd returned to the island. But their weekend together had afforded them the chance to get reacquainted in a way that felt much more intimate.

They'd relived the happy memories of the past while avoiding the land mines of their breakup or Dakota's plans for the future. Subjects they needed to discuss if he had any hope of convincing her to stay on the island and make a life among the friends and family who loved her.

But he couldn't bring himself to prick a pin in the shiny bubble of contentment that surrounded them.

So instead, when they weren't talking about the project or other hotel business, he'd updated her on his brothers Steven and Ellis and their families, showing off photos of his nieces and nephews whom he adored. Dakota recounted some of the investigative reports she was proudest of and shared photos of her travel to Europe and South America.

They'd spent a good part of the day laughing about memories from their past. And they'd joined in with the crowd, dancing during several of the musical performances.

It was the most fun Dex had had in a very long time.

Now they were waiting for the final artist of the night to perform. He should be grateful the day had almost come to an end, so he could return to the hotel, crawl into bed, and catch up on his sleep. But he didn't want his time with Dakota to end.

"I have to admit," Dakota said, breaking into his thoughts, "I was nervous about how this weekend would go. But it's been amazing."

"The festival has been outstanding," he agreed. "But if I'm being honest, what I enjoyed most was getting to hang out with you again, Dakota." He nudged her arm on the armrest beside his. "I'm glad we were able to move past what happened back then."

"Same." She nudged his arm back.

There was something in her sweet smile that made him feel as if he were floating. He clenched his fists, resisting the urge to reach out and squeeze her hand.

Dexter breathed a quiet sigh of relief, thankful that Dakota *wanted* to be there with him. Maybe it was the first step to something more for them. But even if all they'd ever be was friends, he was glad that Dakota was in his life again.

They sipped their drinks in contented silence, her shoulder pressed against him, as they waited for the show to begin.

———

It felt like Dakota had been on her feet for most of the last two days. But as the final concert of the night wound down, she couldn't be happier to have spent this time with Dex. She had no idea what the future had in store. But she was glad that she and Dexter had made amends. He was an important part of her life, so she was grateful that they'd been given the opportunity to rewrite the ending to their story.

She wasn't getting the happily ever after she'd hoped for as a teenage girl. But their story would have a happy ending, nevertheless.

They were rebuilding a genuine friendship. One that had the potential to endure the rest of their lives. Wasn't that better than an intense, but short-lived, affair?

Her fists tightened and her thighs clenched.

She knew the right answer to the question. But her body's reaction to memories of their kiss and of the sensual dreams she'd had about the two of them last night signaled dissent.

Why couldn't the right answer be both?

But there were too many reasons that wasn't an option for them. Their timing wasn't right, and maybe it never would be.

The performance was winding down, and the crowd had already thinned a bit as people made their way to the parking lot and the shuttles, hoping to beat the traffic.

The band leader announced that they were playing their final song, "The Way You Look Tonight." The artist encouraged the crowd to make use of the extra room by grabbing the hand of the person they came with and dancing.

Dakota tensed, her belly doing a flip as she remembered dancing with Dex on Sin's balcony while he sang the same song to her.

"Care to dance?" Dex held out his open palm.

"Thought you'd never ask." She smiled despite her nervousness.

Dex slipped an arm around her waist and held her hand. He swayed to the music, singing softly so only she could hear.

The night they'd danced on Sin's balcony, she'd been attracted to Dexter. Had maybe even felt an inkling of *something* for him. But since then, the gratitude and affection she'd felt for him had grown exponentially. And that mere spark of attraction had become a blazing desire. Electricity zipped along her spine. Her knees felt unsteady. And the ache between her thighs beat as steadily as her heartbeat.

Dexter pulled her into a tighter embrace than he had that night on Sin's balcony. They moved together, her body pressed to his.

She shut her eyes, and allowed herself to get lost in the moment. To hold on to it for as long as she could. But sadness and longing filled her chest. She'd missed the warmth of Dexter's embrace. The security she'd always felt in his arms. The comfort she felt in his presence. The love and friendship they'd once shared.

Would it ever feel this right with anyone else?

Eyes closed, Dakota inhaled the subtle, masculine scent she'd been admiring for the past two days. Dexter's heat enveloped her as the cool breeze blowing off the nearby bay swirled softly around them.

Finally, the song ended, and the remaining crowd applauded. But Dex still held her in his arms, seemingly as reluctant to release his hold as she was to relinquish the warmth of it. But eventually, he did let her go, and they joined in applauding the band members for their encore performance.

"Ready?" Dex shoved one hand in his pocket and extended the other elbow to her.

It had been such a perfect night. Dakota wasn't ready for it to end. But she nodded reluctantly and accepted the gentlemanly gesture as he escorted her out of the venue and onto the festival grounds. A couple of vendors were still open and selling food. Nestled between them was an old-school, enclosed photo booth.

Dakota pointed to the small line of people waiting for their turn. "I haven't seen one of these in forever. Remember how much we loved goofing off in them?"

The photo album she'd found at his place the day before had been filled with those little strips of photos that came from photo booths.

"I do," he said softly. "The last time I was in one was that day we went to the arcade in Wilmington with Sin and my cousin Rett. I swear, I thought those two were going to kill each other before the night was over."

"Same," she said. She knew she shouldn't care, but something about the fact that Dex hadn't been in a photo booth with anyone else felt satisfying. It was *their* thing. Not some random thing they'd done with other people.

"Then it seems like fate that we happened upon one." She grinned. "Don't you think?"

"You sure you want to stand in that line?"

"I am." She tugged him in the direction of the booth. "Doesn't seem wise to ignore fate."

He stared at her, his gaze soft and his tone wistful. "No, I don't suppose it is."

Dakota removed the hat Dexter bought her the day before and tousled the loose, natural curls she hadn't worn in years. An action inspired by his sweet compliment.

She dug in her small crossbody bag for her tinted lip gloss. "I must look a mess after being out here all day."

"Trust me," Dex said. "You look incredible."

She thanked him, lightly applying her lip gloss.

"One more day left of our adventure," Dex remarked. "Are you sure you're up to it?"

"Yes. I'll catch up on some sleep tonight and I'll be right as rain tomorrow. Promise. What about you? Think you'll be able to hang in there, old man?"

"Et tu, Dakota?" He gripped his chest. "I've been getting enough of those jokes lately from Em and my brothers."

"Sorry. I didn't realize your age was a sensitive issue for you," she teased. "Relax, buddy. I'm only a couple of years behind you. And until a few months ago, I'd been enjoying my thirties just fine."

"I'm sorry to hear that, Dakota." Dex frowned. "I know the last few months have been rough, but I hope you've enjoyed being home. Your dad, Sin, Nick, and me...we're all grateful you came back."

A slow smile spread across her face as a jumble of emotions welled inside her chest. Gratitude for Dex's thoughtful remark. Thankfulness for the time she'd had to spend with her family and friends. Guilt that she hadn't come home to see her father more often or done a better job of staying in touch with Sin. And a deep twinge of sadness at the thought of leaving them all behind again.

She thanked Dex and tucked her lip gloss back in her bag as the line surged forward. They were next. As she watched the group in front of them pile into the booth and close the curtain, she couldn't help thinking about all of the happy times she'd had growing up on Holly Grove Island with Sin, Dex, and their friends. She had so many wonderful memories of clamming, fishing off the Fox Haven Sound pier, the town festivals, and the quirky town history reenactments. Visiting the gardens and nature preserve on the island. Getting lost in the garden's maze and climbing the steps at the old lighthouse for the hundredth time. Then there were the lazy afternoons spent lying on the beach. Or the fun of kayaking on the sound.

Her mother had drilled it into her head that she was destined for great things that were too big for their little town. Taught her that she shouldn't be satisfied by what Holly Grove Island had to offer. Poked holes in the bubble of contentment that Dakota had felt living there.

They'd traveled often. As a family or just Dakota, Shay, and their mother. Madeline Jones had designed each trip to show her girls that the world was so much bigger than their little town. To make them want more. That was why'd Dakota had fallen in love with New York. Why Shay preferred to be a California girl. That had always been the underlying message with their mother.

Run. Run and don't look back.

Before their mother had gotten sick, she'd never pressured them to return to Holly Grove Island. She'd preferred traveling to visit them instead. Enjoyed crowing to the ladies back home about her eldest daughter living in LA and married to a successful Hollywood executive and her youngest daughter breaking into the news industry in New York.

But being back home reminded Dakota that she'd once been very happy living there. Made her wonder if she could be again. Until the memory of her mother's voice shook her.

Don't let anything distract you from your path. And if you fall off the horse, a few bumps and bruises will heal. Get up, dust yourself off, and get right back at it again.

Dakota craned her neck and pressed her fingers to the tension there. Her mother was right. She'd gotten burned, and deep down she was afraid it would happen again. That was the real reason she was entertaining thoughts of an idyllic life back in her familiar small town.

This isn't what you really want. She whispered the words in her head. *You're just scared.*

Dakota released a slow, quiet breath.

"Everything okay?" Dexter placed his large hand on her back, removing it just as quickly when she startled at his touch.

"Yes, I'm fine." She forced a smile much bigger than necessary. "Just thinking . . . about what pose I should strike when it's our turn."

"Pose?" His eyes widened with surprise. "We're taking this all the way back to high school, huh?"

"Might as well go for the complete experience, right?" She shrugged with a silly grin. "Besides, it would be nice to have something to add to that photo album you've been holding on to all this time, wouldn't it?" She turned back to face the booth. The curtain rustled and the people inside giggled. "And maybe I'm building a photo album of my own. Starting with these photos. So make it good."

"Yes, ma'am." The rumble of Dex's deep chuckle made her smile. She was glad she could think of that sound now with fond memories, rather than the pain it usually conjured.

The black curtain slid open and the group of friends spilled out.

It was finally their turn in the photo booth. A sudden wave of nervousness swept over Dakota.

Dex stepped forward and swept his hand toward the inside of the booth. "Ladies first."

Dakota slid onto the bench against the far wall, making room for Dexter's long legs and wide shoulders. She remembered these booths being larger. But then her hips and ass were much fuller now than they'd been then. Dexter was bigger, too. His shoulders seemed wider and his chest and biceps were more developed than they'd been back then. And his thigh, pressed against hers, was thicker and more muscular now than it had been when they'd piled into one of these things with their friends ages ago.

"Okay, let's do this." She struck one silly pose after another as the camera flashed again and again.

Once the flashes stopped, Dexter moved to draw the curtain back and exit the booth, but Dakota grabbed his arm.

"Why do I feel like I'm the only one who's really into this?" She shoved his shoulder. "You're dialing it in here. I know you can do better than that. This is supposed to be fun, Mr. Serious. It isn't going on your LinkedIn profile."

Dexter laughed. "All right, all right. Just promise me that these photos won't end up on some I Hate My Ex website and we've got a deal."

"I wish I could claim not to believe a website like that existed," she said. "But I've done revenge porn stories, so

I'm honestly not surprised. And yes, you have my word. Are you ready for real now?"

He nodded. "Okay, let's do this."

They moved from one goofy pose to the next, laughing and giggling, until they turned in the same direction, his lips hovering just above hers. Dakota froze. Dex did, too. Both of them simply stared at the other as the flashes continued.

Her heart thumped hard against her chest. She should turn away. Pretend the moment hadn't happened. Especially after that kiss at his place. But she couldn't bear to be the first to pull away.

He'd been the one to put a stop to the kiss before. He would need to be the one to halt it again. Because no matter how much she knew that she shouldn't, she desperately wanted his lips on hers. His hands roaming her skin.

She swallowed hard, her skin overheating. Her cheeks felt like they were on fire. Dakota was about to pull away when Dexter suddenly cupped her cheek, dipped his head, and ghosted his lips over hers.

Her heart beat faster and her eyes fluttered closed as he pressed his mouth to hers, his kiss gentle and tentative. Building slow and steady. She sighed softly, her lips parting. Dexter slipped his tongue inside her mouth. The taste of the Long Island iced tea she'd consumed mingled with his cranberry juice and vodka.

Dakota's hands trembled and her body filled with heat. She lightly gripped his sides, needing his solidity to anchor her. Because she felt like she was floating away on a cloud of contentment. Like this couldn't possibly be real.

But it was. Every touch. Every gasp. Every sensation. The feel of his sensual lips against hers. The pressure of his thumb against her cheekbone. His fingers sifting through her hair. The glide of his tongue against her own. The tightening of her nipples against his hard chest. And the insistent throb between her thighs.

Dakota wanted to straddle Dexter's lap. To feel his steely length against her sex. To slip her hands below his waistband and stroke the velvety skin she remembered so well.

There was a hard knock against the wall, jolting them both.

"This is the photo booth, not a kissing booth. Get a room, you two," some smart-ass called from the other side of the black curtain. A din of laughter followed.

Dex released her, his gaze studying hers as they tried to catch their collective breath.

"Dakota, I'm...sorry." His expression was filled with regret, while she felt none.

She'd only wished that they'd been back in her hotel room, where no one would've bothered them. Dakota wiped the lip gloss from his mouth with her thumb, not acknowledging his apology.

Dexter groaned, adjusting himself before he slid the curtain back and stepped out. He reached for her hand and helped her out of the booth. Then he grabbed their photos out of the slot under the gazes of the long line of people waiting for their turn, many of whom flashed them knowing grins or hooted.

He took Dakota's hand and they headed toward the parking area. Suddenly, Dexter let go of her hand as if he'd only just realized that he was holding on to it. He gave her a quick, apologetic smile before pulling out his phone and opening the ride share app.

Neither of them spoke.

It was just as well. What was there to say that they didn't already know?

They were intensely attracted to each other. But Dexter only wanted friendship. She wanted more. Sex more, *not* relationship more. And yet they'd kissed again. Because she was apparently a masochist of the highest order.

"Our driver will be here in less than five minutes," Dexter informed her in a tone that was all corporate. There was none of the playfulness and familiarity that she'd heard for the past two days. A reminder that he was her boss and this was a business trip. That they'd crossed the line and they needed to step back into their designated boxes. Where things were nice and safe.

"Okay. Good." She nodded, acknowledging both messages.

Dakota took a subtle step away from Dexter. She folded her arms over her chest, suddenly self-conscious that the hardened tips of her breasts were visible through the fabric of the sleeveless, slate-blue knit tennis dress she wore.

There was just one more day of the festival. *And two more nights at the hotel*, the little voice inside her head reminded her.

She could get through one more day with Dex. This time they'd stay focused on their reason for coming to this little island in New England.

They weren't here for a walk down memory lane or to reconnect as friends. They were professionals, here to do a job. And that's what they would do.

Anything else would simply be a distraction, leaving one or both of them hurt.

When the vehicle arrived, Dakota slid inside first, scooting as far toward the other door as possible. She clicked her seat belt, then pulled out her phone to scroll through her work and personal emails.

The silence between the two of them seemed to echo off the interior of the small SUV as the driver chattered on obliviously. Dexter politely engaged with the man as the two talked about the festival. The best places to eat around town. How epic the after-parties were. But Dakota kept her attention on her phone.

When she raised her head, it was only to admire the boats gliding past in the bay or to watch the people milling about.

She could swear that the skin on her shoulders was burning from the heat of Dexter's gaze. But she couldn't bear the awkwardness of glancing over to see if she was right.

When they arrived at the hotel, she hopped out of the car while Dexter paid. She fled toward the lobby, trying to reach the elevator before he could catch up with her.

He'd made it clear he wasn't willing to risk his career for a tryst with her. She'd unequivocally affirmed her plans to leave Holly Grove Island.

There was no viable path for them.

What more did they need to say to each other?

"Dakota!" Dexter called her name twice more before she finally halted her steps, just before she'd reached the entrance of the hotel. She turned to him slowly.

Why does he have to look so damn good right now?

His expression was so sincere, like a hurt puppy. She couldn't hate the man, even if she wanted to. "Dakota, I'm sorry. I shouldn't have done that."

"You've made that abundantly clear. Boss plus employee equals career disaster. I get it." She managed a barely-there smile as she ran her fingers through her hair. "Meet you for breakfast downstairs again at nine?"

"Yeah, sure. That'd be great," he said absently, running a hand over his head.

"Good. I'll see you then." She turned on her heel and left. In the reflection of the glass entrance of the hotel, she saw him turn and walk away instead of following her inside.

A part of her was relieved they wouldn't have the awkward climb together in the hotel elevator. But another part of her hated to see him leave.

Chapter Twenty-Three

Dexter had gone for a walk around the small island town, so different from his own, to clear his head. Hungry again after their long day, he stopped in an Irish pub and grabbed a burger, the house fries, and a glass of Irish whiskey.

Despite the late hour, the place was bustling with patrons and there was a live band playing. He sighed as he bit into one of his steaming-hot fries.

Dakota would like this place.

She'd always loved little holes in the wall with amazing food and lots of character.

Dexter shook his head. He'd come here to forget about Dakota and that kiss—their second in two days—and yet she was all he could think about. The taste of her mouth, the softness of her lips, how it felt to have her body nestled against his.

He'd reminded himself of all the reasons he shouldn't want her. Reminded himself that while this might be a nostalgic fling for her, every moment, every touch, every kiss rocked him to his very foundation. Poked at the wound she'd left on his heart, making it bleed. After all this time,

Dakota Jones could still bring him to his knees with a look or the pout of her lush lips.

He'd known the photo booth was a bad idea. That it would take them too far down memory lane while putting them in dangerously close proximity. More than the car ride or their dance at the end of the show. But he hadn't known how to articulate the reasons they shouldn't do it without revealing the truth.

He was still very much in love with her.

Dexter wanted Dakota so badly he could taste it. And he didn't want one night or even a few months with her. He wanted to go to bed each night knowing her gorgeous face and sweet smile would be the first he'd see every morning. He wanted her honeyed voice to be the last one he heard every night.

He'd tossed and turned last night, visions of Dakota walking toward him on the beach in a white dress shifting through his head. And the dream that had shaken him most... the two of them in that glass elevator together with two kids of their own and another on the way. Happy and in love.

Dexter took another bite of his burger and fought off thoughts of Dakota, of the mistakes he'd made in the past, of the hard choice he was forced to make now.

Whatever this is, son... all I ask is that you be honest with her about it this time.

Oliver's words had been floating in his brain since their talk on the man's front porch.

Chief Jones hadn't tried to interfere or put a stop to the relationship they were rebuilding. Nor had he advised Dexter to stay away from his daughter, as he had long ago when he'd realized they'd become more than running partners and friends.

He'd simply asked that Dexter have the decency to be honest with his daughter. A fair request going forward. But telling her the truth about the past could hurt her in a way she might never recover from. He wouldn't do that to her. Not when there was no indication it would be worth the pain and anguish that he'd have to put her through.

Dexter paced his hotel room. He'd returned after his meal, showered, and hopped into bed. But he was restless, his brain going a mile a minute and his body aching with desire.

Maybe he'd been looking at this all wrong. Maybe this was something the two of them simply needed to get out of their systems so they could move on.

The dream is always better than the reality.

It was something his father had always said. The implication had depressed him. That the dream of having a wife and a family had been far more appealing to his father than reality and the countless responsibilities that went along with it. But over the years, he'd come to realize that there was quite often truth in those words.

The fantasy of being a star college football player was far different from his day-to-day life. The discipline, the grueling workouts, the sacrifices, the injuries. There had been relationships, jobs, and apartments that started off seemingly perfect. Glittering with hope and promise. Only to quickly devolve into the stuff of nightmares. Or at the very least, turn out to be a colossal disappointment.

Perhaps what was happening between him and Dakota was the same. A mirage masquerading as an oasis in the desert, it only *appeared* real. In reality, its quenching "waters" would be nothing more than a mouth filled with sand.

They were both consumed with their desire for one another. But would the reality live up to the fantasy?

Dexter stood in front of the mirror and glanced down at the small shaving kit he'd placed on the bathroom counter.

Maybe it was time to find out.

———

Dakota had returned to her room, hit the shower, then gone to bed. Okay, that wasn't exactly true. She'd gotten to know the removable showerhead quite intimately; then she'd gone to bed, hoping that the temporary high would stave off her cravings for the man she was obviously still incapable of resisting.

She'd actually managed to get a couple of hours of sleep. But then she'd awakened hungry and eaten the salsa and chips she'd picked up at the hotel shop earlier that evening. She'd managed to spill some of the salsa on her nice comfy pajamas, so she was glad she'd thrown another nightgown in her bag.

Dakota picked up the book about the history of the jazz festival she'd purchased in the gift shop the day before. She would read until she dozed off to sleep again.

There was a knock at her door. She checked her phone. It was well after midnight.

Maybe someone came *to the wrong room.*

She stayed in bed, not moving as she stared at the door to see if they would go away.

There was another, harder knock. This time she recognized the voice loudly whispering her name.

First she was surprised, then annoyed.

Dexter Roberts seemed determined to torture her. Why else would he come to her room this late when he'd made it clear he only wanted to be friends?

Dakota glanced down at her nightgown. It wasn't overtly sexy. But it wasn't the kind of thing she'd wear to answer the door.

She slipped out of bed and put on the robe hanging in the bathroom. Dakota loosely tied the belt around her waist, unlocked the door, and cracked it open just enough so Dexter could see her face.

His ruddy, copper-colored skin was flushed, and he stammered, then cleared his throat when he greeted her. But he didn't sound like he was drunk. He seemed...flustered. Nervous.

It was unlike Dexter. His claim to fame had been his unreadable expression. He'd been as good at shielding his true feelings as he'd been at surprising the defense with his signature no-look pass. He'd focus on one player downfield, as if he'd intended to throw the ball to him, only to pass it with pinpoint accuracy to an entirely different player.

Dakota opened the door wider. "Dex, what is it? What's wrong?"

"I know it's late," he said, not answering her question. "But is it okay if I come in?"

Dakota held open the door, allowing him to step inside. He wore a button-down shirt over a simple white tee and a pair of jeans.

Dexter closed the door behind him. But before she could ask again what was wrong, he'd cradled her face in his hands and captured her mouth in a hungry, deliberate kiss. The tentativeness he'd displayed in the photo booth was gone.

Dakota gasped in surprise. But after the initial shock, she pressed her fingertips to his back. She needed to know this was real. Not one of the dreams that had left her tossing and turning in bed for the past two nights.

He tipped her head back, sweeping his tongue inside her mouth and gliding it along hers as he kissed her harder and deeper. She worried that this kiss would end in the same frustrating stalemate as the others. But then he loosened her robe and slipped his large hands beneath the garment as he pulled her to him.

"I want you, Dakota. Here. Now." His voice quaked with a need that made her tremble and the space between her thighs ache for him. He dropped a featherlight kiss on the shell of her ear, sending a shiver down her spine.

"Yes." She nodded, wetting her lips with her tongue. "Please."

His mouth quirked in a lopsided smile as he leaned in and nibbled on her lower lip. He sucked it between his, then kissed her again. One hand braced her back. The other glided over her bottom. He gripped her flesh, bringing her body flush against his.

Dexter's growing length pressed hard against her belly, evoking a quiet gasp from her, which his greedy kiss swallowed before the sound could escape her lips.

A jolt of electricity trailed down her arms and legs, causing a steady pulse between her thighs and the beading of her sensitive nipples, crushed against the hardness of his chest.

Dakota slipped one shoulder out of the robe, and Dexter shoved the fabric off the other shoulder, helping her shrug off the garment. She returned the favor by helping him out of the button-down and T-shirt. Dakota took a moment to admire his strong chest and the fine smattering of hair that trailed down below his waistband.

She looped her arms around Dexter's neck, crushing her mouth against his, hungry for more of his kiss. He palmed her bottom, hauling her against his hardened length. Dexter groaned, deepening their increasingly desperate kiss.

The carnal sound had always given her a heady sense of power over him. He was bigger, faster, taller. But her touch and kiss brought such a strong, disciplined man to his knees.

Dexter lifted her, and she wrapped her legs around his waist as he carried her to the bed, a few feet away. He deposited her there, crawling onto the bed after her.

"You smell like coconut and vanilla," he murmured as he kissed her shoulder.

"It's my body wash." Her response was automatic, though she doubted he cared about such an insignificant detail at a time like this. "Glad you like it."

"Almost as much as the woman wearing it." His beard abraded her skin as he trailed hot kisses along her neck. "But you know what I can't stop wondering?"

She shook her head, unable to form a string of intelligible words. He'd found that spot on her neck that was an erogenous zone for her. That turned her blood to hot, molten lava and rendered her incapable of basic speech and sensible decisions.

"For the past month I've been wondering if you taste as good as you look."

Oh shit.

She nearly came undone at the mere thought. She and Dex had been young, her sexual experience limited to him. They'd never done *that*. The mere thought of his lips on her there made her heated skin tingle with anticipation.

"I've been wondering the same about you." She surveyed the beautiful man hovering over her. She inhaled his intoxicating scent, her hands roaming the expanse of his strong chest.

Dexter's mouth curled in a wicked smile that sent tingles down her spine. "Me first."

He pressed hot, openmouthed kisses to her chest. Then he helped her lift the nightgown over her head, tossing it onto the floor before he resumed the trail down her body. He sucked her taut, sensitive nipples, grazing them gently with his teeth before soothing them with a lap of his tongue and a tender kiss. He lavished attention on one, then the other before gliding down her body, laying erotic kisses on her belly, then dipping lower.

The sound of her heartbeat filled her ears and her breath came harder and faster as he neared the damp space desperately longing for his mouth.

Every inch of her skin was so sensitive, he could probably blow on her aching clit and she would shatter into a million satisfied pieces. He seemed fully aware of how desperately she needed him there. He teased her with slow, lingering kisses. Seemed to enjoy heightening her anticipation. To relish every murmur as he kissed a path down her body. He hooked his thumbs in the waistband of her panties, tugging the silky fabric down her legs. She lifted her hips, permitting him to remove the barrier to his touch.

He shifted so his shoulders were beneath her thighs as he kissed lower and lower, still avoiding the slick, sensitive bud. Her pulse raced and her body trembled with anticipation.

Finally, he licked her there.

"Oh God," she whimpered. The first flick of his tongue sent a wave of pleasure through her, her belly tensing. Back arched and pulse pounding, she gripped the sheets, riding the delicious sensations until he'd taken her over the edge, her body quivering and spent.

Dex sighed contentedly, then kissed his way back up her body, over her belly, then through the valley between her breasts. He nibbled on her neck, then grazed the skin behind her ear.

Dakota brushed her fingertips over his skin, sweeping them up his spine as he lay beside her wearing a satisfied smile.

"That was...amazing." She dragged a thumb along his lower lip, then pressed her mouth to his.

He grinned, a mischievous glint in his dark eyes. He whispered gruffly, "Babe, that was only the beginning."

———

Dexter stood, retrieving the strip of foil packets from his back pocket. He tossed them on the bedside table, then he shed his remaining clothing and sheathed himself.

He was revved up enough from the way Dakota had fallen apart after he took her over the edge with his mouth. But watching her appreciative stare as her breath hitched turned him on in a way words couldn't describe. Her eyes followed the gentle bobbing of his painfully hard length with every movement.

"He missed you, too," Dex said as he climbed beneath the covers beside her.

"Oh yeah? On a scale of one to ten, how much would you say he missed me?"

"Definitely a twenty." He kissed her neck.

"Not mathematically possible," she countered, giggling as he nibbled on the tender flesh behind her ear.

"But dickmatically possible," he assured her.

Dakota dissolved into laughter.

He sifted her shiny, mahogany curls through his fingers.

"A lesser man's confidence might be shaken by the giggling," he teased.

Her smile deepened as she turned to face him. "Which is why I make it a policy never to deal with *lesser* men."

"Touché." He pressed a soft kiss to her lips, then another.

He'd always loved kissing Dakota. But there was something truly incredible about the ones they'd shared these past few days. Each touch of their lips ignited a fire inside him, making him crazy with need. Desperate with want.

Dakota was the first woman he'd ever loved. She had a power over him no other woman possessed. That no other woman ever would.

He tangled his fingers in the curls he'd always adored. Reveled in the delicious sensation of Dakota's soft, bare skin against his. Without breaking their kiss, he found the space between her thighs. He delved one finger, then another inside her slick channel. His thumb teased the taut, sensitive bundle of nerves as he glided his fingers in and out of her. He swallowed every moan, every curse coming from her lips.

Dakota ground her hips against his hand, her breathing increasingly shallow, her gasps and soft murmurs intensifying. The movement of her hips became more demanding with every stroke. She gripped his shoulders, her fingernails biting into his flesh, straddling the line between pain and pleasure, without breaking the skin.

He curled his fingers inside her. She sucked in a deep breath, her eyes widening as her mouth formed a sensual little O. She tensed, her legs quivering as she called out his name.

There is no sweeter sound.

Dex kissed her. Cradled her as she slowly descended. Positioned himself at her entrance and savored every ounce of pleasure as he inched inside her. He drove his hips forward, intoxicated by the overpowering sensation as her body welcomed his.

God, he loved that blissful expression on her gorgeous face.

If only for tonight, Dakota was his again.

He clasped their joined hands above her head as they moved together. Until he tumbled over the edge, free-falling into a deep abyss of pleasure that rocked him to his very core.

Dexter rolled onto his back and gathered her in his arms. He kissed her forehead, damp with perspiration.

He loved this woman. Wanted her in his life forever. But if all they had was tonight, he would never, ever regret it.

Chapter Twenty-Four

Beams of sunlight broke through the curtains and fell across Dakota's face, waking her. Her eyelids fluttered as she slowly regained consciousness. She rolled onto her back and sighed contentedly. Then eyes fully open, she jerked to a sitting position.

Dexter.

She'd slept with Dexter Roberts. Not in her head, where it was safe and no one need know. In the *real* world, where there were consequences and repercussions.

Dakota checked her phone. It wasn't quite seven thirty, and Dex was gone. The scent of his skin still clung to the pillow and sheets. His clothes were gone, too, except for the T-shirt hanging on the edge of the chair.

She was still very naked. Climbing out of bed, she pulled on his T-shirt and stumbled to the bathroom, groggy and half-awake. She'd neglected to put on her silk bonnet, so her curls were a tangled mess. She washed her face and brushed her teeth.

Dakota pressed a hand to her trembling belly as she recalled the comfort, warmth, and intimacy she'd felt falling asleep in Dexter's arms last night. Before they'd been teenagers, both still living with their parents. So sleeping over was something they hadn't done. Her chest expanded at the memory of her cheek pressed to his heart as he snored quietly after drifting off.

Had he left in the middle of the night after she'd fallen asleep? Or early this morning?

Either way, he'd dipped, avoiding the awkward morning-after conversation.

And maybe that wasn't such a bad idea after all.

Dakota took a quick shower, then slipped on her robe. The click of the lock drew her attention to the door as it swung open.

Dexter stepped inside. Handsome, beard trimmed, and smelling like he'd just stepped out of the shower himself. He set down a bag and a tray with two steaming cups of coffee.

Her heart raced as she stood there staring at him, not quite sure what to say.

"Hey." She gave him an awkward, low wave.

"Hey." He smiled, leaning down to kiss her cheek.

The chaste kiss felt odd after their sensual night together. What did it mean?

"I thought you went back to your room." She fiddled with the belt on her robe.

"I did. I left a little before seven to shower, shave, and get ready. I hoped to get back here in time to bring you breakfast in bed." He held up the bag. "I hope you still like everything bagels with cream cheese."

You remembered.

"I do. Thank you." She opened the bag and removed the warm, freshly toasted bagel. "And I assume one of those is for me." She indicated the two beverages.

"Yes." He checked the labels on the cups and handed

one to her. "Thought you might like the crème brûlée latte."

Her smile deepened and her tummy went all fluttery.

It's just coffee and a bagel, girl. Don't get so emotional.

"Excellent choice. Thanks, Dex." She folded one leg beneath her and sat on the edge of the bed, while he sat at the little desk that seemed barely big enough for his large frame. The amusing image alleviated a little of the tension in her chest.

Morning-after small talk was the absolute worst, even with someone she knew as well as Dexter. Still, she was determined not to make this awkward. If he didn't want to discuss last night or what it meant, they didn't have to. If he wanted to resume a just-friends, business-only relationship, they could do that, too. And if he wanted a replay of last night's toe-tingling, back-breaking, make-you-scream-my-name performance...well, her mother didn't raise any fools. She was *definitely* down for that.

Either way, she wouldn't put any pressure on him. And she wouldn't allow this—whatever it was and whatever it meant—to interfere with their stellar working relationship.

"Fantastic bagel," she mumbled, her mouth half-full. "Here's what I was thinking we should tackle today..."

They planned the day and discussed the project over their bagels and coffee. As if she weren't completely naked underneath her robe. As if they hadn't spent the previous night making love in the bed she was sitting on, the scent of their sex still lingering in the air.

When they'd finished eating, he gathered the trash and dumped it. Then he turned back to her. "I guess we should talk about last night."

"I guess we should." Dakota smoothed the robe over her legs, making sure nothing was exposed. "And maybe I should start by saying that last night was absolutely incredible. In fact, this entire weekend has been amazing."

"But…" He furrowed his brow, his jaw tense.

She reached for his hand, holding it in hers. "But in a few months, I'll be gone, and I have no idea exactly where I'll end up. So if you're looking for a relationship…"

"And what if I'm not?" Dexter's lowered gaze followed his thumb as it stroked the back of her hand. But even without seeing his face, she could feel his disappointment.

"You'd be open to keeping this casual?" She lifted his chin, needing to see his eyes.

He shrugged after a long pause. "Why not? We're both adults, and this is what we both want. Maybe we just need to get each other out of our systems. Gain some closure."

The words were right, but his tone was unconvincing. But would it be wrong of her to accept him at his word?

Dakota was enjoying getting to know Dex again. And she'd enjoyed every minute of their weekend together. Maybe he had a point. They could be grown-ups about this. Have fun and enjoy each other's company. Then walk away as friends.

Dexter was an amazing man. Sweet, funny, thoughtful, brilliant, and creative. If she'd planned to stay on Holly Grove Island, she'd jump at the prospect of a second chance with him. Because she really did care for him. But she wasn't staying. And Dexter wouldn't leave.

"If you're *really* not looking for a relationship right now, I'd be open to a repeat of last night." Her mouth twisted in a naughty grin. "And not just for the weekend."

He kissed her palm, but his half smile didn't reach his dark eyes. "Then, it's settled."

"What about your job?" Dakota cupped his cheek, his

beard tickling her palm. "As much as I want this, Dex, I can't let you jeopardize your career for a fling with me."

Dex nodded reluctantly. His brows knitted. "Then we keep this between us."

"If that's not something you can deal with, Dexter, I understand." Dakota pressed a kiss to his lips, hoping he wouldn't say no.

"I can." He pulled her closer to the edge of the bed and kissed her again.

Dakota pretended not to notice the pained look in his eyes or the furrowing of his brows that indicated otherwise. She needed to believe that this time, when they parted ways, everything would work out fine...for both of them.

"By the way, here's your spare room key. I borrowed it this morning." He produced the keycard from his back pocket.

"Keep it." Dakota stood in front of him, loosened the belt, and let her robe drift to the floor. "I have a feeling you'll need it again."

———

Dexter lay awake with Dakota sleeping in his arms after their final day at the festival. They'd made love again that morning after their talk. Had he known she wasn't wearing a stitch of clothing beneath that robe, he'd probably have tumbled into bed with her the moment he'd returned and found her awake.

They'd both been reluctant to leave her room. But this was a business trip. And the resort had footed the bill for them to attend all three days of the event. So they managed to tear themselves from the bed, shower together, get dressed, and return to the festival grounds.

She looked gorgeous in a floral, sunny yellow backless dress. He hadn't been able to resist putting a hand on her waist as he guided her through the crowd, caressing the soft, smooth skin of her back with the pad of his thumb.

Dakota had donned her straw fedora and a pair of dark shades. He'd worn his mirrored sunglasses and a baseball cap pulled down over his head. They'd strolled through the festival grounds, alternating between walking hand in hand or with his arm wrapped around her waist, like they had when they were two starry-eyed teens in love.

His chest flooded with warmth and his heart swelled with affection for Dakota. But he silently reminded himself that, for her, this was neither love nor a relationship. Because in a few months, she'd move on. So the depth of his feelings for her didn't matter.

For Dakota, this was a short-lived fling. A little fun before she moved on with the rest of her life. For him, this was a taste of everything he'd hoped for when Dakota had returned to town. Only it was temporary, like her employment at the resort and his position as the DOO.

He should be glad Dakota wanted to keep their relationship short-term and a secret. It saved him from having to choose between her and the position he'd worked so hard for.

Dakota stirred in his arms, as if she could sense how perturbed he was as he lay awake, trying to convince himself that it wouldn't hurt like hell when he had to let her go.

But maybe he'd finally be able to give up chasing the ghost of relationships past and move on with the rest of his life. A life without the one woman he wanted more than anything.

Chapter Twenty-Five

◆━━●━━◆

Dakota spread out her blanket and flopped down in the beach chair beside Sinclair's on a Saturday afternoon. She pulled down the wide-brim fedora hat Dexter had bought her at the festival and readjusted her shades.

"What's with the movie-star-in-hiding look?" Sin asked. "Is the paparazzi out?"

"No. Why?" Dakota sat up quickly, her pulse racing as she glanced up and down the beach.

"It was a joke, hon. Relax." Sin shoved her shoulder; then she pulled a cranberry-walnut chicken-salad sandwich on a croissant wrapped in plastic out of her bag and waved it. "Hungry? Or did Ms. Lila already bring y'all something to eat last night?"

Dakota thanked her friend for the sandwich and nodded. "Yes, she did." She unwrapped her sandwich. "And honestly, I felt like a third wheel on their date."

Her father had had his surgery in Wilmington two weeks ago. Ms. Lila had spent most of the day of the operation at the hospital with Dakota, keeping her company. And she'd been fussing over her father and bringing him specially made, off-menu meals since.

Sin unwrapped her own sandwich. "So they're finally admitting that they're dating now?"

"Not exactly. He refers to her as his *lady friend* and says they just really enjoy each other's company. Then he finds a way to change the subject."

"Well, that's progress, kind of...I guess." Sinclair nibbled on her sandwich. "How long before you need to go back home and check on your dad?"

"I'm off duty. Ms. Lila is playing nurse this afternoon." Dakota cringed the moment she said the words, and her friend descended into raucous laughter. "God, that sounded so much better in my head."

Now she'd never scrub the idea of her father and Ms. Lila playing doctor from her brain.

"You've been back home a couple months now. I'd'a thought you'd be used to the idea of Ms. Lila being your new stepmama by now."

Dakota shot her friend a look.

"What? You've always liked Ms. Lila," Sin said.

"I still do, and like I said, this isn't about me. I don't think my dad is ready to move on." Dakota bit into her croissant. It was amazing.

"Your dad was super supportive and understanding when you told him the truth about Marcello, right?" Sin reminded her. "So maybe you can return the favor by helping him to move on. Maybe he's ready but he doesn't know how. Or maybe he's concerned about how you and Shay will react."

Dakota chewed thoughtfully as she considered her friend's words. Telling her father the truth about what had happened in New York and why she'd kept it from him had been one of the most difficult conversations she'd ever had. She'd expected him to be angry and disappointed. For him to say that he'd told her so about the television industry or life in New York. But he hadn't done any of that. He'd hugged her tight and told her that he loved her and that none of what had happened changed how proud he was of her. And he'd assured her that she was welcome to stay with him for as long as she liked.

At the hospital, the day of the surgery, she'd confessed the truth to Ms. Lila, too. The only person she hadn't told was Dexter, despite the fact that they'd been secretly seeing each other since their trip to New England.

While she and Dex were at work, or out with mutual friends, they carried on as coworkers and old friends. Except for a lingering touch here or the rare stolen kiss, there was no indication of the raging desire between them. And they hadn't told anyone else. Not even Sin.

She'd even spent two of the three nights her father had stayed over at the hospital following his surgery at Dexter's place.

As Sin prattled on, Dakota was lost in daydreaming about Dex. Remembering when he'd made breakfast for her at his condo. Something she hoped he'd be able to do again soon, but this time after she'd awakened in his bed.

"You didn't hear a word I said, did you?" Sin stared at her, one of her perfectly arched eyebrows cocked.

"I did. You said…umm…okay, what was it you were saying?"

"What's going on with you, Dakota?"

"I've been a little worried about my dad because of the surgery. But other than that, everything's fine." Dakota nibbled on her sandwich.

"And how is work going? You haven't talked much about your trip with Dexter, since you've been back," Sin said.

Dakota averted her gaze from her friend's, her cheeks hot. "Work is good."

Sin tilted her head, studying Dakota for a moment. Suddenly her friend's eyes widened. "Wait. That's it, isn't it? You two hooked up during your trip, didn't you?"

Dakota chewed slowly, her brain churning. She deserved some privacy, even in their little town. But her only options were to lie to Sin or come clean. She chose the latter.

"Yes." Dakota made the admission under her breath.

Sin started squealing like a prize hog at the county fair.

Dakota squeezed her friend's arm. "You *cannot* tell anyone about this, Sin. There could be real blowback for Dex at his job if anyone found out."

"Right, of course. I'm just so glad that the two of you are back together—"

"We're not *together* together, Sin," Dakota assured her.

"So if it's not a relationship, what would you call it?" Sin pushed her shades on top of her head and peered at Dakota.

"It's more of a situationship." Dakota shrugged. "It's nothing serious, and there's no need to start shopping for bridesmaid dresses, if that's what you're thinking."

"First: disappointing. I've proven that I look good in even the butt-ugliest of bridesmaids dresses." Sin batted her eyelashes and posed, making Dakota laugh, too. "Second: Does Dexter know that he's in a…what did you call it again…a *situationship*?"

"Yes. I mean…I think so. We talked about it. About why I wasn't looking for a relationship. Why we needed to keep things on the down low. And we both agreed." Dakota swigged some of her sweet tea.

"Hmm…I'm guessing it went like this…You told Dexter you weren't looking for anything serious right now.

So rather than losing you, the option behind door number one, Dex agreed to this little fling y'all *think* you're having that was behind door number two. Sound about right?"

"No—I mean...yes. Kind of," Dakota stammered. "I certainly didn't trick him into this arrangement, if that's what you're implying."

"Of course not, sweetie. All I'm saying is that Dexter Roberts has been waiting nearly two decades for a second chance with the love of his life." Sin shrugged. "Can't blame the boy for snatching up the crumbs you offered him."

"Did Dexter say I was the love of his life?" Dakota's throat suddenly felt dry.

"He didn't need to, honey. It's in the eyes." She waved two fingers that formed a V in front of hers for emphasis. "Sadly, you and Dex are 'bout the only folks in town who can't see it." She squeezed Dakota's arm. "Look, sweetie, no one would like to see the two of you together again more than me. But I don't want to see either of you get hurt. So please be completely honest with each other about where this is going."

"You're a good friend, Sinclair."

"True." Sinclair batted her lashes and struck her best Southern belle pose. "But my motives here are completely selfish. I just got my best friend back. I can't afford for things to blow up between you two again." Sin took a sip of her tea, then slipped her shades back on.

"I won't let that happen again, Sin. I promise."

"I know you won't." Her friend leaned back in her beach chair. "Because I will hunt your tail down wherever you go. We are *not* breaking up the band again. Period. No, ma'am!"

Dakota lay back in her chair, too. She couldn't help

glancing toward Sin's building in the direction of Dexter's condo on the second floor, wondering if he was home.

They hadn't managed to see each other outside of work since her father had returned home from his surgery. They'd been communicating mostly via text message, but she missed him desperately. She was tempted to show up at his door unannounced.

"Saw his car pull out of the parking lot this morning," Sin said without turning her head.

"How do you do that?" Dakota asked.

"Can't give up all my trade secrets, darlin'." Sin shrugged. "And I know you and I had planned a little movie marathon later, but I promise not to whine about Dex friend-jacking you if you decide you'd rather spend the evening with him. At least, I won't complain about it this time. If it becomes a habit, we're gon' have to negotiate friend time."

"Thank you for understanding, Sin."

Dakota picked up her phone and typed out a text message to Dexter. He replied almost immediately. He was at his mother's house, but he was excited to see her at his place later that night. Dakota's heart skipped a beat, and she couldn't help smiling.

She settled back in her beach chair and turned to watch as the waves licked the shore, Sin's words replaying in her head.

Dexter Roberts has probably been waiting nearly two decades for a second chance with the love of his life.

Was she really the love of Dexter's life? Was he hers?

Long ago, she'd been sure that he was. That was why she'd been so angry all these years. What they'd had was special, and he'd thrown it away. But that morning at his condo, when he'd confessed that he hadn't wanted her to give up her dream for him, his words had struck a nerve.

Dexter was right. She would've regretted giving up her ambitions for him. She only wished she could've had the career she wanted and the man she loved, too.

———

"So are we just going to keep pretending that bounce in your step for the past couple of weeks isn't because of your little weekend getaway with Dakota?" Emerie Roberts opened the box containing a new air filter for her car and handed it to Dex.

"The festival was amazing," Dex said, glad he was nearly finished changing the oil in his sister's car. Em had been pestering him about Dakota since that night at the Foxhole. When he and Dakota had returned from the trip to the jazz festival in New England, she'd redoubled her efforts. "And it's an excellent model for what we plan to do here. It's even on an island. It was helpful to be able to see the potential of an event like that."

"And it seems the two of you got along pretty well. I haven't seen you this happy in a really long time," Emerie said gleefully.

Dexter was trying to be the patient older brother, but he had his limits. He knew that his sister had always liked Dakota and that she was excited about the prospect of the two of them getting back together. But they'd agreed to keep their relationship under wraps, and with good reason. His career was on the line. So he had to keep hoping that his petulant little sister would eventually grow bored or take a hint.

"We've been getting along well enough since she returned to the island." He shrugged as if it were no big deal. "And yes, working together has helped."

"So, are you two a couple now, or what?" Em burst into a fit of giggles when he gave her his *that's enough* look. "It's a fair question," she said. "You can tell me. I won't say anything."

"Except to your best friend, Nick, who would probably mention it to his mother, who would then tell Dakota's father—who lives next door." Dex pulled a rag from his back pocket and cleaned up Em's engine. "Do you see where I'm going with this?"

"What I got out of that little story is that you'll neither confirm nor deny couplehood. In my book, that's a yes every day of the week." Em folded her arms, looking smug.

"Em." Dex lowered his voice. "I'm Dakota's superior. Us dating...it wouldn't be a good look. Especially when I'm essentially on probation for this position."

"I hadn't thought of that. That sucks." Em frowned. "But it just means that the two of you have to be discreet about your relationship for now."

"There is no..." Dex released a slow breath and lowered his voice again. "There is no relationship," he said. "Even if I was interested in one, hypothetically speaking, Dakota isn't, and she plans to leave the island as soon as Oliver is one hundred percent."

"So this is basically a vacation fling, then?" Em folded one arm across her body as she gripped her chin. "Problematic. Not because I have a problem with hookups overall—"

"For the record, *not* something I needed to know." Dex gave Em a pointed look.

"Like I was saying," she continued, unbothered. "It's not the principle of the matter that worries me. It's that...well, does she know?" Em asked.

"Does she know what?"

"Does Dakota know that you're still in love with her?"

Heat swarmed over Dexter's face, and it felt like he'd been punched in the gut. He stuck his head under the hood of Em's car again and checked the windshield wiper fluid level. "That's enough of playing nosy kid sister, Em. I can take care of myself."

"I know you can." His sister sighed. "You're a good guy, Dex. And I'm not saying that because you're my big brother. You're always looking out for everyone else. Digging the rest of us out of jams. Fixing things for us. Maybe it's time someone started looking out for you."

"That's sweet, Em. It means a lot, but I'm fine." Dex topped off the windshield wiper fluid, his back to his sister.

He really did appreciate the sentiment. If it were up to him, he'd shout to the rooftops that he was in love with Dakota. Take her out every chance he got. Go to sleep with her each night and wake up beside her each morning. But it wasn't that simple. And the way things stood right now, the more people who knew about them, the more chance that word would get back to the wrong people. It could spell trouble for both of them.

"You should tell her, Dex. We don't get many second chances in life. Not for things that really count. Don't let Dakota walk away without telling her how you really feel. You'll never forgive yourself if you do."

Dexter sighed quietly and clenched his teeth. When had his little sister gotten so damn wise? She was dropping the kind of knowledge he'd expect from his mother. More importantly, Emerie was right about him regretting it if he didn't tell Dakota how he felt. Still, he wasn't willing to tell Em that explicitly.

Instead, he glanced over his shoulder and acknowledged

his sister's plea with a small nod before turning and screwing the top back on the windshield wiper fluid bottle.

His phone vibrated. He pulled it from his pocket and read the message that flashed on the phone's lock screen.

At the beach with Sin. If you're not busy later, would love to come over to your place tonight. Miss you.

An involuntary smile slowly spread across Dexter's face. His heart danced at the thought of spending some alone time with the woman who held his heart in the palm of her hand. Even if Dakota seemed completely oblivious to that fact.

Something had slowly shifted since Dakota had returned to the island. Prior to her arrival in town, he wouldn't have considered himself miserable or even unhappy. But he had become complacent. He was preoccupied with work and seeing after his mother and sister. Enjoyed spending time with his nieces and nephews and playing at the Foxhole once a month with the band. So he hadn't even realized that there was something missing in his life. That despite being surrounded by people, many of whom he loved, there was a loneliness and a wanting inside him that he kept himself busy enough to ignore.

But being with Dakota had laid that deficit bare. Exposed the feelings he'd tried so hard to bury. He needed love and companionship. The kind he'd really only experienced once in his life. And that had been with her. The girl he'd let get away. The one woman he'd never been able to forget.

He was in love with Dakota and being with her made him happy. Em was right on that count, too. Maybe he'd get shot down if he told Dakota how he felt about her, but at least he'd have no regrets.

——

Dakota shrugged on Dexter's discarded T-shirt and followed the trail of clothing that led from Dex's master bedroom back to the front door, stooping to collect each piece. She stacked them on the chair while she grabbed two bottles of water from the fridge and made a plate of grapes, cherries, and orange slices.

"Fuel and rehydration." Dex slid back under the covers after slipping out of the master bathroom. "Great idea."

She handed him the plate and bottles of water before dropping their discarded clothing onto a chair.

"Okay, so I might've been a tiny bit eager to get you into bed." Dexter nodded toward the pile of clothing they'd begun discarding the moment she entered his condo. He set the water bottles and tray on his bedside table, then pulled her down onto his lap, so she was straddling him. He pushed her loose curls aside and kissed her neck. "But you can't blame a brother for missing you."

Dakota looped her arms around his neck and pressed her forehead to his momentarily. She placed a soft, lingering kiss to his lips. "I missed you, too. But there's something I need to tell you."

"What is it, Dakota?" He studied her with anticipation, not with the usual panic she'd seen in men's eyes whenever a woman said she needed to talk.

"I didn't intend to tell Sin about us, but she's known both of us forever, so she figured it out. But I made her promise not to tell anyone. She understands the stakes for you, so I know she won't say anything."

"Well, I guess there's a theme today because Em figured it out, too," Dexter said. "She also knows it could jeopardize my job, so she won't tell anyone else."

Dakota was relieved that Dex wasn't upset that she'd confirmed Sin's suspicions. And there was a part of her that was glad Sin knew. Dakota had loved spending that last day at the festival holding hands and being affectionate with Dexter. She'd enjoyed the comfort of his embrace. The way they'd stolen kisses whenever they could. And the way he'd looked at her...he made her feel like she was the center of his universe. The way she thought she'd once been. Back when he was the center of hers.

Dexter slipped the T-shirt over her head, glided his fingers into her hair, and pulled her mouth to his. There was so much passion and hunger in his kiss. Like he was determined to make up for every single lost moment between them.

Dakota's stomach fluttered in response, and her heartbeat quickened. She ached with want. As if they hadn't just made love a short time ago.

She gasped against his mouth when Dexter suddenly flicked one stiff peak with his thumb. He broke their kiss, closing his warm mouth over her other breast.

Dakota shuddered at the sensation of his tongue on her heated skin and arched her back, giving him better access. Bracing her hands on his strong shoulders, she shifted to her knees on either side of him as she glided her sex over his hardened length, the outline visible through his black boxer briefs. Dakota whimpered with pleasure at the sensation, and she relished how the movement elicited a groan from deep inside his chest.

They'd had hot, passionate sex against the living room wall while they were both still fully clothed nearly the instant she'd entered the condo. Then they'd fumbled their way into the bedroom, making out and shedding their clothing along the way.

She shouldn't be ravenous for him again, but she was. Dakota wanted Dexter to kiss and make love to her. To make up for the decade and a half they'd spent apart. To establish memories she could cling to once they went their separate ways.

Dexter flipped her over onto her back. He shed his boxers, reached into the bedside table for one of the foil packets, and sheathed himself. He captured her mouth in a greedy, devouring kiss. Both of them were ever aware of the short-lived nature of their affair and the underlying urgency to make every stolen moment together count.

When he slid inside her, she reveled in the sensation of being filled by him. The taste of his kiss. The way the hair on his bare chest abraded her skin. He reached between them, his fingers strumming the sensitive bundle of nerves like the strings of a guitar. Until she fell apart in his arms, her body tensing and her legs trembling as she was overcome by waves of pleasure. His hips moved slowly and steadily, his brows furrowed and his gaze intense, until he followed her over the cliff, his body stiffening and a low moan emanating from his sensual lips as he cursed softly and called her name.

Dex fell back onto the pillow beside Dakota, his chest heaving, and his breathing labored. She sank into the comfort of his embrace as he wrapped her in his arms and pulled her closer, their bodies slick with sweat despite the cool temperature in the room.

"That was...whew..." Dex blew out a long breath and sighed.

"I know, right?" Dakota pressed her cheek to his chest, her eyes drifting closed as she listened to the slowing of his erratic heartbeat. "Back then it was great, but this…is…amazing. I'm pretty sure you've ruined me for all other men."

"Good." He raked his fingers through her hair, worn in loose, natural curls, then kissed the top of her head. "Because you're the only woman I want in my bed, Dakota."

Everything about their afternoon together was perfect. Part of her wished she could lie there blissfully in Dexter's arms forever. But another part feared that if she lay there a moment longer, she would never be able to bear their impending separation.

Dexter distracted her from the somber thoughts swirling inside her head when he rubbed her back and hugged her to him one more time before excusing himself from the room. Dakota rolled over, already missing his warmth and scent, the solidity of his firm chest, and the comfort of his strong arms. A stark reminder of the fleeting nature of the relationship that had quickly become so important to her.

Suddenly her chest ached, and she blinked back the tears stinging her eyes.

As amazing as the past few weeks with Dex had been, what they shared was only temporary. And this time, when they went their separate ways, she was determined to walk away with her heart intact.

———

When Dexter returned from the bathroom, Dakota had put on her panties and bra and she was digging through the clothes piled on the chair.

"You're leaving?"

Dakota jumped at the sound of his voice. As if she'd hoped to get dressed and slip out before he'd returned.

"I thought I'd stop at the ice cream shop and pick up

a pint of black walnut ice cream for my dad before they close." She tugged her sundress over her head, then stepped into one sandal, then the other. "He's been a model patient, so I'd like to do something nice for him."

The dreamy gaze Dakota had given him moments ago was gone, replaced by a distant look in eyes that wouldn't meet his. Her posture suddenly seemed stiff and her speech tense.

What the hell happened in the five minutes since I left the room?

"I was hoping you'd stay the night." He tugged on his boxers and tried his best to mask his disappointment by keeping his voice even, despite the growing panic he felt inside. Dakota's sudden need to escape felt like it was about so much more than Dakota deciding to reward her father with his favorite ice cream. It felt like a deliberate choice to pull away from him.

"That sounds really nice." She smiled sadly as she braced her hands on his bare chest and lifted onto her toes to press a quick kiss to his lips. "Rain check?"

"I... Yeah, sure," he stammered, running a hand over his head. He sighed heavily, then forced a wooden smile. "I'll make you breakfast again. This time in bed."

He'd wanted to talk to Dakota. To level with her about his feelings. And if she was receptive to the idea of moving this from a fling to an actual relationship... well, then he would have to be honest about what happened seventeen years ago. To tell her the *whole* truth. Because they couldn't start a serious relationship with that secret hanging over them.

"What's wrong, Dex?" She narrowed her gaze. "You look like you lost your best friend."

He did—seventeen years ago.

Don't let Dakota walk away without telling her how you really feel.

"Dakota, I love you." The words came out in a breathy whisper. His heart raced and the sound of rushing blood filled his ears. He stroked her cheek and swallowed what felt like a pebble in his suddenly dry throat. "I've never stopped loving you. And these past weeks have only confirmed what I'd already been feeling since you returned to town."

"Dex, that's…really sweet, I…" Her eyes lit up, a soft smile curving her sensual lips. But then suddenly, her brows furrowed, and her eyes were shiny with what looked like unshed tears. She blinked rapidly, averting her gaze as she sank her teeth into her lower lip. "But you know I can't stay. I was clear about that."

"I haven't always lived here on the island, you know," he reminded her. The words weren't something he'd contemplated. In fact, they were the very opposite of everything he'd been trying so very hard to achieve in his career. But faced with the reality of losing Dakota again, it was his only play.

Seventeen years ago, Dakota had been prepared to make a huge sacrifice to support his dream. He loved her and was determined to have her in his life. So why wouldn't he be willing to do the same for her now?

"I know, but you've worked so hard to get back here. You even managed to land the exact job you wanted." She shook her head. "Dex, I can't take that away from you."

"Dakota…" He reached for her, his voice faint.

"I have to go, but we can talk about this more later. I'm not leaving anytime soon."

"Of course." He tried to force a smile, but he couldn't manage it. Not when her words seemed so final.

She pressed a kiss to his lips, grabbed her purse, and slipped out the door.

Dexter stood frozen, his muscles suddenly tense, brows furrowed and his throat tight. His lungs constricted in his chest, and for a moment it seemed his heart beat more slowly.

"Shit." He rubbed his forehead, then locked the front door behind her.

He shut his eyes against the vision of her leaving playing on a loop in his head.

He'd completely botched it. He'd made his fumbling, awkward plea, and she'd rejected it. Dakota wouldn't even entertain his offer to leave the island with her. A spontaneous declaration that had surprised even him.

Maybe if he'd waited longer or told her in a more romantic setting, she would've reconsidered. Or maybe there was nothing he could ever say that would induce Dakota to stay.

Chapter Twenty-Six

Dakota walked up to Helene's Homemade—the storied ice cream shop on Main Street that was practically synonymous with summer for any kid who grew up on the island. The place was a favorite of both native islanders and tourists. Owned by the third generation of a local family, Helene's had been around since long before Dakota was born.

The small, locally owned shop had some of the best ice cream around, but it required patience as the clerks chatted with each patron and allowed them to try free samples of their countless flavors. Dakota stood in the line, which started well beyond the shop's front door, and pulled out her cell phone. She scanned her job alerts, something she hadn't done in some time. Further proof that she'd gotten too comfortable with life here on the island.

Don't lose track of your plan. You're here to regroup, not to establish roots.

"Dakota! Imagine running into you here."

Angela Gilson.

Dakota groaned quietly, then turned slowly, wearing a cursory smile. "Why would it be a surprise, Angela?

We came here together as kids with our mothers plenty of times."

"I guess I didn't think you TV types ate real food, the camera adding ten pounds and all that." Angela made a point of sizing Dakota up, especially looking at her bottom. "But it seems you've certainly relaxed your standards since you've been home."

Dakota's cheeks flamed. She was well aware she'd put on a few pounds since she'd returned. But that didn't stop her from wanting to throat punch Angela for bringing it up.

"Is there something you want?" Dakota turned back around and moved forward with the line. A part of her considered leaving after Angela's remark, but that would only validate her little mean-girl routine.

"I hear that you're trying to organize a music festival here on the island."

The event wasn't public knowledge yet. They'd only discussed the possibility with the town commissioners, one of whom was Maybelline Gilson, Angela's mother. So she didn't need to ask Angela how she'd learned about the proposed festival. Neither did she need to ask what she thought of the idea. Her derisive tone made that abundantly clear.

"I've proposed a handful of festival ideas over the years. No one has ever taken them seriously. But I guess in a cut-throat city like New York, you learn to do whatever it takes to come out on top. Then again, you were always pretty good at that anyway."

Okay, now Dakota was *pissed.*

She whipped around, her arms folded. "What the hell are you talking about, Angela?"

The woman behind Angela covered her young son's ears. Dakota mouthed an apology.

"I hear that you talked Dexter into taking you to some expensive festival in New England for a long weekend. Just the two of you. You always did have a way of convincing him to do nearly anything for you. The poor lovesick fool adored you so much he even 'broke up' with you"—Angela used air quotes—"just to save your precious future. Because the great Dakota Jones was too good to go anywhere but NYU. Like you were more special than the rest of us."

All of the arguments and finger wagging Dakota had planned died when Angela mentioned the breakup.

"You don't know what you're talking about." Dakota resisted the urge to shove the woman.

But the truth was, Angela *did* seem to know what she was talking about. Dexter had only admitted to her a few weeks ago the real reason for their breakup. So how on earth did Angela Gilson, of all people, know the truth?

"Sorry, I forgot you didn't know the *real* reason he broke up with you," Angela said smugly.

Dakota grabbed the woman by the arm and led her away from the line.

"Hey! We lost our place. You do realize the store will be closing soon," Angela whined.

"Then I guess you'd better talk fast." Dakota glared at her. "And if you're lying, I swear I'll dig up every buck-toothed, braces-wearing picture I can find of you and post them online." She shoved a finger in the woman's face. "Now spill what you know."

Angela flipped her dark extensions over one shoulder and batted her long, thick eyelashes. She sat on a nearby bench and indicated that Dakota should sit in the seat beside her.

"I'd prefer to stand, thanks," Dakota said, her patience wearing thin.

"Suit yourself." Angela shrugged. "Dexter never wanted to break up with you. Your mother put him up to it."

"That's a lie, and I told you if you lied—"

"It isn't a lie." The woman looked genuinely outraged by the accusation. "Your mother offered Dexter five grand if he'd break up with you."

"My father would never have given her a portion of their savings for a foolish scheme like that." Dakota should've known this pathetic, jealous troublemaker was full of lies.

"Of course not. But it was not long after your mother's wealthy aunt died. She left your mother some money, and she was willing to use most of it to sabotage your relationship with Dexter."

Dakota's spine stiffened and her heart started to beat harder. The part about her mother's aunt leaving her some money was true, though Dakota had never known exactly how much or how her parents had used it. She also knew that her mother hadn't wanted her to stay with Dex after he went off to college. She'd tried everything in her power to convince Dakota that she should focus on school and her career, not some boy.

"If that was true, why wouldn't my mother have offered me the money instead?"

Angela laughed. "Are you kidding? You've always been as stubborn as a mule. The more your mama tried to talk you out of being with Dex, the more in love with him you proclaimed you were. Her only hope was to appeal to Dexter's love for you."

"So you're saying that Dexter broke up with me for the money?" Dakota's legs suddenly felt weak. She dropped onto the bench beside Angela.

"Told you that you were gonna wanna have a seat."

Don't throat punch her. Don't throat punch her. Don't—

"And no. Dexter Roberts is too honorable to have given up the *love of his life* for money. He was hurt and angry on your behalf that your mother would even offer him a deal like that."

Now, that sounds like the Dexter Roberts I know.

"So if everything you've said is true, why did Dexter break up with me?" Dakota couldn't believe she was asking the question of Angela. But if there was any truth to what the woman was saying, she needed to know.

Angela sighed, her mood shifting from contemptuous to something that almost seemed like admiration. "Your mother tried to convince Dex that if you stayed together he would ruin your life. That you'd be sidetracked from the career you'd been planning for since you were ten. He promised that he'd never let that happen, and he reminded her of how independent her daughter was. But then he came home for Christmas and you—"

"I told him I was changing my plans to go to NYU. That I was following him to Texas A&M instead." Dakota pressed a hand to her forehead. "It was one of my gifts to him. That's when he said he wanted to break up."

Dakota had always believed Dex broke up with her because he was seeing someone else at school and didn't want her following him there. But that wasn't it at all. He'd promised her mother he'd never let her derail her career for him, and then she'd gone and done just that.

"Like I said, he was head over heels in love with you. And was willing to sacrifice being with you so you could have the life your mother always dreamed of," Angela said, the mocking tone back in her voice.

So you could have the life your mother *always dreamed of.*

The words played over and over in Dakota's head. Dex's father and Dakota's mother hadn't been so different. Her

mother had always told the story as if Dakota had chosen
to be a big city reporter of her own volition. But in reality,
it had been a goal that her mother had always guided her
toward. Because her mother had been a local reporter for
her small town's newspaper. And she'd had aspirations of
going into television broadcasting.

Because of her inquisitive nature, Dakota had come to
love journalism. Especially once she'd started working on
hard-hitting stories that impacted people's lives. But she
hadn't come to the decision on her own.

"How did you know all of this?" Dakota asked.

Angela's cheeks flushed, as if she did in fact have the
capability to be ashamed. "When your mom got really sick,
she'd come to visit my mother sometimes, when she felt
up to it. They'd talk on the screened porch. You know the
one where we would listen to them through the vents when
we were kids?"

Dakota jumped to her feet, startling Angela. Angela
held up her hands in defense, as if she feared Dakota was
going to attack her. But as much as she'd enjoy seeing
Angela Gilson land in those prickly bushes behind her, feet
in the air, the woman wasn't worth spending a night in the
town jail.

She turned and headed toward her father's truck, not
bothering to say goodbye.

Chapter Twenty-Seven

Dexter was doing push-ups in his bedroom when there was a sudden banging on the front door. It was the kind you'd expect when the building was on fire or there was an evacuation order. He hopped to his feet, searching for a T-shirt.

But then came another round of the urgent banging. He tossed the shirt over his shoulder and strode to the door. Dex looked through the peephole, surprised at the source of the noise. He swung the door open.

"Dakota? The way you're knocking, I thought you were a sheriff's deputy trying to clear the building." He chuckled, but his demeanor shifted immediately when he saw that her eyes were watery and her chin trembled, as if she were on the verge of tears. She clutched at her stomach, her shoulders rounded.

"Sweetheart, what's wrong? Your hands are shaking. Is your father okay?" Dex reached for her, but Dakota flinched, pulling her hand just out of his reach. As if the thought of him touching her was repulsive.

Her reaction knocked him on his ass. His muscles tensed and his heart thudded in his chest. Whatever had happened earlier to make Dakota pull away...*this* was ten times worse. She hadn't even said whatever it was that she had come to say. Yet he could see it in her eyes. Disappointment. Fury. Pain.

"My dad's fine." Dakota dragged her fingers through her hair, not looking at him directly. "Is it okay if I come in for a minute?"

"Of course." It was an odd question, since he hadn't wanted Dakota to leave in the first place. He stepped aside, so she could enter the condo.

"I need to ask you a question, Dexter, and I need you to be completely straight with me. No bullshitting. Promise me that." She lifted her chin, finally meeting his gaze.

Dexter took a deep breath, then exhaled slowly. It was a loaded request. One that felt like the beginning of the end for them. Still, whatever it was that she'd come there to ask him, he wouldn't lie to her about it. *Couldn't* lie to her about it. Regardless of the consequences for either of them. Because he loved her.

It was the same reason he'd fought so hard to keep the truth from her. Because he loved her and didn't want her to be hurt by the truth. He'd spent his entire life trying to *fix* things. And people. And while his propensity for problem solving made him outstanding at his job, it was exhausting and sometimes backfired in his personal life.

As a kid, he'd tried to be the glue that would mend his parents' broken relationship. The star player that would make his father's derailed life a *little* less disappointing. The bridge between his father and grandfather's fractured relationship. And he'd been willing to make a painful sacrifice to prevent Dakota from throwing away her aspirations while also shielding her from the ugly truth.

But he realized now that had *never* been his call to make. It was Dakota's life, not his. Even back then, he should've trusted her to make the right choice for herself and then respected her decision. Whatever it may have been. He couldn't fix his past mistake. But he could do the right thing now.

She deserves the unfiltered truth.

He nodded, swallowing hard, his throat dry. "Of course, Dakota. Ask me anything."

"First…can you put on your shirt? I can't have this conversation right now with you looking like *that*." She waved her hands in front of his abs, her appreciative gaze trailing down his chest and settling on the outline visible through his black basketball shorts before she shut her eyes and folded her arms.

Maybe she'd been hit by the memory of what had happened between them up against the wall behind her just a few short hours ago.

He obliged her, putting on his shirt. "Can I get you some water? Tea? A glass of wine?"

"No. All I want is the truth," she whispered, her voice breaking as her gaze locked on his. "I just ran into Angela Gilson in the line at Helene's Homemade."

Shit.

Dexter sucked in a quiet breath. Any story with a setup of *According to Angela Gilson* would not end well. But there was also a good chance that it would amount to nothing more than vicious gossip or contrived innuendo.

"Did my mother ever offer you money to break up with me?"

Dakota's pointed question felt like a ton of bricks being dumped onto his head. He'd long hoped she'd never need learn of the drastic measures her mother had gone to in order to separate them. But regardless of what would happen between them, she deserved to know.

"Yes." He sagged against one of the barstools, his response a harsh whisper. "Right before I left for college, she offered me five thousand dollars to break things off with you."

She pressed a hand to her mouth, fat tears rolling down her cheeks.

He would've done anything to erase the betrayal and pain she must be feeling. And though he had the over-whelming desire to take her in his arms and comfort her, it was the last thing she wanted from him right now. Anger and disappointment were evident in her scowl and the way she glared at him.

She didn't want anything to do with him. The way she hovered near the entrance of the condo, he was afraid that she planned to dash out of the door at any moment.

"Did you take it?"

"No. I never even considered it." It hurt that she believed he would've accepted her mother's offer.

"Your family could've used that money, and you ended up breaking up with me anyway. So why didn't you take it, Dex?" She wiped angrily at the tears that ran down her face.

She'd been all he really wanted back then. Not a pro football career or fame. He'd just wanted *her*. And he'd given up any hope of being with her because he'd thought he was acting in her best interest. So her needing to ask that question...it hurt like hell.

"I loved you, Dakota. I would *never* have taken a bribe to walk away from you."

"But you *did* walk away, Dex. And this time I want you to tell me the truth about why. I need to know."

Dex sat on the edge of the kitchen stool, his pulse pounding. His heart felt as heavy as it had that day. The day he'd broken her heart and his.

"As long as I'd known you, the only thing you'd ever said you wanted to be was a reporter. And not just any reporter. You wanted to be the best. And you were convinced that the only way that would happen was if you moved to New York and went to NYU for your undergrad and grad school." He swallowed roughly, his mouth suddenly parched and his throat dry.

"Your mother had approached me several times to say that we were too young to be so serious and that if I wasn't careful, I would ruin your life. I assured her that wouldn't happen because I loved you more than anything, Dakota." He huffed, his chest heaving. "And after all this time, that hasn't changed."

"Then why did you break up with me?"

"I promised your mother I wouldn't do anything to derail your life. But then I came home for Christmas that first year of college and you'd decided to trash all of your carefully laid-out plans to follow me to school in Texas," he said. "It was *exactly* what your mother was afraid of."

"I know that you both cared about me, but it was *my* life, Dex." Dakota slapped her chest with her open palm. "So it wasn't your choice or hers to make. You didn't even have the decency to talk to me about it. And then you made a decision that completely changed the trajectory of our lives." Her voice broke, more tears streaming down her face.

"I know, it was a colossal mistake, but..." He choked back the emotion clogging his throat and scrubbed a hand down his face. "But I swear to you, Dakota, I did it because I loved you and I wanted the best for you. I wanted you to be happy—"

"I *was* happy, Dex," she interrupted, her hand shaking as she wiped away tears. "Being with you made me happy. And you took that away from me, away from us, without even consulting me. You should've trusted me to make my own decision."

"I know we were happy together then. But so were my parents in the beginning. And I couldn't help thinking of my dad. How resentful he was that his life didn't go according to plan and it was because of me. I couldn't bear the thought of you one day resenting your life with me, the way my father did. Or that you'd regret the things you hadn't done in your life, like your mom. So I ended things between us, hoping we'd eventually find our way back to each other." Dexter rubbed at the insistent ache in his chest, wishing, as he had so many times before, that he could have that pivotal moment in his life back. That he'd made a different decision. "No one was more thrilled than I was when you returned home. It was the first time I'd laid eyes on you since your mother's funeral."

"You *weren't* at my mother's funeral." She scowled, her eyes blazing with both hurt and anger.

"I *was* there, sweetheart," he said softly. He wanted to hold her to his chest. Rain kisses on her forehead and face. But the way she paced the floor several feet away from him, tension in her shoulders and her brows furrowed, made it clear that she didn't want his comfort. "I would never have missed being there."

"No, you weren't," she repeated the words, louder this time, her voice trembling. "I know because I looked for you. Despite everything that happened between us, I needed to know that you were there. That some small part of you still cared. It was the most painful day of my life, Dex. And everyone in town was there except for you."

"I was there, Dakota," he said again, his heart aching. It had been another missed opportunity. "You wore that black dress with the jacket that your mother bought you for church. The one you swore you'd never wear because you said it made you look like someone's great-grandmother." His mouth pulled into an involuntary smile at the memory, despite the gravity of the conversation. "You refused to wear it, but your mother liked you in it, so she never returned it. She always hoped you'd change your mind because it was smart and—"

"Sensible," she finished her mother's words. "You *were* there." She pressed a trembling hand to her mouth and her eyes drifted closed momentarily. Her shoulders seemed to sag with relief. She took a few steps toward him, and for the first time since she'd walked through the door, he felt hopeful. "But why didn't I see you?"

"I sat at the back of the church. I couldn't not be there, but you were already hurting so badly." He inhaled deeply, remembering the pained look on her face when she'd entered the church that day, clutching her father's hand. How it had torn him up inside to see her hurting, knowing there was nothing he could do. "You were furious with me. The last thing I wanted to do was agitate you at a time when you were already suffering. So I didn't come to the house to pay my respects, but I did send something. Lemon meringue pie." He smiled faintly. "Your favorite."

Every day—for the two weeks she was in town after her mother's funeral—a mini lemon meringue pie had been delivered from the local bakery with a simple note: *From the people who love you here on Holly Grove Island.*

"That was you?" she stammered, her eyes wide. "I don't understand. Why didn't you just come to the house?"

"I was terrified you couldn't forgive me," he admitted.

"And the idea of closing the door on us forever…I didn't want to take that chance."

"One last question." She sniffled, tipping her chin and meeting his gaze. "Were you ever going to tell me the truth?"

His eyes drifted closed, his gut twisting in knots. He wanted to just say yes; it was what she needed to hear. But the truth wasn't that simple, and he wouldn't keep it from her anymore. Not even to protect her. "That depends."

"On what?" Dakota folder her arms, her eyes narrowed and her lips pursed. She was irritated by what she must've considered a flippant response.

"I've given it a lot of thought these past couple of months, and I decided I would only tell you if things became serious between us," he admitted. "I wanted to protect you, Dakota. But we could never have an honest, long-term relationship with that secret lodged between us."

"Why not tell me the truth either way?" Her voice trembled as she wiped angrily at the tears that wet her cheeks. "The way you tell it, you're the valiant, self-sacrificing hero. Maybe that would've tipped the scales in your favor."

"Your mother's gone, Dakota." His voice was a gruff whisper. "She isn't here to defend herself and give you her side of the story. So you two can fight and hash it all out and then make up, the way you always did. I didn't want to risk tarnishing your memory of her for no reason."

Dakota blinked back a fresh wave of tears. He handed her a napkin, and she accepted it, dabbing at her eyes. "Thank you for responding honestly." She sighed heavily, seemingly spent. "It's late. I should go."

"Dakota." He reached out and caught her wrist before she could turn and walk away. "Sweetheart, I know you're angry, and I don't blame you. But you have to know that at the time, I thought I was doing right by you."

"And since?" She tipped her chin, her watery gaze meeting his.

He was buoyed by the fact that she hadn't pulled her hand from his. "I've regretted not having you in my life every single day."

Dakota's eyes widened and her lips parted slightly. A soft sigh escaped her mouth as she dropped her gaze. She tugged her hand from his and made her way to the door.

He'd hurt her enough, but she'd demanded complete honesty. She deserved to know the truth about *everything*.

"There's one more thing I need to tell you." He called out to her as she grabbed the doorknob. She paused but didn't turn back to look at him. "I know, Dakota." It killed Dexter inside to be the one to dredge up the pain and embarrassment she must feel. "About what happened in New York with that director you were dating."

She turned around, completely mortified. Her shoulders were tense as she wrapped her arms around herself, her gaze on the floor in the distance. "Did Nick tell you?"

"Nick knows?" He was surprised by that bit of news. But he shouldn't have been. Of course she would've leveled with Nick about any liability she felt she might bring to the team. "No. I've known for a while." He took a few steps toward her, hoping she'd look up at him, but she didn't.

"I guess there's another confession I should make first." He scrubbed a hand down his face, wishing he could spare her any further hurt and embarrassment. "I've kind of followed your career. Your Facebook page, your Instagram account. I liked watching your investigative stories." The words caught in his throat, and he inhaled deeply. "I guess I needed to know that the sacrifice I made was worth it because you were out in the world living your dream." Dex folded his arms. "So when the negative comments started coming in on some of your posts...I learned everything pretty quickly."

"I've been such a fool." Her eyes finally met his. "Half the town probably knows."

"There are others who do," he confirmed. "But the general consensus was that you're our girl. A native Holly Grove Islander. You will always be one of us, and we protect our own. The people who know the truth wanted this town to be a safe space for you. A shelter in the ugly storm brewing outside of it. That's why no one has brought it up to you or to Chief Jones."

Dakota pressed a hand to her open mouth as she stared at him. She shuffled backward, her back pressed against the door. Her voice came out shaky. "I can't believe that you...that they...I was so sure that..." She huffed, momentarily giving up on her attempt at coherent speech.

"The people here care about you, Dakota. *I* care about you." He patted his chest. "And about Chief Jones, too."

Dakota inhaled deeply, as if to calm herself. "I've been so wrong about so many things. About so many people. About this town." Her voice was faint, as if she was talking more to herself than to him.

"I know there are some busybodies here. But most of us are good people, and we care about one another. Whether you stay or go, Dakota, don't ever forget that."

Dakota looked up at him, like she was noticing him again for the first time. She nodded as she turned to leave. "I won't."

Dexter sat on the edge of the barstool again and groaned. She was gone. And just like the day things had ended between them seventeen years ago, she took a piece of his heart with her, which he feared he'd never get back.

———

Dakota pulled into her father's driveway and headed straight to the swing on the front porch. She rocked in the padded swing where she'd sat with her mother, excitedly planning her future. It had always been a fond memory. But now her entire body trembled with hurt and anger as she thought about how hard her mother had pushed her to take up her mantle. To have the dream career that Madeline Jones had never gotten to achieve for herself.

How could her mom have done something so under-handed as bribing her boyfriend to walk away? Convincing Dex that he needed to be some sort of martyr if he really loved her? What her mother had done had altered the course of her life. How could she have taken such a decision upon herself without consulting her? Worse, how could Dex have let her?

He should've loved and trusted her enough to let her make her own decision, rather than trying to be the knight in shining armor who selflessly saved the day.

"Mind if I have a seat?" Her dad stood in front of her on his crutches.

She was so lost in thought she hadn't heard the door open or her father's crutches thudding against the floor-boards. Dakota wiped away the tears that streaked her face and nodded. Her eyes didn't meet his.

Her father sat beside her and draped an arm over her shoulder. She laid her head on his chest, her tears wetting his shirt.

"What's wrong, sugarplum?"

Dakota sat up and looked at her father. "Did you know that Mom offered Dexter five thousand dollars if he'd break it off with me?"

Her father grimaced, shifting his gaze to the house across the street from theirs. "Your mother told me during the final months of her life. But before then, I didn't have a clue about it." He was silent for a moment. "Dexter finally told you, huh?"

"Only after I confronted him. Angela Gilson told me while I was in line at Helene's Homemade."

"Did you get a pint of Helene's black walnut?" he asked hopefully.

"No!" Dakota said indignantly. "And I'm glad I didn't." She poked his arm. "Why didn't you tell me once you knew?"

"Maddie begged me not to." He rubbed his bearded chin and sighed. "She knew she didn't have long. She didn't want the time she had left with you girls to be filled with anger and resentment. I couldn't deny her that."

Dakota was disappointed her father hadn't told her. But she needed the comfort his broad shoulder had always provided more.

"How could Mom do this to me...to us?"

"Kota, I know you must be angry with your mom right now. But what she did—no matter how wrong it may have been—she did because she loved you and wanted the very best for you. She wanted you to have all of the opportunities she didn't."

Dakota lifted her head, her eyes meeting his. "I think that's what hurts most. It feels like she was rejecting us. Like our family was one big mistake to her. Doesn't that bother you?"

"Your mom never regretted marrying me or having you

girls. She loved you. You were her entire world." He shifted on the swing. "That was the problem. She was thrilled to have her family at the center of her universe. She just didn't want us to comprise her *entire* universe. Your mom wanted more. A career, a life outside of the family. Doesn't mean she didn't love us."

"If she wanted to have a career, why didn't she?" Dakota turned toward him.

There was something her father wasn't saying. She needed to know what it was.

Oliver rubbed his chin, averting his gaze. "I wanted her to stay home once she got pregnant with your sister. It was a matter of pride for me. I didn't want my wife to have to work, especially once we had children. My dad had always managed to provide for all of us, no matter how bad things got. I felt I needed to do the same."

"You *forbade* her from working?" The words tasted bitter on her tongue. Like something awful she needed to spit out.

"You know your mama. No one could *make* Madeline Jones do anything," he said fondly. "But it was something we fought about after she was pregnant. Something we hadn't thought to discuss before. Your mother gave up her career because she wanted to be at home with you girls. In the end, it was a sacrifice she was willing to make. But a sacrifice nonetheless."

Dakota wrapped her arms around her body as a chill seeped into her skin. "I appreciate the sacrifices Mom made for us, but that didn't give her the right to interfere in my life or make my decisions for me."

"I know." He wrapped his arm around her and rested his chin on atop her head. "But you've always been as stubborn and determined as your mother. And it's not like your mother and I hadn't talked to you about why following some boy off to college would be a grave mistake. But anything we had to say to you about Dexter...It was like we were talking to a wall. You were as in love with that boy as Madeline and I were when our parents told us we were too young to get married." He chuckled, the sound rumbling in his chest. "Guess she figured it was a lost cause, so she took her argument to Dex. She said she didn't think she'd have much luck with him, either, but Dexter surprised her. He surprised us both with the sacrifice he was willing to make for you. That man loves you, Dakota. He always has. And I can't help thinking he always will."

Her father's words should've made her ecstatic. Dex loved her, and he'd made a painful sacrifice to prove it. So why didn't that make her feel better? Instead, all she could think of was what she and Dex might've been, had it not been for her mother's calculating interference.

Tears slid down her cheeks and she tried to muffle her cries in her father's chest. She ached for the pain she and Dex had both suffered. The years they'd spent apart. The moments they would never get back. She cared very much for Dexter, but he hadn't respected her right to make her own decision any more than her mother had.

Her dad squeezed her shoulder. "I know this is hard for you to accept right now, but hopefully one day you'll realize how much they both loved you. How much he still does. I won't meddle in your affairs. You've had enough of that. But I will tell you that Dex has proven he's a stand-up guy, willing to go to bat for the people he loves, even at great sacrifice to himself. Seems to me that a person would be mighty lucky to have someone like that in their corner."

"Dex said it today, that he loves me." Dakota swallowed hard. "Said he always has."

"But you doubt it?" her father asked.

"No. I believe him." Dakota sat up, running her fingers through her hair as the scene replayed in her mind. "I love him, too. But if we don't have trust and honesty, is love enough?"

"True." Her father nodded sagely. "But sometimes we find it difficult to be completely honest with the people we love. Whether it's 'cause we're trying to protect them or ourselves." He patted her arm.

Oof! An uppercut to the jaw that left her flat on her back and down for the count.

Her father was right. She hadn't been honest with the people she loved, either. And while she hadn't wanted to hurt her dad or disappoint him and the rest of the town, it was her own pride she had been most concerned with protecting.

Even if his actions had been misguided, at least Dexter had acted selflessly.

"I'm sorry I lied to you about why I lost my job." Dakota lowered her gaze to her hands, her face filled with heat. "But it was so humiliating, and I felt so stupid." She swiped a finger beneath her eyes. "It was nice to pretend it hadn't happened. Even if it was only in the safe, warm bubble of Holly Grove Island."

Her father nodded. "I get that, Kota. Wrong thing, right reasons. I've been there a time or two myself." He cleared his throat. "Like when you asked me about whether there was anything going on besides friendship between me and Lila Gayle."

Dakota pulled her legs onto the swing and wrapped her arms around them as she turned her body to face her father. "And is there?"

A soft smile slowly spread across her father's handsome

face as he turned toward her with a dreamy look in his eyes. "Little by little, Lila Gayle and I have grown closer over the years since she lost Ed and I lost Madeline. We bonded over the loss of our spouses, I guess. Things kind of took off from there."

"Do you love her, Dad?"

"Yes, I do," he answered without hesitation. "I haven't said those exact words to her, mind you, but I most definitely do love her."

"Wow, Dad. That's... *huge*." Dakota squeezed her father's hand and widened her smile.

She was happy that her father had fallen in love again. That he'd found companionship with someone as sweet and loyal and all-around wonderful as Ms. Lila. But the idea of someone else taking up space in her father's heart felt... *odd*. That was her problem, not his. It was something she would have to get used to. Until then, she'd plaster a big smile on her face and do exactly as Sin suggested.

Maybe you can return the favor by helping him to move on. Maybe he's ready, but he doesn't know how.

"Dad, if you feel so strongly about Ms. Lila, why haven't you been explicit about your feelings for her?" she asked. "Are you afraid she doesn't feel the same?"

"No. It's not that. I'm pretty sure she loves me, too." The light she'd seen in his eyes dimmed. He rubbed the back of his neck and heaved a sigh. "I guess I've been worried about how you and your sister would feel about me falling for someone else. That you would think I was trying to replace your mother."

Dakota released her father's hand and hugged her legs again. "I'm not proud of it—the thought did cross my mind at first. But I realize now that this isn't about replacing

Mom. That woman was a bona fide original. No one's ever gonna replace her."

They both laughed.

"Ms. Lila isn't Mom, but she doesn't need to be. She just needs to be good to you and to bring you joy. I can already see that she does." Dakota gave her father a teary but genuine smile.

She was grateful her father found love and companionship again. That he wouldn't live out the rest of his life alone. And she honestly believed her mother would be, too. Because for all her faults, Madeline Jones truly loved her family. And she'd wanted the best for them. Even if she wasn't always right about exactly what that was.

"I'm so happy that you've found someone special again, Dad. Ms. Lila's a gem. So if you love her, *tell her*. Don't leave her wondering. She deserves to know how you feel."

The corners of her father's eyes were wet. "Thank you, Kota. Your blessing means a lot to me. I know it'll mean a lot to Lila, too."

They sat in silence, staring at the darkening sky. She thought about her parents' room, filled with her mother's things. At one time, she might've considered those items her last connection to her mother. But she didn't need *things* to remind her of her mom. And neither did he. Her mother was a part of her life every day. She would always have her memories of the woman who'd taught her so much. But maybe it was time to let some of those things go.

Things like her mother's old clothing and mostly evaporated bottles of perfume. And some of her mother's philosophies which no longer served Dakota and that she didn't want to pass on to her future children. But that was okay.

"Dad, I've been thinking...maybe it's been hard for you to tell Ms. Lila how you feel because you haven't really let go of Mom. I mean...you haven't gotten rid of any of her things. It's like you're expecting her to walk back through that door any day now. How could you possibly move on?"

He grimaced, rubbing the knee that had been replaced. "Didn't seem right to get rid of her things."

"I know." She squeezed her father's shoulder. "But it's time, for both of us. So I've been thinking...why don't I go through your room and box up Mom's stuff. I won't get rid of anything right now," she added quickly. "I'll put it in the storage space in my suite. Then the next time Shay is in town, we can go through the boxes together and decide what to keep. We can donate the rest—so someone else can get enjoyment from Mom's things. All right?"

Her father was somber. But after a few moments of quiet contemplation, he clasped her forearm and gave her a watery smile as he lay his other hand over his heart. "Okay, Dakota. It'll be nice to know her things are going to someone who'll appreciate them. Thank you for taking this on; I know it won't be easy for you either." His smile deepened a bit. "And the way you said 'the next time Shay is in town' makes it sound like you intend on sticking around a while." There was a hopeful lilt in his voice.

I did say that, didn't I?

"I don't know, Dad. I thought I knew *exactly* what I wanted for my life. Had it planned down to the most minute detail, so I always knew what was supposed to come next." Dakota sighed. "Before my career self-destructed, I was following that path perfectly. Even though it meant sacrificing a little piece of my soul. Or playing along with the politics behind the scenes, even when I knew I should be speaking out against them."

"I'm sorry, sweetheart. I had no idea things were so challenging." Her father frowned and placed a hand on her arm. "I wish you'd confided in me."

"Me, too. But it didn't really fit my 'successful reporter living the life in the big city' narrative." She laughed bitterly, regretting all the times she'd decided against being frank with her father about how things had been going in her life. "Honestly? I love being an investigative reporter and the part where I get to make a real, tangible difference in people's lives. But I was stressed out all the time chasing the next big story. And somewhere along the way, it became more about achieving the next rung of success in my career, not about enjoying my life."

"Doesn't sound like a very pleasant way to live, Kota." Her father's voice was warm and sympathetic, not judgmental—which she appreciated. "Maybe this career reset could turn out to be a blessing in disguise," he noted. "Have you thought about what you'll do next?"

"I have no clue what's next for me, or if I even want to continue pursuing a career in broadcast news right now. But I'm living in a place that I truly love. I'm doing fun, interesting work that I enjoy and for which I'm being well paid. I'm working with brilliant people I respect, while surrounded by my friends and family."

"Sounds like the perfect setup to me." Her father beamed.

"Except that if I stay, I can either keep the job I love or be with the man I love—but neither of us can have both." She nibbled on her lower lip, her chest heavy and her mind racing with all the various possibilities.

"Sounds like one hell of a complication." Her father frowned. "But you're a smart, determined woman. I know you'll figure this out. And I'm right here if you need me." He reached for his crutches, waving her off when she offered to help him up. "Gotta learn to manage on my own eventually," he said, climbing to his feet with a quiet groan. "I'm gonna head to bed. Maybe we can start on that project you talked about this weekend."

"Sure, Dad. I'll check with Lila Gayle in the morning to see if she has a few boxes I can use to get started." It wasn't lost on her that her father had avoided saying *boxing up your mother's things*. Baby steps. For both of them. "I'm going to stay out here a little longer, but I'll be in in a bit. Good night."

Dakota put one foot down on the wooden porch boards and pushed off, setting the swing in motion as she stared up at the night sky filled with twinkling stars. Something she and her mother had often done on bright, cloudless nights like this. Gazing up at the stars had always made her think of her mother fondly. But tonight she felt a jumble of emotions about the woman she'd always revered: disappointment, anger, and betrayal among them.

"Your mother wasn't perfect, Dakota," her father said from the other end of the porch, where he stood with one hand on the knob. "None of us are. But she loved you—loved all of us—fiercely. I wouldn't have traded the years we shared together for anything in the world. I hope you're lucky enough to find the kind of love your mother and I shared. And who knows, maybe you already have."

Her lips quirked in a soft smile and her heart fluttered as she thought about Dexter's bumbling, but sincere, declaration of love earlier that night.

She couldn't help wondering if she'd already found that kind of lasting love, too.

Chapter Twenty-Eight

• • •

In the fourteen hours since his encounter with Dakota, Dexter had been agitated and restless. Angry with himself for not leveling with Dakota back then. Disappointed in himself for not telling her the whole truth once she'd returned to Holly Grove Island. Wondering if he'd blown any chance of reconciling with her again.

Whenever he was in a foul mood, it was usually improved by a chat with his mother. Marilyn Roberts wasn't afraid to say the things he needed but didn't necessarily want to hear when he'd screwed up. And today she was serving up her observations with wicked-sharp wit and mouthwatering leftovers: her famous pot roast, savory smashed potatoes, and one hell of a raspberry and peach hand pie.

"You're doing it again." His mother folded her arms on the table and stared at him.

"Doing what again?" Dexter stacked their plates.

"That thing you do where you feel the need to ride in on your white horse and save the day because you don't trust us to figure out how to fix our own problems." Her words were direct, but her voice was filled with a warmth and affection that made his heart swell.

That was his mother. She served up the bitter truth, sweetened with a taste of honey.

"And exactly who is this *us*?" He leaned back and folded his arms, too.

His mother repositioned her chair. Chairs they'd had as long as he'd been alive. "Me, your father, your siblings, your employees, random townsfolk, Dakota...Need I go on?"

Dexter groaned inwardly. None of this was news to him. Still, he hated being reminded of his innate, persistent need to "fix" the lives and problems of everyone around him. It wasn't the first time his mother had told him as much, reminding him that he wasn't responsible for everyone else's happiness. But damn if that last name hadn't struck a nerve. It spoke to a wound that ran deep and had never really healed but was now torn open and bleeding afresh for both of them.

And he had no idea how to fix it.

"Isn't that why you two aren't together now?" His mother hiked an accusing brow. "If you hadn't allowed Madeline to rope you into her half-baked scheme—"

"It wasn't a scheme," he countered defensively as he rubbed his temple, which had begun to throb. "In our own ways, each of us wanted what was best for her."

"What right did you or Madeline have to decide what was best for Dakota?" His mother stabbed the cloth-covered table with her index finger. Her tone harbored an unspoken *uhn-hmm*. "Maybe if you'd discussed the situation with Kota, she might've agreed with you. But, sweetheart, you took away her choice. And you did it again by not telling her the whole truth when you had a chance. *Before* Ms. Run-Tell-Dat, Queen of the Tattletales, beat you to it."

"I just want Dakota to be happy, Ma. That's all I've ever wanted for her."

"I know, honey." Her tone softened as she squeezed his hand. "But it's up to Dakota to decide what that is. Sometimes it takes us a while to figure it out. That's part of being human. But the real question is: Does being with Dakota make *you* happy? I remember how the two of you lit up like the Christmas tree on town square whenever you were together. If you both still feel that way, well, then maybe this thing is worth fighting for."

Being with Dakota did make him happy: then and now. He remembered every moment he'd spent with her since she'd returned to Holly Grove Island. Even during their tense exchange at the Fourth of July Festival, he'd felt a hint of hopefulness. That the intense passion with which she disliked him meant that something worth saving still lay beneath the surface. Like the teeming wildlife that survived fire by burrowing deep belowground so it could one day emerge and repopulate the charred landscape. He'd just needed to find a way to reawaken the affection they'd once shared.

He was thankful that he had, because the past few weeks with Dakota had made it clear that she was the only woman for him. He couldn't imagine going back to life without her. Even if it required him to give up the thing he'd wanted most.

"I still love her, Ma. Dakota is amazing, and there is no woman in the world I'd rather be with. I can't lose her again."

"That's wonderful, honey." A tearful smile lit his mother's glistening eyes. "I would love to see you and Dakota finally get your happy ending, but what about your job at the resort?"

"Still trying to work that out." It was a dilemma to

which he had yet to find a suitable solution after lying awake, tossing and turning, all night. But he'd prioritized the issues at hand, and what was most important to him was salvaging his relationship with Dakota.

After their seventeen years apart, the torch they'd once carried for each other still flickered. And after their getting reacquainted, the flame burned even brighter. There had to be a reason neither of them had gotten seriously involved in all this time. The past few weeks had left him with no doubt of why that was. They were *meant* to be together.

So he'd talk to her. Plead his case. Try to make her understand. He loved her and wanted to be with her. Even if it meant leaving everyone and everything else behind. He could find another resort, another job. But he'd never find anyone else like Dakota.

———

Dakota sat on the floor of her bedroom late Sunday afternoon, a stack of photo albums spread out in front of her. She'd spent the morning going through her mother's things with her father and toting them up to the third-floor storage. But she couldn't bring herself to put the albums in the dark, dusty old space.

For the past two hours, she'd been sitting up in her room flipping through the pictures of her family, friends, and the people of Holly Grove Island. People she'd known most of her life. She'd traced the evolution of her style, for better or worse.

It had prompted her to pull out the photo albums that had been shoved in the back of a high shelf in her closet. These photos were solely hers. Pictures of her and her high school friends. And a ton of snapshots of her and Dex.

Him looking handsome in his high school football uniform. Her running track. The two of them and their friends at the beach or at bonfires. Her unfortunate experiment with bangs. Sin's series of high school boyfriends.

"Dakota, Lila's here and we're going out to dinner. Don't wait up for me." Her father's giddy voice and the sound of Ms. Lila's bashful giggle floated through the smart speaker in her room. He'd initially resisted using them, but since his surgery, he'd become an avid user of the drop-in feature. "But you've got company."

Sin.

She'd tried to stop at her friend's condo when she'd left Dexter's last night, but Sin had spent the night at her cousin's place in Wilmington. She'd updated her friend on her conversation with Angela and her discussion with Dexter, and Sin had promised to stop by as soon as she'd returned.

"Thanks, Dad. Send her up, and don't get too wild tonight. You know that knee is still healing." She ended the call, because it was something her father never seemed to be able to manage. Then she continued flipping through the pages of the album and came across a photo of Sinclair with a teased hairdo that made her friend look like a French poodle.

"Oh my God, Sin. Do you remember when you were going through your *Designing Women* big-hair phase?" Dakota called out when she heard footsteps approaching.

"I didn't think it was so bad."

Dakota's attention jolted toward the doorway. "Dexter, what are you doing here?"

"I'm here to see you, beautiful." His gaze was soft as his mouth curved in a lopsided grin. "Chief Jones sent me up here. I'm a little stunned by that myself."

She climbed to her feet, dusting off her frayed cut-off jeans. Her T-shirt was smeared with dirt from hauling things into the storage space.

"Remember," she whispered conspiratorially, "as far as my dad knows, this is the first time you've ever been in my room."

"I think that ship has sailed. When your dad sent me up here, he made a point of saying, 'Dakota's in her room on the third floor, but I'm sure you remember where it is.'" Dex did a fairly good imitation of her father, complete with the Oliver Jones stare of intimidation.

"Not funny, Roberts." Dakota folded her arms, resisting the urge to laugh. The only sounds in the room were the ticking of the clock and the whirring of the fan. "And you still haven't told me what you're doing here."

"Like I said, I'm here to see you. More specifically, I came to apologize again. I've had a really long time to think about what happened back then. Wishing I'd done things differently. That I'd tried harder to give you the world *and* stay together."

"I wish you'd given us a shot at that option, too." She sighed, running her fingers through her hair. "I didn't need you to give me the world, Dex. I was prepared to do my own dragon slaying. I just wanted to do it with you by my side."

"I understand that now." He shoved a hand into the pocket of his relaxed-fit jeans and leaned against the doorframe. "And I'm here to grovel shamelessly for your forgiveness...for keeping the truth from you then and now."

She liked the sound of *groveling*. And the hot image of Dexter, shirtless and on his knees, that flashed into her brain didn't hurt either.

"Have a seat." She removed a photo album from the desk chair, then gestured for him to sit there before she took a seat on the foot of the bed.

Dexter looked at the spot she'd cleared off for him, several feet away from her; then his dark eyes shifted toward the space beside her on the bed. He nodded toward it. "Would you mind if I sat there instead?"

Yes. Very much.

There was so much they needed to talk about. And she needed to do it with a clear head. Something that was difficult to maintain when he was sitting less than a foot away on her bed. The bed they'd made love in for the first time all those years ago.

"No, not at all." She slid over, making room for his large frame. She sifted her fingers through her hair, tugging her wild curls over one shoulder.

The mattress shifted beneath them as Dexter sat beside her. He turned his body toward hers, folding one leg on the bed to accommodate the position.

She drew in a quiet breath, her heart racing and her temperature rising. His subtle, familiar scent teased her senses. And in a room cooled only by a fan on such a hot day, his body heat seemed to wrap itself around her.

He swallowed, his Adam's apple bobbing. "Dakota, I'm sorry I hurt you. I should've been straight with you about my concerns when you declared you were changing schools for me. Then we could've talked things out. I've regretted not giving you that opportunity every day since." Dexter placed his large hand on top of hers, linking their fingers.

Her eyes drifted closed involuntarily as the heat and electricity from his touch trailed up her arm. The memories of him holding her hand as they strolled through the

Newport festival grounds that final day filled her brain. She forced them to the back of her head.

She'd given a lot of thought to this conversation with Dexter. And she needed to ensure that the parts *above* her neck remained in control. Not her treacherous heart, which missed him desperately. Nor the body that vibrated with energy at his nearness and craved his touch.

He squeezed her hand. "Dakota, these past few weeks with you have been beyond amazing for me. When I said that I love you, I meant every word. I honestly can't imagine going back to life without you."

She raised her eyes to his, her heart squeezing in her chest at his raw, seemingly sincere declaration of love for the second time in less than twenty-four hours. Butterflies fluttered in her stomach as she shifted her gaze to their joined fingers. Her breathing suddenly became shallow and her pulse raced.

The words she wanted to say to him hovered on her tongue.

I love you, too. And I want to be with you.

Returning his feelings was the easy part. Figuring out how this would all work in real life and if they could trust each other moving forward—*that* was the hard part.

"What about your job?" Dakota stroked his stubbled cheek. "You've worked hard to get where you are, Dexter, and you deserve this. I have no doubt that you'll be appointed as the permanent director at the Holly Grove Island Resort, and I can't be the reason that you lose out on such an incredible opportunity."

He pressed her palm to his lips, his whiskers tickling her skin. "I appreciate you wanting to safeguard my career. But I've been up all night thinking about what it is I want most." He smiled, his eyes filled with emotion. "And what I want, unequivocally, is to be with you, because you, Dakota, are my heart. You have been since the day I first kissed you on your front porch. And I've been stumbling around without it since the day I let you walk out of my life, waiting for a second chance."

Dakota withdrew her hand and pressed her palm to her lips as she blinked back the tears that clouded her vision. Her hand was trembling.

"Sweetheart, what's wrong?" Dexter cradled her face.

Dakota sniffled, her voice breaking as she met his gaze. "That's the sweetest thing anyone has ever said to me."

He breathed a sigh of relief and then a soft smile curved his lips. He tugged her onto his lap, so she was straddling him. "Good, because I meant every word of it."

Dexter slid his fingers into her hair, bringing her mouth to his. His scent was intoxicating, and she felt safe in the comfort of his strong arms. When his lips glided against hers, she lost herself in his kiss. Her body thrummed with electricity and the anticipation of his touch.

Which was why she'd needed space. So that they could have this conversation with clear heads while fully clothed.

Dakota pressed the heels of her palms against Dexter's chest, breaking their heated kiss. She searched his dark eyes. "Are you saying that—"

"I'm saying I love you, Dakota. And I want to be *wherever* you are." He traced her cheekbone with his thumb. "Seventeen years ago, I was willing to give you up so that you could have the world. So yes, I'm willing to make this concession to have you back in my life."

"But you're finally on the verge of moving back home full-time, so you can be near your family." Dakota cradled his face, her voice quivering as she choked back tears, moved by the sacrifice he was willing to make for her. "You'd leave Holly Grove Island, your job, your family? For me? But you've always wanted—"

"*You*, Dakota," he said, his voice breaking slightly. "More than anything, I've wanted you back in my life. Sweetheart, there are hotels and resorts all over the world. I'll find another job, but I can't find another Dakota Jones and I don't want one. I have the original. I lost you once, and I've regretted it ever since. I don't want to lose another moment with you, Dakota. And I don't care if it's here on Holly Grove Island, in New York City, or in the middle of Alaska. I just want to be with you. The rest will work itself out."

Dakota's eyes stung, and her heart felt as if it might burst. She kissed him, her arms looped around his neck.

"I love you, Dex. And maybe one day I'll take you up on your offer." She held back a smirk in response to his sudden look of panicked confusion. "At some point, maybe I'll decide to return to my career in broadcast news. But I'm not ready to leave Holly Grove Island just yet."

"You're staying on the island?" Dexter's eyes lit up, then he wrapped her up in a tight hug. "Baby, that's fantastic. I couldn't be more thrilled, and I know that your dad and Sin will be, too. I can't wait to tell…" He paused suddenly, frowning. "But then that means—"

She held up a hand. "Before you say anything, I've been thinking about my job situation now that working at the resort is off the table. Let me show you something."

Dakota climbed off of Dexter's lap and grabbed her phone. She opened up an app and handed it to him.

Dexter read the screen carefully, then raised his gaze to hers. A wide smile spread across his face. "You're starting your own marketing and communications consultancy?"

"Yes!" she said, giddy with excitement. "Ever since our meeting with some of the local business owners and then the presentation to the town, I've had several requests for help with marketing, PR, and event brainstorming from local businesses. So I'll start working with people here and then branch out from there."

"Babe, that's brilliant. I'm thrilled for you." He pulled her onto his lap and kissed her again.

"I've been able to save a little while I've been working for the resort," she said as he kissed her neck, the short whiskers of his beard tickling her skin. "I realize that it will take a little time for me to build the consultancy to a sustainable level. So, I'll put some feelers out for work here or off-island in the meantime."

His chuckle vibrated against her collarbone, where he was trailing kisses. "Don't worry, babe." He kissed her jaw. "Got a comfortable savings to tide us over, just in case."

"*Us?*" They were really doing this—officially making a go of this relationship.

"Us." He repeated the word as he gazed up at her. The dreamy, content smile on his face made her heart swell in her chest and butterflies flutter in her belly. "You and me, Dakota. For as long as you'll have me, which I hope is a mighty long time. Because we've got a lot of time to make up for."

They were a couple now. *We* and *us* were words she'd have to get accustomed to using.

She smiled at Dexter—a blur through the tears that filled her eyes and slid down her cheeks. They'd been given a second chance at making a life together. This time they weren't naive kids who had no idea what life was really about. The time they'd spent apart had shown them both what was important in life. *Who* was important. Family.

Friends. And someone who loved you unconditionally, even when you screwed up.

"One more thing. Promise me that from now on, we will always be completely honest with each other." She studied his handsome face. "No matter what."

"I promise. You're the girl I let get away. The one woman I could never get out of my head. I loved you then. I love you now. And I will always, always love you, Dakota."

"I love you too, Dex."

She kissed him, her chest swelling with the deep affection she felt for him and with the unexpected contentment of being back on Holly Grove Island. Dakota was *exactly* where she belonged; surrounded by the people she loved in the place that would always feel like home.

Epilogue

— • • • —

Thanksgiving

Dakota felt like she, Lila Gayle, Sin, and Dexter's mother, Marilyn, had been cooking for at least three days straight in preparation for Thanksgiving, only to have the crowd of friends and family they'd invited to her father's house for dinner devour it in what felt like mere minutes.

They'd prepared a baked turkey, a fried turkey, and a ham. There were scalloped potatoes, sweet potato casserole, baked macaroni and cheese, corn bread dressing, green bean casserole, and honey buttermilk dinner rolls to complete the carb overload. The dessert table overflowed with sweet potato pie, apple pie, blackberry and peach cobbler, and of course, Dakota's favorite—lemon meringue pie.

Nick and Dexter had borrowed Nick's mother's dining room table to help accommodate their guests: Oliver and Lila Gayle, newly engaged and planning a simple, outdoor Christmas Eve wedding ceremony in the gazebo on the town square; Dakota and Dexter; Dexter's entire family—including his brothers and their wives and children and his father, James, whom Dex was working on forging a closer relationship with; Lila Gayle's eldest son, Daniel, who'd moved back to town and was renovating the bait shop himself; Sin and her parents, Terri and Troy; and Nick and his parents.

Her sister, Shay, and her husband had stayed in California to celebrate Thanksgiving with his family, but she'd promised to come home for their father's wedding to Lila Gayle on Christmas Eve.

"Hey, beautiful." Dexter slipped his arms around Dakota's waist and kissed her neck from behind while she stood at the sink scrubbing dishes from the mountain of pots and pans. She'd gotten a head start on the kitchen while everyone else played cards or hung out together. "Can I talk to you for a minute?"

Dakota relaxed in the comfort of Dexter's embrace and inhaled his subtle cologne. They'd been together officially for three months. But Dakota would never tire of the hugs and kisses they shared.

Dexter had been appointed as the permanent director of operations at the HGI Resort at the end of ninety days. And the resort group's management staff had been so impressed with the two festivals she'd developed for HGI and the way she'd handled community relations with the island's residents that they'd engaged her as a consultant to work with both the Myrtle Beach and Holly Grove Island Resorts.

Though she spent a few nights a week at Dexter's place, she officially still lived here with her father—until he and Lila Gayle got married in a few weeks on Christmas Eve. Then she would be moving into Dexter's condo.

"Sure. What's up?" She turned around. "Looking for a spades partner?" She nodded toward the ruckus coming from the dining room, where there were rise and fly games of both spades and bid whist going on. "If so, let me wash a few more of these dishes first."

"There's something I want to show you." A sexy smile curved his sensuous lips and a mischievous grin lit his dark eyes.

Dakota gasped and punched him in the gut playfully. She leaned in and whispered so that only Dex could hear her. "I am not sneaking up to my room for sex with you in a house full of people, Dexter Roberts."

"Noted." He chuckled. "But *that* isn't what I want to show you. Not this time." He waggled his eyebrows and laughed. "But after you see what I want to show you, you might at least want to make out with me a little." He chuckled.

Dakota shook her head. Whatever Dex's surprise was, she was grateful for a reason to abandon the dish of baked-on macaroni and cheese that was ruining her nails. Maybe soaking it would help.

"Sure." She grabbed a dish towel and dried her hands. "Lead the way."

Dexter slipped his hand in hers and led her toward the back door. He grabbed their jackets off a hook by the door and helped her into hers. Then they stepped outside in the cool, crisp November air. The chilly wind whipped across her face, and Dakota could see her breath in the air.

She rubbed her hands together and blew on them. "I'm assuming there's a really good reason for us to be out here freezing our buns off?"

"I assure you that there is." He took her hand again and led her to the front of the house. They stood out in the street in front of the pale-pink clapboard house with white trim. Light glowed from all of the downstairs windows, but the windows on the second and third floors were dark. Dex spread his arms out, his face brimming with excitement. "What do you see?"

Okay, I'll bite.

"My dad's place." She pulled her jacket around her more tightly as the wind blowing off the Atlantic Ocean whipped down Cypress Lane. "The house I grew up in."

"Exactly." He pointed. "And now that your dad and Lila Gayle are getting married, the place will be empty."

"My dad plans to update the place and add it to his list of rental properties." She frowned. It made her sad to think of strangers making themselves at home in the lovely old Victorian that had been the setting for so many special memories in her life and in her relationship with Dexter. But it made sense for her father to either sell or rent the place. It would be a shame for it to sit empty.

Her father had suggested that she buy the place to keep it in their family. But as a brand-new business owner, she couldn't afford it just yet. So she'd suggested that her father rent out the property for a year or two. By then she'd be able to make the purchase.

"What if he didn't rent the place? What if he sold it to us instead?" Dex asked excitedly.

"Us?" She wished she could take back the word as soon as the light in his eyes dimmed in response to it. She pressed her hands to his chest, lifted onto her toes and pressed a quick kiss to his lips. "I mean, I'm interested in keeping the house in our family, of course. But with my consultancy being so new—"

"That's why I suggested that we buy it together." He grinned, pressing another kiss to her lips. "I've been look-ing to expand my real estate holdings and it would be a really great investment. More importantly, think how great it would be to raise our children here in the same house where you and your sister grew up."

Dakota stared up into Dexter's dark eyes. Her belly fluttered and her knees suddenly felt weak. It warmed her chest that he was willing to make such an offer.

"Dex, that's incredibly sweet of you, and I appreciate the offer. But I honestly couldn't ask you to do something so generous for me." She clutched at his jacket.

"You didn't ask," he said. "I offered. Because this is something I really want to do for you, but also for *us*. Please," he added before she could object. "Let me do this for us."

Dakota turned to look at the house that had been synonymous with home for the entirety of her life. The house that still held memories of her childhood and of her mother. Memories of growing up with Shay, playing hide-and-seek, and sliding down the original wooden banisters.

She and Dex were only a few months into their renewed relationship, but they'd already talked about getting married the following year. And about wanting to start a family. She wanted her children to have a connection to the home that had been in their family for four decades.

"It would be amazing, wouldn't it?" she mused, already thinking of ways they could update the place and make it their own while honoring its history and connection to her parents.

Dakota turned back to look at Dexter's wide smile, his eyes dancing with excitement.

"Say yes, Dakota. Please." He leaned in and kissed her forehead.

She bounced on her heels, her pulse racing and a throaty laugh erupting from her lips. Dakota nodded excitedly. "Okay, yes. Let's do it."

He whooped with excitement, lifting her off her feet and swinging her around, both of them laughing before he kissed her again.

Dakota couldn't be happier. She and Dexter had been given a second chance at love right there on Cypress Lane. In the town, on the street, and in the very house that had always meant so much to them.

Don't miss Sinclair and
Garrett's story in
Return to Hummingbird Way!

Coming Fall 2021

About the Author

Reese Ryan is an award-winning author of romantic fiction with captivating family drama, surprising secrets, all the feels, and a posse of complex, flawed characters. A panelist at the 2017 *Los Angeles Times* Festival of Books and recipient of the 2018 Donna Hill Breakout Author Award, Reese is an advocate for the romance genre and diversity in fiction.

A Midwesterner with deep Southern roots, Reese currently resides in semi-small-town North Carolina, where she's an avid reader, a music junkie, and a self-declared connoisseur of cheesy grits.

You can learn more at:
  ReeseRyan.com
  Twitter @ReeseRyanWrites
  Facebook.com/ReeseRyanWrites
  Pinterest.com/ReeseRyanWrites

For a bonus story from another
author that you'll love, please
turn the page to read
Kiss Me at Sweetwater Springs
by Annie Rains.

If Lacy Shaw could have one wish, it'd be that the past
would stay in the past. And with her high school reunion
coming up, she has no intention of reliving the worst four
years of her life. Especially when all she has to show
for the last decade is how the shy bookworm blossomed
into…the shy town librarian. Ditching the event seems the
best option until a blisteringly hot alternative roars into
Lacy's life. Perhaps riding into the reunion on the back of
Paris Montgomery's motorcycle will show her classmates
how much she really has changed…

FOREVER

Chapter One

Lacy Shaw looked around the Sweetwater Springs Library for the culprit of the noise, a "shhh" waiting on the tip of her tongue. There were several people reading quietly at the tables along the wall. A few patrons were wandering the aisles of books.

The high-pitched giggle broke through the silence again.

Lacy stood and walked out from behind her counter, going in the direction of the sound. She wasn't a stickler for quiet, but the giggling had been going on for at least ten minutes now, and a few of the college students studying in the far corner kept getting distracted and looking up. They'd come here to focus, and Lacy wanted them to keep coming.

She stopped when she was standing at the end of one of the nonfiction aisles where two little girls were seated on the floor with a large book about animals in their lap. The *shhh* finally tumbled off her lips. The sound made her feel even more like the stuffy librarian she tried not to be.

The girls looked up, their little smiles wilting.

Lacy stepped closer to see what was so funny about animals and saw a large picture of a donkey with the heading

"Asses" at the top of the page. A small giggle tumbled off
Lacy's lips as well. She quickly regained control of herself
and offered a stern expression. "Girls, we need to be quiet
in the library. People come here to read and study."

"That's why we're here," Abigail Fields, the girl with
long, white-blond curls, said. They came in often with their
nanny, Mrs. Townsend, who usually fell asleep in the back
corner of the room. The woman was somewhere in her
eighties and probably wasn't the best choice to be taking
care of two energetic little girls.

"I have to write a paper on my favorite animal," Abigail said.

Lacy made a show of looking at the page. "And it's a
donkey?"

"That's not what that says," Willow, Abigail's younger
sister, said. "It says..."

"Whoa!" Lacy held up a hand. "I can read, but let's not
say that word out loud, okay? Why don't you two take that
book to a table and look at it quietly," she suggested.

The little girls got up, the older one lugging the large
book with both hands.

Lacy watched them for a moment and then turned
and headed back to her counter. She walked more slowly
as she stared at the back of a man waiting for her. He
wore dark jeans and a fitted black T-shirt that hugged
muscles she didn't even have a name for. There was probably an anatomy book here that did. She wouldn't mind
locating it and taking her time labeling each muscle, one
by one.

She'd seen the man before at the local café, she realized,
but never in here. And every time he'd walked into the
café, she'd noticed him. He, of course, had never noticed
her. He was too gorgeous and cool. There was also the fact

that Lacy usually sat in the back corner reading a book or people-watching from behind her coffee cup.

What is he doing here?

The man shifted as he leaned against her counter, his messenger bag swinging softly at his lower hip. Then he glanced over his shoulder and met her gaze. He had blue crystalline eyes, inky black hair, and a heart-stopping smile that made her look away shyly—a nervous remnant of her high school years when the cool kids like him had picked on her because of the heavy back brace she wore.

The brace was gone. No one was going to laugh at her anymore, and even if they did, she was confident enough not to find the closest closet to cry in these days.

"Hey," he said. "Are you Lacy Shaw, the librarian here?"

She forced her feet to keep walking forward. "I am. And you are?"

He turned and held out a hand. "Paris." He suspended his hand in midair, waiting for her to take it. When she hesitated, his gaze flicked from her face to her hand and then back again.

She blinked, collected herself, and took his hand. "Nice to meet you. I'm Lacy Shaw."

Paris's dark brows dipped farther.

"Right," she giggled nervously. "You didn't need me to introduce myself. You just asked if that's who I was. Do you, um, need help with something? Finding a book maybe?"

"I'm actually here for the class," he said.

"The computer skills class?" She walked around the counter to stand behind her computer. "The course instructor hasn't arrived yet." She looked at the Apple Watch on her wrist. "It's still a little early though. You're not late until you're less than five minutes early. That's what my mom always says."

Lacy had been wanting to offer a computer skills class here for months. There was a roomful of laptops in the back just begging for people to use them. She'd gotten the computer skills teacher's name from one of her regular patrons here, and she'd practically begged Mr. Montgomery over the phone to take the job.

"The class runs from today to next Thursday. It's aimed toward people sixty-five and over," she told the man standing across from her, briefly meeting his eyes and then looking away. "But you're welcome to attend, of course." Although she doubted he'd fit in. He appeared to be in his early thirties, wore dark clothes, and looked like his idea of fun might be adding a tattoo to the impressive collection on his arms.

Paris cleared his throat. "Unless I'm mistaken, I *am* the instructor," he said. "Paris Montgomery at your service."

"Oh." She gave him another assessing look. She'd been expecting someone...different. Alice Hampton had been the one to recommend Paris. She was a sweet old lady who had sung the praises of the man who'd rented the room above her garage last year. Lacy never would've envisioned the likes of this man staying with Mrs. Hampton. "Oh, I'm sorry. Thank you for agreeing to offer some of your time to our senior citizens. A lot of them have expressed excitement over the class."

Paris gave a cursory glance around the room. "It's no problem. I'm self-employed, and as I told you on the phone, I had time between projects."

"You're a graphic designer, right?" she asked, remembering what Alice had told her. "You created the designs for the Sweetwater Bed and Breakfast."

"Guilty. And for a few other businesses in Sweetwater Springs."

Lacy remembered how much she'd loved the designs when she'd seen them. "I've been thinking about getting something done for the library," she found herself saying.

"Yeah? I'd be happy to talk it over with you when you're ready. I'm sure we can come up with something simple yet classy. Modern. Inviting."

"Inviting. Yes!" she agreed in a spurt of enthusiasm before quickly feeling embarrassed. But that was her whole goal for the library this year. She wanted the community to love coming in as much as she did. When she was a child growing up, the library had been her haven, especially during those years of being bullied. The smell of books had come to mean freedom to her. The sound of pages turning was music to her ears.

"Well, I guess I better go set up for class." Paris angled his body toward the computer room. "Five minutes early is bordering on late, right?" he asked, repeating her words and making her smile.

He was cool, gorgeous, *and* charming—a dangerous combination.

———

Paris still wasn't sure why he'd agreed to this proposition. It paid very little, and he doubted it would help with his graphic design business. The librarian had been so insistent on the phone that it'd been hard to say no to her. Was that the same woman who'd blushed and had a hard time making eye contact with him just now? She looked familiar, but he wasn't sure where or when they'd ever crossed paths.

He walked into the computer room in the back of the

library and looked around at the laptops set up. How hard could it be to teach a group of older adults to turn on a computer, utilize the search engine, or set up an email account? It was only two weeks. He could handle that.

"You're the teacher?" a man's voice asked behind him.

Paris whirled to face him. The older man wore a ball cap and a plaid button-down shirt. In a way, he looked familiar. "Yes, sir. Are you here for the class?"

The man frowned. "Why else would I ask if you were the teacher?"

Paris ignored the attitude and gestured to the empty room. "You have your pick of seats right now, sir," Paris told him. Then he directed his attention to a few more seniors who strolled in behind the older man. Paris recognized a couple of them. Greta Merchant used a cane, but he knew she walked just fine. The cane was for show, and Paris had seen her beat it against someone's foot a couple of times. She waved and took a seat next to the frowning man.

"Paris!" Alice Hampton said, walking into the room.

He greeted her with a hug. After coming to town last winter and staying at the Sweetwater B&B for a week, he'd rented a room from Alice for a while. Now he had his own place, a little cabin that sat across the river.

All in all, he was happy these days, which is more than he could say when he lived in Florida. After his divorce, the Sunshine State had felt gloomy. He hadn't been able to shake the feeling, and then he'd remembered being a foster kid here in Sweetwater Springs, North Carolina. A charity event for bikers had given him an excuse to come back for a visit, and he'd never left. Not yet, at least.

"I told all my friends about this class," Alice said. "You're going to have a full and captive audience with us."

Nerves buzzed to life in his stomach. He didn't mind

public speaking, but he hoped most were happy to be here, unlike the frowner in the corner.

More students piled in and took their seats, and then the timid librarian came to the door. She nibbled on her lower lip, her gaze skittering everywhere but to meet his directly. "Do you need anything?"

Paris shook his head. "No, we have plenty of computers. We'll just get acquainted with them and go from there."

She looked up at him now, a blush rising over her high cheekbones. She had light brown hair spilling out of a messy bun and curling softly around her jawline. She had a pretty face, made more beautiful by her rich brown eyes and rose-colored mouth. "Well, you know where I am if you do need something." She looked at the group. "Enjoy!"

"You hired a looker!" Greta Merchant hollered at Lacy. "And for that, there'll be cookies in your future, Ms. Lacy! I'll bring a plate next class!"

The blush on Lacy's cheeks deepened as her gaze jumped to meet his momentarily. "Well, I won't turn down your cookies, Ms. Greta," she said.

Paris watched her for a moment as she waved and headed back to her post.

"The ink in those tattoos going to your brain?" the frowner called to him. "It's time to get started. I don't have all day, you know."

Paris pulled his gaze from the librarian and faced the man. "Neither do I. Let's learn something new, shall we?"

An hour later, Paris had taught the class of eleven to turn on and turn off the laptops. It'd taken an excruciating amount of time to teach everyone to open a browser and use a search engine. Overall, it'd gone well, and the hour had flown by.

"Great job," Alice said to him approvingly. She patted

a motherly hand on his back that made him feel warm and appreciated. That feeling quickly dissipated as the frowner headed out the door.

"I already knew most of what you taught," he said.

Who was this person, and why was he so grouchy?

"Well, then you probably didn't need this class," Paris pointed out politely. "Actually, you probably could've taught it yourself."

The frowner harrumphed. "Next time *teach* something."

Paris nodded. "Yes, sir. I'll do my best."

"Your best is the only acceptable thing," the man said before walking out.

Paris froze for a moment, reaching for the memory that the frowner had just stirred. *Your best is the only acceptable thing.* His foster dad here in Sweetwater Springs used to say that to him. That man had been nothing but encouraging. He'd taught Paris more about life in six months than anyone ever had before or since.

Paris hadn't even caught his student's name, and there was no roster for this computer skills class. People had walked in and attended without any kind of formal record.

Paris watched the frowner walk with slow, shuffled steps. He was old, and his back was rounded. A hat sat on his head, casting a shadow on his leathered face. All Paris had really seen of him was his deep, disapproving frown. It'd been nearly two decades since Paris had laid eyes on Mr. Jenson, but he remembered his former foster dad being taller. Then again, Paris had been just a child.

When Paris had returned to Sweetwater Springs last year, he'd decided to call. Mrs. Jenson had been the one to answer. She'd told him she didn't remember a boy named PJ, which is the name Paris had gone by back then. "Please, please, leave us alone! Don't call here again!"

she'd pleaded on the line, much to Paris's horror. "Just leave us alone."

The memory made Paris's chest ache as he watched the older man turn the corner of the library and disappear. He resisted the urge to follow him and see if it really was Mr. Jenson. But the Jensons had given Paris so much growing up that he was willing to do whatever he could to repay their kindness—even if it meant staying away.

———

Lacy was checking out books for the Fields girls and their nanny when Paris walked by. She watched him leave. If you flipped to the word *suave* in the dictionary, his picture was probably there.

"I plan to bring the girls to your summer reader group in a couple weeks," Mrs. Townsend said.

Of course she did. That would be a convenient nap time for her.

"I always love to see the girls." Lacy smiled down at the children. Their father, Granger Fields, and his family owned Merry Mountain Farms in town where Lacy always got her blue spruce for the holidays.

Lacy waved as the little girls collected their bags of books and skipped out with Mrs. Townsend following behind them.

For the rest of the afternoon, Lacy worked on ongoing programs and plans for the summer and fall. At six p.m., she turned off the lights to the building and headed into the parking lot.

She was involved with the Ladies' Day Out group, a gaggle of women who regularly got together to hang out and have fun. Tonight, they were meeting at Lacy's house to discuss a book that she'd chosen for everyone to read. They were in no way a book club, but since it was her turn to decide what they did, Lacy had turned it into one this time.

Excitement brimmed as she drove home. When she pulled up to her small two-bedroom house on Pine Cone Lane, she noticed two of her sisters' cars already parked in the driveway. Birdie and Rose had texted her during the day to see what they could do to help. Seeing the lights on inside Lacy's home, they'd evidently ignored Lacy's claims that she didn't need anything and had used her hideaway key under the flowerpot.

"Honey, I'm home!" Lacy called as she headed through the front door.

Birdie, her older sister by one year, turned to face her. "Hey, sis. Rose and I were just cleaning up for you."

"Great." Lacy set her purse down. "Now I don't have to."

"What is this?" Rose asked, stepping up beside Birdie. Rose was one year younger than Lacy. Their mom had been very busy those first three years of marriage.

Lacy looked at the small postcard that Rose held up.

"You were supposed to RSVP if you were going to your ten-year class reunion," Rose said. "You needed to send this postcard back."

"Only if I'm going," Lacy corrected.

"Of course you're going," Birdie said. "I went to my ten-year reunion last year, and it was amazing. I wish we had one every year. I wouldn't miss it."

Unlike Lacy, her sisters had been popular in school. They hadn't had to wear a bulky back brace that made them look like a box turtle in its shell. It had drawn nothing but negative attention during those long, tormenting years.

"It's not really a time in my life that I want to remember,"

Lacy pointed out as she passed them and headed into the kitchen for a glass of lemonade. Or perhaps she should go ahead and pour herself something stronger. She could tell she might need it tonight.

A knock on her front door made her turn. "Who is that?" Lacy asked. "I scheduled the book discussion for seven. It's only six." Lacy set down the glass she'd pulled from the cabinet and went to follow her sisters to the door.

"About that," Birdie said a bit sheepishly. "We changed the plan at the last minute."

Lacy didn't like the sound of that. "What do you mean?"

"No one actually read the book you chose," Birdie said as Rose let the first arrivals in. "Instead, we're playing matchmaker tonight. What goes together better than summer and love?"

Lacy frowned. "If you wanted summer love, I could've chosen a romance novel to read instead."

Birdie gave her a disapproving look. Lacy doubted anyone was more disappointed about tonight's shift in festivities than her though.

Chapter Two

Paris hadn't been able to fully concentrate for the last hour and a half as he sat in front of his computer working on a job for Peak Designs Architectural Firm. His mind was in other places. Primarily the library.

The Frowner, as he'd come to think of the old man in his class, was forefront in his mind. Was it possible that the Frowner was Mr. Jenson?

It couldn't be. Mr. Jenson had been a loving, caring guy, from what Paris remembered. Granted, loving and caring were subjective, and Paris hadn't had much to go on back then.

Mrs. Jenson had been the mother that Paris had always wished he had. She'd doted on him, offering affection and unconditional love. Even though Paris had been a boy who'd landed himself in the principal's office most afternoons, Mrs. Jenson had never raised her voice. And Mr. Jenson had always come home from his job and sat down with Paris, giving him a lecture that had proved to be more like a life lesson.

Paris had never forgotten those lessons. Or that man.

He blinked the memories away and returned his attention

to the design he was working on. It was good, but he only did excellent jobs. *Your best is the only acceptable thing.*

He stared at the design for another moment and then decided to come back to it tomorrow when he wasn't so tired. Instead, he went to his Facebook page and searched Albert Jenson's name. He'd done so before, but no profiles under that name had popped up. This time, one did. The user had a profile picture of a rose instead of himself. Paris's old foster dad had loved his rose gardens. This must be him!

Paris scrolled down, reading the most recent posts. One read that Mr. Jenson had gone to the nursing home to visit his wife, Nancy.

Paris frowned at the news. The transition must have been recent because Mrs. Jenson had been home when he'd called late last year. She'd been the one to pretty much tell him to get lost.

He continued to scroll through more pictures of roses and paused at another post. This one read that Mr. Jenson had just signed up for a computer skills class at the Sweetwater Library.

So it was true. Mr. Jenson, the foster dad who'd taught him so much, was also the Frowner.

———

Lacy had decided to stick to just lemonade tonight since she was hosting the Ladies' Day Out group. But plans were meant to be changed, as evidenced by the fact that the book discussion she'd organized had turned into the women sitting around her living room, eyes on a laptop screen while perusing an online dating site.

"Oh, he's cute!" Alice Hampton said, sitting on the couch and leaning over Josie Kellum's shoulder as she tapped her fingers along the keys of Lacy's laptop. Not that anyone had asked to use her computer. The women had just helped themselves.

Lacy reached for the bottle of wine, poured herself a deep glass, and then headed over to see who they were looking at. "I know him," she said, standing between her sisters behind the couch. "He comes into the library all the time."

"Any interest?" Josie asked.

Lacy felt her face scrunch at the idea of anything romantic with her library patron. "Definitely not. I know what his reading interests are and frankly, they scare me. That's all I'll say on that."

She stepped away from her sisters and walked across the room to look out the window. The moon was full tonight. Her driveway was also full, with cars parked along the curb. She wasn't a social butterfly by any means, but she looked like one this evening and that made her feel strangely satisfied.

"So what are your hobbies, Lacy?" Josie asked. "Other than reading, of course."

"Well, I like to go for long walks," Lacy said, still watching out the window.

Josie tapped a few more keys. "Mmm-hmm. What's your favorite food?"

Lacy turned and looked back at the group. "Hot dogs," she said, earning her a look from the other women.

"Do you know what hot dogs are made out of?" Greta wanted to know.

"Yes, of course I do. Why do I feel like I'm being interviewed for one of your articles right now?"

"Not an article," Birdie said. "A dating profile."

"What?" Lacy nearly spilled her glass of wine as she

moved to look over Josie's shoulder. "What are you doing? I don't want to be up on Fish In The Sea dot com. Stop that."

Birdie gave her a stern look. "You have a class reunion coming up, and you can't go alone."

"I'm not going period," Lacy reiterated.

"Not going to your class reunion?" Dawanda from the fudge shop asked. She was middle-aged with spiky, bright red hair. She tsked from across the room, where she sat in an old, worn recliner that Lacy had gotten from a garage sale during college.

Lacy finished off her wine and set the empty glass on the coffee table nearby. "I already told you, high school was a miserable time that I don't want to revisit."

"All the more reason you *should* go," Birdie insisted. Even though she was only a year older, Birdie acted like Lacy's mother sometimes.

"Why, so I can be traumatized all over again?" Lacy shook her head. "It took me years to get over all the pranks and ridicule. Returning to the scene of the crime could reverse all my progress."

"What progress?" Rose asked. "You never go out, and you never date."

Lacy furrowed her brow. "I go to the café all the time."

"Alone and you sit in the back," Birdie pointed out. "Your back brace is gone, but you're still hiding in the corner."

Lacy's jaw dropped. She wanted to argue but couldn't. Her sister was right.

"So we're making Lacy a dating profile," Josie continued, looking back down at the laptop's screen. "Twenty-eight years old, loves to read, and takes long walks in the park."

"I never said anything about the park," Lacy objected.

"It sounds more romantic that way." Josie didn't bother to look up. "Loves exotic fruit…"

"I said hot dogs."

This time Josie turned her head and looked at Lacy over her shoulder. "Hot dogs don't go on dating profiles...but cute, wagging dogs do." Her fingers started flying across the keyboard.

"I like cats." Lacy watched for another moment and then went to pour herself another glass of wine as the women created her profile at FishInTheSea.com.

After a few drinks, she relaxed a little and started feeding Josie more details about herself. She wasn't actually going to do this, of course. Online dating seemed so unromantic. She wanted to find Mr. Right the old-fashioned way, where fate introduced him into her life and sparks flew like a massive explosion of fireworks. Or at least like a sparkler.

———

An hour later, Lacy said goodbye to the group and sat on the couch. She gave the book she'd wanted to discuss a sidelong glance, and then she reached for her laptop. The dating profile stared back at her, taking her by surprise. They'd used a profile picture from when she'd been a bridesmaid at a wedding last year. Her hair was swept up and she had a dipping neckline on her dress that showed off more skin than normal. Lacy read what Josie and her sisters had written. The truth was disregarded in favor of more interesting things.

Lacy was proud of who she was, but the women were right. She wasn't acting that way by shying away from her reunion. She was acting like the girl in the back brace, quietly sitting in the far corner of the room out of fear that others might do something nasty like stick a sign on her back that read KICK ME! I WON'T FEEL IT!

"Maybe I should go to the reunion," she said out loud. "Or maybe I should delete this profile and forget all about it."

The decision hummed through her body along with the effect of one too many glasses of wine. After a moment, she shut the laptop and went to bed. She could decide her profile's fate tomorrow.

———

The next morning, Paris woke with the birds outside his window. After a shower and a quick bite, he grabbed his laptop to work on the deck, which served as his office these days. Before getting started on the Peak Designs logo, he scrolled through email and social media. He clicked on Mr. Jenson's profile again, only to read a post that Paris probably didn't need first thing in the morning.

> The computer skills class was a complete waste of time. Learned nothing. Either I'm a genius or the instructor is an idiot.

The muscles along the back of his neck tightened. At least he didn't need to wonder if Mr. Jenson would be back. He read another post.

> Went to see Nancy today. I think she misses her roses more than she misses me. She wants to come home, and this old house certainly isn't home without her.

Paris felt like he'd taken a fall from his bike, landing chest-first and having the breath knocked out of him. Why wasn't Mrs. Jenson home? What was wrong with her?

And why was Mr. Jenson so different from the man he remembered?

Paris pushed those questions from his mind and began work on some graphic designs. Several hours later, he'd achieved much more than he'd expected. He shoved his laptop into its bag, grabbed his keys, and rode his motorcycle to the library. As he walked inside, his gaze immediately went to the librarian. Her hair was pulled back with some kind of stick poking through it today. He studied her as she checked books into the system on her desktop.

She glanced up and offered a shy wave, which he returned as he headed toward the computer room. He would have expected Mr. Jenson not to return to class today based on his Facebook comments, but Mr. Jenson was already waiting for him when he walked in. All the other students from the previous day filed in within the next few minutes.

"Today I'm teaching you all to use Microsoft Word," he told the group.

"Why would I use Microsoft Word?" Alice Hampton asked. Her questions were presented in a curious manner rather than the questions that Mr. Jenson posed, which felt more like an attack.

"Well, let's say you want to write a report for some reason. Then you could do one here. Or if you wanted to get creative and write a novel, then this is the program you'd use."

"I've always wanted to write a book," Greta told Alice. "It's on my bucket list, and I'm running out of time."

"Are you sick?" Alice asked with concern, their conversation hijacking the class.

"No, I'm healthy as a buzzard. Just old, and I can't live forever," Greta told her.

"Love keeps you young," Edna Baker said from a few

chairs down. She was the grandmother of the local police chief, Alex Baker. "Maybe you should join one of those online dating sites."

The group got excited suddenly and turned to Paris, who had leaned back against one of the counters, arms folded over his chest as he listened.

He lifted a brow. "What?"

"A dating site," Edna reiterated. "We helped Lacy Shaw join one last night in our Ladies' Day Out group."

"The librarian?" Paris asked, his interest piquing.

"Had to do it with her dragging and screaming, but we did it. I wouldn't mind making a profile of my own," Edna continued.

"Me too." Greta nodded along with a few other women.

"I'm married," Mr. Jenson said in his usual grumpy demeanor. "I have no reason to be on a dating site."

"Then leave, Albert," Greta called out.

Mr. Jenson didn't budge.

"We're here to learn about what interests us, right?" Edna asked Paris.

He shrugged. There was no official syllabus. He was just supposed to teach computer literacy for the seniors in town. "I guess so."

"Well, majority rules. We want to get on one of those dating sites. I think the one we were on last night was called Fish In The Sea dot com."

Paris unfolded his arms, debating if he was actually going to agree to this. He somehow doubted the Sweetwater Springs librarian would approve, even if she'd apparently been on the site herself.

"Fine, I'll get you started," Paris finally relented, "but tomorrow, we're learning about Microsoft Word."

"I don't want to write a report or a novel," Mr. Jenson

said, his frown so deep it joined with the fold of his double chin.

"Again, don't come if you don't want to," Greta nearly shouted. "No one is forcing you."

Paris suspected that Mr. Jenson would be back regardless of his opinions. Maybe he was lonely. Or maybe, despite his demeanor, this was his idea of a good time.

After teaching the group how to use the search bar function and get to the Fish In the Sea website, Paris walked around to make sure everyone knew how to open an account. Some started making their own profiles while others watched their neighbors' screens.

"This is Lacy's profile," Alice said when he made his way to her.

Paris leaned in to take a closer look. "That's not the librarian here."

"Oh, it is. This photo was taken when she was a bridesmaid last year. Isn't she beautiful?"

For a moment, Paris couldn't pull his gaze away from the screen. If he were on the dating site, he'd be interested in her. "Likes to hike. Loves dogs. Favorite food is a hot dog. Looking for adventure," he read. "That isn't at all what I would have pegged Lacy as enjoying."

Alice gave him a look. "Maybe there's more to her than meets the eye. Would you like to sit down and create your own profile? Then you could give her a wink or a nibble or whatever the online dating lingo is."

He blinked, pulled his gaze from the screen, and narrowed his eyes at his former landlord. "You know I'm not interested in that kind of thing." He'd told Alice all about his past when he'd rented a room from her last year. After his messy marriage, the last thing he wanted was to jump into another relationship.

"Well, what I know is, you're young, and your heart can take a few more beatings if it comes to it. Mine, on the other hand, can't, which is why I'm not creating one of these profiles."

Paris chuckled. "Hate to disappoint, but I won't be either." Even if seeing Lacy's profile tempted him to do otherwise.

———

At the end of the hour, Paris was the last to leave his class, following behind Mr. Jenson, who had yet to hold a personal conversation with him or say a civilized thing in his direction.

He didn't recognize Paris, and why would he? Paris had been a boy back then. His hair had been long and had often hung in his eyes. His body had been scrawny from neglect and he hadn't gotten his growth spurt until well into his teen years. He hadn't even had the same last name back then. He'd gone by PJ Drake before his parents' divorce. Then there was a custody battle, which was the opposite of what one might think. Instead of fighting *for* him, his parents had fought over who *had* to take him.

"Mr. Jenson?" Paris called.

The older man turned to look at Paris with disdain.

"How was the class?"

"An utter waste of time."

Paris liked to think he had thick skin, but his former foster dad's words had sharp edges that penetrated deep. "Okay, well, what computer skills would you like to learn?"

The skin between Mr. Jenson's eyes made a deep divot as he seemed to think. "I can't see my wife every day like I want to because I don't drive. It's hard for an old man like me to go so far. The nurses say they can set up Skype to talk to her, but I don't understand it. They didn't have that sort of thing when I was young enough to learn new tricks."

"Never too late," Paris said. "A great man once taught me that."

That great man was standing in front of him now, whether he knew it or not. And he needed his own pep talk of sorts. "Come back tomorrow, and we'll get you set up for that."

Mr. Jenson frowned back at him. "We'll see."

———

Lacy was trying not to panic.

A blue circle had started spinning on her laptop screen five minutes ago. Now there were pop-up boxes that she couldn't seem to get rid of. She'd restarted her computer, but the pop-up boxes were relentless. She sucked in a breath and blew it out audibly. Then another, bordering on hyperventilation.

"You okay?" a man's voice asked.

Her gaze lifted to meet Paris's. "Oh. Yeah." She shook her head.

"You're saying yes, but you're shaking your head no." His smile was the kind that made women swoon, and for a moment, she forgot that she was in panic mode.

"My computer seems to be possessed," she told him.

This made Paris chuckle—a sound that seemed to lessen the tension inside her. "Mind if I take a look?"

She needed to say no. He was gorgeous, charming, and cool. And those three qualities made her nervous. But without her computer, she wouldn't be able to pay her bills after work. Or delete that dating profile that the Ladies' Day Out group had made for her last night. *Why didn't I delete it right away?*

"Yes, please," she finally said.

Paris headed around the counter. "Did you restart it?" he asked when he was standing right next to her. So close that she could smell the woodsy scent coming off his body. She could also feel a wave of heat radiating off him, burning the superficial layer of her skin. He was gorgeous, charming, cool, *and* he smelled divine. What woman could resist?

"I've restarted it twice already," she told him.

"Hmm." He put his bag down on the floor at his feet and stood in front of her computer. She couldn't help a closer inspection of the tattoos that covered his biceps muscles. They were colorful and artistically drawn, but she could only see parts of them. She had to resist pulling back the fabric of his shirt to admire the artwork there. What was wrong with her?

Paris turned his head to look at her. "Is it okay if I close out all the programs you currently have running?"

"Of course."

He tapped his fingers along her keys, working for several long minutes while she drifted off in her own thoughts of his muscles and tattoos and the spicy scent of his aftershave. Then he straightened and turned back to her. "There you go, good as new."

"Wow. Really? That was fast."

He shrugged a nonchalant shoulder. "I just needed to reboot and run your virus software."

"You make it sound so easy."

"To me it is. I know computers. We have a kinship."

Lacy felt the same way about books. She reached for her cup of coffee that she'd purchased this morning, even though a jolt of caffeine was probably the last thing her nerves needed right now.

Paris pointed a finger at the cup. "That's where I know you from. You're the woman at the café. You always sit in the back with a book."

Her lips parted as she set her cup down. "You've noticed me?"

"Of course. Why wouldn't I?"

She shrugged and shook her head. "We've just never spoken." And she'd assumed she was invisible in the back corner, especially to someone like him. "Well, thank you for fixing my computer."

"Just a friend helping a friend." He met her gaze and held it for a long moment. Then he bent to pick up the strap of his bag, hung it over his shoulder, and headed around to the other side of the counter. "Be careful on those dating sites," he said, stopping as he passed in front of her. "Always meet at a safe location and don't give anyone your personal information until you know you can trust them."

"Hmm?" Lacy narrowed her eyes, and then her heart soared into her throat and her gaze dropped to her fixed computer. Up on the screen, first and foremost, was FishInTheSea.com. She giggled nervously as her body filled with mortification. "I didn't…I'm not…" Why wouldn't her mouth work? "This isn't what it looks like."

Paris grinned. "The women in my class told me about last night. Sounds like you were forced into it."

"Completely," she said with relief.

He shrugged. "I doubt you need a website to find a date. They created a really attractive profile for you though. It should get you a lot of nibbles from the fish in the sea."

She laughed because he'd made a joke, but there was no hope of making intelligible words right now. Instead she waved and watched him leave.

"See you tomorrow, Lace," he called over his shoulder.

———

That evening, Paris kicked his feet up on the railing of his back deck as he sat in an outdoor chair, laptop on his thighs, watching the fireflies that seemed to be sending him secret messages with their flashing lights. The message he needed right now was "get back to work."

Paris returned to looking at his laptop's screen. He'd worked on the graphic for Peak Designs Architectural Firm all evening, and he was finally happy with it. He sent it off to the owner and then began work on a new agenda for tomorrow's class. He'd be teaching his students how to Skype, and he'd make sure Mr. Jenson knew how to do it on his own before leaving.

Paris liked the thought of reuniting Mr. and Mrs. Jenson through technology. It was the least he could do for them. Technology shouldn't replace person-to-person contact, but it was a nice substitute when two people couldn't be together. Paris suspected one of the main reasons Mr. Jenson even came to the library was because it was one of the few places within walking distance from his house.

Creating an agenda for live communication technology took all of ten minutes. Then Paris gave in to his impulse to search FishInTheSea.com. He found himself looking at Lacy's profile again, staring at the beautiful picture on the screen. Her brown hair was down and spilling over one shoulder in soft curls. She had on makeup that accentuated her eyes, cheekbones, and lips. And even though she looked so different from the person he'd met, she also looked very much the same.

"Why am I on a dating site?" he muttered, his voice blending with the night sounds. And for that matter, why was he staring at Lacy's profile? Maybe he was just as lonely as Mr. Jenson.

Chapter Three

I love the design," Pearson Matthews told Paris on Friday afternoon as Paris zipped down the gently winding mountain road on his bike. The pavement was still wet from the rain earlier this morning. Puddles splashed the legs of his jeans as he hit them.

He had earbuds in place under his helmet so he could ride hands-free and hold a conversation without the roar of the engine interfering. "I'm glad you like it, sir."

"Love. I said love," Pearson said. "And I plan to recommend you to everyone I know. I'm part of the Chamber of Commerce, so I have business connections. I'm going to make sure you have enough work to keep you in Sweetwater Springs for years to come."

Paris felt a curious kick in his heart. He loved this town and didn't like to think about leaving...but he had never been one to stick anywhere for long either. He credited the foster system for that. "Thank you."

"No need for thanks. You did a great job, and I want others to know about it. You're an asset here."

Paris resisted saying thank you a second time. "Well,

please make sure anyone you send my way tells me that you referred them. I give referral perks."

Pearson was one of the richest men in the community, so he likely didn't need any perks. "Sounds good. I'll talk to you soon."

They hung up, and Paris continued down the road, slowing at the entrance to the local library. His heart gave another curious kick at the thought of Lacy for a reason he didn't want to investigate. He parked, got off his bike, and then walked inside with his laptop bag on his shoulder.

Lacy wasn't behind the counter when he walked in. His gaze roamed the room, finding her with two little girls that he'd seen here before. She was helping them locate a book. One little girl was squirming as she stood in place, and Paris thought maybe she needed to locate a restroom first.

"Here you go. I think you girls will like this one," he heard Lacy tell them. "Abby, do you need to use the bathroom?"

The girl bobbed her head emphatically.

"You know where it is. Go ahead." Lacy pointed to the bathroom near the front entrance's double doors, and both girls took off in a sprint. Lacy watched them for a moment and then turned back to her computer. She gasped softly when she saw Paris. "You're here early. Do you need something?" she asked.

Need something? Yeah, he needed an excuse for why he'd been standing here stupidly waiting to talk to her.

"A book maybe?" Lacy stepped closer and lowered her voice.

"Yeah," he said. "I'm looking for a book."

"Okay. What exactly are you looking for?" she asked.

He scanned the surrounding shelves before his gaze

landed back on her. "Actually, do you have anything on roses?"

Lacy's perfectly pink lips parted.

Paris had been trying to think of something he could do for his former foster parents, and roses had come to mind. Albert Jenson loved roses, but his wife, Nancy, adored the thorny beauties. "I was thinking about making a flower garden at the nursing home, but my thumbs are more black than green."

Lacy giggled softly. "Follow me." She led him to a wall of books in the nonfiction area and bent to inspect the titles.

Paris tried and failed not to admire her curves as she leaned forward in front of him. *Get it together, man.*

"Here you go. *The Dummies' Guide to Roses.*" She straightened and held a book out to him.

"Dummies' Guide?"

Her cheeks flushed. "Don't take offense. I didn't title it."

Paris made a point of looking at the other titles that had sandwiched the book on the shelf. "No, but you didn't choose to give me the one titled *Everything There Is to Know About Roses* or *The Rose Lover's Handbook.*" He returned to looking at her, fascinated by how easily he could make her blush. "Any luck on Fish In The Sea dot com?"

She looked away, pulling her hands to her midsection to fidget. "I've been meaning to cancel that. The ladies had good intentions when they signed me up, albeit misguided."

"Why did they choose you as their victim?"

Lacy shrugged. "I have this high school reunion coming up. They thought I'd be more likely to go if I had a date."

"You're not going to your own reunion?" Paris asked.

"I haven't decided yet," she said as she inched away and increased the distance between them.

Unable to help himself, Paris inched forward. He told himself it was because they had to whisper and he couldn't hear her otherwise.

"Have you gone to one of yours?" she asked.

"No." He shook his head. "I never stayed in one place long enough while I was growing up to be considered an official part of a class. If I had, I would." He looked at her. "You should go. I'm sure you could find a date, even without the dating site." Part of him was tempted to offer to take her himself. By nature, he was a helpful guy. He resisted offering though because there was another part of him that wanted to be her date for an entirely different reason.

He lifted *The Dummies' Guide to Roses*. "I'll just check this out and get set up for my class."

Lacy headed back behind the counter and held out her hand to him. "Library card, please."

"Library card?" he repeated.

"I need it to check you out."

He laid the book on the counter. "I, uh, I…"

"You don't have one?" she asked, grinning back at him.

"I do most of my reading on the computer. I guess it's been a while since I've checked a book out."

"No problem." She opened a drawer and pulled out a blank card. "I can make you one right now. Do you have a driver's license?"

He pulled out his wallet and laid his license on the counter. He watched as she grabbed it and got to work. Then she handed the card back to him, her fingers brushing his slightly in the handoff. Every nerve in his body responded to that one touch. If he wasn't mistaken, she seemed affected as well.

There was the real reason he hadn't offered to be her date for her class reunion. He was attracted to Lacy Shaw, and he *really* didn't want to be.

———

Lacy lifted her gaze to the computer room in the back of the library where Paris was teaching a class of unruly elders. From afar, he actually seemed to be enjoying himself. She'd called several people before Paris, trying to persuade them to teach a class here, and everyone had been too busy with their own lives. That made her wonder why a guy like Paris was able to accept her offer. Did he have any family? Close friends? A girlfriend?

She roped in her gaze and continued checking in books from the pile beside her. Paris Montgomery's personal life was none of her business.

"Ms. Shaw! Ms. Shaw!" Abigail and Willow Fields came running toward the checkout counter.

"What's wrong, girls?" Lacy sat up straighter, noting the panic in the sisters' voices.

"Mrs. Townsend won't wake up! We thought she was sleeping, but she won't wake up!"

Lacy took off running to the other side of the room where she'd known Mrs. Townsend was sleeping. Immediately, she recognized that the older woman was hunched over the table in an unnatural way. Her skin was a pale gray color that sent chills up Lacy's spine.

Panic gripped Lacy as she looked around at the small crowd of people who'd gathered. "Does anyone know CPR?" she called. There were at least a dozen books here on the subject, but she'd never learned.

Everyone gave her a blank stare. Lacy's gaze snagged

on the young sisters huddled against the wall with tears spilling over their pale cheeks. If Mrs. Townsend died in front of them, they'd be devastated.

"Let's get her on the floor," a man's voice said, coming up behind Lacy.

She glanced back, surprised to find Paris in action.

He gently grabbed hold of Mrs. Townsend and laid her on the floor, taking control of the situation. She was never more thankful for help in her life.

"Call 911!" Lacy shouted to the crowd, relieved to see a young woman run toward the library counter where there was a phone. A moment later, the woman headed back. "They're on their way."

Lacy nodded as she returned to watching Paris perform chest compressions. He seemed to know exactly what to do. Several long minutes later, sirens filled the parking lot, and paramedics placed Mrs. Townsend onto a gurney. They revived her just enough for Mrs. Townsend to moan and look at the girls, her face seeming to contort with concern.

"It's okay. I'll take care of them, Mrs. Townsend," Lacy told her. "Just worry about taking care of yourself right now."

Lacy hoped Mrs. Townsend heard and understood. A second later, the paramedics loaded the older woman in the back of the ambulance and sped away, sirens screaming as they tore down the street.

Lacy stood on wobbly legs and tried to catch her breath. She pressed a hand against her chest, feeling like she might collapse or dissolve into tears.

"You all right?" Paris asked, pinning his ocean-blue gaze on hers.

She looked at him and shook her head. "Yes."

"You're contradicting yourself again," he said with a

slight lift at one corner of his mouth. Then his hand went to her shoulder and squeezed softly. "Why don't you go sit down?"

"The girls," Lacy said, suddenly remembering her promise. She turned to where the sisters were still huddled and hurried over to where they were. "Mrs. Townsend is going to get help at the hospital. They'll take good care of her there, I promise."

Abby looked up. "What's wrong with her?"

Lacy shook her head. "I'm not sure, honey. I'm sure everything will be okay. Right now, I'm going to call your dad to come get you."

"He's at work," Willow said. "That's why we were with Mrs. Townsend."

"I know, honey. But he won't mind leaving the farm for a little bit. Follow me to the counter. I have some cookies up there."

The girls' eyes lit up, even as tears dripped from their eyelashes.

"I can call Granger while you take care of the girls," Paris offered.

How did Paris know that these sweet little children belonged to Granger Fields? As if hearing her thoughts, he explained, "I did some graphic design work on the Merry Mountain Farms website recently."

"Of course. That would be great," Lacy said, her voice sounding shaky. And she'd do her best to calm down in the meantime too.

———

Thirty minutes later, Granger Fields left the library with his little girls in tow, and Lacy plopped down on her stool behind the counter. The other patrons had emptied out of the library as well, and it was two minutes until closing time.

"Eventful afternoon," Paris said.

Lacy startled as he walked into view. She hadn't realized he was still here. "You were great with the CPR. You might have a second career as a paramedic."

He shook his head. "I took a class in college, but I'll stick to computers, thanks."

"And I'll stick to books. My entire body is still trembling."

Paris's dark brows stitched together. "I can take you home if you're not up for driving."

"On your bike?" she asked. "I'm afraid that wouldn't help my nerves at all."

Paris chuckled. "Not a fan of motorcycles, huh?"

"I've never been on one, and I don't plan to start this evening. It's time to close, and my plans include calling the hospital to check on Mrs. Townsend and then going home, changing into my PJs, and soothing my nerves with ice cream."

Paris leaned against her counter. "While you were with the girls, I called a friend I know who works at Sweetwater Memorial. She checked on things for me and just texted me an update." He held up his cell phone. "Mrs. Townsend is stable but being admitted so they can watch her over the next forty-eight hours."

Lacy blew out a breath. "That's really good news. For a moment there, she looked like she might die. If we hadn't gone over to her when we did, she might have just passed away in her sleep." Lacy wasn't sure she would've felt as safe in her little library ever again if that had happened.

"Life is fragile," Paris said. "Something like this definitely puts things into perspective, doesn't it?"

"It really does." Her worries and fears suddenly seemed so silly and so small.

Paris straightened from the counter and tugged his bag higher on his shoulder. "See you tomorrow," he said as he headed out of the library.

She watched him go and then set about to turning off all the lights. She grabbed her things and locked up behind her as she left, noticing Paris and his motorcycle beside her car in the parking lot.

"If I didn't know you were a nice guy, I might be a little scared by the fact that you're waiting beside my car in an empty parking lot."

"I'm harmless." He hugged his helmet against him. "You looked a little rattled in there. I wanted to make sure you got home safely. I'll follow you."

Lacy folded her arms over her chest. "Maybe I don't want you to know where I live."

"The end of Pine Cone Lane. This is a small town, and I get around with business."

"I see. Well, you don't need to follow me home. Really, I'm fine."

"I'd feel better if I did."

Lacy held out her arms. "Suit yourself. Good night, Paris." She stepped inside her vehicle, closed the door behind her, and cranked her engine. It rolled and flopped. She turned the key again. This time it didn't even roll. "Crap." This day just kept getting better.

After a few more attempts, Paris tapped on her driver's side window.

She opened the door. "The battery is dead. I think I left my lights on this morning." It'd been raining, and she'd had them on to navigate through the storm. She'd forgotten her umbrella, so she'd turned off her engine, gotten out of her car, and had darted toward the library. In her rush, she must've forgotten to turn off her lights.

"I'll call Jere's Shop. He can jump your battery or tow it back to your house," Paris said.

Lacy considered the plan. "I can just wait here for him and drive it back myself."

"Jere is dependable but slow. You don't need to be out here waiting for him all evening. Leave your keys in the ignition, and I'll take you home."

Lacy looked at the helmet that Paris now extended toward her, her brain searching for another option. She didn't want to be here all night. She could call one of her sisters, but they would then follow her inside, and she didn't want to deal with them after the day she'd had either.

She got out of the car and took the helmet. "Okay," she said, shaking her head no.

This made Paris laugh as he led her to his bike. "You are one big contradiction, Lacy Shaw."

———

Paris straddled his bike and waited for Lacy to take the seat behind him. He glanced over his shoulder as she wrung her hands nervously. She seemed to be giving herself a pep talk, and then she lunged, as if forcing herself, and straddled the seat behind him.

Paris grinned and waited for another long second. "You know, you're going to have to wrap your arms around my waist for the ride."

"Right," he heard her say in a muffled voice. Her arms embraced him, clinging more tightly as he put the motorcycle in motion. Before he was even down the road, Lacy's grasp on him was so tight that her head rested on his back. He kind of liked the feel of her body hugging his, even if it was because she was scared for her life.

He knew the way to her house, but at the last second, he decided to take a different route. Lacy didn't speak up, so he guessed her eyes were shut tightly, blocking out the streets that zipped past.

Instead of taking her home, he drove her to the park, where the hot spring was. There were hiking trails and a hot dog vendor too. On her profile, Lacy had said those were among her favorite things, and after this afternoon, she deserved a few guilty pleasures.

He pulled into the parking lot and cut the engine. Slowly, Lacy peeled her body away from him. He felt her shift as she looked around.

She removed her helmet. "Why are we at the park?"

Paris glanced back. "Surprise. I thought I'd take your mind off things before I took you home."

She stared at him, a dumbfounded expression creasing her brow. "Why the park?"

"Because you love to take long hikes. And hot dogs, so I thought we'd grab a couple afterward. I didn't wear my hiking boots, but these will work for a quick half mile down the trail. Your profile mentioned that you love the hot spring here."

Lacy blinked. "You read my dating profile?"

"Great late-night reading." He winked.

She drew her hand to her forehead and shook her head. Something told him this time the head shake wasn't a yes. "Most of the information on my profile was exaggerated by the ladies' group. Apparently, they didn't think the real Lacy Shaw was interesting enough."

"You don't like hiking?"

"I like leisurely walks."

"Dogs?" he asked.

"Cats are my preference."

Paris let his gaze roam around them briefly before looking back at her. "What *do* you like?"

"In general?" she asked.

"Let's start with food. I'm starving."

She gave him a hesitant look. "Well, the hot dog part was true, but only because I added that part after they left."

Paris grinned, finding her adorable and sexy at the same time. "I happen to love a good chili dog. And there's a stand at the far side of the park." He waited for her to get off the bike and then he climbed off as well. "Let's go eat, shall we?"

"Saving someone's life works up an appetite, I guess."

"I didn't save Mrs. Townsend's life," he said as they walked. "I just kept her alive so someone else could do that."

From the corner of his eye, he saw Lacy fidgeting.

He reached for her hand to stop the motion. "I brought you here to take your mind off that situation. Let's talk about something light."

"Like?"

"You? Why did you let the Ladies' Day Out group make you a dating profile if you don't want to be on the site?"

Lacy laughed softly as they stepped into a short line for hot dogs. "Have you met the Ladies' Day Out group? They are determined and persistent. When they want something, they don't take no for an answer."

"You're part of the LDO," he pointed out.

"Well, I don't share that same quality."

"You were persistent in getting me to agree to teach a class at the library."

"True. I guess when there's something I want, I go after it." They reached the front of the line and ordered two sodas and two hot dogs. One with chili for him and one without for her.

Lacy opened the flap of her purse, and Paris stopped her. "I brought you here. This is my treat."

"No, I couldn't—"

She started to argue, but he laid a ten-dollar bill in front of the vendor. "It's just sodas and hot dogs." He glanced over. "You can treat me next time."

Her lips parted. He was only teasing, but he saw the question in her eyes, and now it was in his mind too. Would there really be a next time? Would that be so bad?

After collecting the change, they carried their drinks and hot dogs to a nearby bench and sat down.

"I didn't think I'd like teaching, but it's actually kind of fun," Paris confessed.

"Even Mr. Jenson?" she asked before taking a huge bite of her hot dog.

"Even him. But he didn't show up today. Maybe he dropped out." Paris shrugged. "I changed the syllabus just for him. I was planning to teach the class to Skype this afternoon."

"You didn't?"

He shook his head. "I went back to the lesson on Microsoft Word just in case Mr. Jenson showed up next time."

"Maybe he didn't feel well. He's been to every other class this week, right?"

Paris shook his head. "But he's made no secret that he doesn't like my teaching. He's even blasted his opinions all over Facebook."

Lacy grimaced. "Oh my. He treats everyone that way. I wouldn't take it personally. It's just how he is."

"He wasn't always that way. He used to be really nice, if memory serves me correctly."

Lacy narrowed her eyes. "You knew him before the class?"

Paris looked down at his half-eaten hot dog. "He and Mrs. Jenson fostered me for a while, but he doesn't seem to remember me."

"You were in foster care?"

"Yep. The Jensons were my favorite family."

Her jaw dropped. "That's so interesting."

Paris angled his body toward her. "Do you know what's wrong with Mrs. Jenson?"

Lacy shrugged. "I'm not sure. All I know is she's forgetful. She gets confused a lot. I've seen her get pretty agitated with Mr. Jenson too. They used to come into the library together."

"Maybe that's why he's so bitter now," Paris said, thinking out loud. He lifted his hot dog to his mouth and took another bite.

"Perhaps Mr. Jenson just needs someone to help him."

Paris chewed and swallowed. "I'm not even sure how I could help Mr. Jenson. I've been reading up on how to make a rose garden, but that won't make his wife well again."

Lacy hummed thoughtfully. "I think Mr. Jenson just needs someone to treat him nicely, no matter how horrible he is. No matter what he says to me, I always offer him a big smile. I actually think he likes me, although he would never admit it." She giggled to herself.

Paris looked at her. "You seem to really understand people."

"I do a lot of people-watching. And I had years of being an outcast in school." She swiped at a drop of ketchup at the corner of her mouth. "When you're hiding in the back of the classroom, there's not much else to do but watch everyone else. You can learn a lot about a person when they think no one is paying attention."

"Why would you hide?" he asked, growing increasingly interested in Lacy Shaw.

She met his gaze, and he glimpsed something dark in her eyes for a moment. "Childhood scoliosis. I had to wear a back brace to straighten out my spine."

His gaze dropped to her back. It was long and smooth now.

"I don't wear it anymore," she told him. "My back is fixed. High school is when you want to be sporting the latest fashion though, not a heavy brace."

"I'm sure you were just as beautiful."

She looked away shyly, tucking a strand of brown hair behind her ear with one hand. "Anyway, I guess that's why I know human nature. Even the so-called nice kids were afraid to be associated with me. There were a handful of people who didn't care. I'm still close with them."

"Sounds like your childhood was less than desirable. Kind of like mine," he said. "That's something we have in common."

She looked up. "Who'd have thought? The librarian and the bad boy biker."

"Bad boy?" he repeated, finding this description humorous.

Her cheeks blossomed red just like the roses he'd studied in the library book. She didn't look away, and he couldn't, even if he wanted to. Despite himself, he felt the pull between them, the sexual tension winding around its gear, cranking tighter and tighter. "Perhaps we have a lot more in common."

"Like what?" she asked softly.

"Well, we both like hot dogs."

She smiled softly.

"And I want to kiss you right now. Not sure if you want to kiss me too but..." What was he doing? It was as if something else had taken control of his mind and mouth. He was saying exactly the opposite of what he intended.

Lacy's lips parted, her pupils dilated, and unless he was reading her wrong, she wanted to kiss him too.

Leaning forward, he dropped his mouth and brushed his lips to hers. A little sigh tumbled out of her, and after a moment, she kissed him back.

Chapter Four

Sparks, tingles, the whole nine yards.

That was what this kiss with Paris was. He was an amazing kisser. He had a firm hand on her thigh and the other gently curled around the back of her neck. This was the Cadillac of kisses, not that Lacy had much experience recently. It'd been a while since she'd kissed anyone. The last guy she'd briefly dated had run the library in the town of River Oaks. They'd shared a love of books, but not much else.

Paris pulled back slightly. "I'm sorry," he said. "I didn't mean to do that."

She blinked him into focus, a dreamlike feeling hanging over her.

"All I wanted to do tonight was take your mind off the afternoon."

"The afternoon?" she repeated.

"Mrs. Townsend?"

"Oh." She straightened a touch. Was that why he'd kissed her? Was he only taking her mind off the trauma of what happened at the library? "I definitely forgot about that for a moment."

"Good." Paris looked around the park. Then he stood and offered her his hand. "Want to take a walk to the hot spring before we leave?"

She allowed him to pull her to standing. "Okay."

She followed him because he'd driven her here. Because he'd kissed her. Because she wasn't sure what to think, but one thing she knew for sure was that she liked being around Paris. He was easy to talk to, and he made her feel good about herself.

"Penny for your thoughts?" he asked a couple of minutes later, walking alongside her.

She could hear the subtle sound of water as they drew closer to the hot spring. "Oh, I was just thinking what a nice night it is."

Paris looked around. "I don't think there's a single season in this town that I don't like. The air is easier to breathe here for some reason." She watched him suck in a deep breath and shivered with her body's response.

"I've always wanted to get in a hot spring," Lacy admitted, turning her attention to the water that was now in view.

"You've never been in?" Paris asked.

Lacy shook her head. "No. That was another fabrication for the profile. I've read that a spring is supposed to help with so many things. Joint and muscle pain. Energy levels. Detoxification."

"Do you need those benefits?" he asked.

Lacy looked up at him. "Not really." All she really needed was to lean into him and press her lips to his once more.

Paris sighed as they walked. "So what should I do?"

A dozen thoughts rushed Lacy's mind. "Hmm?"

"I want to help Mr. Jenson somehow, like you suggested."

"Oh." She looked away as she swallowed. "Well, he didn't show up at today's class. Maybe you could stop by and see him. Tomorrow is Saturday, so there's no class anyway. You could check on him and make sure he's okay."

Paris stared at her. "I have to admit, that old man kind of scares me."

Lacy giggled softly. "Me too." She gasped as an idea rushed into her mind. She didn't give herself time to think before sharing it with Paris. "But I'll go with you. It's my day off."

He cocked his head. "You'd spend your day off helping me?"

"Yes, but there's a condition."

He raised a questioning brow. "What's that?"

"I'll go with you if you'll be my date to my class reunion." Seeing Mrs. Townsend at death's door this afternoon had shaken her up more than she'd realized. "I don't want to hide anymore. I want to go, have a blast, and show everyone who tried to break me that they didn't succeed." And for some reason, Paris made her feel more confident.

Paris grinned at her. "Are you asking me out, Lacy Shaw?"

She swallowed. "Yes. Kind of. I'm offering you a deal."

He shoved his hands in his pockets. "I guess Mr. Jenson might be less likely to slam the door on my face tomorrow if I have a beautiful woman by my side. You said he likes you, so..."

Her insides fluttered to life. "My old bullies might be less likely to pick on me if I have a hot graphic designer as my escort."

This made him laugh. Then Paris stuck out his hand. "Want to shake on it?"

She would prefer to kiss on it, but that first kiss

had come with an apology from him. This deal wasn't romantic in nature. It was simply two people helping one another out.

——

Even though Paris worked for himself, he still loved a Saturday, especially this one. He and Lacy were spending the day together, and he hadn't looked forward to something like this in a while. He got out of bed with the energy of a man who'd already had his coffee and headed down the hall to brew a pot. Then he dressed in a pair of light-colored jeans and a favorite T-shirt for a local band he loved.

As he sipped his coffee, he thought about last evening and the kiss that probably had a lot to do with his mood this morning. He hadn't planned on kissing Lacy, but the feeling had engulfed him. And her signals were all a go, so he'd leaned in and gone for it.

Magic.

There'd be no kissing today though. He didn't like starting things he couldn't finish, and he wasn't in the market for a relationship. He'd traveled that path, and his marriage had been anything but the happy ending he'd envisioned. He couldn't do anything right for his ex, no matter how hard he'd tried. As soon as he'd realized she was having an affair, he'd left. He didn't stick around where he wasn't wanted.

Paris stood and grabbed his keys. Then he headed out the door to go get Lacy. He'd take his truck today so that he didn't need to torture himself with the feel of her arms around his waist.

A short drive later, he pulled into her driveway on Pine

Cone Lane, walked up the steps, and knocked. She opened the door, and for a moment, he forgot to breathe. She wore her hair down, allowing it to spill softly over her shoulders just like in her profile picture. "You look, uh...well, you look nice," he finally said.

She lifted a hand and smoothed her hair on one side. "Thanks. At the library, it's easier to keep my hair pulled back," she explained. "But since I'm off today, I thought I'd let loose."

It was more than her hair. A touch of makeup accented her brown eyes, and she was wearing a soft pink top that brought out the colors in her skin. If he was a painter, he'd be running for his easel. If he was a writer, he'd grab a pen and paper, ignited by inspiration.

But he was just a guy who dabbled in computers. A guy who'd already decided he wasn't going to act on his attraction to the woman standing in front of him.

"I'm ready if you are," she said, stepping onto the porch and closing the front door behind her. She looked out into the driveway. "Oh, you drove something with four wheels today. I was ready for the bike, but I admit I'm kind of relieved."

"The bike grew on you a little bit?"

She shrugged one shoulder. "I could get used to it. My mother would probably kill you if she knew you put me on a motorcycle last night."

"I was rescuing you from being stranded in a dark parking lot," he pointed out.

"The lesser of two evils."

Paris jumped ahead to open her door, winning a curious look from her as well as a new blush on her cheeks—this one not due to makeup.

"Thanks."

He closed the door behind her and then jogged around to the driver's side. Once he was seated behind the steering wheel, he looked over. "Looks like Jere got your car back okay." He gestured toward her Honda Accord parked in front of a single-car garage.

"He left it and texted me afterward. No charge. He said he owed you." Lacy's brows subtly lifted.

"See, it pays to hang around me." Paris started the engine. "I was thinking we could stop in and check on Mrs. Townsend first."

Lacy pointed a finger at him. "I love that idea, even though I'm on to you, Paris Montgomery. You're really just procrastinating because you're scared of Mr. Jenson."

He grimaced as he drove toward the Sweetwater hospital. "That's probably true."

They chatted easily as he drove, discussing all of Lacy's plans for the library this summer. She talked excitedly about her work, which he found all kinds of attractive. Then he pulled into the hospital parking lot, and they both got out.

"We shouldn't go see Mrs. Townsend empty-handed," Lacy said as they walked toward the main entrance.

"We can swing by the gift shop before we go up," he suggested.

"Good idea. She likes magazines, so I'll get her a couple. I hope Abby and Willow are okay. It had to be confusing for them, watching their nanny being taken away in an ambulance."

"The girls only have one parent?" he asked.

"Their mother isn't around," Lacy told him.

Paris slid his gaze over. He wasn't sure he wanted to know, but he asked anyway. "What happened to their mom?" He'd heard a lot of stories from his foster siblings growing up. There were so many reasons for a parent to slip out of the picture. His story was rather boring in comparison to some. His parents didn't like abiding by the law, which left him needing supplementary care at times. Then they'd decided that another thing they didn't like was taking care of him.

"Their mother left right after Willow was born. There was speculation that maybe she had postpartum depression."

Paris swallowed as they veered into the gift shop. "It's good that they have Granger. He seems like a good dad."

"I think so too. And what kid wouldn't want to grow up on a Christmas tree farm? I mean, that's so cool." Lacy beelined toward the magazine rack in the back of the shop, picking out three. They also grabbed some chocolates at the register.

Bag of presents in hand, they left the shop and took the elevator up to the third floor to Mrs. Townsend's room. Lacy knocked, and they waited for Mrs. Townsend's voice to answer back, telling them to "come in."

"Oh, Lacy! You didn't have to spend your Saturday coming to see me," Mrs. Townsend said as they entered her room. "And you brought a friend."

"Mrs. Townsend, this is Paris Montgomery. He did CPR on you in the library yesterday."

Mrs. Townsend's eyes widened. "I didn't even know I needed CPR. How embarrassing. But thank you," she told Paris. "I guess you were instrumental in saving my life."

"It was no big deal," he said.

"To the woman who's still alive today it is." Mrs. Townsend looked at Lacy again, her gaze dropping to the bag in her hand. "What do you have?"

"Oh, yes." Lacy pulled the magazines out and offered them to Mrs. Townsend, along with the chocolates.

Mrs. Townsend looked delighted by the gifts. "Oh my goodness. Thank you so much."

"Are you doing okay?" Lacy asked.

Mrs. Townsend waved a hand. "The doctors here have been taking good care of me. They tell me I can go home tomorrow."

Lacy smiled. "That's good news."

"Yes, it is. And I'll be caring for the girls again on Monday. A little flutter in the heart won't keep me from doing what I love."

Lacy's gaze slid to meet Paris's as worry creased her brow. He resisted reaching for her hand in a calming gesture. His intentions would be innocent, but they could also confuse things. He and Lacy were only out today as friends. Nothing more.

They stayed and chatted a while longer and then left, riding down the elevator in silence. Paris and Lacy walked side by side back to his truck. He opened the passenger side door for her again and then got into the driver's seat.

"I'm glad Mrs. Townsend is okay," Lacy said as they pulled back onto the main road and drove toward Blueberry Creek Road, where Albert Jenson lived.

"Me too," Paris told her.

"But what happens next time?"

"Hopefully there won't be a next time."

"And if there is, hopefully you'll be around," Lacy said. Something about her tone made him wonder if she wanted to keep him around for herself too.

A few minutes later, he turned onto Mr. Jenson's street and traveled alongside Blueberry Creek. His heart quickened as he pulled into Mr. Jenson's driveway.

"I can't believe he walks from here to the library," Lacy said as he cut the engine. "That has to be at least a mile."

"He's always loved to walk." Paris let his gaze roam over the house. It was smaller than he remembered and in need of new paint. The rosebushes that the Jensons loved so much were unruly and unkempt. He was in his seventies now though. The man Paris knew as a child had been middle-aged and full of energy. Things changed. He looked over. "All right. Let's get this over with. If he yells at us, we'll know he's okay. The buddy system, right?"

"Right."

Except with each passing second spent with Lacy, the harder it was for him to think of her as just a buddy.

———

Lacy had never been to Mr. Jenson's home before. She'd known that the Jensons kept foster children once upon a time, but it surprised her that one of them was Paris.

"Strange, but this place feels like home to me," Paris said as he stood at the front door.

"How long did you live here with the Jensons?"

"About six months, which was longer than I lived with most."

"Makes sense why you'd think of this place fondly then." She wanted to ask more about his parents, but it wasn't the time. "Are you going to ring the doorbell?" she asked instead.

"Oh. I guess that would help." Paris pushed the button for the doorbell with his index finger and let his hands clasp back together in front of him.

"If I didn't know better, I'd think Mr. Cool was nervous," she commented.

"Mr. Cool?" He glanced over. "Any relation to Mr. Clean?"

This made her giggle until the front door opened and Mr. Jenson frowned back at them.

Lacy straightened. From the corner of her eye, she saw Paris stand more upright as well.

"Mr. Jenson," Paris said. "Good morning, sir."

"What are you doing here?" the old man barked through the screen door.

"Just checking on you. You missed a class that I put together just for you."

"I hear you were trying to kill people at the library yesterday," Mr. Jenson said, his frown steadfast. "Good thing I stayed home."

"Mrs. Townsend is fine," Paris informed him. "We just checked on her at Sweetwater Memorial."

"And now you're checking on me?" Mr. Jenson shook his head, casting a suspicious glare. "Why?"

Paris held up his hands. "Like I said, I missed you in yesterday's class."

Mr. Jenson looked surprised for a moment, and maybe even a little happy with this information. Then his grumpy demeanor returned. "I decided it wasn't worth my time."

Lacy noticed Paris tense beside her. "Actually, the class is free and taught by a professional," she said, jumping in to help. "We're lucky to have Mr. Montgomery teaching at Sweetwater Library."

Mr. Jenson gave her a long, hard look. She was prepared for him to take a jab at her too, but instead he shrugged his frail shoulders. "It's a long walk, and my legs hurt yesterday, okay? You happy? I'm not a spring chicken anymore, but I'm fine, and I'll be back on Monday. If for no other reason than to keep you two off my front porch." Mr. Jenson looked between them, and then he harrumphed and promptly slammed the door in their faces.

Lacy turned to look at Paris. "Are you sure you're remembering him correctly? I can't imagine that man was ever very nice."

"Did you see him smile at me before he slammed that door though? I think he's softening up."

Lacy laughed, reaching her arm out and grabbing Paris momentarily to brace her body as it shook with amusement. Once she'd realized what she'd done, she removed her hand and cleared her throat. "Okay, our well-check visits are complete. Mrs. Townsend and Mr. Jenson are both alive and kicking."

"I guess it's time for me to keep my end of the deal now," Paris said, leading her back to his truck.

Lacy narrowed her eyes. "But my reunion isn't until next Saturday."

"Yes, but I'm guessing you need to go shopping for something new to wear, right? And I can't wear jeans and an old T-shirt." He opened the passenger door for her.

"You can wear whatever you want," she told him as she stepped inside. Then she turned to look at him as he stood in her doorway.

"I want to look my best when I'm standing beside you. And I hear that Sophie's Boutique is the place to go if you want to dress to impress." He closed the door behind her and walked around to get in the driver's seat.

"Are you seriously offering to go dress shopping with me right now?" she asked once he was seated. "Because guys usually hate that kind of thing."

Paris grinned as he cranked the truck. "Sitting back and watching you come in and out of a dressing room, modeling beautiful clothes, sounds like a fun way to spend an afternoon to me." He winked before backing out of the driveway.

For a moment, Lacy was at a complete loss for words. "I mean, I'm sure you have other things to do with your Saturday afternoon."

He glanced over. "None as fun as hanging out with you."

She melted into the passenger seat. No one in her life had made her feel quite as interesting as Paris had managed to do last night and today. Just the opposite—the Ladies' Day Out group, while well-meaning, had made her feel boring by elaborating on the truth.

Paris made her feel other things as well. Things that were too soon to even contemplate.

Chapter Five

Every time Lacy walked out of the dressing room, Paris felt his heart kick a little harder. The dresses in Sophie's Boutique were gorgeous, but they paled in comparison to Lacy.

"You're staring at me," she said after twirling in a lavender knee-length dress with small navy blue polka dots. "Do you like this one or not?" She looked down. "I kind of love it. It's fun, and that's what I want for my reunion." She was grinning when she looked back up at him. "I want to dance and eat all the foods that will make this dress just a little too tight the next morning." A laugh tumbled off her lips.

Paris swallowed, looking for words, but they all got stuck in his throat. His feelings for Lacy were snowballing with every passing second—and it scared him more than Mr. Jenson did.

"Well?" she said again.

"That's the one for sure." He tore his gaze from her, pushing away all the thoughts of things he wanted to do to her in that dress. He wanted to spin her around on the dance floor, hold her close, and kiss her without apology next time.

Next time?

"Oh, wow! You look so beautiful!" Sophie Daniels, the boutique's owner, walked over and admired Lacy in the dress. "Is that the one?"

Lacy was practically glowing. "I think so, yeah."

Sophie turned to look at Paris. He'd met Sophie before, and she'd flirted mildly with him. He hadn't returned the flirting though because, beautiful as she was, he wasn't interested.

But he couldn't deny his interest in Lacy.

"Now it's your turn," Lacy said.

Sophie gestured to the other side of the store. "I have a rack of men's clothing in the back. Let's get you something that will complement what Lacy is wearing but not steal her show."

"As if I could steal the attention away from her," he said while standing.

Sophie's mouth dropped open. With a knowing look in her eyes, she tipped her head, signaling for him to follow her while Lacy returned to the dressing room to change.

"You seem like a nice guy, Paris, and Lacy deserves someone who will treat her well," Sophie said to him over her shoulder as she led the way.

"It's not like that between us." He swiped a hand through his hair. "I mean, Lacy is terrific, but the two of us don't make sense."

Sophie started sifting through the men's clothes on the rack. "Why not? You're both single and attractive. She avoids the spotlight, and you kind of grab people's attention wherever you go."

"I do?" he asked.

Sophie stopped looking through the clothes to give him another knowing look. "Opposites attract is a real thing, and it makes perfect sense." She pulled out a dark purple button-down shirt that would match Lacy's dress. "Do you have black pants?"

"I have black jeans," he told her.

She seemed to think about this. "Yes, black jeans will work. You just need to dress up a little bit. You're a jeans and T-shirt kind of guy, so let's keep the jeans." She nodded as if making the decision. "You, but different."

"Me, but different," he agreed, taking the shirt from her. That's how he felt with Lacy. He was still him but more grounded. And Lacy was still reserved but also coming out of her shell, and he loved watching it happen. "Do you have any bathing suits?" he asked on a whim. "One for me and one for Lacy?"

Sophie's eyes lit up, a smile lifting at the corners of her mouth. "Of course I do."

"I'll take one for each of us then. And this shirt for the reunion," Paris said.

Sophie gave him a conspiratorial wink. "I'll take care of it."

———

Lacy felt like Julia Roberts in *Pretty Woman*. She loved the dress she'd picked out, and she'd enjoyed the way Paris had stared at her as she'd modeled each one before it.

They left the boutique and walked back to Paris's truck. He opened her door, and she got in, tucking her bag in the floorboard at her feet. "That was so much fun. Thank you."

He stood in the open doorway of his truck, watching her. His gaze was so intense, and for a moment, her heart sped up. Was he going to kiss her again?

"I want to take you somewhere else," he said.

She furrowed her brow. They'd already spent nearly the entire day together, not that she minded. "Where?"

He placed a second bag in her lap and winked before shutting the door behind her and walking around the truck.

Lacy peeked inside the bag and gasped as he opened his own door and got behind the wheel. "This is a bathing suit."

"You said you always wanted to go to the hot spring. You and I are on one big adventure today, so I thought it'd be fitting to end our expedition by doing something on your bucket list."

"I don't actually have a bucket list," she noted, looking down at the bathing suit again, "but if I did, this would be on it. I can't believe you got me a bathing suit." Underneath her bright pink suit in the bag was a pair of men's board shorts. "Are we really going to do this?"

Paris looked over. "Only if you agree. Will you go on a date with me to the hot spring?"

A date? Had he meant that the way it'd sounded? Because a date implied that they were more than friends, and that's the way she felt about him right now.

———

The night was alive with sounds of nature. In the past hour, the sun had gone down behind the mountains, and stars had begun to shimmer above as darkness fell.

Lacy came out of the changing room with her bathing suit on and a towel wrapped around her waist. Paris was waiting on a bench for her, bare chested and in a pair of swim shorts.

Her mouth went dry. This wasn't her. She didn't visit

hot springs with gorgeous men. Her idea of fun on a Saturday night was curling up on her front porch swing with a good book. This was a nice change of pace though, and with Paris beside her, she didn't mind trying something new.

"Ready?" he asked, standing and walking toward her. He reached for her hand and took it. The touch zinged from her heart to her toes, bouncing back up through her body like a ball in a pinball machine.

The sound of water grew louder as they approached the hot spring. They were the only ones here so far this evening, which she found odd and exciting.

Paris stood at the steps and looked at Lacy. "You're going to have to drop that towel," he said, his gaze trailing from her face and down her body toward her hips.

"Right." She swallowed and let go of his hand. She was about to remove her towel, but he reached out for her and did the honors. There was something so intimate about the gesture that her knees weakened. The towel fell in his hand, leaving her standing there in just her suit. She felt exposed and so alive.

He met her gaze for a long moment and then folded the towel and left it on a bench. Turning back to her, he reached for her hand again. "Careful," he said quietly, leading her down the steps and into the water.

She moaned softly as the hot water lapped against her skin. "This is heavenly," she finally said once she'd taken a seat inside. He was still holding her hand, and that was heavenly as well. They leaned back against the spring's wall, and both of them looked up at the stars.

"Anywhere I've been in my life," Paris whispered after a moment, "I've always been under these same stars. I've always wished I was somewhere different when I looked up, but tonight, there's nowhere else I'd rather be." He looked over, his face dangerously close to hers.

She swallowed. "Are you going to kiss me again?"

His blue eyes narrowed. "Do you want me to kiss you again?"

"Ever since that first kiss."

His eyes dropped to her mouth. Her lips parted for him. Then he leaned just a fraction, and his lips brushed against hers. He stayed there, offering small kisses that evolved into something deeper and bigger. One of his hands slid up her thigh, anchoring midway. The touch completely undid her, and if they weren't in a public setting, she might have wiggled until his hand slid higher.

"Are you going to apologize again?" she asked once he'd pulled away.

He shook his head. "I'm not sorry."

"Me neither," she whispered. Then she leaned in and kissed him this time. Who was she these days? This wasn't like her at all.

They didn't stop kissing until voices approached the hot spring. Lacy pulled back from Paris. Another couple appeared and headed toward the spring. They stepped in and sat across from Lacy and Paris.

"We have to behave now," Paris whispered in Lacy's ear.

"Easier said than done." She grinned at him.

"And I'm not leaving until this little problem I have has gone down."

"What problem?" she asked, looking down through the clear bubbles. Then she realized what he was referring to, and her body grew impossibly hotter.

They returned to looking at the stars and talking in whispers, sharing even more details about themselves. Lacy could've stayed and talked all night, but the hot spring closed at ten p.m. When she finally stepped out of the water, the cool air was a harsh contrast.

After toweling off and changing in the dressing room, Lacy met Paris outside and got into his truck. He drove slowly as he took her home, their conversation touching various subjects. And the more she learned about Paris, the more she wanted to know.

Finally, he pulled into her driveway and looked at her.

"I'm not sure you should walk me to my door," Lacy said. "I'd probably end up asking you if you wanted to come inside." She nibbled softly on her lower lip. "And, well, that's probably not the best idea."

"I understand." He reached for her hand. "Thank you for the best day that I can remember."

She leaned toward him. "And the best night."

She gave him a brief kiss because there was still the risk that she might invite him inside. She was doing things that were surprising even herself. "The library is closed tomorrow. I can make lunch if you want to come over."

He hesitated.

"I mean, you don't have to, if you have something else to do."

He grinned. "I have work to do tomorrow, but a man has to eat, right? Lunch sounds nice. I'll be here."

"Perfect." She pushed the truck door open before her hormones took over and she climbed over to his side of the truck instead. "Good night, Paris."

"Good night, Lace."

Chapter Six

Lacy wasn't thinking straight last night. Otherwise, she would've remembered that a few members of the Ladies' Day Out group were coming over for lunch after church. No doubt they wanted to nag her about one thing or another. Today's topics were most likely the dating site and her reunion.

Then again, that was all the more reason for Paris to join them for lunch. His presence would kill two birds with one stone. She didn't need a dating site. And she and Paris were going to have an amazing time at her reunion next weekend.

She heard his motorcycle rumble into her driveway first. She waited for him to ring the doorbell, and then she went to answer. Butterflies fluttered low in her belly at the sight of him.

"Come in." She led him inside the two-bedroom house that she'd purchased a couple of years ago. "It's not much, but it's home."

"Well, sounds cliché, but I've learned that home really is where the heart is," he said.

She turned to look at him, standing close enough that

she could reach out and touch him again. Maybe pull him toward her, go up on her tiptoes, and press her lips to his. "By cliché, you mean cheesy?"

Paris pretended to push a stake through his heart. "When you get comfortable with someone, your feisty side is unleashed. I like it." He leaned in just a fraction, and Lacy decided to take a step forward, giving him the not-so-subtle green light for another kiss. He was right. She was feisty when she was with him, and she liked this side of her too.

The sound of another motor pulling into her driveway got her attention. She turned toward her door.

"Are you expecting someone else?" Paris asked, following her gaze.

"Yes, sorry. I didn't remember when I invited you last night, but I have company coming over today."

"Who?" Paris asked.

"My mom."

He nodded. "Okay."

"And my two sisters, Birdie and Rose," Lacy added. "*And* my aunt Pam."

Paris started to look panicked. "Anyone else?"

"Yeah. Um, Dawanda from the fudge shop. They're all part of the Ladies' Day Out group. I got a text earlier in the week telling me they were bringing lunch."

"Well, I'll get out of you guys' hair," he said, back-pedaling toward the door.

She grabbed his hand, holding it until he met her gaze. "Wait. You don't need to leave. I want you here."

Paris grimaced. "Family mealtime has never really been my strong point."

Lacy continued to hold his hand. She wanted to show the women outside that she could find a guy on her own.

She didn't need FishInTheSea.com. She also wanted to show them this new side of herself that seemed to take hold when she was with Paris. "They're harmless, I promise. Please stay."

Paris shifted on his feet, and she was pretty sure he was going to turn down the invitation. "You didn't take no for an answer when you wanted me to teach the computer class at the library," he finally said. "I'm guessing the same would be true now, huh?"

She grinned. "That's right."

"You're a hard woman to resist."

"Then stop trying," she said, going to answer the door.

———

The spread on Lacy's table was fit for a Thanksgiving dinner by Paris's standards. Not that he had much experience with holidays and family gatherings. He'd had many a holiday meal with a fast-food bag containing a burger, fries, and a small toy.

"I would've brought Denny if I'd known that men were allowed at lunch today," Mrs. Shaw said, speaking of her husband. She seemed friendly enough, but Paris also didn't miss the scrutinizing looks she was giving him when she thought he wasn't looking. He was dressed in dark colors and had tattoos on both arms. He also had a motorcycle parked in the driveway. He probably wasn't the kind of guy Mrs. Shaw would have imagined her sweet librarian daughter with.

"Good thing you didn't bring Dad," Lacy's sister Birdie said. "He would've grilled Paris mercilessly."

"Paris and I aren't dating," Lacy reiterated for the tenth time since she'd welcomed the women into her home. She slid her gaze to look at Paris, and he saw the question in her eyes. *Are we?* When the ladies had come through the front door, they'd all immediately begun calling him Lacy's secret boyfriend.

"Sounds like I'd be in trouble if you and I did get together," Paris said. "Your dad sounds strict."

Lacy laughed softly. "Notice that my sisters and I are all still single. There's a reason for that."

Lacy's other sister, Rose, snorted. "Dad crashed my high school prom when I didn't come home by curfew. Who has a curfew on prom night?" Rose slid her fork into a pile of macaroni and cheese. "I thought I'd never forgive Dad for that. I liked that guy too."

"What was his name again?" Mrs. Shaw asked.

Rose looked up, her eyes squinting as she seemed to think. "I can't remember. Brent maybe. Bryce? Could've been Bryan."

"You couldn't have liked him too much if you can't remember his name," Mrs. Shaw pointed out.

Everyone at the table laughed.

"Don't you worry, Rose," Dawanda said, seated beside Mrs. Shaw. "I've read your cappuccino, and you have someone very special coming your way. I saw it in the foam."

"Well, I'll be sure to keep him away from my dad until the wedding," Rose said sarcastically, making everyone chuckle again.

Whereas some read tea leaves, Dawanda read images formed in the foam of a cappuccino. She'd done a reading for Paris last Christmas. Oddly enough, Dawanda had told him he was the only one whose fortune she couldn't read. Dawanda had assured him it wasn't that he was going to fall off a cliff or anything. His future was just up in the air. He had shut his heart off to dreaming of a life anywhere or with anyone.

He didn't exactly believe in fortune-telling, but she was spot-on with that. Some people just weren't cut out for forever homes and families. He guessed he was one of them.

"Dad's first question any time he meets any of our dates is 'What are your intentions with my girl?'" Rose said, impersonating a man's deep voice.

"He actually said that while sharpening his pocketknife for a date I brought home in college," Birdie said. "I didn't mind because I didn't like the guy too much, but what if I had?"

"Then you would've been out of luck," Lacy said on a laugh.

The conversation continued, and then Mrs. Shaw looked across the table at Paris. "So, Paris," she said, her eyes narrowing, "tell us about yourself. Did you grow up around here?"

Paris looked up from his lunch. "I spent a little time in Sweetwater Springs growing up. Some in Wild Blossom Bluffs. My parents moved around a lot."

"Oh? For their jobs? Military maybe?" she asked.

Paris shifted. Ex-felons weren't allowed to join the military. "Not exactly. I was in foster care here for a while."

"Foster care?" Mrs. Shaw's lips rounded in a little O. "That must've been hard for a young child."

Paris focused his attention back on his food. "I guess I didn't really know any different. Most of the places I landed were nice enough." And there'd been somewhere he'd wished he could stay. Six months with the Jenson family was the longest amount of time he'd ever gotten to stay. It was just enough time to bond with his foster parents and to feel the loss of them to his core when he was placed back with his real parents.

He picked up his fork and stabbed at a piece of chicken.

"And what brought you back to Sweetwater Springs? If I recall, you moved here last year, right?" Dawanda asked. "You came into my shop while you were staying at the Sweetwater Bed and Breakfast."

Paris swallowed past the sudden tightness in his throat. He didn't really want to answer that question either. He looked around the table, his gaze finally landing on Lacy. "Well, I guess I decided to come back here after my divorce."

Lacy's lips parted.

Had he forgotten to mention that little detail to her? When he was with Lacy, he forgot all about those lonely years in Florida. All he could think about was the moment he was in, and the ones that would follow.

"That sounds rough as well," Mrs. Shaw said.

Paris shrugged, feeling weighed down by the truth. "Well, those things are in the rearview mirror now." He tried to offer a lighter tone of voice, but all the women looked crestfallen. Mrs. Shaw had already seemed wary of him, but now she appeared even more so.

"And since my husband isn't here to ask"—Mrs. Shaw folded her hands in front of her on the table—"what are your intentions with my daughter?"

"Mom!" Lacy set her fork down. "Paris and I aren't even dating." She looked over at him. "I mean, we went on a date last night. Two if you count that night at the park."

"Last night?" Birdie asked.

All the women's eyes widened.

"It wasn't like that." Lacy looked flustered. "We didn't spend the night together."

Mrs. Shaw's jaw dropped open, and Lacy's face turned a deep crimson.

Guilt curled in Paris's stomach. Lacy was trying her best to prove herself to everyone around her. Now her family and Dawanda were gawking at her like she'd lost her mind. It was crazy to think that she and Paris would be dating. Sophie Daniels had told him at the boutique that opposites attract, but he and Lacy had led very different lives.

"Sounds like you're dating to me. Are you going to go out again?" Rose asked.

"Well, Paris offered to go with me to my reunion," Lacy said.

Mrs. Shaw's smile returned. "Oh, I'm so glad you decided to go! That's wonderful, dear. I want all those bullies to see that you are strong and beautiful, smart and funny, interesting—"

"Mom," Lacy said, cutting her off, "you might be a little partial."

"But she's right," Paris said, unable to help himself.

Lacy turned to look at him, and something pinched in his chest. He'd tried to keep things strictly friendly with her, but he'd failed miserably. What was he going to do now? He didn't want a relationship, but if they continued to spend time together, she would.

"So, Paris, how did you get our Lacy to agree to go to this reunion of hers?" Mrs. Shaw asked. "She was so dead set on not attending."

"Actually, Lace made that decision on her own," he said.

"Lace?" Both Birdie and Rose asked in unison.

The nickname had just rolled off his tongue, but it fit. Lace was delicate and beautiful, accentuated by holes that one might think made it more fragile. It was strong, just like the woman sitting next to him. She was stronger than she even knew.

"Well, I'm glad she's changed her mind. High school was

such a rough time for our Lacy," Mrs. Shaw said. "I want her to go and have a good time and show those bullies who treated her so badly that they didn't break her."

Paris glanced over at Lacy. He wanted her old classmates to see the same thing.

Mrs. Shaw pointed a finger at Paris, gaining his attention. "But if you take her, it won't be on the back of that motorcycle in the driveway. Lacy doesn't ride those things."

"Actually, Mom, I rode on the back of it with Paris two days ago."

Mrs. Shaw looked horrified.

"Maybe he'll let me drive it next time," Lacy added, making all the women at the table look surprised.

"Lacy rode on the back of your bike?" Birdie asked Paris. "This is not our sister. What have you done with the real Lacy Shaw?"

He looked over at the woman in question. The real Lacy was sitting right beside him. He saw her, even if no one else did. And the last thing he wanted to do was walk away from her, which was why he needed to do just that.

———

An hour later, Lacy closed her front door as her guests left and leaned against it, exhaling softly.

"Your mom and sisters are great," Paris said, standing a couple of feet away from her. "Your aunt too."

She lifted her gaze to his. "You almost sound serious about that."

"Well, I'm not going to lie. They were a little overwhelming."

"A little?" Lacy grinned. "And they were subdued today. They're usually worse."

Paris shoved his hands in his pockets. "They love you. Can't fault them for that."

The way he was looking at her made her breath catch. Was he going to kiss her again?

"I guess not."

"They want what's best for you," he continued. Then he looked away. "And, uh, I'm not sure that's me, Lace."

She straightened at the sudden shift in his tone of voice. "What?"

He ran a hand over his hair. "When we were eating just now, I realized that being your date might not be doing you any favors. Or me."

"Wait, you're not going to the reunion with me any-more?" she asked.

He shook his head. "I just think it'd be better if you went with someone else."

"I don't have anyone else," she protested, her heart beating fast. "The reunion is in less than a week. I have my dress, and you have a matching shirt. And you're the one I want to go with. I don't even care about the reunion. I just want to be with you."

He looked down for a moment. "You heard me talking to your family. I've lived a different life than you. I'm an ex-foster kid. My parents are felons." He shrugged. "I couldn't even make a marriage work."

"Those things are in the past, Paris. I don't care about any of that."

He met her gaze again. "But I do. Call me selfish, but I don't want to want you. I don't want to want things that I know I'll never have. It's not in the cappuccino for me, Lacy." His expression was pained. "I really want you to believe me when I say it's not you, it's me."

Her eyes and throat burned, and she wondered if she felt

worse for herself or for him. He obviously had issues, but who didn't? One thing she'd learned since high school was that no one's life was perfect. Her flaws were just obvious back then because of the back brace.

She'd also learned that you couldn't make someone feel differently than they did. The only feelings you could control were your own. The old Lacy never stood up for herself. She let people trample on her and her feelings. But she'd changed. She was the new Lacy now.

She lifted her eyes to meet Paris's and swallowed past the growing lump in her throat. "If that's the way you feel, then I think you should go."

Chapter Seven

On Monday afternoon, Paris looked out over the room-ful of students. Everyone had their eyes on their screens and were learning to Skype. But his attention was on the librarian on the other side of the building.

When he'd driven to the library, he'd lectured himself on why he needed to back away from Lacy Shaw. Sunday's lunch had made that crystal clear in his mind. She was smart and beautiful, the kind of woman who valued family. Paris had no idea what it even meant to have a family. He couldn't be the kind of guy she needed.

Luckily, Lacy hadn't even been at the counter when he'd walked in and continued toward the computer room. She was probably hell-bent on avoiding him. For the best.

"Does everyone think they can go home and Skype now?" Paris asked the class.

"I can, but no one I know will know how to Skype with me," Greta said.

Janice Murphy nodded beside her.

"Well, you could all exchange information and Skype with each other," Paris suggested.

"Can we Skype with you?" Alice asked.

Warmth spread through his chest. "Anytime, Alice."

"Can I Skype you if my wife doesn't want to talk to me?" Mr. Jenson asked. "To practice so I'm ready when she does?"

Paris felt a little sad for the older man. When Paris had been a boy in their home, they'd been the happiest of couples. "Of course. If I'm home and free, I'll always make time to Skype with any one of you," he told the group, meaning it. They'd had only a few classes, but he loved the eclectic bunch in this room.

When class was over, he walked over to Mr. Jenson. "I can give you a ride home if you want."

Mr. Jenson gave him an assessing stare. "If you think I'm climbing on the back of that bike of yours, you're crazy."

Paris chuckled. "I drove my truck today. It'll save you a walk. I have the afternoon free too. I can take you by the nursing home facility to see Mrs. Jenson if you want. I'm sure she'd be happy to see you."

Mr. Jenson continued to stare at him. "Why would you do that? I know I'm not that fun to be around."

Paris clapped a gentle hand on Mr. Jenson's back. "That's not true. I kind of like being around you." He always had. "And I could use some company today. Agreeing would actually be doing me a favor."

"I don't do favors," the older man said. "But my legs are kind of hurting, thanks to the chairs in there. So walking home would be a pain."

Paris felt relieved as Mr. Jenson relented. "What about visiting Mrs. Jenson? I'll stay in the truck while you go in, and take as long as you like." Paris patted his laptop bag. "I have my computer, so I can work while I wait."

Mr. Jenson begrudgingly agreed and even smiled a little bit. "Thank you."

Paris led Mr. Jenson into his truck and started the short drive toward Sweetwater Nursing Facility.

"She sometimes tells me to leave as soon as I get there," Mr. Jenson said as they drove.

"Why is that?"

Mr. Jenson shrugged. "She says she doesn't want me to see her that way."

Paris still wasn't quite sure what was wrong with Mrs. Jenson. "What way?"

"Oh, you know. Her emotions are as unstable as her walking these days. That's why she's not home with me. She's not the same Nancy I fell in love with, but she's still the woman I love. I'll always love her, no matter how things change."

"That's what love is, isn't it?" Paris asked.

Mr. Jenson turned to look out the passenger side window as they rode. "We never had any kids of our own. We fostered a few, and that was as close as we ever got to having a family."

Paris swallowed painfully.

"There was one boy who was different. We would've kept him. We bonded and loved him as our own."

Paris glanced over. Was Mr. Jenson talking about him? Probably not, but Paris couldn't help hoping that he was. "What happened?"

"We wanted to raise him as part of our family, but it didn't work out that way. He went back to his real parents, which I suppose is always best. I lost him, and now, most days, I've lost my wife too. That's what love is. Painful."

Paris parked and looked over. "Well, maybe today will be different. Whatever happens, I'll be in the truck waiting for you."

Mr. Jenson looked over and chuckled, but Paris could tell

by the gleam in his eyes that he appreciated the sentiment. He stepped out of the truck and dipped his head to look at Paris in the driver's seat. "Some consolation prize."

———

Two nights later, Lacy sat in her living room with a handful of the Ladies' Day Out members. They'd been waiting for her in the driveway when she'd gotten home from the library and were here for an intervention of sorts.

"Sandwiches?" Greta asked, her face twisting with displeasure.

"Well, when you don't tell someone that you're coming, you get PB&J." Lacy plopped onto the couch beside Birdie, who had no doubt called everyone here.

"You took your online profile down," Birdie said, reaching for her own sandwich.

"Of course I did. I'm not interested in dating right now."

"You sure looked interested in Paris Montgomery," Dawanda said, sitting across from them. "And you two looked so good together. What happened?"

All the women turned to face Lacy.

She shrugged. "My family happened. No offense. You all behaved—mostly," she told her mom and sisters. "We just decided it'd be best to part ways sooner rather than later."

Birdie placed her sandwich down. "I thought you were the smart one in the family."

Rose raised her hand. "No, that was always me." A wide grin spread on her face. "Just kidding. It's you, Lacy."

Birdie frowned. "I was there last weekend. I saw how you two were together. There's relationship potential there," she said.

Lacy sighed. "Maybe, but he doesn't want another relationship. He's been hurt and..." She shrugged. "I guess he just doesn't think it's worth trying again." That was her old insecurities though so she stopped them all in their tracks. "Actually, something good came out of me going out with him a few times."

"Oh?" Birdie asked. "What's that?"

"I'm not afraid to go to my reunion, even if I have to go on my own."

"Maybe you'll meet someone there. Maybe you'll find 'the one,'" Rose said.

"Maybe." But Lacy was pretty sure she wouldn't find the *one* she wanted. He'd already been found and lost.

"I'll go with you if you need me to," Josie offered. She wasn't sitting on the couch with Lacy's laptop this time. Instead, she held a glass of wine tonight, looking relaxed in the recliner across the room.

"I wonder what people would think about that," Birdie said.

Lacy shrugged. "You know what, I've decided that I don't care what the people who don't know me think. I care about what I think. And what you all think, of course."

"And Paris?" Dawanda asked.

Lacy shook her head, but she meant yes. Paris was right. Her gestures often contradicted what she really meant. "Paris thinks that we should just be friends, and I have to respect that."

Even if she didn't like it.

Chapter Eight

Paris was spending his Saturday night in Mr. Jenson's rosebushes—not at Lacy's class reunion as he'd planned. He'd clipped the bushes back, pruning the dead ends so that they'd come back stronger.

Over the last couple of days, he'd kept himself super busy with work and taking Mr. Jenson to and from the nursing facility. He'd read up on how to care for rosebushes, but that hadn't been necessary because Mr. Jenson stayed on the porch barking out instructions like a drill sergeant. Paris didn't mind. He loved the old man.

"Don't clip too much off!" Mr. Jenson warned. "Just what's needed."

"Got it." Paris squeezed the clippers again and again, until the muscles of his hand were cramping.

Despite his best efforts, he hadn't kept himself busy enough to keep from thinking about Lacy. She'd waved and said hi to him when he'd gone in and out of the library, but that was all. It wasn't enough.

He missed her. A lot. Hopefully she was still going to her reunion tonight. He hoped she danced. And maybe there'd be a nice guy there who would dance with her.

Guilt and jealousy curled around Paris's ribs like the roses on the lattice. He still wanted to be that guy who held her close tonight and watched her shine.

"Done yet?" Mr. Jenson asked gruffly.

Paris wiped his brow and straightened. "All done."

Mr. Jenson nodded approvingly. "It looks good, son."

Mr. Jenson didn't mean anything by calling him son, but it still tugged on Paris's heartstrings. "Thanks. I'll come by next week and take you to see Mrs. Jenson."

"Just don't expect me to get on that bike of yours," the older man said for the hundredth time.

"Wouldn't dream of it." As Paris started to walk away, Mr. Jenson called out to him.

"PJ?"

Paris froze. He hadn't heard that name in a long time, but it still stopped him in his tracks. He turned back to face Mr. Jenson. "You know?"

Mr. Jenson chuckled. "I'm old, not blind. I've known since that first computer class."

"But you didn't say anything." Paris took a few steps, walking back toward Mr. Jenson on the porch. "Why?"

"I could ask you the same. You didn't say anything either."

Paris held his hands out to his sides. "I called last year. Mrs. Jenson answered and told me to never call again."

Mr. Jenson shook his head as he listened. "I didn't know that, but it sounds about right. She tells me the same thing when I call her. Don't take it personally."

Paris pulled in a deep breath and everything he'd thought about the situation shifted and became something very different. They hadn't turned him away. Mr. Jenson hadn't even known he'd tried to reconnect.

Mr. Jenson shoved his hands in the pockets of his pants.

"I loved PJ. It was hard to lose him...you." Mr. Jenson cleared his throat and looked off into the distance. "It's been hard to lose Nancy, memory by memory, too. I guess some part of me didn't say anything when I realized who you were because I was just plain tired of losing. Sometimes it's easier not to feel anything. Then it doesn't hurt so much when it's gone." He looked back at Paris. "But I can't seem to lose you even if I wanted to, so maybe I'll just stop trying."

Paris's eyes burned. He blinked and looked down at his feet for a moment and then back up at the old man. He was pretty sure Mr. Jenson didn't want to be hugged, but Paris was going to anyway. He climbed the steps and wrapped his arms around his foster dad for a brief time. Then he pulled away. "Like I said, I'll be back next week, and I'll take you to go see Mrs. Jenson."

"See. Can't push you away. Might as well take you inside with me when I go see Nancy next time. She'll probably tell you to go away and never come back."

"I won't listen," Paris promised.

"Good." Mr. Jenson looked relieved somehow. His body posture was more relaxed. "Well, you best get on with your night. I'm sure you have things to do. Maybe go see that pretty librarian."

Paris's heart rate picked up. He was supposed to be at Lacy's side tonight, but while she was bravely facing her fears, he'd let his keep him away. His parents were supposed to love him and stand by him, but they hadn't. His ex-wife had abandoned him too. He guessed he'd gotten tired of losing just like Mr. Jenson. It was easier to push people away before they pushed him.

But the Jensons had never turned their back on him. They'd wanted him and he wished things had gone differently. Regardless of what happened in the past, it wasn't too late to reconnect and have what could've been now.

As he headed back to his bike, Paris pulled his cell phone out of his pocket and checked the time. Hopefully, it wasn't too late for him and Lacy either.

———

Lacy looked at her reflection in the long mirror in her bedroom. She loved the dress she'd found at Sophie's Boutique. She had a matching pair of shoes that complemented it perfectly. Her hair was also done up, and she'd put on just a little bit of makeup.

She flashed a confident smile. "I can do this."

She took another deep breath and then hurried to get her purse and keys. The reunion would be starting soon, and she needed to leave before she changed her mind. The nerves were temporary, but the memories from tonight would last. And despite her worries, she was sure they'd be good memories.

She grabbed her things and drove to Sweetwater Springs High School where the class reunion was taking place. When she was parked, she sat for a moment, watching her former classmates head inside. They all had someone on their arm. No one was going in alone. Except her.

She imagined walking inside and everyone stopping to stare at her. The mean girls from her past pointing and laughing and whispering among each other. That was the worst-case scenario and probably wasn't going to happen. But if it did, she'd get through it. She wasn't a shy kid anymore. She was strong and confident, and yeah, she'd rather have Paris holding her hand, but she didn't need him to. "I can do this," she said again.

She pushed her car door open, locked it up, and headed inside. She opened the door to the gymnasium, accosted by the music and sounds of laughter. It wasn't directed at her. No one was even looking at her. She exhaled softly, scanning the room for familiar faces. When she saw Claire Donovan, the coordinator of the event, standing with Halona Locklear and Brenna McConnell, she headed in that direction. They were always nice to her.

"Lacy!" Brenna exclaimed when she saw her walking over. "It's so good to see you." She gave her a big hug, and Lacy relaxed a little more. "Even though we all see each other on a regular basis," she said once they'd pulled apart.

Lacy hugged the other women as well.

"So you came alone too?" Lacy asked Halona.

"Afraid so. My mom is watching Theo for a few hours. I told her I really didn't need to come, but she insisted."

Brenna nodded as she listened to the conversation. "Sounds familiar. Everyone told me that you can't skip your high school reunion."

"This is a small town. It's not like we don't know where everyone ended up," Halona said. "Most everyone anyway."

"Don't look now," Summer Rodriquez said, also joining the conversation, "but Carmen Daly is veering this way."

Lacy's heart sank. Carmen was the leader of her little pack of mean girls. How many times had Lacy cried in the girls' bathroom over something Carmen had said or done to make her life miserable?

Lacy subtly stood a little straighter. Her brace was gone, and whatever Carmen dished out, she intended to return.

"Hi, ladies," Carmen said, looking between them. She was just as beautiful as ever. Lacy knew Carmen didn't live in Sweetwater Springs anymore. From what Lacy had heard, Carmen had married a doctor and lived a few hours east from here. Her vibrant smile grew sheepish as she looked at Lacy. "Hi, Lacy."

Every muscle in Lacy's body tensed. "Hi, Carmen."

Then Carmen surprised her by stepping forward to give her a hug. For a moment, Lacy wondered if she was sticking a sign on her back like she'd done so long ago. KICK ME. I WON'T FEEL IT.

Carmen pulled back and looked Lacy in the eye while her friends watched. "Lacy, I've thought about you so many times over the years. I'm so glad you're here tonight."

Lacy swallowed. "Oh?"

"I want to tell you that I'm sorry. For everything. I'm ashamed of the person I was and how I acted toward you. So many times I've thought about messaging you on Facebook or emailing you, but this is something that really needs to be done in person." Carmen's eyes grew shiny. "Lacy, I'm so sorry. I mean it."

Lacy's mouth dropped open. Of all the things she'd imagined about tonight, this wasn't one of them. She turned to look at Summer, Brenna, and Halona, whose lips were also parted in shock, and then she looked back at Carmen.

"I've tried to be a better person, but the way I behaved in high school has haunted me for the last ten years."

Lacy reached for Carmen's hand and gave it a squeeze. "Thank you. Looks like we've both changed."

"We grew up." Carmen shrugged. "Can you ever forgive me?"

"Definitely."

Carmen seemed to relax. "Maybe we can be friends on

Facebook," she said. "And in real life. Maybe a coffee date next time I come home."

"I'd like that." Lacy's eyes burned as she hugged Carmen again and watched her walk over to her husband. Then Lacy turned her back to her friends. "Is there a sign on my back?"

"Nope," Brenna said. "I think that was sincere."

Lacy faced them again. "Me too. It was worth coming here tonight just for that." Someone tapped her shoulder and she spun again, this time coming face-to-face with Paris.

"Sorry to interrupt," he said, looking just as sheepish as Carmen had a few minutes earlier.

She noticed that he was dressed in the shirt he purchased from Sophie's Boutique. "Paris, what are you doing here?"

"Hoping to get a dance with you?" He looked at the dance floor, where a few couples were swaying.

"I...I don't know," she said.

Summer put a hand on her back and gave her a gentle push. "No more sitting on the sidelines, Lacy. When a boy asks you to dance, you say yes."

Lacy took a few hesitant steps, following Paris. Then they stopped and turned to face each other, the music wrapping around them. "Paris"—she shook her head— "you didn't have to come. As you can see, I didn't chicken out. I'm here and actually having a great time. I don't need you to hold my hand."

He reached for her hand anyway, pulling her body toward his. The touch made her grow warm all over. "You never needed me. But I'm hoping you still want me."

Lacy swallowed. *Yeah*, she definitely still wanted him. She looked at his arms looped around her waist. They fit together so nicely. Then she looked back up at him. "I lied when I said that we could still be friends, Paris. I can't. I want things when I'm with you. Things I shouldn't want, but I can't help it."

"Such as?" he asked.

Lacy took a breath. She might as well be honest and scare him off for good. "I want a relationship. I want to fall in love. I want it all. And I just think it would be too hard—"

Paris dropped his mouth to hers and stopped her words with a soft kiss.

"What are you doing?" she asked when he pulled back away.

"I want things when I'm with you too," he said, leaning in closer so she could hear him over the music. "I want to kiss you. Hold your hand. Be the guy you want a relationship with. To be in love with."

Lacy's lips parted. Since they were being honest... "You already are that guy. I mean, not the love part. We haven't known each other very long, so it's too soon for that. That would be crazy."

"Maybe, but I understand exactly what you mean," he said.

She narrowed her eyes. "Then why are you smiling? You said you didn't want those things."

"Correction. I said I didn't *want* to want those things." He tightened his hold on her as they danced. "But it appears it's already too late, and you're worth the risk."

"So you're my date to this reunion tonight," Lacy said. "Then what?"

"Then tomorrow or the next day, I was thinking I'd go to your family's house for dinner and win over your dad."

Lacy grimaced. "That won't be easy. He'll want to know what your intentions are with his daughter."

Paris grinned. "My intention is to put you on the back of my bike and ride off into the sunset. What do you think he'll say to that?"

She grinned. "I think he'll hate that response. But if you're asking what I think…"

"Tell me," Paris whispered, continuing to sway with her, face-to-face, body-to-body.

"I love it." Then Lacy lifted up on her toes and kissed him for the entire world to see, even though in the moment, no one else existed except him and her.

About the Author

Annie Rains is a *USA Today* bestselling contemporary romance author who writes small-town love stories set in fictional places in her home state of North Carolina. When Annie isn't writing, she's living out her own happily ever after with her husband and three children.

You can learn more at:
  AnnieRains.com
  Twitter @AnnieRainsBooks
  Facebook.com/AnnieRainsBooks

For more from Annie Rains, check out the rest of the Sweetwater Springs series!

Fall in love with these charming contemporary romances!

A VERY MERRY MATCH
by Melinda Curtis

Mary Margaret Sneed usually spends her holiday baking and caroling with her students. But this year, she's swapped shortbread and sleigh bells to take a second job—one she can never admit to when the town mayor starts courting her. Only the town's meddling matchmakers have determined there's nothing a little mistletoe can't fix...and if the Widows Club has its way, Mary Margaret and the mayor may just get the best Christmas gift of all this year. Includes a bonus story by Hope Ramsay!

THE TWELVE DOGS OF CHRISTMAS
by Lizzie Shane

Ally Gilmore has only four weeks to find homes for a dozen dogs in her family's rescue shelter. But when she confronts the Scroogey councilman who pulled their funding, Ally finds he's far more reasonable—and handsome—than she ever expected...especially after he promises to help her. As they spend more time together, the Pine Hollow gossip mill is convinced that the Grinch might show Ally that Pine Hollow is her home for more than just the holidays.

CHRISTMAS ON REINDEER ROAD
by Debbie Mason

After his wife died, Gabriel Buchanan left his job as a New York City homicide detective to focus on raising his three sons. But back in Highland Falls, he doesn't have to go looking for trouble. It finds him—in the form of Mallory Maitland, a beautiful neighbor struggling to raise her misbehaving stepsons. When they must work together to give their boys the Christmas their hearts desire, they may find that the best gift they can give them is a family together.

SEASON OF JOY
by Annie Rains

For single father Granger Fields, Christmas is his busiest—and most profitable—time of the year. But when a fire devastates his tree farm, Granger convinces free spirit Joy Benson to care for his daughters while he focuses on saving his business. Soon Joy's festive ideas and merrymaking convince Granger he needs a business partner. As crowds return to the farm, life with Joy begins to feel like home. Can Granger convince Joy that this is where she belongs? Includes a bonus story by Melinda Curtis!

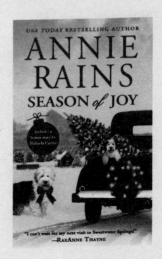

HER AMISH WEDDING QUILT
by Winnie Griggs

When the man she thought she would wed chooses another woman, Greta Eicher pours her energy into crafting beautiful quilts at her shop and helping widower Noah Stoll care for his adorable young children. But when her feelings for Noah grow into something even deeper, will she be able to convince him to have enough faith to give love another chance?

THE AMISH MIDWIFE'S HOPE
by Barbara Cameron

Widow Rebecca Zook adores her work, but the young midwife secretly wonders if she'll ever find love again or have a family of her own. When she meets handsome newcomer Samuel Miller, her connection with the single father is immediate—Rebecca even bonds with his sweet little girl. It feels like a perfect match, and Rebecca is ready to embrace the future...if only Samuel can open his heart once more.

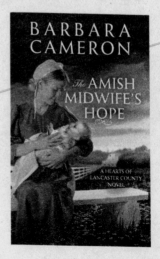

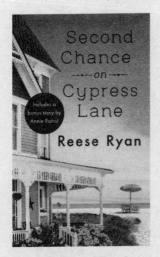

**SECOND CHANCE ON
CYPRESS LANE
by Reese Ryan**

Rising-star reporter Dakota Jones is used to breaking the news, not making it. When a scandal costs her her job, there's only one place she can go to regroup. But her small South Carolina hometown comes with a major catch: Dexter Roberts. The first man to break Dakota's heart is suddenly back in her life. She won't give him another chance to hurt her, but she can't help wondering what might have been. Includes a bonus story by Annie Rains!

**FOREVER WITH YOU
by Barb Curtis**

Leyna Milan knows family legacies come with strings attached, but she's determined to prove that she can run her family's restaurant. Of course, Leyna never expected that honoring her grandfather's wishes meant opening a second location on her ex's winery—or having to ignore Jay's sexy grin and guard the heart he shattered years before. But as they work closely together, she begins to discover that maybe first love deserves a second chance...

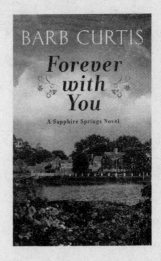